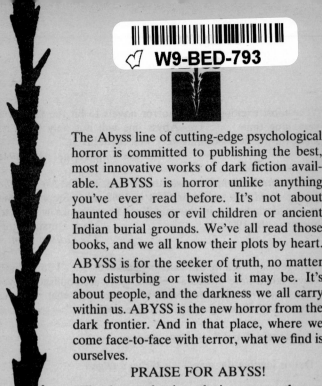

The Abyss line of cutting-edge psychological horror is committed to publishing the best, most innovative works of dark fiction available. ABYSS is horror unlike anything you've ever read before. It's not about haunted houses or evil children or ancient Indian burial grounds. We've all read those books, and we all know their plots by heart.

ABYSS is for the seeker of truth, no matter how disturbing or twisted it may be. It's about people, and the darkness we all carry within us. ABYSS is the new horror from the dark frontier. And in that place, where we come face-to-face with terror, what we find is ourselves.

PRAISE FOR ABYSS!

"Thank you for introducing me to the remarkable line of novels currently being issued under Dell's Abyss imprint. I have given a great many blurbs over the last twelve years or so, but this one marks two firsts: first *unsolicited* blurb (*I* called *you*) and the first time I have blurbed a whole *line* of books. In terms of quality, production, and plain old storytelling reliability (that's the bottom line, isn't it?), Dell's new line is amazingly satisfying . . . a rare and wonderful bargain for readers. I hope to be looking into the Abyss for a long time to come."

—Stephen King

"The new Abyss line of horror fiction has provided some great moments in their first year." —*Mystery Scene*

"Inaugurating Dell's new Abyss Books series, this powerful first novel [*The Cipher*] is as thought-provoking as it is horrifying." —*Publishers Weekly*

"Claustrophobic, paranoid . . . compelling. Dell's new horror line is definitely worth keeping an eye on." —*Science Fiction Eye*

PRAISE FOR *WHIPPING BOY:*

"A powerful and thought-provoking exploration of the nature of human morality and what happens when the ties that bind us to it are cut. This is a book that will stay with readers long after they've finished with it." —Chris Claremont, author of *First Flight* and *Grounded*

"In *Whipping Boy,* John Byrne has created a hell of a novel—in more ways than one. When Paul Trayne works his evangelical magic to ease people's sufferings, all guilt is removed from them, casting them down from the brink of humanity into a degraded, bestial state. The novel follows a large cast of characters who seek the purposed rest offered by a guilt-free conscience and chronicles the struggles of the few who elect to reject the 'gift' and attempt to take back their humanity. It's an exciting book and one you won't forget. When people ask 'Did you like it?' I can only reply 'Guilty, guilty, guilty!' " —Scott A. Cupp, *Mystery Scene*

WHIPPING BOY

BOY

John Byrne

A DELL BOOK

Published by
Dell Publishing
a division of
Bantam Doubleday Dell Publishing Group, Inc.
666 Fifth Avenue
New York, New York 10103

The trademark Dell® is registered in the U.S. Patent and Trademark Office.

ISBN: 0-440-21171-9

Printed in the United States of America

Published simultaneously in Canada

March 1992

10 9 8 7 6 5 4 3 2 1

OPM

The Lord hath made all things *for himself:*
yea, even the wicked for the day of evil.

—Proverbs 16:4

Before

Everywhere he went Ben Carpenter heard talk about the Miracle Show, about "the boy."

Ben found the words increasingly extraordinary: people carried to remarkable eloquence describing events out in the windswept patch of dry grass known around these parts as Gunner's Field. Language Ben Carpenter more associated with science fiction stories—or a pulpit—than with the plain, straitlaced folk he'd grown up with.

He thought himself too hard-nosed to listen; he could fill the pages of his newspaper a thousand times over, every day, were he to start printing fairy tales and rumor. He was not about to believe there were miracles the other side of Pine Tree River, northwest of Faulkner. Not until Mae Ellen Faber came into the office of the *Faulkner Observer*, seven o'clock that Tuesday morning, all bright smiles, a spring in her step.

The rest of the staff had not come in yet. Ben was beginning to become annoyed by the tardiness turning up in even his best people. It was, he'd said to his secretary—who'd seemed thus far unaffected—as if everyone had made a New Year's resolution to slack off and take it easy. It was made particularly galling, to Ben, when he sat down with his morning copies of the Chicago papers he read every day. The big story there was the wrap-up of the Errol Keane Warner murder trial. Every paper was devoting column after column to the kind of top-notch, crack reporting Ben Carpenter viewed as a form of high art, right up there with the paintings of Michelangelo or the works of Shakespeare.

By the morning of Mae's transfiguration—as Ben would come to think of it—the tent show had been in Gunner's Field for three weeks, since the first of the year. Ben could not think of when he had seen Mae as happy as she seemed that day. Normally she was full of the ills of her lonely spinster's life with her invalid mother. Now she floated, tidying, sorting, trilling a tuneless melody that came to Ben as a song of profound joy. He was amazed, when she turned full face. Mae Ellen looked ten years younger. Ben poked his head out of the oak-and-glass cubicle that had served as the domain of a dozen *Observer* editors, fixed Mae Ellen with one of his best glares. Mae was not to be daunted.

"Don't you go looking at me like that, Mr. Carpenter. I feel good today, and none of your sour looks are going to take that away from me."

Ben stepped out of his office, stood just within the low oak railing boxing off the small area around his secretary's desk. "Well, I'm glad to hear you're so chipper, Mae. But I'd love to know what brought on this sudden change of heart."

Mae Ellen crossed from the middle of the three big windows on the far side of the newsroom. "I went out to the Miracle Show." She spoke clearly: a schoolmarm addressing her class, Ben thought. "Now I know you don't hold with such things, Mr. Carpenter, but you just listen before you say anything!"

Ben shrugged. "All right. Say your piece, Mae."

She watched in silence as he settled back on the corner of his secretary's small desk and folded his arms atop his paunch. Then she let it out in one breathless flow, as if, Ben thought, she was being compelled to speak, each word pushed from her mouth by the next, all crowding up to get said. Listening, Ben felt old reporter's instincts bristling. By the time Mae Ellen finished he was on his feet. Her story told, Mae Ellen stood with hands clasped before her, new youth shining from her face in bright contrast to the gray light behind her. Ben could not begin to catalog the fine details of her transformation. He even noticed for the first time what a fine figure Mae Ellen had beneath the unflattering lines of her plain gingham dress. He'd grown used to her stoop-shouldered, shuffling step.

"All right, Mae, I guess I don't need to do more than look at you to know they did you some kind of powerful favor out there." He thought about the other stories, especially the buzzing at Freeman's Groceries and Dry Goods on that Wednesday night, three weeks back, when those who'd gone to the first show returned to talk about it. Ben rolled down his sleeves and reached for his jacket and coat, hung on the stand just inside the gate of his secretary's area. "Guess maybe I should take a look at this place."

"They'll be closed up for the day." Mae looked at the regulator clock by the front door.

Ben smiled. "The best time to see circuses and the like is when they're closed. Then they aren't putting on their public face."

"It's . . . not a circus." Her tone carried personal hurt. She put a hand on his arm, surprising him with her strength of grip. Mae was all surprises today. "It's . . . a very special place, Mr. Carpenter. Paul Trayne is a very special boy."

"Then I'll be on my best behavior." Ben put his hand over Mae Ellen's and squeezed lightly. "I promise."

She let go, smiling. The warmth of it filled the room. "You'll see, Mr. Carpenter. They're fine people, Paul Trayne and his father. The best people." She turned back to her sorting and tidying. "You'll see."

Outside, Ben saw Clarence Nickerson climbing out of his forty-year-old Buick, the massive armored vehicle bulking huge amid frail American compacts and Japanese imports lining Lafayette Street. Police Chief Nickerson, with close-cropped iron-filings hair and solid, bearlike body seemed to Ben one who *should* be driving such a vehicle. Especially with the big, blue steel Sturm Ruger Blackhawk revolver holstered against his hip, so much like the old peacemakers, but for the long barrel and cavernous bore. Ben raised a hand and called "Happy New Year" to his old friend. Nickerson stopped midway into the complex operation of closing the driver's side door and squinted through a fog of myopia Ben knew should have kept him far from the wheel of any car.

Rules bend in interesting ways, for the rule keepers, Ben thought.

"That you, Benny?" Nickerson was the only one who still called Ben Carpenter by the childhood name.

"Yup." Ben added his own weight to the door; a fearsome shriek and clang turned heads up and down Lafayette Street.

"Got time to join me in a cup of coffee?" They were right outside the Double Cup, Faulkner's last, official, old-fashioned diner, and Ben's favorite place to eat breakfast—which, as it happened, he had not done that morning.

"Sure," he said and followed his old friend through the slender doorway into the long, narrow café. There were more people there than Ben would have expected at that hour. It was gone nine o'clock, and most of them, familiar faces all, should have been at work by then. *Unless they took the same resolution as my staff,* he said to himself. As Nickerson lumbered toward the rearmost booth, Ben paused to speak to the olive-skinned man sitting on the stool at the near end of the long counter.

"Phil," Ben said, clapping the man on the shoulder. "Any chance at all I'll be having my garbage picked up any time in the immediate future? Like, before the turn of the century?" Ben's voice dripped with deliberate sarcasm, but Phil Bolland seemed not to notice. He looked at Ben over the rim of his capacious coffee cup and shrugged.

"Been kind of busy, Ben," Bolland said. "Some of my boys been out sick since two, three weeks back. Lot of garbage in a town this size."

"Sure," Ben frowned, "but it's been two weeks. And you don't get much garbage picked up sitting here drinking coffee and making eyes at Mary McKendrick." Ben winked at the blond waitress working behind the counter. She smiled and crossed around the far end of the long bar to Nickerson's booth.

Phil Bolland watched her plump behind as she bent to take Nickerson's order. "Two specials?" Clarence called to Ben.

"Two," Ben nodded, turned back to Bolland. The head of

Faulkner's garbage pickup service was already ignoring him and reading the latest Errol Warner article on the front page of the *Chicago Advocate*. It was the same story Ben had read himself, that morning. Donna Wojciechowski's keen, insightful wrap on the whole horrible, sordid mess. Something of a comeback, Ben had thought, for a woman who, he'd been saddened to note, seemed to have lost the biting edge and razor-sharp instincts that made her one of the finest reporters in the big city.

Still, none of that got Ben Carpenter's garbage picked up. Ben sighed, made a mental note to write a scathing article on the slipshod nature of public service in Faulkner, and crossed to the booth to join Nickerson.

"And what gets you out of your office so early?" the police chief asked. "I can't remember a time when I've seen you out and about before noon."

"Just heading out to this Medicine Show," Ben said. "Mae Faber seems to think it's the most wonderful thing to come this way since, well, cable TV."

Nickerson smiled, showing short, even teeth in a wide mouth. The remark was a small jibe, a reference to his newfound addiction to ESPN. "Mmm. Pete spotted them settin' up. Didn't go check it out for himself." Under fat black eyebrows shot through with spears of white, Nickerson's close-set eyes narrowed.

"Naturally," Ben nodded. Pete Hay was Nickerson's chief deputy, a young man with a fondness for four-letter words and what Ben considered a remarkable ability to be *anywhere* else when there was work to be done. Still, he was something of a fixture in Faulkner, Nickerson's right hand, and Ben found it hard to remember a time—even though Hay was a much younger man—when the deputy had not been an integral part of the civic landscape. His personal proclivities notwithstanding, people liked Pete Hay and trusted him as much as they did his boss.

"He came in and told me about it," Nickerson said. "I checked them out the second day they were here, in an official capacity." Nickerson flipped aside the wide lapel of his bulky winter jacket, showing his badge pinned behind it, a familiar reflex action of which, Ben knew, the chief was not aware. "Doesn't seem to be much out there besides stuff and nonsense," Nickerson said.

Nickerson paused, his expression that of a man groping for a thread of memory. It lasted only for a moment, long enough for Mary McKendrick to bring their specials, a huge, loaded plate each of steak and eggs, home fries, and toast. Nickerson looked back at Ben and said, "Nope."

"Sorry to hear you say that. I was hoping you'd have spotted something . . . well, 'unusual' is about as strong a word as I feel like using. Seems like half the town's been telling me about it." Ben's last words were drowned out by a screech of brakes. The stench of burning rubber came to his nostrils; he turned to see a souped-up '64 Chevy Impala framed in the window of the Double Cup, reversing down Lafayette. Smoke from scalded tires billowed out of the rear wheel wells. Ben recognized the driver, a flat-faced boy named Dwayne Richter. The Impala zoomed away, spinning into the other lane. A moment later it passed the window again as the boy slammed it into forward gear.

"Young idiot." Ben turned back to Nickerson. His old friend was not looking after the Impala. He was busy shoveling forkfuls of egg-smeared steak into his mouth. *He knows who was in that car as well as I do,* Ben thought. *Probably get after him later.*

Nickerson cleared his plate in as much time as it took Ben to complete his traditional routine of cutting his steak into convenient bite-size morsels. Nickerson began searching through his jacket pockets, face brightening as his freckled fist closed on a mashed pack of unfiltered Pall Malls. He extricated a mangled cigarette, pulled a book of matches from the pack, struck one, and lit the cigarette.

Ben raised an eyebrow. "Thought you were trying to quit."

Nickerson looked at the cigarette, small in his big hand, and shrugged. "Alice was out in Gunner's Field, first meeting. Don't know how she knew about it. Plucked it out of the air. She does that. She was sure enough impressed by that boy." Alice was Nickerson's daughter, ten years younger than Ben, a plain woman with big arms and short, thick legs. She'd been taking care of Clarence Nickerson for seven years, since his wife died. In the hundred times Ben had been to the Nickerson house he'd been struck by how *tidy* Alice kept it; she was compulsively fastidious.

"Interesting that she'd be so taken," Ben said. "Alice is a sensible woman."

Nickerson rocked his head side to side, considering. "Sometimes. But she watches those TV preachers too much for my taste. All those phony miracle shows. Just the kind of thing to set her up for some crafty snake-oil salesman."

"From what I hear nobody seems to be actually selling anything out there. They take a donation—not more than five dollars, Ed Austin said—but they don't have anything to sell."

"Bullshit is a product, I'd reckon, if it gets enough people coming back to make donations."

Ben did quick multiplication in his head. *Seventeen thousand people in Faulkner. Nearly eleven thousand of them adults with money to spend. Most of them religious, likely susceptible to a good old, Bible-thumping charismatic revival meeting. If each of them passed by only once, leaving only a dollar . . .*

But so far the turnout at Gunner's Field was much less than that. "Doesn't sound the best way in the world to get rich," Ben said.

"Then maybe it's on the level," Nickerson said, "You go see. Let me know what you think."

"I'll do that."

They parted company outside the Double Cup. Ben walked along the block to the corner of Calhoun, the parking lot where he left his car. The air was brisk against his face, enough to put color in the cheeks. High against the eastern sky, above the rooftops to his right, clouds he thought might bring snow piled over the horizon. He reached his three-year-old Mazda, unlocked it, climbed in, and pulled out of the lot. As he approached Lincoln Avenue, Ben slowed and stopped behind a short line of cars caught by a red light. He saw Deputy Pete Hay crossing from Enteman's Drug Store halfway down the block. Ben rolled down his window and honked the Mazda's horn. Pete saw him and crossed to the driver's side. He smiled, tipping his wide-brimmed hat in an old-fashioned way Ben was not sure how Pete came to adopt.

"Mornin', Mr. Carpenter. What can I do you for?"

"Quick question, Pete," Ben said. "I'm just heading out to the Miracle Show. Clarence said you were the first to see 'em. Setting up, in fact."

"Did he say that?" Pete pursed his lips. "I didn't say that. I mean, I didn't see 'em actually settin' up. Th' tent was already there when I drove by. I just saw it from th' highway as I came up over th' rise out by th' old Tempest place."

Ben didn't ask what the officer was doing out beyond Pine Tree River, well past the northern boundary of Faulkner. Most of the town knew what—or *who*—would beckon Pete Hay to the far side of Gunner's Field.

"Wonder what made Clarence say you'd seen 'em setting up?" Ben said, knowing Nickerson was a fanatic for detail, insisting his deputies get every scrap of information absolutely correct, in even their most mundane reports. The fastidiousness his daughter inherited, along with his looks.

Pete shrugged. "After he came back from checkin' 'em out for himself I got th' impression he didn't really give a shit about what was goin' on out there. Maybe that's why he didn't give it to you quite right." Ben could tell the discrepancy bothered Hay and could see his mind working, sorting through reasons Nickerson might have distorted, even unintentionally, the details of Hay's discovery.

"Maybe," Ben said, deciding not to press the point just now. Wind pushing in through his open window drove a spike into Ben's ear. The light changed and the car behind him honked. Pete shot an angry look at the driver. "Thanks, Pete," Ben said. "Catch you later."

"Sure." Pete Hay stepped back. Ben followed the slow crawl of traffic on through the business district. A glance in the rearview mirror showed Pete stopping traffic with an upraised hand as he continued his slow transverse of the street. Five minutes later Ben was guiding his car off Lafayette up onto Black Rock Highway and the junction with Pine Tree Road. He thought about the changes everyone spoke of in their lives after seeing the boy in Gunner's Field. He thought about his own life, the changes he might have wished to see made in it, if such magic were possible. Ben Carpenter was fifty-two years old and comfortable in his little town, his little life. He'd never married, never had any prolonged romantic involvements. He liked women, enjoyed their company, though he was always vaguely embarrassed by the physical intimacies of sex. In any case, the true love of his life was the *Observer*. There was room for very little else.

The car bounced off the pavement, onto the slush and mud of Pine Tree Road. He'd driven without thought of the passing highway. He glanced out the passenger side window just in time to see the old, abandoned Tempest house standing forlorn on the rise across Black Rock Highway from the turn onto Pine Tree Road. Only a glance. He turned his concentration back to the road ahead. He did not know just how far down this rutted track the tent show was, though it could not be all that far if Pete Hay spotted it from Black Rock. As expected Ben found Pine Tree Road worthy of the title only by virtue of the fact that it ran alongside the Pine Tree River and could not clearly be labeled as anything else. It was too wide to be just a path. In the summer, when the river sparkled and danced in the high sun, this track—baked hard and flat—saw a lot of traffic, day and night: groups of family picnickers, young couples seeking the isolation of sheltering trees along the river-bank. For reasons Ben knew would always remain known only to the city council, the parcel of land the road and river bi-sected was never incorporated into Faulkner proper; the road remained a dirt track, treacherous when the spring thaw turned it to mud, impassable when heavier snows of winter closed over it. The road itself lay one mile beyond the town line, winding west from the main road just north of the bridge that spanned the Pine Tree River.

He spotted the tent, off to the right, the field slightly higher than the road. A broad patch of dry, dead scrub grass was trampled flat, apparently by a combination of human feet and a vehicle rolling back and forth. It stood as high as a man's waist where not weighed down by snow and wet. Ben's first viewing left him unimpressed: a big old canvas tent, unadorned, a small panel truck parked alongside. It might have been a Ford once, Ben thought, but parts had been cannibalized from many other makes. The flaps of the tent were down, the ragged expanse of much-patched fabric fluttering in the cold wind. Ben judged it to be forty feet long by half that wide; a respectable size for a tent, but not as big as might have been expected for a medicine show, at least not by Ben's way of thinking. The walls were a little over eight feet high, rising to about fifteen feet at the point where the canvas roof peaked at the center pole. A small sign, hand-lettered in marker on what looked to Ben like shirt cardboard, was tacked to the left side of the gate opening from the road into the field. Ben paused at the gate, pulled his old Kodak from the glove compartment, and snapped a picture through the driver's side window. The sign said:

SURELY HE HATH BORNE
OUR GRIEFS, AND
CARRIED OUR SORROWS.

Ben frowned. It was a long time since he'd seen the inside of a church, or even opened a Bible, but he recognized the quote from Isaiah, and it bothered him to see Scripture quoted in what was, after all, an advertisement for a medicine show.

Even if they aren't selling anything, he thought.

He pushed down on the accelerator. The car bounced over the edge of the road, up a short incline, and through the gate. He drove across the trampled grass and parked beside the truck. He tooted the horn, three short, sharp blasts, then turned off the engine. He got out. No one appeared to meet him. Ben slung the Kodak round his neck and walked a slow circuit of the tent. So far as he could tell, it was perfectly ordinary, perfectly plain. Along the back, if Ben correctly judged which of the battened-down flaps was the door, he found indications of old paint having been scraped away. Ben stepped back and squinted but could make no sense of the phantom markings. They might have been a logo of some kind, but he would not have put money on it. He continued his circuit. As he came to his car again, the back of the panel truck swung open. A pale-orange light spilled into the gray day; Ben had the fleeting impression of a few sticks of furniture trying to be a room in the back of the truck.

The man who'd opened the doors jumped down onto the trampled grass and closed the truck behind him. He looked how Abraham Lincoln might have looked, Ben thought, clean-shaven and sixty. The same big-boned face, the same tousled hair, except that Lincoln's had been jet black when he came first to the White House; this man's was shot through with gray. There was a gathering of lines about the mouth that spoke of big, wide smiles, but the heavy-lidded eyes held no warmth, no emotion at all that Ben could see, unless it was sorrow. He thrust a broad hand toward Ben. The cuff of his sleeve was frayed a little, and the line of buttons down his shirt front not all of the same family, Ben noticed.

"Welcome, sir," the tall man said. His voice was soft, with just a trace of what sounded to Ben like a Missouri accent. "We are not open, as you can see, but the troubled are always welcome at our door."

Ben took the offered hand and pumped it a few times. The flesh was dry and warm in his grip. "I don't think I qualify as troubled, Mr. . . . ?"

"Trayne. Reverend Robert Johnston Trayne of Three Forks, Missouri." He pronounced it "Missourah." Ben complimented himself on his ear for regional accents.

"Reverend Trayne," he smiled, releasing the man's hand. "As I say, I don't think I quite qualify as troubled. I'm Ben Carpenter. I'm from the *Faulkner Observer*."

"We are all troubled, Brother Carpenter," said Trayne. "Even if we know it not." He gestured toward the front of the tent. "Would you care to step inside, sir? Away from this chill? I fear my old bones are not so . . . resilient as once they were."

"As you like."

Ben followed him to the tent and watched as Trayne untied the strings holding the flaps of the canvas door together. Trayne did not seem one who would be bothered by cold, unless there was some problem Ben could not see. His skin had felt as tough as old leather in Ben's hand, and although the open black jacket he wore was shorter than it might have been, it was a thick, close-weave material that looked to Ben to be serviceable enough in blocking the day's chill. His black trousers were short, too, showing three inches of narrow-boned ankle in dark socks above scuffed brown shoes. Ben supposed the chill might be making its way up, past those high cuffs.

They entered the tent. Inside all was as Ben expected. Rows of folding wooden chairs, about thirty, Ben thought, separated into two roughly rectangular forms by a narrow aisle, arranged before a low stage at the far end of the enclosure. The floor was flattened grasses. "We keep things simple here," said Trayne. "We find the people like it that way. They do not wish to be distracted from Paul."

"Ah, yes," Ben said. "The boy. Your son, is he, Reverend Trayne?"

Trayne nodded his big head and gestured for Ben to sit on the nearest of the wooden chairs. "He has been my only comfort since my wife was taken from me."

Ben drew a small stenographer's pad from his inside jacket pocket, pulled the stub of pencil out of the coils at the top of the pad, flipped to a clean page, and jotted down the name Paul Trayne.

"When was that?" Ben asked. "Your wife's death?"

"Nine years ago," Trayne said.

An expression Ben could not quite read showed itself briefly in the hooded eyes under the heavy brow. Anger? That seemed the most likely, Ben thought. It seemed for all the world that what he read was anger—deep, abiding, but quickly hidden. He made a mental note to probe that area in detail, and before too long, but for the present he asked "How old was Paul?"

"Five."

"Five. That's rough. Old enough to remember a lot." Ben thought about the power the boy was said to have. The way it took away pain. Would Paul himself be carrying such pain? "What was she like, your wife?" Again the phantom flash in Trayne's eyes. "How much pain do you think Paul still carries himself?"

Trayne sighed. It was clear to Ben that the older man did not care for this line, but was not sure how to get out of it. "Susan —my wife—was very attached to Paul. She was . . . young, you see. He was like a toy to her, a doll."

"How young was she?"

"Fifteen, when Paul was born." He stated it so matter-of-factly Ben took a moment to register the number, react to it.

"Fifteen? So, twenty when she died?"

"Twenty when we lost her," Trayne said. "She was weak. She did not understand. It is best left undiscussed."

Ben sensed an iron door descending between them. His reporter's sensibilities were much intrigued by the image of this craggy old man and his child-bride. Calculating back from Trayne's present apparent age and the reported age of the boy, Reverend Trayne must have been at least forty-five when he married Paul's mother.

Ben wanted to know more, but he also wanted to avoid losing Trayne, losing the hook of the conversation. He returned to his earlier tack. "How much do you think he remembers? From before your wife died?"

"Before was another time," said a soft, sweet voice behind Ben. "It does not matter anymore."

PART ONE

The Miracle In Gunner's Field

1

"Look, it's something easy," said Walker Stone. "After the last sixteen weeks I should have thought you'd be glad of it. Glad of an easy one. Think of it as a belated Christmas present."

Donna Wojciechowski kept her back to him and stared out the window of his office, high in the *Chicago Advocate* building. Snow fell across the towers of Chicago. To Donna's left, the city stretching into gray oblivion north and west; to her right Lake Michigan, a sheet of cold blue steel merging seamlessly into the heavy sky. Lakeshore Drive was a dirty black ribbon bisecting her view. Traffic rushed north and south, a constant stream even in the middle of the night. It was nearly noon of a cold February Monday. The *Advocate* tower threw a dark oblong across the curve of the drive, the deserted beach front. Behind Donna, Walker Stone's office was its usual jumble of papers, books, galleys, floppy disks, videocassettes—the clutter of a news editor's life—mixed with his own peculiar memorabilia. Donna turned and found Stone tossing from hand to hand the ten-inch-tall, hard-rubber figure of Froggy the Magic Gremlin that served as his paperweight. Beyond glass walls to Stone's right the bustle of the newsroom was muted to a gentle hubbub.

What he said was true enough. The last four months, covering the Errol Warner case, *had* been particularly intense. The intensity and the fever pitch at which she'd been operating since last Halloween were beginning to wear on her nerves. She *could* use a break, but she was not about to let Walker Stone determine just what the nature of that break would be.

"It's not a break," she said. "It's make-work." Donna was trying hard to control what she saw as her justifiable anger. It wasn't easy. She felt like hell. A team of microscopic construction workers were building something long and spiked behind the bridge of her nose. The condition of her mouth filled her mind with clichés concerning bottoms of birdcages. When she turned, the office tried to swim past her, bright with needle-sharp points of artificial light. She crossed to stand before her boss, mentor, erstwhile bed partner. The cause of her present annoyance lay on the blotter before Stone—small, white, insidious in its apparent innocence.

"Medicine shows," Donna snarled. "Laying on of hands! Crap! *National Enquirer* stuff. Not the kind of assignments you normally give reporters who've come this close"—she held up her thumb and index finger a hair's breadth apart—"to winning a goddamn Pulitzer . . ."

She sighed, caught the sound, held it back. She had a drawer full of prestigious newspaper awards back in her apartment, their inauspicious resting place a clue to the small regard she held for such things. She never—almost never—fell back on flaunting her acclaim to justify herself. Now she'd let Stone goad her into it, and anger and embarrassment crowded close. She seized and diverted the emotion, channeling its power into her assault on Stone. She leaned on his desk, her weight on the knuckles of hands clenched into fists.

"And will you put down that goddamn toy?"

Stone shrugged and set the stumpy-legged figure atop a pile of tear sheets at the edge of his broad blotter. He took off his glasses. From his left breast pocket he drew a short penknife, a little over two inches long. He pulled out the blade with his teeth and began tightening the tiny screws in the frames of his glasses with the tip of the knife. Donna had seen the ritual repeated a thousand times in the years she'd known him. It was as much a part of Walker Stone as his fascination with old TV shows.

"I'll give you the point," he said, and his tone indicated clearly to Donna that he was disturbed by her flash of credentials, "but I'll also take it right back again. You did a fine job with the Warner story. But you've been pushing yourself way, way too hard since . . ." He stopped and shook his head. "But we won't get into that. We'll focus on the fact that you have nothing to *prove,* Donna. Not to me, certainly. You're a fine reporter. Frequently one of the best. Even with your self-destructive tendencies." It was the only way he ever referred to her drinking, these days. "And you stayed dry the whole time you were on the Warner story. But you fell off the wagon the moment you saw your job as done—or is that *not* the grandfather of all hangovers I see behind those bleary eyes?"

"Spare me the lecture, Mr. Perfect."

"I'm not perfect. I'm not pretending to be. I'm just . . ." Stone's voice died away as Donna's face set into the terrible steel mask he'd come to know and hate since the end of their nonprofessional relationship.

"Okay. Have it your way," he said, slipping the spectacles back on his nose. "I'm having lunch with Clay Garber in twenty minutes, so I'm in no mood for a major confrontation. Read it any way your ego wants. Go as an aggrieved martyr done wrong by your boss. But go. Take the break. Do it up in the Wojciechowski way. Show me you've still got the stuff that brought you so close"—he mimicked her gesture—"to the prize Pulitzer."

Donna glowered. The silence between them lengthened.

"You want me to say I'll fire you if you don't go. But I won't. I'm way past being interested in that game." Stone leaned back in the big chair behind his wide, black glass-topped desk. His short, broad feet swung up on the desktop, crossed at the ankles. Shoeless, his red socks, shimmering in the fluorescent lighting, were too bright for Donna's eyes. Stone clasped his hands behind his head. With his thick black beard, plaid shirt, and bright red suspenders he looked to Donna like the editor of a small-town newspaper, circulation 3,752. A man, she imagined, not unlike the one who'd written the article that was now the focus of Stone's attention, the clipping lying on his blotter.

And about that article . . .

"I don't understand why you're so fired up about this, anyway. I mean, what is it about this little fluff piece that's got your whole heart and soul behind it?"

Stone shrugged. "You didn't bother to read it yourself, of course."

Donna snorted. "What you *told* me was enough. Why should I read the damn thing?"

"Oh, I don't know. Something stupid like professionalism, maybe."

"Don't get sarcastic. I don't have to—"

"No, you don't. But you *do* have to take this assignment. There's nothing else."

Donna always found his voice high for a man his size—not tall, but wide, firmly packed. Hard for him to get any real power into it, but he was trying now.

His dark eyes narrowed, heavy brows drawing down over the rims of his glasses. It made him look even more like the fantasy editor Donna pictured. But that image did not jibe with the autographed picture of Howdy Doody and Buffalo Bob Smith on the wall behind him, the huge collection of black-and-white stills from almost every TV show made in the 1950s and '60s facing his desk from the opposite wall. Only an editor as good as Walker Stone could have an office so eclectic, Donna knew.

After a moment he said, "I'm not going to be the scapegoat for you. If you want to keep drinking too much, if you want to self-destruct, fine. But don't come to me for the excuse to do it, Chow." The old nickname dated from silly, giggly days when their affair was barely begun. Now he used it to goad her. It made her want to retch.

"And this has absolutely nothing to do with me getting fed up to here"—she drew the flat of her hand sharply across the bridge of her nose—"with your goddamn holier-than-thou attitude, of course. And it's just coincidence that the time since the last good story you gave me equates exactly to the last time you had me on my back!" Donna's voice rose fast to a keening screech, harsh in her own ears.

Stone winced. His eyes darted toward his closed office door. He looked back, frowned up at Donna. "Why do you have to do that? We may not have had the most beautiful relationship since *Father Knows Best*, but dammit, it was good—very good—for a lot longer than you've ever had a stable relationship. And *you* messed it up. Not me."

He stopped himself with effort. Donna knew he still cared about her—knew it and denied it in much the same way she denied so many other things. Stone was saying more than he wanted, than he meant to say. Donna wondered if Walker Stone was still in love with her. Certainly she would allow no question of her still being in love with him, would resist the suggestion that she had *ever* been "in love" with anyone. Even Steve Binder, and him she had actually gone so far as to marry.

Donna frowned at the *Father Knows Best* reference. Sometimes Stone's fascination with old TV shows was a bigger pain in her butt than the god-awful nickname. She said so.

Stone shrugged again, his plaid shoulders rising to engulf the sides of his head, his hands still clasped behind his neck. "We all have our vices," he said. "Mine happens to be considerably less destructive than some people I could name."

"Don't start . . ."

"Oh? And here I was thinking we'd already started." His sarcasm still cut. After the months of their relationship, when Stone spent what seemed every iota of his effort to be kind and understanding, to help her deal with her drinking, his impatience and anger could still be sharp.

"I got pretty ripped last night, yes." Donna kept her voice ice cold. "I was unwinding after the end of the Warner trial. Now I'm paying for it."

"You're paying for a lot more than that."

"And you want to add to my bill, obviously, by sending me off on—yes!—yet another two-bit assignment." Donna seized the anger burning up under her heart and pushed it down. She would not get into this, would not allow the tired old pattern to repeat. Would not remind Walker Stone that she could stop drinking anytime, giving him the opportunity to sneer and say, *Sure. Like you quit fifty times in the last five years.* It might be even worse, in fact, if he did *not* sneer.

"All right," Stone said, swinging his feet down off the desk. "Have it your way." He picked up the newspaper clipping from his blotter and creased it slightly so that it stood out stiffly from his hand. "It's a two-bit assignment. I am giving it to you because I want to punish you. It's sixty-five miles away. You can drive it in an hour. See some countryside, breathe some clean air." He could not maintain his anger; Donna ignored how much his eyes told her he still cared. His tone softened. "The change will do you good. Stay a week. Do it up in depth." He set the clipping on the desk before Donna, took off his glasses, removed the penknife from his pocket, and recommenced the nervous ritual.

"That doesn't need a week." Donna flicked a finger at the strip of newsprint. The paper, folded, hung limp across the curve of Stone's hairy knuckle.

"You don't know that. Anyway, what's that got to do with anything? If you don't find something worthwhile, make it up. Remember the line in *Citizen Kane*? 'You provide the prose poems, I'll provide the war.' You wouldn't be the first reporter who shaped the facts to fit the story. Everybody does it nowadays. 'Nowadays' meaning roughly since the invention of movable type. Anyway, it might be something after all. Some people believe in miracles. My cousin Tommy springs to mind."

Donna scowled. She'd met Tom Sylvestri three or four times when she and Walker Stone were living together. She was struck by his dark, smooth good looks, his lean, athletic build. "He's a *priest*," she said, "it's his *job* to believe in miracles."

"Maybe. But I've discussed—argued, really—such things with him enough to know Tommy believes in miracles because he thinks they're *real,* not because the Pope signs his paycheck." He laid the clipping on the blotter again and pushed it closer to her. Donna stared at it, the focus of her distress.

If only it had gone unnoticed, she thought. *If only nobody in the clipping service had seen the stupid, piddling little article. If only it hadn't been forwarded to Walker's desk. If only he'd not seen it as perfect assignment for his crazy, drunken ex-girl friend. And if only I hadn't gotten so ripped last night. If only. If only . . .*

"All right." She still did not pick up the rectangle of newsprint. She retrieved her purse from the chair by his desk. "I'll go and check out the Boy Wonder. But you can't honestly believe it's gonna take me a week. Sixty-five miles away. Hell, I could come home every night."

"But I don't want you to. Every time I send you out on a soft story you say I'm handing you some kind of rest cure. Well, okay, I won't deny it this time. We really had something good going there, for a while, Chow, no matter what you think. I hate seeing you ripping yourself apart, and I hate having to play games like this with someone who was onetime one of my best reporters." He fixed her eyes, voice calm. "But until you admit to yourself that you're messed up, this is what you get." He pushed the clipping across the blotter. Donna picked it up, her body language telling Walker Stone she considered it as much fun to touch as used toilet paper. "Don't make it a war zone," Stone said. "I've been through Faulkner. It's about the sleepiest little town in Illinois. Calm. Peaceful. And this is a story about something that makes people feel good."

"Yippee shit."

He glared at her. "That's your assignment. If it's legit, you could win a Pulitzer."

Donna laughed without humor. "If it was really that good, the population of Faulkner would have doubled by now, with all the reporters who'd have moved in on it. The TV goons alone would be crawling all over the place."

Stone shrugged. "Just go and do, okay?"

Donna shoved the offending clipping into her purse, slung the purse over her shoulder, and opened the door. The noise of the newsroom rose around her. The spiky thing behind her eyes grew three inches. She clicked the heels of her boots together and snapped her right arm into a stiff salute. *"Ja wohl, mein Führer."*

Stone said nothing. Donna closed the door behind her as softly as she could, determined she would not give him the satisfaction of hearing it slam.

As Donna reached the revolving outer door in the lobby of the Advocate Building, the light of day was blotted out by a massive shape pushing through on its way in.

"Good afternoon, Commissioner," Donna said.

The big black man squinted, his eyes not accustomed to the

indirect lighting in the lobby. At last he nodded, thrusting out a hand. "Donna. Good to see you. I've been very much enjoying —if that's an appropriate word—your Errol Warner stories. You seem to have reached right inside the man's head."

"Thanks." Donna pumped the huge hand. Police Commissioner Garber had been instrumental in pulling the strings that allowed Donna her access to Warner and therefore her story. "Personally I think I only skimmed the surface. There's a lot more going on inside that man than we know. Than we'll ever know now, I suppose." She shivered involuntarily and changed the subject. "How's Marjorie?"

"Very well, thank you. Her charities and whatnot keep her very busy."

"And the girls?"

"Both away at school. Good grades, high promise."

Donna could tell Garber was not enjoying the exchange of meaningless pleasantries. A man of great power in the machine of Chicago politics, the oldest and closest friend of the mayor, he was not one for chitchat. He'd offended more than one rising politico with that refusal to play the glad-handing game, but he'd also won enormous respect from most of his colleagues and a sizable percentage of the voters of Chicago. Donna included. His own political aspirations were not known, but commissioner of police, even in a city the size of Chicago, seemed to Donna but one rung on the ladder Clay Garber was climbing.

"Well, got to run," he said, at last. "I'm late for . . ."

". . . Lunch with the inimitable Mr. Stone. Yes, I know. He promised you one of his fabulous feasts for being so helpful, right? Good-bye, Commissioner."

"Good morning, Donna."

Donna paused by the revolving door, watching as Clay blended—remarkably well, she thought, for a man his size—into the crowd flowing through the lobby. Before the Warner case she'd had very little real contact with Commissioner Garber, but she liked him. He was warm, friendly; Donna found a great natural strength in the man, a quiet sexuality that, to his credit, she'd never known him to use to unfair advantage. Garber was a man who demanded to be met on his own level, honest, uncompromising ground. A statesman, Donna thought, in a sea of politicians.

Garber gone completely from her sight, Donna pushed through the door to the bustling avenue. She turned left, walking in the shadow of the *Advocate* tower to the parking structure where she'd left her car. Donna retrieved her keys from the garage office, took the tiny, dingy elevator up six levels. A classic Chicago wind blasted down the low, wide concrete tunnel before her. Icicles hung precariously from the thick cables marking the outer edge of each level. Donna wonder what kind of damage one of those icy spikes might do to a soft human form after a sixty-foot drop. She climbed into her Toyota and pulled out of the parking structure, turning toward Route 55 and the trip west and south. Thirty minutes later Donna was cruising along the eastbound road at a steady sixty-five miles an hour. Walker Stone's estimate of one hour's travel time was from the city limits. Most of the trip still lay ahead of her.

She reached across the passenger seat with her right hand and opened the clasp of her purse without looking. She fished around inside the purse until her fingertips found the edge of the damnable clipping. She pulled it out and clipped it to the little notepad holder mounted on her dashboard just to the right of the instrument panel. She looked at the headline, frowned at it, wishing it would somehow turn into something else, something that made sense to her.

THE MIRACLE IN GUNNER'S FIELD

Donna did not believe in miracles and did not want to believe. She wrinkled her long nose at the smudged newsprint, an expression Walker Stone would have recognized. Donna was not one to hide her feelings.

Eyes bobbing back and forth between the road and the clipping, she read again the words that Stone seemed to find so moving—or at least claimed to find so moving:

There is a miracle in Gunner's Field. A bona fide miracle. The kind of thing we used to read about in storybooks when we were all little kids, long before the workaday grind forced us to become grown-ups and look at the world with all the magic scrubbed out of our eyes.

Donna narrowed her own eyes. *He can't be serious. If Walker was a diabetic, the first damned paragraph would've killed him!* She read on.

By now a lot of you have been out to Gunner's Field. You've seen the tent, the old truck. You've met Reverend Trayne, maybe shaken his big, dry hand, looked into those droopy eyes and seen the fire there, the simple, unabashed honesty and love of his fellow man. He looks like Abraham Lincoln. That's the first thing you think to yourself, and when he speaks, when he looks at you, that first impression is confirmed, strengthened. Is it just because Lincoln was an Illinois boy that face works such magic? I doubt it. I think that kind of rugged, honest face reaches across the barriers of state lines, even ethnic and racial differences. Honesty wears no one flag, no one skin color.

And you've seen the boy. Paul Trayne. There's magic in just the name. Simple. Strong. The kind of name you can trust, believe in.

Donna looked back to the road just in time to discover the straight stretch that had allowed her to read so much, uninterrupted, was curving sharply to the left, the south. The outboard tires thudded on unpaved shoulder. Donna brought the car back onto the macadam with a steady pressure on the wheel. No panic, no sudden jerk of her hand. She did not want to skid. She followed the slow curve until the road became straight again, then looked back at the article.

I don't expect there's anything I can say that would do real justice to Paul. If you've seen him, you'll know what I mean. You'll know how it feels to stand inside that ragged old tent, feeling the press of all the others who've come to see him crowded tight around you. Feeling them all breathe as one, breathe in unison with the slow, steady breaths of the boy.

He seems to be breathing for all of you. His head is down, a strand of his wavy orange hair falling over his forehead. The big sea-green eyes are closed. His shoulders rise and fall as he breathes, those narrow, bony shoulders, lost somehow in the folds of his too big shirt.

You'll have felt the pain, too. The anguish that floods up inside when you think about the terrible burden he takes onto himself. The terrible burden that young soul assumes as it drains all the blackness and bile out of your own soul and sets you free.

And wouldn't that be sweet, Donna thought, looking away again, looking toward the heavy clouds rolling low across the gray horizon. *Wouldn't it be sweet to open up your soul and let all the grief and pain and stupidness, all the wounds the slings and arrows of outrageous fortune inflict, and just be . . . free.*

That was the only word for it. Donna felt it now, so suddenly, so strongly she could almost reach out and pluck it from the air. Freedom. That was what the boy in Gunner's Field was offering. And not just freedom from the everyday nonsense, the cuts and abrasions a soul collected as it jostled against other souls. A freedom even from the likelihood of such damage occurring again.

If this is to be believed.

If you've lived in Faulkner any length of time, you know me, know my paper, know the position I've taken on all kinds of things from the Bermuda Triangle to flying saucers, and you know I'm not a man who's quick to believe in things I can't see and feel, touch and taste.

There was the piece of it that would have grabbed Walker Stone, Donna was sure. If he'd written the article himself, he could not have picked words that more completely defined his own view of the universe. His hobby notwithstanding, there was little room for nonsense in Walker Stone's world. He was not above manipulating the facts to create the story he wanted, but it had to be facts he began with, not dreams or illusions.

And that's why I'm putting this into words, right here in the paper, in the hopes that those of you who haven't been out to Gunner's Field yet, those of you who've maybe heard your friends and neighbors talking about Paul Trayne, but who've thought yourselves too busy or too straitlaced to mess about with such foolishness—I'm putting this down in words in the hopes I can reach out to you and make you see how important it is you go out to Gunner's Field and experience Paul's miracle. Let him open his soul to you, open that vessel he has inside and take in all the pain, the meanspiritedness, the troubles and griefs you're carrying around with you. Let him give you the gift he gave me.

It *is* a miracle. Paul Trayne *is* a godsend. And what he offers, what he can give you, is nothing less than the most important thing you'll ever see or do, in all your life.

Go to him. You won't regret it.

"All right," Donna said aloud to the empty car. "I'll do just that."

There was far less sarcasm in her tone than she might have expected.

The sun was low over the rooftops as Donna drove along Faulkner's main east–west transversal, Jackson Street. The going was not easy. There had been heavy snow three times in the last week, and Donna saw no indication of it having been plowed. The streets—all the streets, it seemed—were thick with hardened snow and ice, ruts carved into the surface pulling the wheels of her car this way, then that as she struggled to maintain control.

The eastern faces of the buildings were deep purple shadow, lights warm yellow pools through windows all along the street. As Donna approached the town center, she noticed that Christmas decorations still twinkled in half the storefronts, looking somewhat bedraggled, she thought. It struck her odd that, even in a small town that might not be victim of the crass commercialism of the big city, these had not long since been replaced by gaily frolicking Valentine cherubs.

Directions picked up at a gas station on the western edge of town indicated she'd need to divert to the north around a small town square; ahead of her Donna saw the open space approaching, guarded by a stern-faced statue identified at the gas station as Elihu Faulkner. Donna took this mutton-chopped patriarch to be the founder of the town and wondered if it was ego or respect that bequeathed his name to this collection of buildings and streets. If it was respect, she noted with sadness, it had long since worn off. The statue was rainbowed with graffiti, not a little of it crudely pornographic.

She turned right onto Randolph Street, as directed, and hit the brakes hard. The car started to skid, but Donna held it, waiting with tensed muscles for the slam and crunch as traffic back-ended her. The street behind was empty; the anticipated impact did not occur. Donna rolled down her window and stuck her head out into the cold air.

"Are you trying to get somebody killed?" she bellowed.

In front of her, inches from the bumper, a woman Donna judged to be in her mid-thirties gazed back at her, head tipped to one side in a manner that reminded Donna of a dog trying to comprehend what was being said to it. The woman had stepped off the curb just as Donna rounded the corner. She was pushing a baby stroller and was apparently completely oblivious to how close the sleeping child riding in the plastic seat had come to being crushed under Donna's car. The woman looked at Donna for a moment, then her gaze drifted. She continued on her way across the street without even attempting to answer Donna's angry question. Donna's muscles tensed and relaxed several times as she debated getting out of the car and further confronting the woman.

Ultimately, watching the distracted way in which the woman moved down the opposite sidewalk, Donna decided it would be pointless. She lifted her foot from the brake. She'd been pushing down so hard on the pedal her leg muscles were beginning to ache. She let the car roll forward, turning left onto a short connector that brought her to Faulkner's main street, Lafayette. She turned right, to the north again. She scanned numbers—as many as she could make out in shadowed door-ways—looking for 57 Lafayette, the building Walker Stone's researchers said housed the *Faulkner Observer*.

She wanted to meet the man who'd written the article that brought her here. Ordinarily Donna would have headed straight for the field described in the clipping, but the writer had taken such a profoundly personal approach to his reporting Donna felt compelled to contact him first. He was, she suspected, as much a part of the story as an observer. She found the building, a three-story sandstone block halfway between two intersections. She found no parking open along the curb, pulled alongside a dusty Chevrolet just outside the *Observer* office door.

She climbed from her car to scan the town. Faulkner looked not at all as she'd expected. It was small, plain, and old, and that much matched the image in her mind. She spotted occasional modern intrusions across the worn face of the town: a McDonald's, she noted, and down the block the familiar logo of Radio Shack. Except for them, and the cars at the curb, nothing in Faulkner looked more recent than the turn of the century. Most of it looked older. Abraham Lincoln could have had a law office in one of those buildings, Donna thought. He could have walked on floors still snug against their original walls. But he would not, she thought, have recognized the town she looked at now. Garbage was piled high along the outer edges of the wide sidewalks, dark green plastic bags and mouldering cardboard boxes bursting to vomit their decaying, rank contents onto the street. Even in the cold of the winter air, a workable natural refrigerator if ever there was one, the stench of decayed offal was thick and cloying. The town looked dirty—*used* was the word that came to Donna's mind. In the way a twenty-dollar whore looked used.

She looked up the street, to the north. She could see where the far end of Lafayette ducked under an overpass carrying the highway across the north side of Faulkner. Somewhere beyond that span, according to Ben Carpenter's article, lay Black Rock Highway, and Gunner's Field.

Donna shivered from the cold and negotiated her way around the Chevy and a small mountain of garbage to the doorway of the *Faulkner Observer*. A flight of steps rose almost vertically from the small vestibule just inside the door. To the right of these a hall barely wider than Donna's shoulders ran to a second ground-floor door on what she guessed would be the back of the building. Two frosted-glass office doors opened on the right side of the hall. Donna squinted up into the darkness around the top of the stairs and started climbing. It was hard going; the stairs were steep, her heels high. She grabbed the worn old banister rail with her gloved right hand and pulled herself up the last ten steps. At the top she found herself on a small landing, five feet deep by seven wide. The banister turned into a high rail, cutting just across Donna's middle as she leaned to look back down into the hall. The stench of urine rose from the hall below. She might have been in the worst neighborhood in Chicago, she thought, not an idyllic midwestern hamlet.

She was twelve feet above the street. The only light came from a seventy-five-watt bulb hanging just beyond the railing in an elaborate wrought iron cage. The cage Donna judged to be at least as old as the building in which it hung. The bulb might have been there from the first day, so little life flickered in its yellowed coil. She studied the heavy iron chain and embossed bolt plate from which the light fixture hung. Appreciating the old and hardy, Donna thought the chain and its ceiling fixture looked as if they could hold a couple of tons and might outlast most of the artifacts of the twentieth century just as they had survived the nineteenth.

She turned from the light to find the offices of the *Faulkner Observer* closed and locked. She rapped three times on the frosted glass of the door. It rattled, but no one came. Inside, Donna could see one small light burning, but there was no sign of movement near it. The light cast on the glass the shadow of a mesh that covered the inside of the door, heavy-grade steel by Donna's best guess, a security precaution not at all in keeping with her image of the town. She debated leaving a message for Ben Carpenter and went so far as to take her slim pad of self-adhesive Hasti-Notes from her purse.

Then she had a better idea. Beard the lion in his den, she thought. She clattered back down the wooden stairs and out onto the street. Her Toyota was still double-parked as she'd left it. Donna looked up and down the darkening avenue. Overhead street lights began coming on, phantom yellow glows pulsing weakly in thick glass cages. The wind was cold against her leather-sheathed legs. Her short jacket did nothing to diminish its chill.

There was a phone booth on the corner to Donna's right. She walked over to it, seeking a telephone directory in which she might find a listing for Ben Carpenter. Instead she found the book gone, the slender silver chain that once secured it pinched off, sliced through with metal cutters. She was about to leave the booth again—hesitant to surrender the small protection it afforded from the wind—when she noticed a pile of ashes in the corner, below the phone. She stooped and prodded them carefully with a fingertip. What was left was enough to tell Donna the crisp, blackened pile was the phone book.

She rose. It seemed an unlikely bit of vandalism, she thought, for a small town like this. Yet she would be the first to admit she had no real experience of small towns. For all she knew the people could be just as neurotic, just as discontented as anyone walking the streets of Chicago. She considered this in the light of the security mesh on the *Observer* office inner door. She stepped out of the booth and walked back toward the door to the *Observer*. Next door to the paper's entrance, below their second-floor offices, was a large hardware store.

Donna pushed the door open. A yellow plastic bird mounted on a perch above the lintel squawked as she entered. Donna winced at the shrill, annoying sound. The smell of wood and steel, plastic and paper surrounded her. There was no one in sight. She walked up to the main sales counter in the center of the store. There was a small stainless steel bell, such as she remembered her grade school teachers having on their desks. It sat on the counter next to a sign that said RING FOR SERVICE in a stiff, architectural hand.

Donna wondered if it would do much good, if the bird at the door had been insufficient to announce her. She struck the plunger atop the bell with the flat of her palm. The silver dome emitted a familiar chime. She waited a moment, then struck the bell again. After the first clear sound, she closed her fingers around it to stifle the ring. Still no response. Donna turned her back to the counter and looked around. There was a closed door in the back, behind shelves of pipe, chain, nails, hooks, hoses, handles, and all the other paraphernalia she normally associated with such a place.

Donna walked toward the door, placing her feet flat with each step. She felt uneasy in the still, dim light at the rear of the store. The hair prickled on the back of her neck, as though warning her that any moment someone might step from the concealment of a rack of shelves.

She stopped outside the door and listened. Muffled sounds from within. Male and female sounds, grunting and giggling. Donna frowned. For no reason she could properly identify, the fact that she had been standing at the counter tapping the little bell while whoever was supposed to be taking care of her was humping away in the back room set a slow fuse burning inside her. She rapped sharply on the door. Inside there was the sound of sudden movement, a crash as something fell or toppled.

Donna stepped back from the door, waiting. After a moment it was opened by a pale-eyed girl, her coppery-blond hair askew, plastered to her brow by sweat, her smock disheveled. Her skirt was short enough to show Donna's trained eye reddened knees, as if the girl had been kneeling for some time. In her early twenties, Donna thought, but tired and old beyond her years. Also annoyed, as Donna supposed she might have been, under similar circumstances.

"Yeah, what?" The girl's voice was throaty, rasping on the words.

"Do you have a phone book I could look at? I need to find a local number."

The girl opened and closed her eyes, slowly. Her rust-colored eyebrows rose. She seemed on the verge of saying something particularly nasty, Donna thought, but instead she turned and walked back into the little office-cum-storeroom Donna could see beyond the door. Donna looked in after her, finding a claustrophobic cubicle piled high with boxes, barely enough room for a desk. Behind the desk sat a man Donna judged to be in his late forties, salt-and-pepper hair thinning above a plain, leather-colored face. He parted the hair low over his right ear and swept the result over his crown to cover the baldness. In any other circumstance it might have been a successful disguise, Donna thought. Now, the flap of Bryl-creemed hair had fallen to the side and was standing out from the side of his head, reminding Donna of nothing so much as a convertible with the roof stuck partway up. He wore a brown plaid shirt and, from the way it hung across his belly, Donna could tell even without seeing around the desk that he was not wearing any trousers.

The girl reached around the man, under the desk, produced something that looked to Donna like an old and very dilapidated copy of *Reader's Digest*. She crossed back and handed it to Donna. It was a phone book—five years old.

Donna flipped to the *C*'s. Under Carpenter, Benjamin J., she found an address. She scribbled it on an envelope pulled from her purse.

"How far away is this?" she asked, showing the girl her notation.

" 'Bout fifteen blocks," the girl said. She raised a hand toward the front windows of the store, cocking her thumb to the left. "Go down to Piper, then over five, six blocks."

"Thanks." Donna looked past the girl at the man behind the desk, offering her most knowing smile. "Sorry to have disturbed you."

"S'all right," the man said.

"Din't think so," said the girl.

"Sorry?" Donna did not follow her.

"Din't think you'd come in to buy anything," the girl said.

Donna shrugged. "Maybe next time."

The girl said "Sure," in a weary way that told Donna she knew very well there would be no next time.

As Donna walked away the girl closed the door, sealing herself and the older man in the office again. Just before the door closed Donna heard the girl say something. Donna could not be absolutely sure, but the girl might have called the man "Dad."

Donna shuddered and pushed on out of the store. Outside the day was darkening fast—barely four thirty, the luminous dial of her analog watch informed her. In the east the moon was a pale-yellow crescent against the first bright stars. A light snow had started again, halfheartedly. Small dry flakes drifted by her face, landing on nose and cheek, turning to spots of cold water and disappearing.

Donna shivered. She was glad to be wearing her slacks instead of her trademark short skirt. Donna had good legs— "Damn fine legs," as Walker Stone referred to them: "damnfinelegs," one word—and liked to show them off. But the wind would have been merciless on bare legs.

Donna pulled her cigarette pack from her purse—only two left, she noted—and lit one. She stepped around the Chevy to her car and slid behind the wheel. The engine resisted her for a moment, then turned over with a sickly cough. She moved out into sparse traffic. In the rearview mirror she saw a bulbous old car—a Buick, she thought—move away from the curb. She thought it might be following her, but she did not monitor it as she followed the shopgirl's directions.

She turned left onto Piper Street, the location of Ben Carpenter's apartment. Out of the corner of her eye Donna saw a dark shape cross the lighted intersection behind her as she turned. Her first thought was of the Buick. She slowed and looked back over her shoulder. Nothing.

Now you're getting paranoid, she thought, annoyed at herself.

Donna accelerated, checking house numbers until she found the indicated address. She looked out at a plain-faced, three-story apartment building built close to the year she was born. Donna did not like mid-twentieth-century architecture. The boxes that sprang up in the early 1950s and through the late '60s lacked any kind of soul. They sought functionality and, achieving it, stopped. Splashes of paint were the only concession to humanity's need for beauty in a workaday world.

Donna parked the Toyota in front of Carpenter's apartment block and climbed out. A row of steel garbage cans ran across the front of the building, overloaded with what seemed an incredible amount of garbage for the number of tenants. She remembered being in New York during a garbage strike and wondered briefly how long it would take this tiny town to pile up that kind of sludge.

She walked up the short path to the front door. On frosted glass over the door, peeling gold leaf said THE BEL AIRE. Eighteen windows looked down from the street face; behind ten of these lights burned.

Ben Carpenter's apartment number was 303. Donna hoped that it was one of the illuminated dwellings on the front of the top floor. She looked at her watch again. A quarter after five. She hadn't phoned ahead. There was every chance Carpenter might be out, she knew, but she wanted to catch him unawares, if possible. She did not want him to have the chance to prepare in his mind a story for this out-of-town snooper. She studied the mailboxes on the wall outside the main entrance out of force of habit. No names struck her in any way. She tried the door. It was not locked. She stepped into a small entrance hall. Before her a short flight of steps went down to the right and a slightly longer flight rose to the left. A smell of cooked cabbage floated on the air. She went up the stairs, one, two, three flights.

On the top floor, four apartment doors led off the landing, two to a side, and frosted-glass partitions separated them from the stairs, front and back. Donna crossed to 303—one of the front apartments, as she'd guessed—and pressed the doorbell. She heard the bell ring inside, but nothing else. She put her ear to the door and listened. There was no sound within, no television or radio playing. She rang the bell again and again heard only the muted *dingdong* within. Donna went down the back staircase, a mirror image of the front.

On the second-floor landing she paused. Raised voices came from behind the closest of the four doors that faced into that landing. It sounded to Donna like a man and two women yelling at the top of their lungs. Angry voices. Donna took an involuntary step back. She had not heard that kind of rage in a human voice in a long, long time. It conjured marital memories she did not want recalled. Abruptly there was a loud crash. The voices stopped.

Donna turned down the stairs and pushed open the back door. She wanted nothing to do with whatever angers were raging through that apartment. She focused her thoughts on Ben Carpenter and what she might be able to find out about him.

As she'd hoped, there was a large rectangle of concrete behind the apartment house, with cars parked in numbered stalls. Several of the cars were little more than hulks—stripped, smashed, with pieces scattered across the snow streaked cement. There was strewn garbage here, too.

A three-year-old Mazda was parked in space 303. Donna looked through the window and noted the mileage. Crumpled Chinese takeout cartons filled the floor of the backseat. If this car belonged to Ben Carpenter, she decided, he was something less than the perfect housekeeper.

Carkeeper?

But he was at home, unless he'd gone somewhere that did not require his car.

A night out with the boys? Where do you go for yaks in a town like this? The bowling alley? The Y?

Donna went back to the door she'd just come through and found it had locked behind her. She swore and walked around to the front door again. As she turned the corner, a man and a woman were coming up the path. He was medium height and build, with a substantial paunch. He was carrying a small sack of Chinese takeout. Donna could smell the pungent aromas even at that distance. The woman was slender and pretty in a wholesome, well-scrubbed way that made Donna think of Sunday picnics and lots of children playing around a little house with a white picket fence.

Donna took a chance. "Mr. Carpenter?" she asked. "Ben Carpenter?"

In the light from the door Donna saw one of his eyebrows go up. "Yes . . . ?"

The small entrance hall just inside the front door of Ben Carpenter's apartment held three large green plastic trash bags. One was open at the top; Donna saw more Chinese food cartons crushed in with the rest of the garbage. Donna stepped past them, following the wave of Ben's hand. What she could see of the apartment was warm, plain, friendly. Living room sparingly furnished. Two chairs and a short couch set around a low table, each strong and solid, comfortable without being in any way ornate. Framed lithographs of World War II fighter planes, such as Donna imagined one might buy from an ad in the back of *Guns & Ammo* or *Life.* Two large bookcases crammed with dog-eared paperbacks. A tiny TV.

She liked the feel of the place, comparing it immediately with Walker Stone's high tech box, or her own Spartan three rooms. *A man's apartment,* Donna thought as she settled into an offered easy chair.

"Well, I must say this is a real honor," said Ben Carpenter. "I'm something of a fan of yours, Miss Wojciechowski. Been reading your pieces for, what? Three, four years now? Just what can I do for you?" He seated himself on the couch and turned toward her.

The woman he'd introduced as Mae Faber busied herself with the cartons of Chinese food in the kitchen. "You're sure you wouldn't like some chow mein or some of the sweet and sour ribs? They're very good."

Donna settled back in her chair. "No, really. I'm just after answers. First off—mind if I smoke? Thanks. First off, I'd like to know if you have anything to add to that little tale of yours." She took out her pack of Marlboros—lit one. "It's been nearly two weeks since your article ran in the *Observer,* time enough to do some additional mulling. Any new thoughts? Any, well, change of heart?"

"No," Ben said, his tone unequivocal. "I'd say it's all there in the article. And, of course, it's all true." The way he said it made Donna want to believe him. She finished lighting her cigarette and studied Ben's face through her first cloud of smoke.

"I suppose you'd've realized that, though, from reading what I wrote," Ben said. "Don't think I've ever, well, labored so hard over a piece. Spent all day on it, to get it into the evening edition. You know we have two daily editions of the *Observer?* We're very proud of that. Anyway, I worked hard at that piece, like I say. Locked myself away in my office. Wouldn't even talk to Mae." He looked toward the sounds coming from the kitchen. "I had to get it right. It had to be believable. More than that. Convincing."

Donna smiled around her cigarette. "Well, you certainly seem to have convinced my boss. He sent me packing down here to Faulkner within about ten minutes of reading your story." *Not that I really think for two seconds that he believes any part of this.*

"Who did you say that was, now?" Ben asked.

"Walker Stone," Donna said. "And I didn't mention his name before." She narrowed her eyes behind the screen of smoke. "I think you're the kind of man who'd remember, if I had."

Ben shrugged. "Seems like I might have heard of him, yes. Maybe even met him once, when I was up in Chicago a few years back. Mighty fine paper, the *Advocate*." He looked away for a moment. "How's dinner coming, Mae?"

Mae Ellen Faber poked her head around the edge of the kitchen door. "Two minutes," she said. "Would you like some coffee and Oreos, at least, Miss Wojciechowski?"

"Or would you like something stronger than coffee, Ms. Wojciechowski?" Ben Carpenter asked.

Donna blinked. "Why . . . yes. I wouldn't mind a drink. Thanks."

"What's your poison?" He rose and opened a sliding door on the bottom of one of the bookcases. The low light danced off a row of bottles.

Donna squinted. "Gin and tonic would be fine," she said. "Thanks."

She watched as Ben poured her drink. "Ice?"

"Please."

He went briefly into the kitchen; she heard him bang the ice cube tray in the freezer, then heard ice clink against the glass. When he came back, Mae was with him, carrying a large tray with a tall, slender chrome coffeepot—Donna was surprised by the ultramodern design—and the contents of the takeout cartons neatly arrayed on several small plates. Donna realized she would be the only one drinking hard liquor as Ben handed her the glass.

Oh, well, she thought, *it won't be the first time.*

"Now then," Ben said, settling himself back on the couch, Mae at his side, and reaching for a dark, glistening pork rib, "what can I tell you?" He bit into the meat and chewed with noise and gusto.

"Everything, I guess." The drink's only effect so far was to make Donna want a second one. She placed the glass firmly on the paper coaster on the end of the coffee table. "All your perceptions of this Paul Trayne."

"He's wonderful." This from Mae Ellen. Donna tried to pinpoint the emotional content of the woman's voice, but there were so many layers she could not be sure what was dominant.

Ben placed a square hand over Mae's fine-boned one and smiled. "Mae got me to go out there. After I saw the change in her."

Mae Ellen smiled at Ben, then freed her hand to take a helping of pork-fried rice on a smaller plate. There was nothing to indicate the well-scrubbed good looks Donna registered on first seeing Mae were anything new.

"Change?" Donna asked.

"Improvement," Ben said. He looked at Mae. "I'd say that's a fair word, wouldn't you?" He picked up the plate of chow mein and a spoon and began shoveling the viscous mixture into his mouth.

Mae nodded. "Oh, definitely an improvement." She picked up a spring roll and bit into the end delicately. The hard crust crunched loudly in the small room.

"What was wrong with you before, then?" Donna asked. She took from her bag the small Sony tape recorder Stone had given her for her thirty-fourth birthday and set it on the table, centered between the three of them. "You don't mind . . . ?"

"Not at all," Mae Ellen said.

"She was all folded in on herself," Ben said, picking up another rib. He stirred the tip into the juices of the chow mein before he bit into the meat. "I mean, do you realize we'd worked together all those years and I'd never even noticed she had a bust?"

Donna's head twitched involuntarily. This was not at all the kind of response she'd expected. Donna was not sure where to

go next. "And . . . you're . . . ah . . . pleased with Ben's
. . . ah . . . discovery, Mae?"

Mae smiled, sitting up straighter in her chair, shoulders
back, to reveal the truth of Ben's discovery. "Oh, yes. I mean,
I'd carried a torch for Ben for a long time. But I was afraid to
say anything, show anything, you know? Now we're having the
most wonderful time."

She looked at Donna with eyes very much those of a child
announcing the discovery of some new wonder, revealing the
world to tired, grown-up eyes in a whole new light. "We've had
the most beautiful sex every night since the Miracle Show."

2

Winter night closed tight about Chicago. Stepping from the warmth of the venerable old rectory beside St. Timothy's, Father Tom Sylvestri found it bitter cold, much colder than the day. He pulled his coat collar up and his head down into that shallow ring of protection. He'd forgotten to pick up his hat from the long rack by the rectory door—his mind was wandering as it had far too much in the past two days. He did not feel like going back to retrieve the hat. The wind came down West Addison from the east, across the Lake. It carried knives. Tom closed up the rectory and passed in front of the church, as he always did when he was heading for Balducci's Ristorante. He met old Bert Whipple coming to say his evening prayers. Tom glanced at the clock on the corner of the bank across the street. Just gone eight.

I could set a watch by Bert's coming and going, he thought.

The old man paused to chat for a moment, shifting from one foot to the other, clapping his big mittened hands against the cold. Bert told Tom he'd heard on the radio that the windchill factor was close to seventy below and dropping. Nevertheless, after saying good night and allowing Bert to go into the warmth of the church, Tom walked the eight blocks east to the intersection with North Lakewood Avenue. He wanted to think. The past weeks had given him much—too much—to think about. That was why his mind wandered so. Now he could only think of the meeting that lay ahead, the meeting he would have given anything to avoid.

A shrieking horde of ice demons came swirling in off the Lake, pushing deep past the eastern edge of the city. Chicago had not been dubbed "the Windy City" because of its climate, as most thought, but as far as Tom Sylvestri was concerned, the name worked just as well in that context as it did as a reference to the blustery politicians the city was said to breed. He tipped his head, pushed into the wall of cold air, stared at his feet, and kept walking. Thoughts of guilt and resentment turned his mind back to the young man who was at that moment, Tom knew, also heading toward Balducci's. Tom sighed again.

Joseph. Such a preposterous young man. But with the red hair. The haunted eyes.

Tom shook his head and huddled deeper into his coat. He was feeling a cold now that had nothing to do with the windchill factor.

God forgive me my moment—my long moment—of weakness, Tom thought, adding a silent prayer: *I acknowledged my sin unto thee, and mine iniquity I have not hid. I said, I will confess my transgressions unto the Lord; and thou forgavest the iniquity of my sin.*

A cascade of jumbled memories poured across his brain, too swift, too sweet to be stopped; bodies pressed close in the dark silence that follows physical love. Hands exploring with practiced skill, familiar ease. In the morning, the brush of one stubbled cheek against another. The strangeness of a kiss . . . all so real in his mind, so immediate.

So wrong.

Am I forgiven? his silent thoughts asked a sky pregnant with dark clouds. *I have confessed my sins, but is that really enough, given the nature of the sins? I have done my penance—will be doing my penance, in fact, for some time to come. But is that really enough? Is God really to be satisfied by such a paltry thing as a few Hail Marys when I have transgressed His Law in so blatant a fashion? When I have, in effect, been unfaithful to Him? And if He is not satisfied, is this my punishment, then? Is God really prepared to spend the effort to make miserable the life of one priest? Am I to be forever tormented by the memories of this terrible, terrible failure of the flesh?*

Perhaps that is not unfair, he answered himself. *Perhaps it is no more than I deserve, for letting down the guard I've carried all my life. For letting one poor, fragile soul insinuate himself into my innermost heart, to find in there the ancient sorrow. "The Lord knoweth how to deliver the godly out of temptations, and to reserve the unjust unto the day of judgment to be punished. But chiefly them that walk after the flesh in the lust of uncleanliness . . ."*

Tom realized he'd reached Balducci's. He turned his thoughts away from Joseph Terranova to the mundane, mechanical matter of entering the little restaurant. He stepped through the air lock of the double doors, allowing the outer door to swing closed against the chill before he pushed through the inner. Inside he found the restaurant dimly lighted as always, with pools of dull red light picking out the small tables ranged along each side of the narrow main room. Tom loved the look and feel of Balducci's: a long, narrow place—with arms outstretched, his fingertips would probably reach opposite sides—walls and ceiling old tin plate, elaborately embossed in fifty mismatched patterns and painted a uniform dark red. There were checkered tablecloths, candles flickering in stubby rose glass jars, breadsticks in tall glasses, napkins folded neatly under clean but battered knives and forks that glinted in the light. The aromas from the kitchen caressed his nostrils as he entered. Father Tom's mouth turned to water instantly.

"Padre." The round faced girl who took Father Tom's coat smiled. "It is good to see you. Your usual table?"

"Please, Sophia. And I'm . . . expecting someone."

"*Buòno.* I will bring them to your table." She led him to the back of the restaurant, past the half-dozen other diners, to a small alcove at right angles to the rest of the room. Barely more than a notch in the wall, it held the only booth and afforded a degree of privacy the tables did not. Tom liked it for just that reason. He had chosen a life of public service willingly, without a second thought, but sometimes the public could demand their service when he was in no mood to give it.

An unfortunate attitude for a priest, Tom admitted, but just now he thought himself an unfortunate excuse for a priest.

He slid behind the table and accepted the menu from Sophia Balducci. After six years of coming to this restaurant at least once a week, he really did not need the menu, but it was part of a ritual, allowing the girl a moment to speak to him, undisturbed by other patrons.

"How is everything tonight, Sophia?" Tom asked. He was not inquiring about the menu.

"Fine for me, Padre," she said. Tom studied her face in the candlelight. Not a pretty face, he thought, too broad and flat, but pleasant in an open, honest way. He'd seen her grow from a precocious twelve-year-old to a self-assured young woman. "Enzio got in trouble again last night. Some of his friends stole a car. He was only joyriding in the backseat, so the police let him out on bail, but Papa was ready to kill him."

"And Gina? Any word from her?"

"No, Padre. Eleven weeks, now."

Tom shook his head. He'd heard for the first time only ten days before how Sophia's older sister had vanished without word, without trace. She was nineteen; Tom thought her very quiet, very sheltered. He feared she might have found her way into serious trouble, out in Chicago, unprotected. With the papers full of the Errol Keane Warner case, it was difficult to keep from imagining the worst things happening to a young woman. The worst things, unimaginable things, had happened to thirty-eight young women who'd had the misfortune to cross paths with Errol Keane Warner. And, though he was safely locked away now, there would be those, Tom knew, who would draw not horror from his story, but inspiration.

"I pray for her every night," he said in perfect sincerity, though he frankly doubted if prayers from his particular heart and soul reached as high as heaven.

"You pray for all of us, Padre. That's what Papa says." Sophia's smile was huge. Tom wondered if there was an evil anywhere in the world that could stand against that smile.

"Yes," he said. "But I pray especially for Gina."

"Mie grazie, Padre. And now, some wine? We have a nice red, to go with the fettuccine bolognese."

"How did you know what I wanted?" Tom returned her smile, warmly.

"I saw the way you took a deep breath when you came in. And the way you smiled. And anyway, I know you like the bolognese best."

"That's true." He handed back the menu. "Yes. A small carafe of the red. And the fettuccine. And some of the garlic bread. With cheese."

Tomorrow I can go to the gym and run a few thousand miles around the track, Tom thought, *or swim a few hundred laps. If I must face Joseph, I need bolstering. No . . . I need pampering. I can debate later whether or not I deserve it.*

He watched Sophia walk to the kitchen and vanish through swinging doors. He leaned back. The squeak of the booth's faded Naugahyde reminded him of the sound his office chair made. It brought his thoughts back to the matters now pressing against his mind. But he was not ready to think of them again. Not just yet. Not for another few moments, at least. He studied the paper placemat. He'd seen it a hundred times; the map of Italy, the crude paintings of famous Italian sights. To the right of the longboat a gondolier poled his narrow craft through flooded streets that looked nothing like Venice. In the covered center of the gondola an amorphous lump had less to do with the shape of anything human than the jumbled building blocks behind it had to do with architecture. Tom placed his elbows on the mat and laced his fingers. He closed his eyes, leaning the bony ridge of his inner brow against his extended thumbs. Now he was ready to think about the upcoming meeting with Joseph—how much he dreaded it!

To have failed after all these years! To have been weak, foolish—and with someone who needed my strength, not my weakness. Someone who was crying out for help.

He opened his eyes as Sophia arrived with the carafe of wine and the sliced loaf of garlic bread. The aroma was particularly exquisite that cold night. "You'd better bring two glasses," Tom said, then realized she had. "How did . . . ?"

"You told me when you came in that you were expecting someone," Sophia said. She set the tray on the table. "Don't you remember, Padre?"

"Evidently not. Thank you, Sophia. I guess my mind was . . . wandering."

"*Sì*, Padre." She left him, casting a worried look over her shoulder, a look he fended off with a smile. He poured a half glass of the wine and sipped it. It was, as Sophia promised, a good vintage, healthy and robust, with just the hint of sweetness in the aftertaste. He took a mouthful and held it, pursing his lips, savoring the subtle flavoring.

"Tom . . ."

He swallowed hard. "Joseph. Take a seat."

The young man slipped into the booth, sliding around the other side of the table. Without waiting he took the carafe, poured himself a full glass of wine, and gulped back two thirds so fast Tom knew he could not have tasted it.

"I needed that," said Joseph Terranova. His smile was lame. "It's been a long one today, believe me. A long one."

Tom looked at him, trying to see him with professional eyes, detached and, perhaps, dispassionate eyes. The face was narrow, the chin too long, too pointy for the width of the cheekbones. The deep-set eyes could be piercing. Now they were fogged. The wine was not Joseph Terranova's first drink of the day. Tom was in no mood for anything that might remotely approach small talk. He'd thought the worst over and had disengaged himself—he hoped—from his time of madness with Joseph Terranova. Now . . .

"It's your dime, Joseph," Tom said, hating the artificial dispassion, the coldness he heard in his voice.

The young man looked stung. He refilled his glass. He fidgeted. He struggled out of his bulky jacket—it would have been easier to remove it before sitting, but he had not—and pulled off his overlong scarf. He avoided Tom's gaze throughout the awkward operation. He put the jacket to one side and piled the scarf on top, curling in around itself until it reminded Tom of nothing so much as a multicolored dog turd. Joseph picked up his glass with his left hand, but did not drink. He began chewing at the tip of his right thumb. It was not the nail he chewed, but the surrounding flesh itself.

"Well . . ." Joseph Terranova took his thumb away from his mouth and sipped his wine. "I'm glad you agreed to see me.

Very glad." He finally met Tom's gaze. His eyes were wet. "I
. . . don't know what I might have done, if you'd refused. I
might have done anything. Just anything."

"That sounds like a threat."

"No! No. I wouldn't threaten you. I wouldn't." Another
lame smile. "What would be the point?"

"None. But I doubt that would stop you, Joseph."

*Too hard, too hard! Remember, you're the one who is at fault
here, not Joseph.* "Cease from anger," Tom quoted silently to
himself, remembering the counsel of Monsignor Cameron, his
mentor at the seminary, *"and forsake wrath; fret not thyself in
any wise to do evil."*

His mouth twisted. *A little too late for the last part,* he
thought.

"I . . . wish you'd stop saying my name like that," Joseph
said. "You sound like Father Percival. You sound just like
him." Tom's predecessor at St. Timothy's, a stern old martinet
given to wandering senility at the end, Father John Percival
had shown no sympathy at all for Joseph Terranova.

"What do you have to say, Joseph?" Tom did the best he
could to soften his tone without losing control of the conversation.

"What do you think? Do I have to say it?" Eyes like pools
of oil, slippery, sliding. "I mean, do I actually have to say the
words? The words? Haven't I shown you how I feel? Haven't I
shown you in every action? Haven't I shown you every day
since . . . ?"

"Don't finish that, please. Your voice carries far too well."

"And you're ashamed of me, is that it? Ashamed of me?"

"No." Tom sighed, surrendering to the inevitable. "It has
nothing to do with anything like that. I'm ashamed of *myself,*
Joseph. But what does this accomplish? What do you think is
going to come of this?"

"I . . . don't know. But I thought . . ." His eyes locked on
Tom's. "I mean, it was so different with you. Different from
anyone I'd ever been with before. Anyone. You were so gentle,
so . . ."

"Joseph!" Tom heard the edge returning to his voice but did
nothing to stop it. "You could make this conversation a lot

easier if you'd try to limit yourself to one run of each sentence. I've told you about that before."

Scolding now? Playing the schoolmaster with the rambunctious student? That was never your best role.

Joseph looked crushed, but he was not stopping now. "You and me, we could be so special, Tom." He dropped his eyes, his voice. "It's not foolishness. I love you." He looked up. "There. I said it. Happy now?"

No, Tom thought. *How can I be? When I know what you say is true? And when I know an old and often bitter memory would make it so terribly easy to say I feel exactly the same way about you. Because, truth to tell, that is how I feel . . .*

"Joseph . . ." Tom fought back an urge to place a comforting hand on top of the two that quivered on the table before him, twisting and turning around each other like fighting cats. Such a kindly gesture could only be misinterpreted at this stage. "Joseph, you must be realistic . . ."

"I am." The petulance of a child, an unbreakable barrier against the real world. "I am. I love you. And I know you could love me, too. You do love me. We couldn't have had what we had, couldn't have had those weeks. We couldn't have had that if you didn't love me, too."

His eyes met Tom's again, hard now, defiant. *Call me a liar,* they said.

"You're wrong," said Tom Sylvestri, and he knew it was a lie.

"I'm not wrong!" Again the sudden reddening. The dropping of the eyes, the tone. "I'm not wrong." He was back to repeating himself.

Sophia appeared with Tom's dinner. "Something for you, signor?"

"No." Joseph watched as Sophia fussed a moment with the breadsticks.

"And you, Padre Tom?"

"Nothing more. Thank you, Sophia."

"Go away," Joseph snapped.

Sophia looked shocked and hurt. Tom glared at Joseph. "That was uncommonly ignorant, even for you."

"Then you tell her." Joseph would meet neither's eyes. "You tell her to go away."

Tom shook his head. "I'm sorry, Sophia . . ."

"No, no. Nothing to apologize for, Padre." She shot a blade-sharp glance at the side of Joseph's head. "Call me if you need anything."

"I will. Thank you." Tom turned back to the table. He sprinkled a fine layer of Parmesan cheese over the fettuccine and waited for Joseph to speak again. When the silence had stretched to more than a minute, Tom said, "I suppose you think you can impress me by being rude to my friends, is that it?"

"I'm . . . sorry. I'm . . . upset. You must understand that I'm upset. Say you understand. That I'm upset."

Tom closed and opened his eyes, slowly, three times. "Yes. I understand that you're upset. But I do not understand what you expect me to do about it. *That I haven't already done . . . ?* He softened his tone, just a little. "Really, Joseph, I don't."

"You . . . could . . . leave the priesthood." A sudden rush. Fiery color back in the gaunt face. "You could. You could leave the priesthood."

"For you?"

"For me. For me. Why not for me?"

Tom wiped the corners of his mouth with a napkin. The fettuccine was delicious, but there was a sour taste in his mouth, destroying his pleasure. At the very least he knew he'd never be able to look at Sophia in quite the same way again. "You . . . presume too much, Joseph. Even if you were right, and I did love you . . ."

"I am right. I am. You know I am."

"Let me finish, dammit . . ." Tom dropped his chin onto his chest. He counted to ten, then to ten again. He looked up. Joseph's eyes were wide. "There now," said Tom Sylvestri, "see what you've made me do? I'll have to give myself a hundred Hail Marys for that. And the Stations of the Cross."

"Tom . . ."

"No, Joseph. It's my turn, now. You've said what you came to say. You've said you love me. And, all right, I won't deny that in another world, another time and place, I might return that love. But I can't. Period. Finished. End of discussion. I'm a priest, Joseph. I have made a decision to serve God and my fellow men, in that order. And while our Father may understand this particular cross I bear, He does not approve. It's all right for me to . . . be as I am, so long as it has no more to do with my life as a priest than . . . than the urges any other priest might feel. We're none of us more than human. None of us immune. But we make a solemn oath when we take to the priesthood. In a moment of weakness I broke that oath—and I'm sorry, terribly, terribly sorry that you had to suffer for my weakness—but it was just that: a weakness. A *passing* weakness. It cannot be repeated. *It will not be repeated.*"

"I'll kill myself. I will. I'll kill myself."

Tom pushed his plate away. In the flickering candlelight his companion's face looked soft, womanly. The deep eyes were darkly shadowed, as if mascara had run from the tears he'd shed.

"All right," said Tom, not believing he said it. "If you think that's the only solution, go ahead and be damned."

"I'm damned anyway, aren't I? Damned for being gay. Damned for living my life the way it came to me."

"God sets trials for all of us . . ."

"Oh, now you're going to preach at me! You're going to preach to me! Sermon number thirty-seven, for faggots and other lowlife. The great God Almighty makes you queer to test you. To test you. Like he makes somebody else a hunchback or a leper." Joseph was on his feet, grabbing for his coat and scarf. "Well, screw Him! Screw your great God Almighty. Screw Him, screw Him, screw Him!" He was almost hysterical. Tom rose to grab him, to shake him, but Joseph ducked away. "And screw you too! Screw you, you goddamn faggot priest! GODDAMN FAGGOT PRIEST!"

He ran. Halfway down the narrow length of the restaurant his feet tangled in his trailing scarf. He tripped, crashing full length through a table of four. Linguine flew. Voices snarled. A big man surged after him, but Joseph was faster. He ducked under a badly aimed fist and out the door. Tom could not find the strength to go after him, though everything told him he should. He sank back into his booth. He poured a glass of wine and drank it in a single draught. The aftertaste was like vinegar.

The vinegar they gave our Savior as He hung upon the cross, Tom thought, immediately shaking his head. *No. I do not belong in that company.*

He rose again and turned to seek out Sophia and his coat. He saw her standing at the cash register by the front door. Her dark eyes were like saucers. Tom strode past two Vietnamese waiters doing their best to rescue some semblance of a dinner from the exploded table. The four disrupted diners eyed him as he passed. He took his coat and handed Sophia the twenty-five dollars he knew would cover the meal and gratuity. She was looking at him as if he had become a stranger.

Which I probably have, he realized with great sadness.

"Padre . . ." Her voice trembled. "That man . . . what he said . . . what he called you . . ."

Tom pulled his coat collar up around his ears. "Yes, Sophia?"

"Such a terrible thing . . ." She could not bring herself to ask the question he saw in her eyes.

Of course, he thought. *Doesn't everyone think those called to the priesthood are a little strange? Don't they have to be a little odd, to sacrifice the pleasures of the flesh for the mysteries of the Church?* Tom Sylvestri felt very tired. Weary with the games, the lies, the charade.

"Not so terrible," he said. He stepped to the inner door and pushed it open. People were coming in the other way. A gust of frigid air crashed around him. "Not so terrible," he said again, in unconscious imitation of Joseph Terranova. "Not when you know it's true."

Donna Wojciechowski lay on the couch in Ben Carpenter's apartment, seven hours after their interview. She'd asked where she might find a good hotel, but Ben shook his head.

"No need to go looking for a hotel," he'd said. He thumped the couch beneath his broad rear. "This folds out into a mighty comfortable bed."

Donna started to protest but Ben waved any objection aside.

"I'm not going to come sneaking out in the middle of the night and try to rape you. Mae won't let me." He'd smiled, as if, Donna thought, he found the idea quite comical. She found nothing humorous in the concept whatsoever, and her expression said so. Ben, however, seemed unable or unwilling—*or uncaring*—to read her face, and simply bolstered his suggestion with logic. "You want to go and see Paul as soon as possible, right? Tonight is out of the question, but I can drive you out there myself in the morning. Fair enough?"

Donna had balanced the alternatives and decided she could probably deal with Ben Carpenter should he make the move he'd denied.

"All right." She'd sighed, releasing in a long, slow exhalation the breath she then realized she'd been holding for quite some time.

"Fine. I've got some pajamas that'll fit you." Ben paused. "You don't have any bags, right?"

Donna felt a flush of color in her cheeks. He was reading her too well. Her tone, her attitude, possibly even her words had told him she'd come to Faulkner ill prepared. "No," she'd said. "No bags."

Now, with Ben's flannel pajamas soft against her skin and the cool, blue-white streetlight just below the living room window painting the ceiling above her with dark parallel shadows of the venetian blinds Ben had lowered, Donna kept going back to the words of their interview. She wanted—professionalism demanded—some flaw in the perfect picture Ben and Mae painted. Yet she found herself believing, the more she thought about what they'd said. She was never much one for daydreams herself, and Stone's training had only reinforced her natural pragmatism, but the honest enthusiasm of Carpenter's simple little article was given greater and greater power by their words. At times it seemed to Donna as if Ben and Mae were united in some kind of religious chant, their words carrying such potent emotion, such conviction.

But she was here to do a job, and increasingly—perhaps to spite Walker Stone—she wanted to do the job to the best of her considerable talents.

Donna swung the inside of her left wrist up over her face.

Her watch said 2:34 A.M. She sighed. Friday had become Saturday. She was not going to get any sleep tonight. She needed a drink. A parade of pythons did slow circuits through her lower intestine. Her mouth felt again like the bottom of that hoary old birdcage. She let her mind drift around the conversation of —now—last evening.

"We've had the most beautiful sex every night," she heard Mae Faber saying, "since the Miracle Show."

Donna rolled off the sofa bed and walked the three paces to the desk by the window. She finished the cigarette, tumbled the pillar of ash into the ashtray on the desk's knotty pine top, stubbed out the butt. The exhalation that followed turned into a series of coughs, built to truly spectacular proportions. She tried to stifle the sound so as not to draw the attention of Ben and Mae, hopefully sound asleep in the next room. She did not want to face them so soon after the embarrassing hour or so of listening to their rambunctious lovemaking. Ben's moans and Mae's strangely girlish squeals were still fresh in Donna's mind.

The fit left Donna gripping the edge of the desk as if the room were in an earthquake. Finally she straightened and released the desk. She reached out to the venetian blinds over the window to her left and parted the horizontal slats. She looked out over the darkened face of Faulkner. The snow had stopped. Her car was covered with a soft, smooth layer, an inch or two thick by Donna's estimation. The snow rounded out the shapes of the spilled garbage up and down the street, casting strange, Rorschach shadows. Streetlights made crystalline circles on the pavement, sparkling like fairy dust. Where they were lit. Donna noted now, for the first time, that half the lights she could see were dark. The closest, half a block away, looked shattered, as if it had been shot out with a rifle. There were no people abroad, no cars moving.

Donna thought of a similar hour, looking off the balcony of her apartment. There was always some sort of traffic moving on the streets below her nineteenth-floor view. South she would see the lights moving in and out of O'Hare and Midway airports. In the time she'd lived with Walker Stone, she'd seen that a big city really never sleeps. From his apartment the pageantry of Chicago's nightlife was always on display. Faulkner might have been a photograph, pasted to the outside of the glass.

Donna sighed. She opened her purse and extracted her tape recorder. She dug around under the jumble of oddments cluttering the big bag and found the earphone. She plugged it into the tiny jack, hooking the porous, dark sponge pad over her ear. She pressed rewind, then play.

She heard her own voice say, "Maybe I should get out there and see this boy for myself. Tonight."

"Not tonight," said Ben's low, even tones, tinny through the fingernail-size speaker. "He had a pretty busy time of it last night, what with having to tend to almost two thousand people, all with a needing. Reverend Trayne wants him to rest for a while."

"So it affects him, then, whatever this is he does? It tires him?"

"Not tires so much," said Mae's voice. "It's hard to describe. But it does affect him. Not surprising, when you consider what he does."

"Which is what, exactly? I mean, the mechanics of it. How does he work his . . . magic?"

"It's not magic." Donna remembered the sour look on Mae's face.

"Sorry. Poor choice of words. And I call myself a writer. But, tell me. If you can. What was it, exactly, that made you accept his . . . gift."

Mae had collected herself and shifted to sit up straight, thinking. Donna saw in her mind the tiny fan of creases that spread above the bridge of Mae's nose. She was groping for something, Donna thought, that was now very, very difficult to grasp. When Mae spoke, finally, it was to verbalize exactly that.

"It's very hard," she said. "It's so hard to think how I was, how I felt, before Paul. I mean, it's all there. All still there. But it doesn't matter anymore. When I try to think of it, when I try to remember how I felt, it's like a voice in my head says 'Never mind.'"

Ben nodded. "That's just the feeling exactly. 'Never mind.'"

"But—" Donna heard the edge of frustration in her voice— "you *can* remember, if you try? I mean, it's important that I get a sense of what was going through your head when you first went to see Paul Trayne."

"Well, just curiosity, at first," Mae said. "Faulkner is a small town. Not much happening on a day-to-day basis, you know? So, when something like this comes along, naturally a body wants to go and have a look. So that was all it was, at first."

"At first?"

"Well, yes. By the time I got there, got into the tent . . ." Again the creasing of the brow, the puzzled twist of the lips. "It's funny. I went just out of curiosity, you know? I wasn't feeling down, or anything. But by the time Paul was ready it had changed. I was feeling pretty depressed, as a matter of fact. I find it hard to believe that was ever possible, that anything could have depressed me, but that's what I remember. There were a lot of familiar faces there, that night. And a lot of them had been mean to me, over the years. Well, maybe 'mean' is too strong a word. Careless. You know. The way people can be."

Donna nodded encouragingly.

"Well, seeing them sort of, I don't know, sort of got to me, a bit. It was funny, really. I used to see those people every day, on the street, in the shops, the movie theater, and it never really bothered me that they'd said and done things that had been hurtful. But just then, in the tent, waiting to see what was going to happen, I felt very down in myself."

"So, I guess you were pretty much ready for whatever Paul Trayne had to offer, hmm? How about you, Ben?"

Ben had scratched his chin, remembering. "Pretty much as Mae describes. Maybe it was thinking about what Paul Trayne was offering, but when I went to the session that night I started to think about all the things I'd like to see sponged off my personal slate." He'd smiled. "And, of course, they were."

Donna heard herself sigh. This course was going nowhere, she'd thought. Time to retrace. "Tell me again about the way it affects him."

"I really can't," Mae said. "You'd think maybe it would tire him, even just the time involved. But it didn't seem to. And the people kept going up. By the end of the evening he was on his knees, with tears pouring down his cheeks, but the people kept going up to the stage. The ones who had already been up told them to. Paul's pain doesn't matter, you see. Only that we accept his gift."

"Then, it hurts him? Physically?"

"Yes." Mae frowned for a moment, shrugged. "But the agony he feels . . . well, that's just part of the burden he takes onto himself."

Donna heard herself say, "In the article you mentioned the Biblical quote by the gate, Ben. About bearing griefs and carrying sorrows."

" 'Surely he hath borne our griefs, and carried our sorrows,' " Mae quoted. "It's from Isaiah. Isaiah fifty-three four."

"Uh-huh. Now . . . ." Donna heard the beginning coyness in her own voice, wanted to scream. *What kind of games am I playing with these people?* "I'll admit I'm not big on the Bible. Is that a reference to Jesus?"

"It's a prophecy," Mae said. Donna could still see her smile, with understanding, not condescension. "It's from the chapter that predicts the suffering of the Messiah. The rest of the verse is; '. . . yet we did esteem him stricken, smitten of God, and afflicted. But he was wounded for our transgressions, he was bruised for our iniquities: the chastisement of our peace was upon him; and with his stripes we are healed.' "

"It refers to Paul as if it were written for him," Ben Carpenter's voice said.

There was a long pause on the tape. Donna remembered Mae turning to Ben. Remembered the way their eyes locked, the way some secret, telepathic message seemed to pass between them.

Donna switched off the tape recorder. She did not need to hear the exact words to know what had happened next. Ben and Mae had dissolved into quasi-religious rapture. They still spoke to Donna, still acknowledged her presence in the room, but she was no longer important to them. She did not—could not—understand. She remembered, too, a feeling of being on the outside, a feeling of need. Need to be part of that wonder.

Somewhere in that feeling, she recognized now, was the gene-sis of her thoughts on the compulsion in their words.

When Ben came back to awareness of her, he'd invited her to stay the night. They'd talked about inconsequential things for another forty minutes or so, by Donna's reckoning, Ben finishing his Chinese takeout, Donna far too many gins.

Donna's stomach churned as she turned away from the tape recorder and flopped back on the bed. Feelings of disgust and self-loathing—all too familiar—crowded around the front part of her thoughts. She thought again of Stone's words, his re-minder of her former status in the community of reporters in Chicago and the nation.

Got to get your act back on track, kiddo, she thought, know-ing as the words formed in her mind that she had the power, if not the immediate inclination to do so. Walker Stone might have been right. The Warner story might have been a fluke— the mesmerizing awfulness of it, the endless horrible details, making everything in her own life seem so small and unimpor-tant that for a while—a short while—she'd been fired up again, driven again.

But it hadn't lasted more than a day past her greatest coup, the interview with Warner himself. She'd come close again to the Pulitzer with that one, she thought, if she did not actually win it. But it had been like walking naked through hell, sitting in the interview room, alone with the smooth-faced young man who had, in a period of less than eight months, systematically tortured and killed thirty-eight women—girls, really, not one older than nineteen.

She'd talked to him for three days, three long days, learning every detail of his life—Warner had held back nothing, once he'd been apprehended, but Donna was the first to get it all in sequence, in print—every detail of his thinking. Only one thing remained closed to her, one part of his mind. No matter how hard she tried, no matter how hard the police psychiatrists tried, no one could get into the part of Errol Keane Warner's brain that held his true feelings about what he had done. The guilt, the grief that simple common sense told Donna, told everyone he must surely be feeling. He was not, so far as any-one was able to determine, a complete sociopath. He understood clearly the difference between good and evil, right and wrong. But his feelings were locked away, buried deep, deep down in a hidden recess of his mind.

"When he does confront it all," the psychiatrists Donna interviewed all agreed, "it will be as if part of his brain exploded. No human psyche could tolerate that kind of grief and guilt being unleashed all at once."

And what would happen, Donna wondered now, standing by the window of Ben Carpenter's living room, if Errol Warner met Paul Trayne? What would be the effect of this "gift" of Paul's on the strange, twisted psyche of the worst mass murderer Chicago had seen since John Wayne Gacy?

It felt odd to find herself thinking along such lines. She didn't want to let herself go into this assignment so willing to buy into the whole story, and yet . . .

She'd been the one to end the conversation with Ben and Mae. Not by turning off the tape recorder and smiling demurely, as was her usual routine, but by becoming suddenly, violently sick. It began with a coughing fit; it ended with a bolt for the bathroom. She'd not made it fast enough. Her spew stained Ben's faded carpet and spattered over her blouse and slacks. These latter hung now from the shower rail, Donna's hopes they would be presentable by morning hanging with them. She was trapped, unless she felt like walking almost naked to her car through the freezing winter night.

"Shit," she said, digging the heels of her hands into her eyes. *Don't you dare cry, bitch,* she warned herself. *Don't you dare!*

But tears came, and Donna eventually released herself to uncontrollable sobbing, collapsing back on the bed, curling into a tight little ball around the daggers sprouting from the backs of the pythons in her gut.

This was what she could thank Steve Binder for, she thought. Her long-departed, probably deceased ex-husband. He'd taught her to drink. "It'll loosen you up," he'd said, working his practiced seduction on a virginal Donna.

It certainly had. But even he had grown tired of sex with a drunken teenager, eventually. About the time he started insisting she do it sober, their marriage began to disintegrate. Donna found it impossible to stay sober from the very first drink. Most of her marriage, she came to realize, was a blur consisting of bad booze, worse sex, and screaming fights.

"Christ, you're a cold bitch," Binder said, in the last days. "I don't know what I thought I was getting into, marrying you. Half the time you're about as much fun as humping a hollow log."

"Well, you'd know," she remembered shouting. "Or is that maybe the only thing you haven't humped since we've been married?" Donna could hear herself, hear so clearly. Barely twenty. A young voice, shrill in its anger. Hating him. Hating what he'd done to her. Hating herself for letting him do it. "You haven't exactly gone without," she'd yelled, "whatever I might have wanted or needed. You never cared whether I was ready, or interested, or . . ."

"That's my right," he'd said. He'd tried to use his magnificent voice on her. The same voice that turned her head inside out the first time they met, made her forget all her years of fear and confusion.

"Donna the dyke," they'd called her in high school, with that special brand of subtlety unique to teenage boys. All because she was so afraid of sex, so afraid of getting pregnant, as her mother had, without a husband to give her child a name. Her mother drilled that into her. But the other kids could not understand how she could be normal—a teenager's definition of normal—how she could have normal needs, normal feelings, and still be able to deny herself the wonders they were uncovering in their clumsy, fumbling ways. Steven Anthony Binder, with his mellifluous voice, his practiced hands, brought Donna to the edge of her prison cell, to the door, then slammed it in her face because she did not respond fast enough.

Another dozen years passed as Donna fought her way up from the pit into which that failed and foolish marriage had hurled her. And fight she had, against all the odds that piled up in her way. Against the chauvinism that still walled the news media, that old-boys' club she wanted so desperately to penetrate. She'd met Steve Binder at a journalism class, lost her way in the years with him, then went back to school, back to the fight. She was strong, she was beautiful. When she was not drinking—and she was able to spread wider and wider apart

the bouts with the bottle in those days of consuming drive—
her mind was razor-sharp and laser-quick. It was this that, perhaps even more than her stunning physical presence, first
brought her to the attention of Walker Stone. He adopted her
first as a protégée, then a confidante, then a lover. He sensed
the turmoil in her soul and probed after it, always kind, always
helpful.

"All the sensitivity of a brick," Walker Stone said, when
he'd finally coaxed the story of her failed marriage out of
Donna.

But that was only part of the story. There was also Viveca.

Donna's mother had not lived long enough to meet Walker
Stone. She would never have approved of him. Not of someone who told Donna to seek out only the best in herself. To
settle for nothing less.

Dear Viveca, Donna thought. *How much you loved seeing
me punished for your sins. Your bastard daughter being put
through the wringer because you'd made her so terribly afraid
of anything a man might do to her. Made her so afraid she had
to get stinking drunk before she could let the first man she
thought she might be in love with even lay a hand on her!*

Damnation, thought Donna Wojciechowski, *it's a miracle
I'm not the dyke they used to say I was!*

She looked at her watch again. The minute hand had crept
to within its own breadth of the hour. An idea was forming.
Partly it came from the need she was feeling to believe Ben
and Mae, to be a part of the special, select club they now
belonged to. Partly it came from the surge of paranoia she felt
over that need. She pulled herself across the bed and reached
for the telephone on the end table beneath the window. She
tapped out the long distance code that would connect her to
Walker Stone's home line and waited for the muted chime of
the automated system's request for her calling card number.
She tapped this out on the dial, then heard the recorded voice
say "Thank you."

The phone rang ten times, Stone's answering machine
picked up. "Stone," said the mechanically altered voice, higher
than his normal one. "You know what this is, and you know
what to do. Here's the beep . . ."

"Walker? It's Don. Are you there? Pick up if you're there." Despite Ben and Mae, asleep in the next room, she shouted into the phone. "Pick up, Walker!"

He picked up. "Christ Almighty, do you know what time it is, Donna?"

She was surprised to hear him swear, but she did not comment. "I own a watch, yes. This is important. This story . . ."

"What story?" Donna could hear Stone coming awake as he spoke, focusing. "Oh, the Boy Wonder. Yeah. What about it? Isn't it something that could wait until a decent hour? I only got home about three hours ago."

"I don't want to lose any time on this, Walker. I . . . want you in on this. Soon."

"It's that good?" Stone cleared his throat. Donna pictured him in her mind, sitting on the edge of the bed they'd shared a few hundred times. She knew he'd be naked, knew the black hair covering almost every square inch of his body would look like thick dark fur against the white sheets.

"Tell me about it, Don. In words of one syllable."

"I can't. Because I don't have anything solid." She paused. "Do you still trust my feelings, Walker?"

"With reservations. Say on."

"There's something definitely happening in this town. Happening to the people. Some kind of . . . No. I can't put a name to it. There are no words. But . . . Walker, if this is genuine, if this boy Paul Trayne is the real article, he could be the most wonderful thing that ever happened to the world. Or the most dangerous. I think we should get the story out as fast as possible. This morning, even, if we can. Get people who could really understand this looking into it."

"What's turned you into such a devout believer, though, Don? I sent you down there as my champion debunker . . ."

"You also warned me not to prejudge the story. Who knows, maybe I actually listened. Or maybe it was seeing the town, talking to Ben Carpenter. I swear to God, Walker, this is a man who could put the televangelists to shame. When he talks about Paul Trayne, you just . . . I don't know . . . I guess I'd have to say he just makes you *want* to believe him."

"Go on." Stone's tone told Donna she was sorely lacking in the convincing abilities she'd found in Ben.

"Not much more to tell over the phone," she said. "You really have to be here. And . . . I'd like you to be here."

A pause. "You want me to come to Faulkner? Why?"

"I don't know." It was true. Donna could not find a real reason to be calling Stone, to be asking him—pleading with him—to join her. Nothing beyond Ben's unassailable conviction. "I just know this is something you should see, you should judge. Then, if it's real, you could get some of your influential friends to pull strings and . . ." She stopped. She did not know what she was going to say next. The words had come in a rush, and now they were gone, dried up.

Another pause, longer this time. "Don . . ." Stone didn't want to say what was coming next. Donna knew the signs. She also knew the question.

"I'm sober, Walker. Not stone cold sober, I won't lie to you. I drank myself stupid tonight, and I vomited most of it into Ben Carpenter's john. I'm sitting here shivering in borrowed PJs because my clothes are hanging in the bathroom after a quick rinse in Ben's sink. But I'm okay now."

"That's hardly an impartial judgment, Don."

"I know," she said. "I also know I'm thinking about as clearly as I ever have. And I'm excited and scared and a whole bunch of other things I can't explain. Just come, okay? You were all full of how this was an hour drive. Test that for yourself."

"All right." He'd sounded unconvinced, but he was yielding. "You'll come?"

"I'll come. But only because it's you, Donna." Another pause. "You understand that, don't you?"

"Sure. See you soon." She hung up before anything more could be said. As she cradled the handset the significance of Walker Stone's words imprinted themselves on her consciousness.

He's only coming because it's you. Because he still loves you.

3

"Sorry to get you down here for this, so early an' all, Father. But your name was the only one we found on him. The only person we could notify."

"That's quite all right, Officer." Father Tom Sylvestri heard his voice echo back harsh and empty from the stone walls around them. It was very much in keeping with the way he felt, harsh and empty, as if his soul had been removed, the place it once occupied scoured with a steel brush.

Joseph is dead, his thoughts repeated, over and over. *After all the threats, he's really dead. Finally dead. And it's my fault. My fault. How could it be otherwise?*

He found the sound of their footfalls terribly loud. A single line of fluorescent lighting snaked through the pipes and conduit above him, flickering, making dark blue shadows dance in the corners of his eyes.

"Here we are, Father." The uniformed officer knocked on an unmarked door set into the old stone of the wall. After a moment the door opened and a small man with a pale, fleshy face and tiny eyes looked out. He looked, Tom thought, like some underground creature startled by an intrusion of light and life from above. The simile was appropriate. They were, by Tom's reckoning, at least sixty feet below the level of the snow-swept streets of Chicago. A hundred feet above him, somewhere, in a high security holding cell, awaiting his transportation to Joliet, Errol Keane Warner would be sitting, Tom thought, alone with whatever thoughts came to such a man. It was strange, Tom thought, and yet so typically human, that even at a time like this he could not keep his mind from straying to thoughts of the monster up there on the fifth floor, the monster who had filled the minds and hearts of all Chicago with so much dread.

"Terranova," said the officer to the man with tiny eyes. The other man squinted at Father Tom. "For ID," said the cop.

The man nodded and stepped back, pulling the door wide. Tom followed the officer into a small room. He found walls painted a faded hospital green, a square table, a chair, and three filing cabinets set side by side. Beyond the table another door stood closed. There was a heavy combination lock set just above the knob. On the table Tom noted a flask of coffee, a mug half filled, a half-eaten sandwich lying on crinkled wax paper. Next to this an issue of *Playboy* lay open to a series of pictures of an opulently fleshed, bronze-haired young woman. Her legs were long and athletic, her breasts impossibly huge and firm. The smooth flow of her flesh made Tom feel slightly queasy. Since he was not normally disturbed by the sight of sumptuous female flesh, he put his feelings down to the place, his reason for being there. The pictures made Tom Sylvestri think of a tasteless joke Joseph Terranova told him in a lighter moment as they lay in each other's arms and Joseph sought any way he could find to keep Tom from thinking what he was doing there.

"These two old queens are standing on a street corner," Joseph said. "Old queens standing on a street corner. And this incredibly zaftig woman walks by. Incredibly zaftig. Tits out to here. And one of the old queens sighs. He sighs. And his lover says, he says, 'Hey, you're not thinking of going straight on me are you?' And the other old queen, he says, 'No, no. It's just when I see something like that, I sometimes wish I'd been born a lesbian.' "

"Something wrong, Father?" asked a voice not part of the memory.

Tom realized he was smiling a little, visibly, at the memory. He looked into the questioning eyes of the uniformed officer.

"No. I was just thinking about something Jos . . . Mr. Terra-nova told me once."

"Were you good friends?" They were walking now through the room that lay on the other side of the combination-locked door, along a wide passageway between stainless steel doors set in vertical rows. Tom was struck by the impression of a grotesquely outsized safety deposit vault.

"We . . . knew each other," he said, and his brain screamed *Hypocrite!* "He was a parishioner at St. Timothy's. We met when he was doing volunteer work for some of the rehab programs I run. He was . . . quite religous."

The cop simply nodded. They'd reached almost the end of the long passage. The man with the tiny eyes—Tom found him-self wishing more of these people wore name tags—checked the numbered paper slipped into the holder on one of the stainless steel doors and grabbed the big handle. He pushed it up and pulled it back, and the door swung back silently on well-oiled hinges. The outward swing of the door activated a mechanism inside the revealed chamber. As Tom watched, the platform nestled within rolled outward six inches or so. Tiny Eyes stepped around the door. He grabbed a protruding hori-zontal bar on the platform and pulled the tray halfway out. He flipped back the sheet.

Tom looked down at the long, pinched face. Joseph looked years younger, a child. Tom Sylvestri had delivered enough absolutions in his career to know the oddly rejuvenating effect of death. With all the muscles relaxed—rigor had passed out of Joseph by now—the face lost years.

A cruel contradiction, Tom thought, *that in the first hours of death we should look as if we had so much more life left in us.*

"Sure looks peaceful, don't he?" said the cop. The man with tiny eyes had not spoken at all as yet.

"I understand it's a very peaceful death, freezing," Tom said. The cop who'd contacted him had told of the way Joseph's body had been found. "The pain goes away, feeling goes away. You just . . . drift off to sleep."

I pray it was peaceful, Tom thought. *You deserved peace at the end, poor Joseph. More peace than ever I brought you.*

He put out a hand and stroked the lank hair away from the

pale, cold brow. He looked up as he realized what he was doing. Neither man seemed surprised by his action. Priests were excused many things.

The cop said, "It's being treated as a suicide, you know? Because of the notebook. It takes time to sit there and write out what he wrote. He woulda known he'd be freezin' to death, sittin' there on the lakeshore." He shrugged. "So it's being treated as a suicide."

Tom nodded. He was taller than the policeman. The officer was standing so close by his side Tom had to twist his head at an uncomfortable angle to see the man's face properly. "I'm almost certain it was. He was . . . very high-strung."

The cop cleared his throat. "Would you happen to know if he was a fa—a homosexual, Father? The stuff in that notebook I told you about . . . well, some of the guys thought it coulda gone either way, you know? Like he might have been writin' about a dame, but . . ."

Tom blinked. "Why? Does that make a difference?" It seemed a ridiculous prejudice now, if prejudice it was. Joseph was dead, frozen as he sat scribbling in a notebook, sitting on the rocky shore of Lake Michigan. What possible difference could his sexual preferences make now?

"The coroner will want to know," the cop said, "before he does the autopsy. So he can be on the watch for, well, AIDS an' like that."

"Oh, yes." Tom considered. Joseph was extraordinarily flamboyant—*a kind word,* Tom thought—in life, but he was not sure he'd publicly come out. Still, there was no reason to guard such a secret, if secret it was, now that Joseph Terranova was a corpse. He had no living relative that Tom knew of, and certainly he knew as much—more—about Joseph Terranova than anyone. "I believe he was gay, yes," Tom said. The distance in his words rang loud and hollow in the metal walled room. "What made you ask?"

"We found a card in his wallet. Same place we found your name. Membership card in, well, one of them *clubs.* You know the kind? Straight until eleven, midnight, then . . . So we thought we'd better ask."

"Yes." Tom frowned. Did Joseph still frequent such places?

The AIDS scare had virtually closed down many gay hangouts in the bigger cities. It would be very like Joseph to continue to go to such a place, living dangerously in the only way he could. A momentary fear inserted itself in Tom's thoughts, and he tried to ignore it. He would have plenty of time later to worry about anything he might have caught from Joseph Terranova.

"There are scars on his wrists. Old scars." A strange voice. Tom looked up. It was the man with tiny eyes. "He'd tried to kill himself before."

It was not a question. Tom nodded. "Twice, I think. Twice that I know of."

The cop nodded too. "Highest suicide rate I know, homos," he said. He coughed again. "Sorry, Father. Language."

Tom smiled. "I'm a priest," he said, "not a cloistered nun." He used the redundant phrase for the sake of his lay listeners. To them, he knew, anything in a habit was a nun. "I've heard a few words stronger than that in my day, Officer."

And used them.

"Well . . ." The cop nodded again, this time to the man with tiny eyes, who pulled up the crisp white sheet and pushed the tray back into the deep box of the morgue drawer. He closed the door silently, rubber seals meeting cold metal without a sound. "Would you like a cup of coffee, Father?" the cop asked. "Or something stronger, even? I think the captain has some brandy."

Tom smiled again. "For medicinal purposes, no doubt. No, thank you, Officer. I think I will be getting back to my church." He paused at the door as they reached it. "The notebook you mentioned. Is that necessary as evidence, or . . . ?"

The cop shook his head. "No. We've already got it set aside to send to the next of kin, if we ever find any."

"I wonder . . ." Tom felt the words coming all in a rush now. "I wonder if I might have it?"

The cop's eyebrows went up. "I . . . well, I guess there ain't no real reason why not, since you were his priest an' all. C'mon upstairs and I'll get his things released to you. You can sign the forms, and maybe you can save us the trouble of looking for his next of kin."

Tom nodded. "I'd be happy to."

* * *

The morning was warming quickly, but Donna froze crossing the distance to Ben's car. Her blouse and slacks were not completely dry from their rinsing. They clung like ice. Donna pulled her coat tighter around her and stuffed her hands in the pockets. When she reached the car Donna stopped hunching in on herself, resigned to the cold, resigned to the misery. Mae's breakfast—delicious, Donna deduced from the way Ben polished off his portion—sat in the pit of her stomach, a tight and utterly indigestible lump. Still, that was better than an empty stomach, and the bland, undirected conversation over Ben's plastic plates had served to sponge away some of the fog around Donna's brain. She was starting to work. With the morning—the real morning, when the sun rose and small, brave birds sang in bare trees—she'd awakened to the aroma of bacon and eggs. Her stomach, empty, tried to invert itself. Donna had tasted bile on the back of her tongue. She'd sat up and seen Mae's shadow move on the wall of the small kitchen opposite her.

"That's a helluva rude way to wake a girl up," she'd said.

Ben's face appeared around the door jamb. "How's that?"

"Making those disgusting cooking smells." She'd wrinkled her nose, and Ben and Mae had laughed.

"You'll need something after last night," Mae said. "I don't imagine your stomach has much to digest but itself."

"No," Donna said, curling her lip at the too vivid imagery of the quip. "I don't suppose it does." She swung her long legs over the edge of the sofa bed and stood. She was surprised to find herself steady on her feet. "Can I take a shower?"

"Go ahead. Clean towels in the closet by the bathroom door." Ben returned to the business of watching Mae prepare breakfast.

Now she looked at her watch, realizing it was probably the twentieth time she'd done so since climbing out of the shower. Eight o'clock.

Too soon to see if any of the local watering holes are open.

In any case, there were other rituals to observe, the careful rituals of denial. Even so low in spirit, Donna clung to her rules of order. No hard liquor before ten. She settled back in the passenger seat as Ben eased the Mazda out of its place and turned out onto the street. Faulkner was alive with morning traffic. The still picture of the night before had become a bustle of cars, trucks, men, women. Even some children darted and called along the main street.

Playing hooky? Donna wondered. She remembered all the times she'd cut class, starting when she was about twelve. She remembered, too, how guilty it had made her feel.

So much of her life disgusted her. So much of everything she did seemed designed to make her hate herself, as if she was studying the available paths from some lofty vantage, directing herself like a little marionette, this way and that.

No, no, Don, her angry, sneering inner voices told her. *That's the way to a nice, stable husband and a family. You should go this way, toward divorce and a miserable little apartment and . . . a drinking problem.* The last three words came faster than she could block, and in Walker Stone's voice.

I do not have a problem, she thought again. *I drink only gin, and that never before ten A.M.*

Unconsciously she stole a look at the dashboard clock. It was faster than her watch, but not enough. Eight-oh-six. Still too soon for a drink, but not too soon to ask Ben to stop at a drugstore so she could pick up a fresh pack of cigarettes.

On their way again, Ben drove offensively, dodging in and out of the slower local traffic. He came close to running down more than one pedestrian. Donna found herself looking back and forth for any sign of a police car. She saw only that the people of Faulkner did not appear overly disturbed by Ben's recklessness. They did not frown, did not raise eyebrows. Nothing in their faces carried condemnation, or even the kind of mild reproach one city dweller might direct against another who accidentally broke the invisible barrier separating each from the other.

"We don't mind." That was what these faces seemed to say. *"We don't mind. Drive like a lunatic. Be a drunk. Be filled with self-hatred. Walk down the street talking to yourself if that's what you want. We don't mind."*

It was on all the faces that they passed. *Contentment?* Donna wondered.

Contentment made her think of sheep, mindlessly munching in the field, oblivious to their ultimate destiny as someone's dinner. These people were not mindless. They were active, alive. They smiled, they nodded, they talked to each other. The people of Faulkner just looked . . .

Donna hunted for a word but could not find one. There was nothing in her vocabulary, her life experience, to match the pleasant faces she saw all around her.

Or the sight that greeted her as they came close to the viaduct carrying traffic across the road they traveled. This side of the highway was a block of buildings Donna had not been able to see from her position outside the *Observer* office when she'd first arrived and reviewed the town. Or, more precisely, it was a block of what had been buildings. Now they were blackened hulks, charcoaled timbers and beams thrusting up from the ground like the fingers of some unfortunate victim of the Inquisition, burned at the stake. A whole block, she saw with amazement, burned to the ground. As they passed she turned to look back at the faces of the buildings fronting on the remnants of the holocaust and saw that they were blackened with grime and smoke.

"Must've been a helluva fire," Donna said.

"Hmm?" It was almost as if Ben had not noticed the scene.

"Back there. That whole block burned to the ground. Anyone killed?"

"Ah . . ." Ben seemed to be searching for the information. "Oh, yes. Fifteen. There was a residential hotel there. Cheap one."

"Fifteen killed?" Donna turned to look back, but the site was already on the other side of the viaduct, blocked from her view. "Where was the fire department?"

Ben was a moment in answering. "They didn't come," he said at last. It seemed to Donna that this struck him not at all odd.

Ben turned right onto Pine Tree Road, following the river-bank, Donna peering ahead for some sign of the Miracle Show. The road was a mess. Two thousand cars and trucks had passed that way in two weeks. Most of them in the last four days. The way was deeply rutted. Ben had trouble holding the wheel, as the car bounced now into a left-hand rut, now a right, following the shifting tracks in the road. He tried to get up onto ground between the ruts, but it was slush and mud; each time the front wheels managed the rise, the effort of getting the rear wheels up would propel them down into the groove again.

When they reached Gunner's Field, the Mazda practically turned itself, trapped in the sweep of ruts carved by all those wheels that had gone before it. Ben pulled in past the gate, still marked with its little cardboard sign. He stopped in the center of the flattened grass area, now much larger than his article's description. Donna climbed out of the car and found the grasses mushy underfoot. The day was just warm enough to have melted some of the snow. Broad, shallow puddles winked in the sunlight. Again Donna regretted her petty decision not to bring a change of clothes. She could have used some flat-soled hiking boots, even gumboots, in that field. Her two-inch heels sank into the mud, forcing her to walk with a backward-leaning gait that made the muscles in her calves scream after only a dozen steps.

Leaving Ben to cross directly to the old truck, Donna walked up to the big tent and peeled back the edge of the door flap. Inside she found darkness and a stale odor unlike anything she'd ever smelled before. Donna put it down to wet canvas and stepped into the tent. It was twenty degrees warmer inside. Donna's breath vanished from the air around her. She pulled from her purse the pack of cigarettes and re-created the steam in smoke. The taste of the tobacco overpowered the odd odors of the tent.

She looked around, slowly. There was, as Ben predicted, nothing remarkable here. In the womblike darkness Donna felt small, isolated. Felt the need for a drink somewhat more acutely than she had even on the drive to Gunner's Field. She strolled around the perimeter of the tent, her mind drifting. All the petty annoyances, all the psychological scars she'd accrued in her life, bubbled at the edge of her thoughts. Something to do with her anticipation over the meeting she was about to have with Paul Trayne?

Am I really so weak, really such a dependent personality that

I'd throw all my hopes out to this boy even before I get a look at him?

It was similar, she realized, to Ben and Mae's descriptions of their own feelings. Donna was not about to let herself wander down that path. She shook off the sensation and went on with her inspection of the tent. The chairs were still arranged as Ben Carpenter described them; the stage was just as she'd expected it. As her circuit brought her to it, she stepped onto the low, broad platform. Boards creaked under her hundred and forty pounds. She turned and faced the array of seats, dark in the darkness of the tent. Her eyes adjusted. Sunlight filtering through the walls took on a brownish cast. Dark shadows on the canvas roof indicated places where snow had not melted. Holding her breath, Donna could hear water running slowly down the slope of the roof, dripping into growing puddles around the perimeter of the tent.

She stepped off the stage. There was nothing of interest in the deserted tent. She went back outside, walked around the outer edge, and came up to the parked van to find Ben and Reverend Trayne waiting for her.

"This is the young woman?" Trayne asked, inclining his head to Ben.

Donna smiled her very best smile and thrust a hand out. "Donna Wojciechowski, *Chicago Advocate.* You must be Reverend Trayne."

Heavy lids blinked. "Yes." He took Donna's hand.

"I guess Ben's told you I read his little piece on you and your son," Donna said. "My editor thought I should follow up on it." She kept the big smile firmly in place. She pumped Trayne's hand as she spoke, releasing it only when she was ready. "Can I meet Paul?"

Ben shook his head, a small movement. "He is resting. Like I said, the night before last was very busy . . ."

"I really only want to ask him a few very simple questions," Donna said, still smiling. She was beginning to feel a real need to see, to meet this boy. She shaped a flat-out lie and handed it to Trayne: "I've already got everything I need, really, except a few words from the horse's mouth. Is Paul in the truck?" She took a step forward.

"Yes." Trayne put out a long arm to block Donna's forward movement. "But we prefer to keep our quarters private."

"I can understand that. But surely you can understand my position? I have a job to do. Meeting your son is part of that job. The whole job, really."

Trayne looked at Ben; a questioning glance, Donna thought. Ben's face did not change, but Donna could tell Trayne was not at all used to this kind of argument, however politely she might be phrasing it.

Donna guessed that his height and big Abraham Lincoln face kept most people in check. But she pressed on. "Just a few words?"

Trayne seemed to her to be considering. She fancied she could see the pattern of thought flashing behind his dark eyes. Obviously they could not afford to shun publicity here, if their "work" was to get done. As many people as possible would need to know of, and believe in, the boy Paul. News, especially out of a metropolis like Chicago, would reach a lot of people. Maybe even get picked up by the national wire services.

"Might not be a bad idea," Ben said, offering his own weight to Donna's argument. "If Donna can convince her boss to give this story the kind of coverage it really deserves . . ."

"All right," said Trayne at last, "but not in the truck. In the tent. I'll bring him to you."

Donna let the smile down a notch. Her cheeks were beginning to ache. "Thanks."

She turned away from Trayne, and she and Ben crossed to the front of the tent and walked up to the stage. She lifted one of the folding chairs, gave it a half turn, and sat. Her weight drove the legs a couple of inches into the ground, a sensation she found unnerving. She pulled out another cigarette, lit it from the stub of the first, and blew a large smoke ring that faded quickly into the subdued light around her.

She looked at Ben Carpenter, silent and a little distant in the semidarkness, and made what seemed to her an inevitable comparison to Walker Stone. She frowned at the thought of Stone, of his reasons for sending her on this story. Out of the corner of her eye Donna saw the tent flap open and close and two figures of very different dimensions enter. She rose to face them. The boy was still in his nightshirt. The hem flapped about his thin legs below his old robe.

"Hello, Brother Carpenter. Good morning, Ms. Wojcie-chowski," said a soft, sweet voice. "I am Paul Trayne."

Donna looked into the smiling face of a perfectly normal teenage boy, a trifle more clean-cut than she was used to seeing. His dark orange hair was neatly trimmed and combed straight back, a feeble effort to control the luxuriant waves that threatened to spill the hair over the boy's sleepy face. That face was well scrubbed, rosy cheeked. Donna saw no acne or other adolescent disorders. His eyes were big and bright; they twinkled. His smile was warm. Donna liked Paul Trayne instinctively but did not feel ready to swoon over him, as Ben and Mae had.

"Hello, Paul," Ben said. Donna heard the tone of unvarnished adoration still in the man's voice.

"Hello, Paul," Donna said. "It's a pleasure to meet you."

Paul continued to smile, but Donna saw the ghost of pain around his clear eyes. "The pleasure is mine. Do you mind if I sit? I'm not really awake yet." As if for punctuation he stifled a yawn, covering his mouth with a small, almost delicate hand.

"Please do. Your father explained you've been through quite an ordeal in the past few days."

"There is so much work to do. So much Father says must be addressed. Cleansed. I appreciate, Miss Wojciechowski, this opportunity to inform a greater number of my gift. My service for the people."

"And what kind of service is that, Paul?" Without a word to Ben or Paul Trayne or his father, Donna slipped from conversation to interview. "How would you define what you do?"

"I relieve suffering," Paul said. "Not as a doctor does, with medicines, nor even as a priest might, with kind words and the solace of the Bible. But directly, by assuming onto myself the burdens people bear. The grief. The sorrows."

"Like the sign on your gate? Do you really think that applies to you, Paul?"

"Father selected it," Paul said, eyes far away for a moment. "I have not read the Holy Bible. Not all of it." His gaze came back to her and fixed her. Donna felt a tremor go down her spine. "I find it too sad," Paul said.

"Sad? I haven't read it myself in years, but I've heard enough to believe it's only about good things. Miracles. Salvation."

"Mostly," Paul nodded. "It is a wonderful book. The words are fine and true. But there is much suffering in them. Much pain. It makes me very sad that I could not be there to help those people, too. It makes me very sad whenever I hear of anyone who has a needing." Ben put a hand on Paul's shoulder; Donna saw his fingers tighten in a gentle squeeze. Paul lifted one of his own pale hands and laid it lightly, briefly, over Ben's thick fingers.

"Yes." Donna nodded. "Ben told me that's what you call it. A 'needing.' What does that mean to you, exactly?"

"It's a term Father invented," Paul said. "These poor people come to me, their hearts and souls all filled with needless sorrows. They have a great desire to empty themselves, to unburden themselves, so they can get on with their lives more properly. That's their needing, Ms. Wojciechowski. To be free of these sorrows."

"What kind of sorrows?"

Paul shrugged. "Guilt, mostly, I suppose. The kinds of silly, unnecessary guilt so many people carry." Donna could hear the weariness in Paul's voice, but it was overlaid by the strength of his words. The conviction she heard in his calm, steady tone.

"And you take it from them?" she asked. "Do you mean that literally, Paul? Their guilt becomes your guilt? How does that work?"

"I do not know the . . . way of it. I only know it happens. I look into a person's face. I look into their eyes, and through their eyes into their soul. I see them as the pure, unsullied beings they were meant to be. And I take away everything that does not belong to that image."

Donna nodded. "And where does that bad stuff go, Paul? Into you? Over you? Around you?"

"Into me." He sighed, a heavy, ragged sound that made his whole body tremble. There was pain in his young face. Donna felt the need to put out a hand, to press one of his, which were resting lightly on his knees, palms up. She resisted, but with effort.

"And you feel this guilt yourself, Paul? You . . . I'm not at all sure how to phrase this, exactly . . . you *become* guilty?"

"I have not committed the thousand little sins they feel their guilt for," he said. His eyes were moist, his soft voice calm. "So I am not truly guilty, no. But I *do* feel their guilt. I feel it for them."

"So you're some kind of . . . whipping boy, Paul?"

Paul cocked his head. "I do not know that term, Ms. Wojcie-chowski."

"It comes from medieval times. The sons of kings could not be punished themselves, directly. No one but the king had the authority to punish a prince, and the king was too busy running the kingdom. So they had servants—more like slaves, I guess— who were punished instead. If the young prince was bad, his whipping boy was beaten for it."

Tears were flowing fast on Paul's cheeks. "That . . . seems so very cruel. The whipping boy had committed no crime him-self?"

"No. That was the point, I guess. Somehow that was sup-posed to be punishment enough for the prince or whoever the real bad boy was. The idea that someone else was suffering for his misdeeds. That's how I understand it, anyway."

"And you see this as something like what I do?" Paul asked.

Ben nodded before Donna could speak. "Yes. Yes, Paul. That's a very good analogy. I wish I'd thought of it."

Donna nodded, too. She was beginning to treat Paul Trayne's words with a large degree of respect. She reminded herself that her self-appointed prime function here was as a debunker. "On the basis of what you say, anyway, it seems like a good catch phrase. If you take on the guilt of others—if you experience their guilt, without ever having actually done the thing they feel guilty about—well, that seems about as much like being a whipping boy as I can think of."

Paul stared at the palms of his hands for several seconds. His gaze came back to Donna's face. Again she felt the thrill run down her spine. Ben was onto something after all, she thought.

"Does this mean you believe in what I'm doing here, Ms. Woj-ciechowski?" Paul asked. "Does it mean you believe in me?"

"Not yet," Donna said. It felt like a lie, but it would give Paul a basis for understanding her. "One of the very first stories I got, back when I was with the *Sun-Times,* was exposing a fake faith healer . . ."

"I am not a faith healer." There was hurt in his young voice. The effect could not have been more pronounced had Donna openly called him a charlatan. Ben's brow furrowed, his mouth tightening to a thin line.

This time Donna did put out the hand to touch Paul's. "You've got to admit that this setup of yours . . . Well, to an outsider, a nonbeliever, it looks like just another flimflam. Another way to part the good people from their hard-earned dollars."

"They take only small donations," Ben reminded her.

"I know that, too. But I've seen that worked as a scam. A small donation, until the victim is hooked, and then it becomes a bigger donation, then an invitation to become part of the church—"

"I'm not representing a church," Paul said.

"—and that means an even bigger donation, of course, and before you know it you're signing over your whole salary and living on a stipend the church or temple or whatever pays you. And I know you're not a church, Paul. But as I say, I've seen the game played, just this way, too many times to just buy into your story, boom, like that."

Paul studied her face, eyes hardened, squinting around the heavy tears. "What can I do to make you understand, Ms. Wojciechowski? To make you believe?"

It wouldn't take much, Donna thought.

But she said, "I don't have to believe in you, necessarily, to present an unbiased story. I'll admit I came into this expecting some kind of standard-issue con, but I'm open to convincing otherwise." She met his gaze with one just as firm. "Just don't look to convert me, okay?"

"I am not in the profession of conversion," Paul said.

Donna shrugged again. "I didn't say you were. I'm just a reasonably impartial observer here, Paul. I want to see what's going on. I'd like to come as close to finding out if it's legit as I can, yes. In fact, I'd flat-out love it if you really had this wonderful cosmic power, if you really could make everything nice-nice just by being there. But . . . well, I've got to see for myself, right?"

Paul nodded. He looked away for a moment, his eyes unfocused. His face went slack. Donna had the impression he was sorting through something, the contents of his soul, perhaps. Sorting through the guilt and sorrow he'd accumulated from four thousand people who'd come to this tent in just over two weeks.

"Perhaps"—his eyes came back to hers—"I could relieve you, right now."

Donna's left eyebrow went up. "Me?"

"You have a needing, do you not? When I look into your eyes, Miss Wojciechowski, I see much sorrow. Much self-hatred."

Do you really? Donna thought. *A fifteen-year-old boy can read me that well?*

Maybe he could. For a moment she was frightened. She was also aware, for the first time, that the elder Trayne had left the tent while she was speaking with his son. She seized that to momentarily deflect Paul's intent.

"Would your father approve?" she asked. "He didn't even want me to talk to you, until I promised to keep it simple and short."

Paul smiled. "And you have not really done that, have you?" He rose. With Donna still sitting he seemed taller than she'd first thought. His eyes were older, wiser. She saw some of the Paul Trayne that Ben Carpenter wrote about. In that moment she wanted to feel the touch of that power, feel the freedom, the unburdening of the soul promised by Paul's gift. The sensation lasted less than a second before all the ancient horrors thundered back around her, the self-hatred, the loathing, to crush her brief, fragile hope of escape.

Paul put a hand on her shoulder, so gently she could not feel it through her jacket. "Will you give me your pain?" he asked.

Donna rose, Paul's hand rising with her, until he was reaching up to touch her shoulder. "Suppose I say 'no,' Paul?"

Donna asked, knowing that was absolutely the last thing she wanted to say. "Can you . . . take the stuff out of me against my will? Are you that powerful?"

Paul paused for a long moment, then shook his head. "Father says the needy must *give* me the guilt, the pain. It must be their choice. I must take it."

It was not quite an answer, but Donna let it by, for now. "Can you take just a little? Like, skim the worst of it off the top, but leave the rest intact? So I'd have a frame of reference?" She was thinking of the way drinking distorted her perceptions. How everything was skewed; she knew it was skewed, but she did not know how it was skewed. She looked at Ben. His eyes were on Paul, his face bright with love and devotion. She felt full of trust for Paul, but she did not want to be so utterly mesmerized.

"No," said Paul, flatly. Then he paused, considering. "At least, I don't think so." He looked back up into Donna's eyes. "I haven't ever really tried to take only part of what I find." He took his hand away, walked a few paces away from her, stood with his back toward her. He grew silent, head down. Donna thought for a moment he was praying. He turned partway back, looking over his right shoulder at her. "I suppose the choice really belongs to you after all, Ms. Wojcie-chowski," he said. "I must not take what is not freely given. Everyone always *chooses* to give me all. If you chose to give me less, I can take no more."

Donna sucked on her lower lip, nodded. "Okay," she said. "That sounds reasonably . . . well . . . safe. Let's give it a try."

"I will need Father," Paul said. "He is always present, when there is a needing."

Donna nodded. "Shall I come with you?"

"No. Wait here. I won't be long." He walked the length of the tent and stepped out through the flap of the door. As it swung open and closed, Donna saw the snow had started again. She walked back to the stage and stepped onto it. She stood with her back to the door. She took out her cigarettes and lit one. The first puff tasted old and horrible, as usual. She filled her lungs with smoke. It tasted sour; it made her want a drink.

What a wonderful collection of bad habits you have, my dear, she thought. *If you only bit your nails, you'd have a complete set.*

She was being unfair to herself, she thought. As bad as her habits might be, with booze and cigarettes leading the pack, she had never tried drugs, never engaged in indiscriminate sex. She blew a smoke ring, wondering again where the mad puppeteer of her life had first begun to steer her wrong. She thought back to a conversation she'd had with Walker Stone, early in their affair. After one evening's lovemaking she'd lain in the warm embrace of his arms, feeling strangely good about herself for a change, listening as he drifted in and out of memories of youth, of wasted moments. Stone invariably became philosophical after sex. Out of his wanderings he'd suddenly looked down into her eyes and said "If you could pick a moment to start again, knowing what you know now, what do you suppose that moment would be?"

Without a moment's hesitation Donna said, "Birth."

She thought about that now, standing on the low stage in the old tent. Had it really all started to go bad that far back? Born out of wedlock, Donna was the only child of Viveca Wojciechowski, a Polish immigrant who'd come to the United States seeking the streets of gold she'd heard of and, at age seventeen, found herself pregnant by a foreman at the factory where she worked. Donna remembered the only picture she'd ever seen of her mother at that age. Viveca had been very different, physically, from her daughter. Short, tending to gawkiness, but with a massive, matronly bust, huge and incongruous above scrawny, big-kneed legs. The face was sweet, childlike; clearly Viveca had been attractive enough, in her bosomy, naïve fashion, to entice a man nearly three times her age.

"Entice" was an unfair word, Donna knew, but she could think of none better. She was, at this late stage of the game, not entirely willing to believe Viveca quite so innocent as she insisted. Whatever the case, so far as Donna could determine, the encounter that created her in Viveca's womb was the young Polish girl's first and only sexual experience. Viveca never spoke of it directly, but passing years gave Donna knowledge in hindsight; she came to understand that Viveca's loss of virginity had been considerably less pleasant than, say, her own.

Donna had never been able to learn who her real father was, other than the most insubstantial suggestions. Whoever he might have been, he'd given Viveca money for an abortion, which instead she'd added to her small savings, moving herself and her unborn child to Illinois, there to establish a foothold in Chicago. In that strange city, unknown to her, knowing nothing of her, Viveca Wojciechowski was able to present herself as an immigrant widow. She bought a secondhand wedding ring and wore it for the rest of her life—less than twenty years, as it happened. From *Life* magazine she clipped a picture of a handsome young airman, framed it expensively, and kept it on the mantelpiece in her one-room apartment.

"My Feodor," she would say, her voice thick with accent all her short life. By the time she was thirty, she believed her own fantasies. It was not until Donna was eighteen that she, herself, learned something of the truth. By then it was too late to probe, to ask her mother for the details Viveca had always kept hidden. Donna—for Donna Reed, who Viveca decided had a truly American-sounding name—was born five months after her mother arrived in Chicago. Viveca was by then a waitress in a small café just off the Loop, taking English courses at night. Donna grew up never hearing a word of Polish, knowing almost nothing about her mother's family or background until she was well into her teens.

By then she had come to despise her mother, despise the terrible fears Viveca planted in her. When Donna was sixteen she left their tiny apartment on the south side of Chicago and struck out on her own. After she moved out she did not see her mother again for nearly two years. Finally, a week before Viveca's thirty-sixth birthday Donna called her and arranged a meeting. She'd thought her mother sounded glad to hear from her again, pleased to hear that she was doing well, was not dead or—worse in Viveca's mind—pregnant. They met in the same restaurant Viveca had once worked in, all those years ago. It was very different from the place they both remembered. It was clean and modern. Instead of greasy hamburgers and greasier fries it served sandwiches named for famous sons of the Second City. Donna arrived fully twenty minutes before the meeting was scheduled to take place. She'd spent the whole morning selecting just the right wardrobe, arranging her hair—very long then, normally worn in a single fat pigtail—and making up her face to look fresh and natural, the way she thought her mother liked. Viveca had come in, seen her, and crossed the restaurant. Her face was utterly without expression. Donna, with the blinding clarity of hindsight, knew she should have seen that for a warning, an omen. She did not. She rose to greet her mother and kiss her on the cheek. Viveca accepted the greeting, seated herself, and waved a hand for Donna to do likewise.

She looked old, Donna thought. Much, much older than her thirty-six years. Donna had friends who were in their late thirties and older; none of them looked as old as Viveca. Donna had no way of knowing, then, that those extra years carved upon her mother's face were the work of the growing uterine cancer that would eventually kill her.

Donna started the conversation. She tried not to gush, but there were two years' worth of significant events she wanted her mother to know. Some of them were very, very important. She was enrolled in a night course in journalism, for instance. Most significant, most difficult for Donna to keep in the proper chronological order, she had met a man. Someone she thought a wonderful man. A dream. Viveca listened for nearly ten minutes without so much as a word. When Donna finally paused, she skewered her daughter with a glare born in the most frozen wastes of Hades and said a single syllable.

Eighteen years later Donna pushed her mother and her horrible, hissed "Slut" to the back of her mind, prayed she would not start to weep now, here, in this place that made her feel so strangely vulnerable.

"Well, Donna?" Ben Carpenter's voice, bringing her back to the here and now.

"Well, indeed," she said, turning to face him. "If he's not sincere, he should be. Or he should be in Hollywood. That kind of talent could make millions in movies."

"He's sincere." Again, the absolute lack of hesitation in Ben's voice, the sureness of his conviction. Donna realized with some annoyance she was beginning to envy him that. She was afraid, as the realization came, that it would color her reactions.

"Miss Wojciechowski?" Donna turned at the sound of Reverend Trayne's voice. He and the boy had come back into the tent as Donna wandered the avenues of her past. As she watched, Robert Trayne removed his dark jacket, rolled up his sleeves. It added to his Abraham Lincoln image: the Illinois rail-splitter, ready to dirty his big hands in a good, hard day's work. He came and stood before Donna. With the advantage of the stage, her eyes were two inches above his. She thought he looked uncomfortable, having to incline his head slightly in order to meet her gaze. He was far more accustomed to looking down at people.

"I want you to know, Ms. Wojciechowski," he said in his steady, somber voice, "that I am completely opposed to this."

Donna shrugged. "We don't have to do it, Reverend Trayne." She used his title as a softener, to win him a little more to her side. "If you think Paul is too tired . . ."

"I have already told you he is exhausted," Trayne said. "However, he says he senses in you a great needing, and I know how much it pains the boy to let such things go unattended." He looked at Ben, a hard, accusing look, Donna thought. A look that said, *This is all your fault.* Then his deep, dark eyes drifted down to look at Paul, standing silently by his right side. Donna was warmed by the parental love and devotion she saw in Trayne's face.

"Therefore I have decided to allow this, just this once," Trayne finished.

Ben released a long-held breath. "That's great!"

Paul smiled. "Thank you, Father. You will not regret it."

"So," Donna said, dropping her cigarette to the stage, stubbing it out with the toe of her right boot, kicking the crushed butt onto the grassy floor of the tent, "what's the drill? Do I sit, stand, kneel . . . ? What?"

"Generally those with a needing stand in front of the stage," Paul said. "That puts my eyes more at their level."

Donna nodded, stepped off the stage. Ben stationed himself at her side. The Traynes stepped up on the stage together and turned to face them. "Do we touch, or hold hands?" Donna asked. She was aware of a strange ingenuousness in her questions. She was not being sarcastic, was not poking fun in any way. She was trying to be helpful, to make it as easy as possible for Paul to perform his miracle.

"No physical contact is necessary," said Paul. Already Donna could see his eyes were drifting away. "Just be still a moment, please."

She waited. Donna did not know what to expect, but she thought that if she was totally aware of how she felt before it came, it might make it easier to spot—and resist—whatever Paul did to her.

But he says he's not going to do anything. It has to come from me, he said. I have to give, so that he can take.

Paul stood perfectly still, hands loose at his sides. He'd changed from the nightshirt to the same green corduroys and white shirt Ben had described in his article. Paul's bare feet were tucked into ordinary white sneakers.

"There is a needing here," Reverend Trayne said. "Only one, now. Not so many as Paul has had to take upon himself before, but still a *burden*. You do understand this, don't you?" Donna flinched at the sudden sharpness in Trayne's voice. "What he takes from you, he keeps," Trayne said. "Your pain becomes *his* pain. Your sorrow becomes *his* sorrow. You are released, but the burden becomes *his*. His to carry, until the end of his days. You bring him your needings, your pain, your grief and sorrow, knowing this?"

There was a long pause. Donna realized Trayne was actually awaiting a response. "Er . . . yes," she said.

"Then let it be done," said Robert Trayne. He stepped back, behind Paul.

"Who has a needing?" Paul Trayne's voice was stronger, more mature than Donna heard before. His green eyes were wide and facing her, but he did not see her.

Ben nudged her, gently. Donna took a step forward. "I guess that's me," she said, hating the flippancy in her voice. She glanced over her right shoulder at Ben, but he was standing with his head bowed, eyes closed. She looked back at Paul.

The world became a better place.

4

Father Tom Sylvestri climbed the low, flat cement steps to the front doors of St. Timothy's and stepped through into the outer foyer. Something he'd done, he estimated, five thousand times in the six years he'd been with the church. On at least half those times, as today, he'd looked up at the flat gray face of St. Timothy's, appalled by the utterly soulless line and form of this building meant to be God's house. The rectory, old and venerable as it was, had far more of the look and feel Tom thought appropriate to a church. In fact, he knew that some of his older parishioners—those who still remembered when this piece of ground had been the perfectly manicured lawn of the old mansion—often joked that the house was, in fact, the real St. Timothy's, and this twentieth century addition simply "the box it came in."

It was only slightly less cold immediately inside than it had been on the street. Tom's breath steamed as he closed the door behind him. He walked slowly down the length of the nave to the crossing, genuflected before the tall, stylized altar in the rear of the chancel, and crossed to the right, behind the choir, to the small office just off the short corridor that connected St. Timothy's with the rectory. It was scarcely worthy of the term "office." Barely six feet on a side—the tall, narrow door had to open outward or it would have struck against the furnishings—and nearly sixteen feet in height. The effect, as John Percival had warned Tom Sylvestri, was much like sitting at the bottom of a well. Tom took off his coat and hung it on the peg on the inside of the door. He hung his scarf on top of the coat, his hat on top of that. He pulled the door shut. In a short time he would be called upon to take the first of the day's confessions. He had something to do, something urgent, before that ritual began. He owed it to his parishioners to get this done, to clear his mind—he prayed—before tending to the needs of their souls. He flipped on the light switch by the door. The single lamp hanging on its long cord threw a pool of yellow-white light onto the small desk and chair that, with the prayer stool in the corner, were the room's only furnishings.

Above the desk, in a tall, narrow niche in the wall, a slender, old-fashioned statue of the Virgin raised her right hand in what seemed to Tom a greeting gesture. Her face was smooth, the features carefully shaped, the curve of eyebrow, the turn of lip all considered and executed for maximum emotional impact on the viewer. The result was perfect, in Tom's eyes. Impassive, peaceful. He pulled out the tall, always uncomfortable chair and seated himself at the desk. He looked up into the Blessed Mary's calm, unquestioning face. To his chagrin Tom found himself remembering another of Joseph Terranova's jokes.

"God decides to take a vacation," he'd said, his voice more breathless and nervous than ever as he tested Tom's tolerance. "He decides to take a vacation, so He goes to a travel agent. He goes to a travel agent and He says, 'I want to go somewhere peaceful and quiet.'

"And the travel agent says, he says, 'I've got just the place, Sire. Earth!'

"But God shakes his head. 'No,' He says. 'Where else have you got?'

"But the travel agent is insistent, see, he's insistent, because he thinks Earth is just the place, and he says, 'But you can't do better than Earth, Sire! Look at all the things it's got going for it!' "

Tom remembered with sadness how Joseph's habit of repeating everything disappeared when he spoke in the voice of others. When he recited dialogue, when he assumed the various characters in a funny story, his manner of speaking became clear and precise.

" 'There's skiing and surfing,' " Joseph continued in the voice of his mythical travel agent, " 'and beautiful beaches, and mountains.'

" 'I know,' says God. 'I made them. But I don't want to go to Earth.'

"Well, the travel agent is really put out by this, Earth being his favorite place, his favorite. And he asks, 'Why, Lord? Why don't you want to go to Earth, if you know how wonderful it is?'

"And finally God just sighs and says, He says, 'I don't want to go to Earth because I went there two thousand years ago, and I got a little Jewish girl in trouble and I haven't heard the end of it since.' "

Joseph paused then, awaiting some kind of reaction: anger, chastisement. Tom remembered the way Joseph's eyes seemed brimming with tears, though they remained dry. He quivered with anticipation.

Tom smiled, genuinely amused by the joke, poor taste though it might show.

"You really think that was funny? You really do?" Joseph seemed almost appalled.

"Yes," Tom said. "Certainly I've heard worse. And I happen to think God has a fine sense of humor. I should think He would probably find it funny too."

Joseph had leaned back in his seat—they'd been in a restaurant on State Street, away from the likelihood of encountering familiar faces on what Tom now realized amounted to their first "date"—and tried to select the proper reaction.

"God has a sense of humor?" Joseph shook his head. "I suppose He must, if He made me."

Tom's smile died. "There's no reason to talk like that. There's nothing wrong with you that calming down and facing reality wouldn't fix."

Joseph had laughed, a silvery, affected thing, a young girl's laugh. Several patrons at nearby tables turned, Tom recalled; one or two frowned when they saw not a pretty young woman but a strange, pinch-faced young man.

"You talk to me about facing reality," Joseph said, "and yet here you are, a faggot priest."

Tom had not allowed himself to react visibly to Joseph's gibe. "You gave me your word not to use such language," Tom said.

"I've offended you? My joke didn't offend you, but the truth does?"

"The truth never offends," Tom replied. "But you don't mean that as a statement of truth. You mean it as an insult. You're like a drug addict mocking the addictions of others."

Joseph picked up his wineglass from the table in front of him. He studied Tom over the rim of the glass as he sipped, then set the glass down directly in front of him. Tom had sufficient training in lay psychology to recognize a barrier being thrown up. Joseph folded his slender arms across his narrow chest, completing the symbolism. "Then you admit you're . . ."

". . . a homosexual," Tom completed the sentence. "Yes. What would be the point in denying it, at this moment?"

What indeed? Tom thought, months later, alone in the tall, narrow office.

He lowered his eyes from those of the Virgin and reached inside his jacket for Joseph's notebook. He set the book on the desk and framed the little blue cover in his hands, the tips of his thumbs touching, the index fingers angling in to hold the notebook in place. He shifted to a more comfortable position on the uncushioned chair and opened the notebook to the first page. The page was thick with Joseph's tiny, precise print, all capital letters, three lines of writing in each space between the ruled blue lines on the page. He tried to imagine what it must have been like for Joseph, sitting in the darkness of the lakeshore, feeling his life ebb out into the cold, cold night. He'd hurt his hand, according to the police. Torn a piece from one finger, probably climbing the chain link fence on the lake side of Lakeshore Drive.

Tom tried to imagine all the thoughts and feelings his lover would have experienced. They'd shared a bed, a piece of a life. It should be possible to know what Joseph had been thinking. . . .

Tom shook his head. How could he pretend to understand Joseph? He'd been insensitive enough that he'd failed to realize Joseph Terranova was serious in his threat of suicide this time. He'd as much as dared him to do it, challenged him to prove himself by . . . Tears were hot in Tom Sylvestri's eyes. He drew a handkerchief from his pocket and wiped his eyes.

Forgive me, Joseph, he thought. He looked again at the rows of cramped printing on the little page.

Tom began to read.

"Ms. Wojciechowski. Are you all right?"

Paul's voice.

A long way away.

He sounded very tired to Donna. But when she opened her eyes, when she focused, he smiled.

"I was so worried," he said. "I sensed a resistance in you. I was not sure I'd finished the task properly."

"You did," Donna smiled up at him. She was sitting but could not remember how she came to be. It did not worry her. She knew she must have blacked out, fainted. That did not worry her, either. She straightened and took in more and more of her surroundings. Still in the tent. Ben still there. The older Trayne. The soft drip of melting snow. The strange smell. The shadows on the canvas walls. It seemed right to her that the wonderful gift of Paul Trayne should come from a place like this. Simple, clean, without ostentation.

"Yes, I'm sure I did, now," Paul said. He crossed to one of the chairs near Donna and sat. He put out a hand to touch hers, lightly, gingerly. "There was so much inside you. So much sadness. So much anger."

Donna nodded, aware now of a strange vacancy where all that had been. She could still remember each portion of it, it appeared, but the feelings connected with those slices of her life were gone. She could think of Steve Binder and not feel the instant flash of revulsion and rage. She could think of her mother and not feel diminished, dirty. She could even think of Walker Stone and not feel the need to run from the feelings she'd begun to share with him. It was as if each of those intense emotional packages had been carefully sliced out, surgically removed from her psyche, leaving memory without feeling.

"I'm sure your mother really loved you," Paul said. Donna saw the flash of pain in his face, the physical manifestation of that same pain she would have felt, she knew, if he'd said the same thing only a few moments ago.

"You . . . know about that?"

"Yes."

"You can read minds, Paul?"

"No. But I take the grief, the guilt, the pain. It becomes mine. So I know. I know about your mother. What she said." He shook his head. "She could not have meant it. She was your mother. She must have loved you. All mothers love their children."

Reverend Trayne had crossed to stand close by Paul. His big hand closed on the boy's shoulder, and it looked to Donna as though the gnarled fingers tightened enough to hurt.

"It doesn't matter," Donna said. It really didn't. She could take out the entire scene now, the once-so-terrible scene, and look at it, and see her mother, and hear the "slut" as clearly as she ever did, and . . . nothing. No emotion. No anger. No pain. Not even a sense of relief at the *absence* of the old emotions. Just nothing.

"This is quite astounding," Donna said. A thought was forming in the back of her mind. A crazy thought. If everyone could feel as she felt now . . . if the whole world could know the touch of Paul Trayne's gift . . .

"I wonder . . ." She probed carefully, not entirely sure, just yet, where she was going with this. "Do you know if there's a limit to the number of needings you can absorb at a single go? There were something like, what? A thousand people here the other night. Your uncle said that knocked you out pretty good."

"But I did it." Paul smiled, a child proud of a high grade in arithmetic. "And I am recovered now. The weariness does not last. Only the . . . things I take from people. The things they give me, I mean."

"But it knocked you out, like I said," Donna repeated. "Is that your limit, Paul? One thousand?"

"They did not all have needings," Paul said. "There may not have been more than eight hundred who actually had needings."

Donna felt her heart sink. *Eight hundred divided into the population of the world,* she thought. *Twelve million days to do the world.*

It was a silly notion anyway. The enormity of it began to press down on her.

Think what you're asking. He feels the grief he takes on. As if it were his own. And there's no indication it wears off after a while. If he took on the sorrows of eight hundred people the other night, they're still inside him. Along with the others from the nights before. And they'll be there for the rest of his life.

She sidetracked that kind of thinking and went on. "Then you think that might be your limit? Eight hundred? What if you did smaller groups, but closer together?" She needed to find a way around his physical limitations. Part of her mind told her this was not something she needed to consider, that Paul's well-being was not an issue. But another part told her not to risk killing the golden goose.

"I don't expect I really have a limit," Paul said. There was a quality in his voice Donna thought almost boastful, bragging. "The very first time I took another's sorrows . . . I was only five." He looked up at his father and frowned. "I don't really remember it all that well . . . I was exhausted for a month. After only one."

Donna felt her heart rising again. "Then . . . then you think you may be getting stronger, as time goes on? Each time you take the sorrows of a big crowd it knocks you back a bit, but the next time you can take a bigger crowd, and not be out for quite so long?"

"Oh, I am sure of it. That's the way Father describes it, anyway." He looked back at Trayne, who simply nodded his big head. It surprised Donna that this discussion had already occurred. Did Trayne have in his mind the same thought she did? Suspicion reared its ugly head, then just as quickly vanished. It was one of those negative reactions that would not cling to Donna's mind anymore.

"Have you spoken of, well, plans for Paul? Plans beyond Faulkner?" Donna asked Robert Trayne.

"Yes," Trayne said. It seemed to Donna, for a moment, too short a moment for her to focus on, that Trayne was having trouble speaking, that—there was no other way to phrase it— his mind was elsewhere. "Yes," he said again. "Paul's gift must spread beyond this place. Out into the whole world."

His voice was growing stronger. He was beginning to sound more like a fire-and-brimstone Bible thumper, an arch-Evangelical. "There is great and terrible corruption in the world. All the world. I have spent my life battling it. God gave me the strength, the means. But it was insufficient, until He gave me Paul. Paul has the power to flush the corruption out. He is a tonic, to vent the bowels of all mankind. To spill the poisons that corrupt the soul."

"Father wants me to bring my gift to as many people as possible," Paul said, his voice much softer, much more reasonable than Trayne's. "He's talked of taking us up to Chicago."

"Anything beyond that? Like New York?" Donna saw Trayne's eyes flash, his lip curl.

Paul's eyes went very far away. "We have talked of that place." His soft voice was barely more than a whisper. "A place of many needings."

"You could say that." Donna leaned into his line of sight, bringing his focus back to her. "What do you think you could do in a place like that, Paul? There are an awful lot of people."

"I think that's why Father wants to go first to Chicago. It is smaller. Perhaps its people are happier."

"It all depends on how you define 'happy,' kid," said a high voice from the other end of the tent.

Donna turned. She looked quickly at her watch. "You're early," she said.

"I came on wings of angels," Walker Stone said, advancing into the tent. "Or, at least, on wheels of Mercedes." He ignored Trayne and Paul for a moment, stuck out a hand toward Ben. "Walker Stone."

"Ben Carpenter. You're the one who sent Donna down here."

"That's me. As she may have told you, I thought it would be

a nothing little story that would keep her occupied for a while." He looked down at Donna, still in her seat. "When she called me at three o'clock this morning I changed my mind."

He looked past the older Trayne at Paul and extended his hand again. "So you're this Boy Wonder." Paul rose to take his hand. He gripped Stone's hand firmly, without hesitation. His sea-green eyes did not waver when they met Stone's. He released Stone's hand and sat down again next to Donna.

Stone turned to Reverend Trayne. Donna's impression was that he had been deliberately ignoring the man, trying to goad him. It would have been a typical thing for him to do, Donna thought. Stone liked to put people off their guard. She smiled, knowing such tactics would not work on Trayne. He was, Donna knew, beyond such manipulation.

"I guess that makes you Reverend Trayne," Stone said. It would not have surprised Donna at all to know that Stone looked into the big, craggy face and saw not Abraham Lincoln at all, but Raymond Massey.

Trayne hesitated a moment before accepting Stone's hand, and Donna was pleased to note this had precisely the unbalancing effect on Stone that he'd been trying to work on Trayne. "I am," said Trayne, his voice even more compelling than when Donna had first heard it.

Unable to flummox the older man, Stone turned his attention back to the boy. "I don't know what you've got cooking here, kid," Stone said, "but whatever magic you've been working in town seems to have made an impression on my most cynical girl reporter here."

Donna was not annoyed by Stone's words, though she guessed he meant her to be. "At least it got you excited enough to come and see for yourself," she said. She remembered the genuine caring she'd heard in his voice that morning. It no longer seemed to matter, but something within told her she should make Stone aware that she remembered. "Thanks."

"My pleasure." Stone hooked a chair and seated himself very close to Paul Trayne. He took off his glasses and reached beneath his coat and jacket for the penknife. He twiddled the screws for a moment. As her heartbeats measured off the passing seconds, Donna found herself wanting to scream at Stone, at his familiar ritual.

Then the small voice said, *Never mind. Never mind. What does it matter?* She relaxed and waited until Stone was ready.

Stone snapped the short blade back into place and returned the knife to his pocket. He leaned forward, staring into Paul's face. "Tell me what you do here, son."

"He gives the gift of life, sir." Trayne said.

"That's pretty impressive." Stone said, not turning. " 'The Gift of Life.' " His capitalization of Trayne's words was as obvious as it was sarcastic. "How does he do that?"

"By taking away the things that lessen life."

"At the risk of repeating myself," Stone said, "how does he do that?"

"Did you see the sign on the gate?" Trayne asked. " 'Surely he hath borne . . .' "

"I saw it." Stone was curt. "It still doesn't answer my question."

Trayne frowned. Donna sensed again that Stone was being deliberately antagonistic. She was not particularly bothered by it, so long as it was not directed toward Paul himself. If that was how Stone wanted to behave, it did not affect her in any way.

"I have a special gift," Paul Trayne said. "I have the ability to take—"

"Yes, I know about that, too," Stone said. "From Mr. Carpenter's article. You're both missing the point of my question. I'm asking *how* you do it. The exact mechanics. Is it a new mutation? Is it some kind of telepathy? Are you up for the lead in a new version of *My Favorite Martian?* What?"

Paul shriveled in Donna's eyes, shrinking back before the barrage of questions. "I . . . I . . ."

Stone held up a hand. "Take it easy, kid. I'm not really going to eat you alive." He turned to the older Trayne. "Well? What's my answer?"

Trayne spread his big, broad hands. "I am a simple man, sir. I found my answer in God's own Holy Bible."

"And you really think a quote written, what, two thousand

years ago? More? That it answers what's up with your boy here?"

"As well as anything can," said Ben Carpenter. "You just have to take it at face value, Mr. Stone. Believe me, Paul does what he does, and it works. I'm living proof of that."

"Well, unfortunately I had no knowledge of you before I read your article, Mr. Carpenter. You could be changed now, maybe for the better, but I don't know. On the other hand"— Stone turned to Donna—"this lady here is definitely modified from the original model. And that worries me."

"It shouldn't," Donna said. "It doesn't worry me."

Nothing worries me. Not anymore.

"Uh-huh. Could you go for a drink right now?"

It was more than an idle question, Donna knew. Stone was a teetotaler, but his Mercedes had a fully equipped bar in the backseat. "Are you asking or offering?" Donna said.

"Neither," Stone said. "I don't know what I'm doing." He stood up. "I'm going to have to take a look at this Miracle Show firsthand, obviously. Is there a . . . performance tonight?"

Trayne nodded. "At seven o'clock."

Donna reached a hand across to Paul again. "You're up to it?"

He smiled. "I must be. There is work to be done."

Donna frowned. *He sounds so drained, so exhausted. And yet he must go on tonight. He must continue bringing his gift to the world. His own well-being is a secondary consideration.*

Stone did not understand the full texture of what he heard, but he intended to. He put a hand on Donna's shoulder. "Will you ride back to town with me? I . . . feel the need to ask you some more questions. In private."

Donna rose. She still had some things she wanted to discuss with Paul, but she knew they could wait, for now.

"All right," she said. "I have nothing to hide."

The drive back into Faulkner could have been tense, but Donna was pleasantly surprised to discover she did not find it so. Ignoring Stone's sideways glances, she helped herself to a glass of gin from the backseat bar, reaching over the front seat in what she knew must surely be a most unladylike pose. She settled back in the passenger seat with her drink, cradling it carefully as they drove.

"So," Donna said, after they had gone a half mile down Pine Tree Road, "what is your lecture of the day, Herr Professor?"

Stone looked away from the road long enough to fix Donna with a baleful glare. It slid across her and drifted away into the netherworld to which she thought all such looks must depart, having failed to fix themselves upon their target. "Cut the crap, Don," he said. "I've seen Trayne. I've seen the boy. I am monstrously unimpressed."

"To phrase a coin," Donna said over her glass, "you ain't seen nothing yet."

"Then tell me what there is to see. Tell me what I'm missing."

Donna shook her head, holding her drink carefully to avoid spillage as the Mercedes lurched off the rutted road onto the highway. "You've got to see. You've got to experience."

"Like you did? What's the matter with you, Don? You . . . well, I'd almost say you were drunk, if I didn't know you drunk. But I do, and this is different."

Donna nodded. "Better."

"I wouldn't say that. Just different. Almost as if . . ." He glanced her way again. "Almost as if you didn't give a damn about anything anymore."

"Not so," Donna said. It was not a protest, such as Stone expected. Her voice was calm. She spoke with the sureness of absolute conviction. As if by saying "Not so" she presented Stone with a point of view as indisputable as gravity.

" 'So,' " Stone countered. "Very 'so,' in fact."

He accelerated to pass a lumbering farm truck, weaving too far into the oncoming lane. A small Chrysler came straight at them, its horn blaring. Stone pulled the wheel hard right, cutting in front of the truck and around the Chrysler. The other car's horn faded into the distance, still going full blast.

"Close," Donna said. Somehow she'd managed to hold onto her drink in the wild maneuvering. "You'll never get saved that way."

"Saved? Have you been born again, Don? Is that what this is all about?"

Donna thought about it for a moment. "No," she said at last. "It's not that. At least, not in the sense of being a born-again Christian, or like that. This is not a religious conversion."

And what does it matter what it is, so long as I feel this good?

"Then what?" Stone asked. "That man Trayne seemed as quick to brandish the Bible as any other thumper."

"Mm. He's religious. Paul too. He thinks his gift comes from God. But it's not a religious feeling, Walker. Not like any I've ever been exposed to, anyway." She thought of her devoutly Catholic mother, wearing away her fingers on the rosary, bruising her big, bony knees on cold stone floors every Sunday.

"What then? Please, Don. Tell me what it's all about."

She sipped her drink and studied the road ahead. She knew she could not put it into words. There was no common thread of experience she could define for Stone. Without it, she might as well be speaking Swahili. After her contemplative silence stretched into more than a minute, Stone slowed the car and pulled onto the shoulder. The outboard wheels of his Mercedes sank deep into the snow, but the car remained stable. He put the gear shift in park and swiveled in his seat to face his erstwhile lover.

She sure looks better, he thought.

But he still despised the sight of a liquor glass in her hand. There was a new vigor about Donna Wojciechowski. Nothing Stone could define; a straightness to her back, perhaps. A firmness to the thrust of her jaw. Definitely there. In her eyes, her tone. Mostly it was in the way she would not rise to any bait. It came to Stone that it was as if the old Donna had died here, in quiet little Faulkner. And the new Donna? Stone had not decided if she was the ghost of the old, or some errant spirit who had moved into the unoccupied cadaver.

"Look, Chow," he said, seeing no flash of anger in her eyes, "I know we've had a lot of harsh words between us, but it was you that broke off our relationship, and that's always left me with a feeling of unfinished business."

"You want to try again, is that it?" She finished her drink and set the empty glass on the dashboard. "Why not? I don't mind. Pull your pants down." She laughed. It did not quite sound like Donna's brand of sarcasm, but Stone was not about to make a fool of himself playing along with whatever game she was up to.

"I'm not making a pass here, Don. I'm admitting that I still care about you . . ."

"I know. I realized it last night. Or this morning, rather, crack of dawn."

"Then level with me. Is this kid some kind of hypnotist? Did he slip you some kind of mickey? Do you know what he did?"

"I know what came out the other end, Walker. That's all. And, believe me, if you could try a sample, you'd be just as hard-pressed to explain it, and just as eager to make sure everyone else in the world joined the club." She leaned forward. "Remember the quote by the gate? That's what this is all about. Paul Trayne takes away the nastiness. Absorbs it. Makes your guilt and grief and sorrow his own, and leaves you . . . well, his word is 'cleansed.' It's a good word for the way I feel."

"Cleansed? And yet you still need a drink." More than anything else, that seemed to be the nail that tore the fabric of Donna's tale, at least in Stone's mind.

Donna rolled her eyes. "I still need a drink. Yes. I'm still an alcoholic, okay? Only it doesn't *matter* anymore. It doesn't need to be anything I'm tying myself in knots over."

"That's the first time I've ever heard you use that word," Stone said.

"What word?"

" 'Alcoholic.' At least in application to yourself."

Donna blinked. It had come out of her so easily she'd not even noticed it. *Of course, that's part of the pattern. I'm not afraid of the word anymore. I'm an alcoholic. Big hairy deal.* She shrugged.

Stone put the Mercedes back into drive and pulled up onto the highway. "I want to get you looked at," he said. "Before we let this thing go much further, I want to call some doctors and have them prod and probe a bit."

"And if I object?" It seemed odd to her that she might, in fact, find a reason to object to what Stone was suggesting.

There seemed so little else in her life, in the world, worth objecting to.

"I wasn't really offering a choice," Stone said.

Donna scowled but said nothing.

Stone had learned from Ben Carpenter the name and location of Faulkner's best hotel. He drove there, taking Donna with him. Stone wanted her near. It took awhile to get suitable rooms arranged. The desk clerk displayed a puritanical reluctance to provide adjoining rooms for an unmarried couple. Donna sat in the lobby, thumbing through a year-old issue of *Vogue* until Stone reappeared, with the manager, and they were escorted to their chambers. The first thing Stone did, in their rooms, was unlock the connecting door.

"I want this left open," he said. "It's not like we have a great deal to, well, hide from each other, and I want to keep an eye on you."

Donna flopped on her bed, the lobby copy of *Vogue* still in her hands. "Suit yourself," she said. She went on reading outdated movie reviews.

Stone frowned at the perfect, airbrushed face of the cover girl interposed between his eyes and Donna's. He went into his own room. There he quickly unpacked his overnight bag. He'd noticed ruefully that Donna had no luggage. He went through the motions of hanging his three-days' change of clothes in the closet. He slipped his suspenders off his shoulders, kicked off his shoes, and flopped onto one of the twin beds in his room. Without thinking he reached for the penknife in his right breast pocket and began tightening the screws in his glasses.

Stone could hear the turning pages of Donna's magazine through the open door. He finished the adjustment to his glasses and slipped the closed penknife back in his pocket. He laced his fingers behind his head and stared up at the ceiling. Memories of early days with Donna Wojciechowski floated across the front of his brain.

Life with Donna, he called it, though he knew that the sharpest, strongest memories could never find a place on TV, not even on cable. He'd never known sex so good, for one thing—after the strange unpleasantness of their first time, their Christ-

mas Eve, anyway. Donna was the third woman with whom
Stone had had a prolonged relationship and, like Steve Binder,
he was shocked and even crushed when he finally discovered it
was not nearly so great for Donna. Unlike Donna's ex-husband, Stone tried to be understanding. He'd reached down into
his heart and found a big handful of compassion. He could not
quite understand what it was that blocked Donna's complete
release to the pleasures he offered, but he was going to keep
talking and listening, day after day, for as long as it took to find
out.

Donna meant that much to him. If he were the marrying
kind—Stone thought himself too emotionally unstable to commit to any kind of binding relationship—he would have
popped the question to Donna after the first night they spent
in the same bed. He'd already decided she was funny, clever,
and, when she wasn't drinking, sharp as a tack. Finding her so
much his idealized bed partner would have clinched the deal,
in another reality. Yet he knew Donna never allowed herself to
think of their relationship as anything but an affair, something
that one entered ready to walk away from. He was glad he'd
not known that going in. He would have dropped all interest in
Donna right away, and that would have cost him moments that
were still very precious to him. Despite all the pain and anger
that had passed between them, and sometimes still passed,
Stone cherished the good points of *Life with Donna* as much as
anything in his life.

"Don?" he called.

"Mmm?"

"Care to take another shot at telling me what happened?"

"He made me all better."

Stone sighed. "You must be able to do better than that." He
heard the bedsprings moan in the next room. Donna appeared
in the doorway, framed between his red-stockinged feet. She'd
left the copy of *Vogue* on the bed behind her. Stone noted the
long ash that dangled precariously from her cigarette.

"Why?" Donna asked.

"Because you're a lady who's spent a considerable amount
of time over the past few years trying to destroy herself, mostly
because she has an incredibly poor opinion of herself, and she

can't quite manage to drag herself low enough to satisfy her destructive urges." Stone was frankly flabbergasted to have completed his speech. He'd never managed to get so much out without Donna interrupting, or leaving. He couldn't, for the moment, think where to go next.

Donna shrugged. She looked around his room, spotted an ashtray, and disposed of her cigarette. "Everything you say is perfectly true." She crossed to the foot of his bed and sat. "It's just . . . what Paul does . . . just makes it all seem so unimportant. All the crap I've collected in thirty-six years, washed away."

"That's quite a trick, if it's real." Stone sat up, swinging his feet off the edge of the bed. "Look, Don, I won't fool with you, okay? This scares me. It scares me when I look at you now and try to connect you to the lady I had a fight with yesterday. The lady who was ready to rip my heart out and stomp on it. Or was I misreading you?" There was no sarcasm in his voice.

"No," Donna said. "At least, I don't think so."

She looked away. On the other side of the room, parallel to the bed, was a low oak dresser with a mirror above it. Donna looked into her own face, and Stone followed the direction of her gaze. He was uncomfortably aware, as he always was, of how much taller she was than he.

Donna's thoughts were not on this. "I have trouble myself," she said, "making that connection. It's like I'm somebody new." She shook her head. "No, that's not it either. I'm still Donna Wojciechowski. I still have all the memories. I still remember every emotional scar." She looked back at Stone. "It's just that they don't matter anymore. And from the way I feel now, they never will again. It's as if new scars I might accumulate in the years to come . . . well, it's like I've been armored against them, you know? As if something has wrapped itself around my soul and is protecting it from anything else that might do it damage."

"I don't think I care much for the sound of that," Stone said. "An armored soul seems like a lonely place to be. I wonder what somebody might do, if they had a soul that didn't care about injury. Its own, or anyone else's."

"It's not like that," Donna said. "It takes away all the hurt.

What could be wrong with that?" She rose. "I'm hungry. Why don't you buy me lunch?"

Stone reached out and caught the hand hanging nearest to him. She did not pull away as he'd expected. "Don . . ."

She leaned to place a finger of her free hand across his lips. "Don't say anything else now, Walker. Just come out to the show tonight and see for yourself what Paul can do."

She freed her hand and crossed to the door of his room. "Lunch?"

"Yes. All right. I guess I am a bit hungry. I skipped breakfast this morning."

Stone pushed his feet back into his shoes, pulled his galluses back into place, and picked up his jacket from the back of the chair. He followed Donna out into the hall in search of food. He watched the way she walked, a few paces ahead of him, and felt old stirrings that had never really died.

Bestdamnlegs in the world, he thought. He'd never cast the lead for *Life with Donna.* Donna Wojciechowski was one of a kind.

Donna turned, as if she'd read his mind. Stone smiled, weakly, but all she said was "I think I could go for a burger or two. How about you?"

"Sounds good." He pressed his thumb against the heat-sensitive button that summoned the elevator and looked into Donna's eyes. They were still dark ringed, but the look of the caged beast was gone.

With disgust Stone realized he missed it.

5

Father Tom Sylvestri finished his reading. He closed the dark blue covers of the little notebook and leaned his head into his hands, resting the weight on his elbows. Altogether he'd read the last words of Joseph Terranova three times as he sat in the little room behind the choir. Outside, in the church, people had gathered for confession. Some had waited over an hour before leaving, muttering under their breath oaths they would have to report at their next confession. Some still waited, as the day stretched into the afternoon. Tom was utterly oblivious to their presence. With each reading he found greater and more subtle nuance, greater and greater demonstration of skill in the pure craft of writing.

You were good, Joseph, Tom thought. *You were very, very good. What a great pity the world never knew. What a greater pity you never let the world know. I never took you seriously. Never for a moment. Your mannerisms, your extraordinary affectations—they all made me think you were just a clown, a silly boy in a man's body. But you had talent. Real talent. Rare talent.*

He leaned back. The image of the Virgin looked down on him without comment or condemnation.

It's my fault he killed himself, Tom said in his mind, addressing his words to the beatific face in the little niche. *I let myself be weak. I let old memories, old needs cloud my thoughts, sap my will. Because of that the world lost someone who could have been a great writer.*

Tom's mind raced. Was there something he could do? Some way he could make amends—a foolish concept, given the gravity of the sin—for the untimely death for which he now felt so responsible? If he could get the work published, perhaps. There were more than enough posthumous novels and plays. Works that friends and relatives arranged to see in print after the writer had given up.

The whole work is about us. It's about Joseph and me, yet there is nothing in it to identify me. . . .

He felt an immediate shame at such a petty consideration. In a fit of childish pique—what else could he call it?—he'd confessed his secret sin to Sophia Balducci; now he worried that the rest of the world might know? He lifted the notebook in his right hand. He slipped it into his inside left breast pocket, rose, gathered his hat, scarf and coat, and stepped back into the main part of the church. He avoided the eyes of the metal Jesus and the following glares of the present representatives of his flock. Tom crossed the church to the door into the residence. He hung his things on the pegs by the side door and went quickly into his study. He pressed the buzzer by his desk, hearing the distant sound of the bell in the kitchen.

A moment later, Mrs. Buck appeared at the door. "You rang, Father?"

"I need to be alone for a while, Mrs. B. Put up one of your impenetrable shields, would you?" Tom tried to keep his tone light, but the woman had known him too long.

"Is there a problem, Father Tom?"

"Yes, but it's nothing you need concern yourself with."

"Concerning myself with you and your problems is what I get paid for," she said.

"And you would do so even without the remuneration, I am sure," Tom replied. He put out a hand, cupping her elbow and turning her gently back the way she'd come. "Just protect me from callers for a while. I'll be fine."

She did no more than meet his gaze with the firm and steady look he'd known for nearly eight years now, since his earliest days working with Father Percival, before the old man surrendered dominion over St. Timothy's to Tom. Mrs. Buck shook her head and departed without another word.

Tom returned to his desk. He sat down and lifted the old black rotary phone from its position on the far right corner. He settled it before him and pulled open the center drawer of the desk. He lifted out his personal telephone book and flipped through the pages to the back.

If I am to get this work of Joseph's seen by the right people, he thought, *I am going to have to learn very quickly who those people are.*

He ran a finger down the long list of names under *S*. He found Walker Stone's office number and dialed.

Forty-five seconds later he hung up, somewhat perplexed to have learned Walker had gone south, to Faulkner, to follow up a story about a boy who could work miracles.

When Walker Stone and Donna Wojciechowski returned to Gunner's Field that evening, a place had been saved for them just inside the gate. Just as well. Cars were lined up three deep on either side of the road, crushing bushes, grazing old trees. On the river side some were so far over as to be on the verge of toppling into the icy water. Ice was packed in against the shore, a thin layer stretched across the breadth of the narrow river. As they passed, the ice cracked and popped as water moved under it. The sound imitated the crunch of snow under feet. When they climbed from the Mercedes the air was cold against their faces.

Donna huddled closer into the topcoat Stone had loaned her. It was three times too big—if Stone was not as tall as Donna, he was wider—but with its lining of artificial fur it was deliciously warm. Her legs and feet still suffered. None of Stone's boots fit her. A pair of his thick winter socks just made her feet too big for the boots she had. Donna found physical discomfort one of the things that still bothered her. Perhaps that was just as well, she decided. The human body would destroy itself a thousand times over, every day, but for the ever constant warning signal of pain.

"Must be all of Faulkner out here tonight," she said, making conversation to take her mind off the cold in her feet.

Stone looked up and down the lines of cars. "I think your boy's fame has spread well beyond McLean County by now." He looked into her eyes, higher than his even when she sank into the snow. "You really think this is a good thing, Don? I'm not going to kid you and say I trust your judgment—" He paused, but again it was not a hostile response. "But you've seen the effect of this first hand."

"From what it's done to my own head, I feel like it's a good thing." Donna thought about Ben, about Mae. There was no ill effect of Paul Trayne's gift that she was aware of.

The field was packed with people. Stone made a quick estimate of close to two thousand but knew it could easily be more. The tired old canvas tent was at the center of a mass of human flesh packed as tight as they could press. Out toward the edges the crush relaxed, but not much. Stone felt distressed by the mass: so many people seeking a thing, a gift he could not believe truly existed. Not in this world, at least. And Stone put very little trust in other worlds.

"Most of these people have wasted their time, surely," he said to Donna in a voice as low as he could manage. Even so, some of the closer faces turned toward him, frowning.

"I don't know," Donna said. "I've never seen Paul work a whole crowd. I was alone when he . . . did me." Now that seemed something that should bother her. Paul had not deigned to grant Ben Carpenter a special sampling of his gift, but for the big city reporter . . . No. It slipped away from her, as Ben Carpenter had slipped away the night before, behind the shield of complacency. *Never mind,* said the voice.

Stone noticed the flicker of doubt in her expression. "Something?"

"No. Nothing." It was a lie, but she had lied to Stone before and felt no increase in bad karma from this deception. In fact, she felt nothing at all. "Want to try to get closer?"

Stone surveyed the wall of flesh before them. "We might try to circle around, I guess. I can't imagine it'll do much good."

Donna stamped her feet on the frozen ground. "Beats standing here," she said. She headed off to the right. Stone followed.

The crowd—Stone upped his estimate to closer to three thousand by the time they were halfway around—formed a

circle around the tent. Donna saw faces she was already beginning to think of as familiar. Faces she'd seen on the streets of
Faulkner. She knew none of them by name, but she felt a kind
of kinship between herself and these strangers. A spirit born
out of shared experience. They were—or would soon become
—members of the same small and select club.

But that club was growing, growing too fast and freely to
really be considered all that "select" anymore. That made her
feel good, to know in her heart the gift of Paul Trayne was
spreading out so quickly to those who needed it. How far could
it reach? How fast? How long would it take, realistically, to
bring his gift to the whole sore, festering world? In Faulkner
the effect was geometric. One person touched by Paul brought
two more, they brought four, they brought eight . . .

"You Miz Wojciechowski?" The voice was slightly nasal and
came from the right, beyond the perimeter of the crowd.
Donna and Stone turned to find themselves facing a tall, lean
young man with broad shoulders and narrow hips barely able
to support the broad belt from which hung his holstered pistol.
Rust-colored hair lay in a light fuzz around the sides of his
head under the broad brim of his Smoky Bear hat. A moustache of like hue decorated his upper lip. The five-pointed star
of his badge glinted on his dark leather jacket.

Donna felt a sudden sinking in her heart. "There's . . .
there's not been any . . . trouble? Paul . . . ?"

"No, no. He's fine. He's fine. Just the crowd's gettin' a tad
too big out here." Pete Hay gestured toward the pressing
throng. "The chief thought me an' some of the other officers
better come out tonight and keep an eye on things." He
looked past Donna at Stone. "You'd be Mr. Stone, then? Ben
Carpenter told Chief Nickerson you'd come up to Faulkner."

"Down," said Stone, "from Chicago."

"Down." Hay shrugged off the correction. "Wouldn't have
thought, few weeks back, that this place'd be worth shit to a
big city newspaper."

Nor would I, thought Stone, but he said, "News is news . . .
Deputy, is it?"

"Hay. Deputy Pete Hay."

Stone nodded. "News is news. Maybe you could answer me a few questions, though, as long as you're here?"

"If I can." No reservation in his tone, Stone noted, his immediate thought being that Hay had already fallen under Paul Trayne's spell. He made that his first question, phrased discreetly.

"Nossir," Hay said, flint in his voice. "I don't hold with this kind of shit. Not at all."

"Then why not close them down, Deputy?"

"If it were up to me . . ." Hay shook his head. "But Clarence—that's Chief Nickerson—says leave 'em be. And, anyway, they're not breakin' any laws I can find."

"How hard did you look?"

"As hard as I needed to, Stone," Hay growled. Stone was mindful of the absence of a "Mr." in front of his name.

"Okay. Sorry, Deputy. I just wanted to be sure."

Hay shrugged. "They leased this field from ol' Tom Hackett. He owns this whole parcel, over to the Faulkner town line, and back that way"—he tipped his narrow head toward the dark northern horizon—"to the edge of Marcy Kavelhoff's property. They got themselves all the right papers to allow this kind of lawful assemblage. All filed proper over t'the city hall."

"Could the papers be forged, d'you think, Deputy?"

"Can't imagine how." Hay stroked his moustache with a freckled finger. "True enough this Trayne fella could've forged the papers he has with him," he said, "but like I said they're all filed over t'the city hall." Stone thought him about to say more, but Hay simply shrugged again.

"Then . . . I guess that's not my story," Stone said. "What about Trayne, Deputy? The older one. Did you run any checks on him? Or on Paul, for that matter?" When Stone said the boy's name he saw Donna's eyes flicker in his direction.

"Did what I could to find out what there was to find out about th' Traynes," Hay said. "Called over t'the Missouri state capital and asked about this Three Forks Reverend Trayne says he's from. It's real, but it's a fly speck. One of those teeny little places that doesn't really exist. You know, a bunch of houses, maybe a place that works as a general store, and all the folks that live there have got round to callin' it Three Forks, but it's never been officially incorporated under that name. Still, I got to wonderin' why they'd left."

"Oh? Why?"

"Well, like I said, this Three Forks don't add up to much as a town, but from what I was able to find out, seems there'd be more than enough around there to keep this kid and his pappy busy."

"Like?"

"Like the highest per capita crime rate in the state, for one. Population's less than three hundred, from what anyone could tell me, but they've had twenty-six murders in the last ten years. Over fifty armed robberies. Twenty rapes."

"And that's the town Trayne and the kid come from?" Stone whistled.

"Yeah. Seems like if they wanted a place to start this crusade of theirs, they'd been born right into it. But they left. They came here."

"Did you check on Trayne's credentials? If he's really a Reverend . . . ?"

Hay shrugged once more. "Doesn't take a whole helluva lot to call yourself a Reverend," he said. "And as long as he insists this ain't a church, ain't nothing like a religious gathering, I can't rightly say that he's breaking any laws. S'pose I could look it up, if you really think that it's an issue . . . ?" His tone was all Stone needed to know that was a dead end. If he'd known Pete Hay as well as the people clustered around them, Stone would have been surprised to hear the policeman had gone out of his way to do even as much investigative research as he had.

"Guess not," Stone said. "What about the boy, then? Anything like child labor laws being violated here?"

Hay frowned. "That's a point, all right. The boy's under age, or looks it, anyway. Miss Wojciechowski . . ." Donna turned at the sound of her name. It seemed to Stone that her eyes drifted for a moment, as if trying—he knew he was being far too subjective—to refocus on the real world, without quite achieving it. "You've talked to this boy," Hay said. "What's your impression of his age?"

Donna thrust her tongue into her cheek as she thought

about it. "From what he said, he's about fifteen. He . . . feels older. Wiser. But fifteen is all the years he's got behind him. Why?"

Stone realized she had not heard what they had been saying and spoke to prevent Hay telling her the gist of their discussion. "Nothing," he said. "Background. For the story."

Donna was content to accept the half-truth. She looked back toward the crowd, collecting faces again. One of the faces she saw, away to one side, was Mae Ellen Faber. Mae was coming toward Donna, although she did not seem to have spotted her yet. She was simply walking, circling the crowd, as Donna and Stone had done, but from the opposite direction. When she came within easy hailing distance Donna raised a hand and called her name. Mae was looking toward the mass of people, to her right. She turned at the sound and smiled.

"Miss Wojciechowski. It's so good to see you here again."

" 'Don,' " said Donna. "How are you this evening, Mae?" Donna noticed the older woman was not dressed much more sensibly than she was herself. Mae wore only a light coat over her print dress, and ordinary shoes. Unlike Donna, she did not seem to mind the cold.

"I'm very well . . . Don. Isn't it wonderful to see all these people? All come to see Paul."

"It's great." Donna nodded, looking quickly at Stone to see if he was going to disagree. He was still talking to Pete Hay.

"I'm glad," Donna added. Somehow this turnout seemed— felt—like a personal achievement. A thing Donna herself could be proud of, although she'd had absolutely nothing to do with it. "Have you seen Paul yet tonight? Is he all right?"

"Yes, he's fine. Still a little tired, but . . . He asked me not to say anything about this, but he seems to get stronger after each . . . what would you call it? Meeting?"

"Session?" Donna suggested. "He's doing the same kind of work that a psychiatrist does. Doing it a lot better, but doing the same work. Psychiatrists call their little meetings 'sessions.' "

Mae nodded. "Anyway, he seems to be getting stronger. As if doing this good work bolsters him." She looked away toward the lights of Faulkner reflected against the low sky. "Not that

that matters so much, I guess, as long as he gets the job done. . . ."

Donna looked over the heads of the crowd, toward the tent. The roof was thick with snow; it looked like a child's drawing of a mountain, a sharp white peak that had nothing to do with natural lines. "D'you think I could see him?" Donna asked. "Before the session starts?"

"I don't see why not." Mae started back the way she'd come.

"Hold on a sec," Donna said. She stepped closer to Stone.

". . . really would like to get some people to look at her," Stone was saying. He broke eye contact with Hay as Donna addressed him.

"I'm going to talk to Paul, before this all gets started up again." Donna fixed her eye on his. "I'd rather go alone, if that's okay with you."

Stone's face said it wasn't, but his voice said, "Don't suppose there's any way I can stop you if I want to, is there?"

"Not short of sitting on me, no." She turned and walked away, joining Mae, quickly disappearing from Stone's line of sight.

"Do you know that woman?" Stone asked Hay.

"Mae Ellen Faber," Pete said. "Works over t'the *Observer*. It was her got Ben Carpenter to come out here, the first time."

"Really?" Stone's eyebrows rose above the rims of his glasses. "How?"

"Carpenter was impressed with the change in her after she came out here, Clarence said. Guess I was too, after I talked to her."

"But not enough to sample the boy's wares for yourself?"

"No. My girl friend wanted to come look . . . That's her place bordering this plot, Marcy Kavelhoff. I told her 'no way.' "

"Why?"

"Told you. Don't hold with this shit."

"Again, why?" Stone was beginning to like Pete Hay. The man was a trifle coarse by Stone's standards—Stone himself almost never used profanity—but they agreed on this point, that whatever Paul Trayne offered there was something very wrong with it. Still, Stone wanted to make sure they were really operating on the same wavelength.

"Don't believe in it," Hay said. "Don't think the kid can really do what they say."

"And yet, by your own admission the Faber woman was . . . well, 'cured' is the only word that springs to mind."

Hay nodded. "I keep findin' myself thinkin' about it like that too. Funny."

"You don't trust Paul Trayne and his ilk, obviously."

"Not by half," Hay agreed. "Don't know as I'm what you'd call an especially religious man, Mr. Stone. I mean, church on Sunday an' all, yes, but, well, living it day by day, the way you're supposed to . . ." He sighed.

"I wonder. I don't like this air of . . . disinterest that seems to go hand in hand with young Trayne's wonder cure. I mean, here's Donna, who used to be ready to climb down my throat if I so much as looked sideways at her and now . . ."

"Now she doesn't seem to care anymore?"

"Yeah. Or, almost yeah, anyway. It's more . . . subtle than that." Stone shook his head. "And once upon a time I thought I might be a writer!"

"Wouldn't be too hard on myself, if I were you. Seems like most folks are havin' trouble puttin' it into words, what Paul Trayne does. And you're tryin' to report it secondhand."

"Mmm. You're a bunch up on me on that one, Deputy. I only have Don to judge the change in. You've got a lot more people you know, people who've been . . . there's that word again, 'cured.' "

"True enough. But I don't think I can put a finger on the exact way th' change works any better'n you, Mr. Stone. They're all happier, but like you said, it seems to be because they don't give a shit anymore. At least, not about anything but Paul Trayne. And they care a helluva lot about Paul Trayne."

"Oh? I saw the enthusiasm in Don. Is that symptomatic?"

"Seems like. It was that that sent Carpenter out here, when he saw it in Miss Faber. Prob'ly you should talk to him first-hand."

"Maybe. Listen, Deputy, I let Donna go off on her own, but

I'm not altogether sure that was such a great idea. What say you and I go and pay the Traynes a more . . . professional visit?"

"Not much I could do, Mr. Stone. I've already checked their papers and all."

"Say you're just concerned about their safety, then. With all these people. I mean, that's pretty much the truth anyway, right?"

"Surely is." Hay smiled a smile most conspiratorial. "Let's go see what we can see, shall we?"

Donna found Paul Trayne sitting on a wooden stool set against the back of the tent. He wore a faded corduroy jacket that matched his trousers in color and cut; bony wrists showed well beyond the cuffs. An old hospital screen was set around him, forming a small, roofless canvas chamber, barely more than three feet on a side. All this Mae Ellen had already seen; it passed largely unnoticed as she poked her head around the side of the screen.

"Hello, Paul," she said. "I've brought someone to see you. Oh, I'm so sorry. Did I wake you?"

He sat with his head back against the canvas wall of the tent; to anyone coming upon him like that, he would look as though he were asleep. His breathing was slow and rhythmic. His mouth hung slightly open. His hands rested on his knees, palms facing up. Paul's head came up as Mae entered. His eyes opened. Mae was struck again by the crystal clarity of his deep green irises. The cold breeze that infiltrated his waiting area lifted slender strands of his hair. He smiled, showed the gap between the top incisors.

"Ms. Faber. I'm very glad to see you again." He seemed to notice Donna as an afterthought. "You too, Ms. Wojciechowski. You did not bring your friend? Mr. Stone?"

"Good to see you, too, Paul," said Donna. "Walker's here, wandering around somewhere. I think he's with Deputy Hay." She paused, studying his young face. The dark eyes were shadowed, but the weariness was gone. He looked, in fact, considerably stronger. "How do you feel?" she asked.

"I am well," Paul said. He looked past Donna at the crowd

visible beyond the edge of the screen. "There are a lot of people, tonight." He shrugged. "There is so much needing here. So many who need my help. And Father says my work will not be done until I have touched as many people as the span of my life will allow." He sighed, and his whole body seemed to Donna to deflate. His shoulders sagged, and for just that moment Donna would have had no trouble believing Paul Trayne was a thousand years old. Then he straightened, his face and eyes fresh and clear again.

"I want to help them." His Huckleberry Finn smile made Donna forget the cold in her feet.

"When do you think you'll be starting, Paul?" Mae asked.

"When Father returns," Paul said. "He is mingling with the crowd now. He has a certain . . . sensitivity. He wants to make sure the correct people are served first." He looked into Donna's eyes. She saw fire behind his pupils, as though a fever raged there, waiting to burst out. "Those who have the greatest needing. Those least able to help themselves."

Paul looked away. "When do you think you'll be returning to Chicago?"

Donna hadn't given it much thought. "Soon, I guess." A painful longing seized her, like a hunger. "I . . ."

"Yes, Donna?"

"I wish you were coming with me. I mean . . . I wish you could come to Chicago and . . . help people there."

Paul smiled. "I have thought about this. But . . . It would be difficult to get the people to come to me, don't you think? I mean, Faulkner is a small town. We were able to depend on word of mouth. But in a big city like Chicago . . ."

Donna realized their conversation had turned all the way back to the point at which Stone had interrupted them with his arrival that afternoon. Thoughts she'd had then, sidetracked until this moment, came flooding back.

"If you had a good publicist, you could get to all the people, I think. It would just be a case of handling it properly. Making sure you talked to the right people first. The highly placed people."

"Do you know such people, Donna?" He sounded, she thought, quite impressed.

"Some of 'em. And they know others, and they know others." She squatted down beside Paul's seat and put a hand on his, which was still palm up on his knee. "I could do this for you, Paul. I could open up Chicago for you. I know I could. And from Chicago, you could go out into the world . . ."

"Oh-h-h!" It was Mae Ellen, still standing behind Donna. "Oh, wouldn't that be wonderful?"

"It would be . . . as I had hoped it would be," Paul said. He flipped his other hand over, pressing Donna's fingers between his palms. Sudden heat suffused her body. Paul's bright eyes were like flames. "If you could do this thing, Donna, you would be among the first in the new Kingdom. The Kingdom of Peace and Tranquility."

"Without sorrow," Donna heard her own voice saying.

"Without grief," Mae Ellen chimed in.

Paul Trayne nodded. He rose. He seemed taller, stronger. Donna swallowed hard. An undeniable sexuality flowed out from Paul, seeping into Donna Wojciechowski through her eyes, her mouth, her pores.

"Will you help me, Donna?" Paul asked.

"Oh, yes," she said. "Oh, Paul, I'll do anything."

She meant it.

Three thousand people in a space a tenth the size of an average football field. Almost all of them crowded into a knot measuring no more than sixty feet from side to side, a tent in the middle.

Walker Stone shook his head. A lot of those pressed bodies were in the tent, seated on the folding chairs, or standing six or more deep around the inner walls. Stone could not see this, from his position at the outer edge of the crowd, but he could imagine it, as he could imagine the respectful distance this tremendous crush would be keeping from the small stage. The quiet, peaceful self-control these people maintained fascinated him the most. No raised voices, shoving, pushing, pulling, fighting. Those who arrived late moved into the outer edge of the mass—absorbed into it, Stone felt with a shiver of revulsion—and drew from it the quiet reserve, the patience this place demanded.

It's like they're in a shrine. A holy place. As if the Virgin is going to come floating over the grotto at any second.

Unconsciously he craned his neck and scanned the dark sky. There were only stars, bright and sparkling directly overhead, the lights of Faulkner reflecting against the low clouds to his back.

He felt uncomfortable being here. There was an element in all this that he had not told Donna. An element he was trying to push out of his brain, because he did not want it there, did not want to believe in the power of Paul Trayne. And yet, undeniably, while he'd talked to the boy that afternoon, Stone had felt a great need to believe in him. Had felt all the old sores, the psychological scars working their way through the layers of mental cotton wadding he'd packed around them, to fire slender, bright, painful laser beams into his brain. All the little hurts—and the not so little hurts—he'd accumulated in forty-two years. They had all begun to make themselves known again, make their presence felt, and with them had come the feeling that Paul Trayne could help, would help, if only Walker Stone would open himself and let the boy work the power of his miraculous gift.

A murmur rose from the center of the crowd, from the tent. *Paul,* Stone thought. *He's made his appearance.*

He wished they could have got to Paul before that happened, to see the boy before he began his show, but Chief Clarence Nickerson had arrived and slowed Hay down long enough to be brought up to date on the evening's events, and then taken his place at Stone's side. It annoyed Stone that Hay allowed himself to be shuttled off like that. Nickerson seemed less enthused by Stone's idea than his deputy had been. Now it was too late.

Stone shuddered at the thought. *Too late for what?*

Alarms were clanging, deep in his subconscious, but he did not know why. He knew that logically he should be glad of anything that freed Donna Wojciechowski of her personal demons. He'd appreciate some salve like that himself. Unbidden his mind turned to thoughts of Elizabeth Barnes, the girl who'd so casually twisted his heart inside out in journalism school. There were still times when he found himself contemplating very dark thoughts about her. Thoughts that had, he hoped, very little to do with the sane, sensible man he believed himself to be. Thoughts that disturbed him deeply. He would not have complained if they simply vanished into the cold night air.

Then why don't you take advantage of what this kid has to offer? Why aren't you in there now, having your own personal "needing" taken care of?

Stone knew why: he was a man who liked to be in control of his own destiny. He'd fought all his life to maintain control in all things. And this, whatever it was, took away control. It made everything fine, but it was not fine because of anything the subject—the word "victim" came first to Stone's mind—had done for himself or herself.

I wonder if that might not kick back, some day? Can we really be happy, as human beings, if we're handed paradise on a silver platter?

There was just enough old-fashioned puritan ethic in Stone to answer "no" to that question. He thought—hoped—human-kind needed more than soft, creature comforts and a blanked-out conscience. He shivered again, as the murmuring from the middle of the crowd took on a chantlike quality. It rose and fell in slow, rhythmic undulations, now soft, now louder. It was spreading through the crowd.

"I don't remember anything like this in Ben Carpenter's article," Stone said to Clarence Nickerson. He felt uncomfortable in the chief's massive presence, overwhelmed, after the taller but considerably narrower Pete Hay.

The chief of police shook his head. He didn't seem bothered by the sounds. "Wasn't there," he said. "And they didn't do this the other night, either. Still, seems peaceable enough."

Stone stood on tiptoe, a waste of time on the soft, muddy ground. He tried to look over the heads of the crowd. He could not see any more than the top of the tent. "Something new added, then," he said. He did not like the feel of it.

With Nickerson leading, his broad shape parting the crowd like the prow of an icebreaker, Stone walked over the churned, muddy ground toward the center of the problem. They reached the back of the tent, the small screened area.

Stone stepped behind the screen and found the back door,

the disguised flap through which Paul Trayne made his entrance each night. He took off his glasses and pressed his right ear close to the canvas, the better to hear through the wall of the tent. Unconsciously he drew the penknife from his pocket and began tightening the little screws in the frames of his glasses as he listened. The murmuring rose and fell around him. It spread to almost everyone in the crowd, man and woman, adult and child alike. For a long moment that was all he could hear. Then Robert Trayne's clear trumpet voice sounded above the hubbub.

"There are many needings here," Trayne said. "Many, many more than Paul has ever had to take upon himself before. You do understand this, don't you?" A sharpness to Trayne's voice, Stone thought. A lecturing tone. "What he takes from you, he keeps. Your pain becomes his pain. Your sorrow becomes his sorrow. You are released, but the burden becomes his. His to carry, until the end of his days."

"Yes," said a single voice through four thousand mouths. Stone actually jumped at the sound. All those people, speaking as one. Everyone in the crowd! How were they all hearing Trayne? Could they all be reacting out of some kind of mob hypnosis? Only those inside heard Trayne, but were the others saying whatever they heard the fortunate few say, automatically, not caring what it meant, what they might be committing themselves to?

"And you bring him your needings, your pain, your grief and sorrow, knowing this?" Trayne went on. His voice was almost . . . scolding?

What the hell is he doing?

Belaboring the obvious was the first thing Stone thought of, but that was too simple. There was more here, something Robert Trayne was trying to create in the throng: a thought, a feeling.

"Yes," said the single voice, louder than before.

"Then let it be done," said Paul Trayne.

Stone turned to speak to Nickerson, close by his side. Words never formed. His glasses slipped from his left hand. The penknife tipped slowly out of his right and impaled itself in the ground a fraction of an inch from his foot. Stone did not notice. A dagger of burning steel penetrated the front of his skull. He did not feel anything else for quite a long time.

"How is he, Donna?"

"I'm not sure, Mae. I'm no doctor, but I'd almost think . . . well, it looks to me like he had a stroke or something."

"Has anything like that ever happened to him before?"

"No. At least, I don't think so. Not in the time I've known him."

"Do you think he'll be all right?"

"Oh, Paul. I didn't hear you come in. I don't know. I . . . I was going to say, 'I think so,' but I really don't know."

"You sent for a doctor?"

"Yes. Chief Nickerson sent one of his officers. Pete Hay. He should be back soon."

"Then there is nothing to worry about, is there, Sister Wojciechowski?"

"Hmm? Oh, no, Reverend Trayne. I wasn't worried. No, as you say, there's nothing to worry about."

"Nothing at all."

"No. Nothing at all."

Voices. Distant voices. Echoing down long, dark corridors; a joining of halls that stretched away in every direction, spokes of some infinite, unimaginable wheel. They grew louder and softer, went up and down, like summer thunder across Lake Michigan or a distant murmured chant. Stone floated in and out of his own life, now today, now yesterday, now ten, fifteen, twenty years ago, propelled by the voices. He saw himself, felt himself to be as he was, as he had been, as he never was, all at once, each completely separate from the other. Those voices. He thought they belonged to the here and now—although he could not be sure what the here and now was—and he thought he recognized them. He was certain he recognized Donna's, at least. He'd heard that voice in enough permutations to be sure it was her voice, somewhere out there, echoing down the infinite halls.

She was talking to someone—Mae Faber?—about someone who'd had an accident. Or, no, not an accident exactly. Something nasty had happened to someone and they were discussing him. There was something missing in the way they spoke. Stone thought—the thought slipped away from him, replaced by his ninth birthday, when his uncle came drunk to little Walker's party and smashed the birthday cake against the wall —replaced by the screaming match with Donna in his office— replaced by his first love affair, his first act of physical love— replaced by the blinding pain of his broken leg, the one and only time he went skiing—replaced by his original thought, that something was missing from those voices. It began to drift by him, that thought. He tried to grab it, to hold it. He did not seem to have any arms, any hands. Nevertheless he managed to hold the thought long enough to complete it. They were empty, those voices. They were discussing something awful, yet there was no more emotion in them than if they were discussing the weather. Less. People could get mad about the weather. Could generate considerable emotion about the weather.

But these voices—he was sure it was Donna and Mae—were discussing someone who'd had a stroke, they thought, with no more concern than if they'd been exchanging recipes. Another voice joined in. The voice Stone was sure was Donna's identified the newcomer as Trayne. In his drifting, dreamlike state, hovering between one disjointed moment of his reality and another, Stone could not connect the voice to Paul Trayne's father. The older Trayne's voice was soft, strong. It never seemed to grow louder. It never seemed to get angry. It was calm and peaceful, even a little flat. The voice Stone heard was emptied of tone, of meaning. It sounded the way Stone thought voices might sound to the seriously autistic, the way he'd heard voices sound to those who could no longer fathom meanings and could take only the emotional content of a voice to tell them what was being said.

And the voice Walker Stone heard was cold as frozen steel, cold as the deepest, blackest pit of Hades.

Donna sat with Stone in the back of the ambulance as it jerked and skidded its way along the quagmire that was Pine Tree Road. It was nothing more than a modified van, that ambulance. The ride, uncomfortable under even the best conditions, was made no better by the clutter of medical equipment—oxygen cylinders, tubes, hoses, lengths of silvery metal that did not reveal their purpose in their shape—and the awkward position Donna was forced to adopt in order to keep herself from falling on top of Stone.

In any other situation he might have enjoyed that, she knew, but he was oblivious. That, at least, was the verdict of the doctor, a thick-faced older man named Zeldenrust. From the reverential tones with which everyone—including Nickerson, Donna noted—addressed the physician, she guessed him to be someone of considerable importance in Faulkner. She wondered why he, and not some underling, was now bouncing along Pine Tree Road with her. She decided it was not important enough to wonder about too long. She looked at Stone. He lay on his back, strapped to the stretcher, eyes closed. His lips hung loose. As the truck bounced and his head lolled, his cheeks moved and made an odd little sucking sound. A drop of saliva had worked its way over the left side of his mouth, through the tangle of his moustache, and was creeping along the line of his beard toward his ear. Donna studied the slow, slick path the droplet traced and wondered what had happened to this man who'd once meant so much in her life.

She'd learned of Stone's collapse when Chief Nickerson burst into the tent demanding to know if there was a doctor there. There was not. No one seemed to know any basic first aid. That struck Donna as somewhat odd, in a gathering of however many thousands of people, that no one should ever have picked up some first aid training. She wondered for a moment if, in fact, there were people there who could have helped Stone, but simply held back, no longer interested in such things, now that they had felt the touch of Paul Trayne's magic.

After all, Donna admitted now to herself, that was her own reaction. She had a pretty good knowledge of various lifesaving techniques, but, standing to one side of the stage, eyes locked on Paul Trayne, she'd felt no interest in offering aid to Stone. It was not that she still harbored any animosity toward him. Far from it, since she harbored ill feelings toward no one anymore. His condition was simply unimportant. Only Dr. Zeldenrust's insistence, in fact, put her here, now, in the ambulance. She would much rather have been back at the Miracle Show with Paul.

It had been nearly two hours into the session when Nickerson burst in. Paul had been tending to the needings of many, many people. He swayed as he stood on the stage, seeming to welcome the respite brought by Nickerson's interruption. Donna could see in the faces of the gathered needy that they resented the intrusion. They could tell Paul was tired, exhausted from all he had taken on in that one evening, but their eyes flashed resentment as Nickerson came up through the crowd. He elbowed people out of his way, bulldozing his way to the stage.

"There's been an accident," he said. "Behind the tent." He turned and sought out Donna. "It's Mr. Stone." Then he looked back at Paul. "He's had some kind of an attack."

Donna had seen a frown pass across Paul's smooth brow. Genuine concern, even for a man who was very nearly a stranger. A hostile stranger at that. It seemed odd to her, especially after that now-familiar voice said *Never mind.* So Donna had gone with Nickerson, out through the back door of the tent, to find Stone slumped by the stool Paul had occupied a few hours earlier. Stone was sitting on the ground, his trousers soaked through with the wet from the ground, as if he'd been sitting there over an hour.

Now, in the ambulance, Donna looked down at Stone's face. So coarse, so poorly made, set against the image of Paul Trayne in her mind. Hard to believe she ever thought she might love this man, even in her own strange, self-destructive way. Odd—no, very nearly impossible—thinking of pleasures being wrought in her by his caress, his kiss. Odd, too, thinking that those same pleasures once disturbed her, distressed her.

Like being given an award I hadn't earned. Like I was being given credit for someone else's work. That's how it felt. Like something I didn't deserve.

Stone was skilled in lovemaking, to be sure. With him on one lost Christmas Eve Donna had experienced a climax more intense than any she had ever known. So much so she knew in that moment that it was in all likelihood her first true orgasm. Yet those few moments of dizzying ecstasy served only to drive her into a deep, unrelenting depression that had sapped all love and joy from the event, retroactively. For the old, self-hating Donna Wojciechowski what could have been an awakening of new life had very quickly turned into a plunge into greater darkness. She had come to hate Walker Stone, hate his face, his lips, his touch. So, typically, she had been utterly unable to tell him this and had let the affair drag on, forcing herself to talk to him, to sleep with him, to work with him, loathing every second of it. Until he released her, by confronting her with her own emotions, forcing her to explode into a blind white rage that shattered their relationship forever. At least, freed from the burden of their affair, she could turn back to her job and find there some solace as the rest of her life crumbled around her. Then her job began to crumble, too, as Stone reduced the importance of the assignments he gave her to pursue, until . . .

Well, until this. And this has turned out to be the most important assignment ever. For anyone. Anywhere.

She started thinking of Paul again. She'd drifted miles, light-years, away when the lurch of the ambulance stopping startled her back to the world. She looked out into the night and discovered they had completed their journey into Faulkner. Outside the window of the ambulance, the Harrison District Hospital was a low, squat building, a single story for the most part, excepting a narrow, three-story addition that rose in the back, newer, in a conflicting architectural style. Warm yellow light burned behind the big windows around the entrance on the face of the building, but for the most part, Donna saw the rest of the structure was dark.

She looked at her watch. Almost midnight. It occurred to her to call Stone's secretary in Chicago, tell her what had happened to Stone.

Why? asked that gadfly voice. Donna had no answer.

The back of the ambulance opened. A wall of ice cold air toppled in to smash over her.

"Jesus!" said Donna. She leaped from the back of the ambulance, almost knocking down one of the uniformed attendants at the door. She pushed past and raced up the low flight of steps into the hospital.

The warmth of the lobby closed around her, carrying the smell of ether and a thousand other hospital smells. Donna cherished the respite from the bitter cold outside. The front doors swung open again and the two attendants hurried in, bearing Walker Stone. He was still unconscious on the stretcher. Dr. Zeldenrust followed, barking orders. He took quick care of all that needed to be done with Stone, then crossed to Donna.

"We need you to fill out some forms, Miss Wojciechowski," he said. His pronunciation of Donna's name was flawless, even, she noted with nostalgia, properly accented.

"All right. Where?" Donna could think of things she'd rather be doing, but the intensity of Dr. Zeldenrust's expression made it plain she would not be allowed to leave until she had completed what he saw as her duty. Since she was not in any sort of mood for an argument, she complied. He led her to the admitting desk and Donna dutifully rolled off such details as she knew of Stone's life. It didn't take long. Stone was an only child, his parents both dead now. He'd never been married. So far as Donna knew, until now, he'd never even been sick.

Does this constitute sick?

"Sick" meant to her diseased, infected. What had happened to Stone was something else. "Stricken" suggested itself. She finished with the forms and thought about leaving. She remembered the genuine love she'd sensed from Stone and wondered if she should hang around to see how he was when the doctors were finished with their prodding and probing. As Stone's pet phrase passed through her mind, Donna remembered the specialists he'd intended to summon from Chicago.

Did he? she wondered. *And if he did, when are they going to get here?* It had become vitally important to Donna that no one examine her.

6

"I think he'll be all right now," said Dr. Maurice Zeldenrust, pulling shut the door of Walker Stone's hospital room. Donna got a glimpse of Stone, propped up on pillows on the cantilevered bed set against the far wall of the small private room. "I'm not certain, you understand," Zeldenrust added, "but his respiration is normal, and his blood pressure is good." He shook his heavy, wavy-haired head. "I've never seen anything quite like it in all the years I've been practicing medicine."

To Donna's right, Clarence Nickerson stared at the door behind the doctor, squinting at its smooth green surface, as if, she thought, willing his eyes to develop X-ray vision. "It looked like a stroke to me."

"No," Zeldenrust said, and there was no equivocation Donna could hear in his tone. She leaned against the wall across the corridor from Stone's room and studied Zeldenrust. It was he who had come out in the ambulance from Faulkner, he who had examined Walker Stone, still lying as Donna found him on the cold, wet ground behind the Traynes' tent. And it was on the couch in Dr. Zeldenrust's office that Donna spent the dreamless hours between their arrival at the hospital and Nickerson's summoning of her to hear the doctor's report.

"No," Dr. Zeldenrust repeated, "there are none of the signs of stroke. No loss of mobility. No indication of hemorrhaging."

He looked at Nickerson directly. "Decribe to me again how it happened. What you saw."

Nickerson shook his big head. "Nothing to describe, Mo. We'd been standing in back of the tent for some time. Couple of hours or more. Listening to the show inside. I kept trying to get him to go inside, but he kept saying no, he wanted to wait in back like that."

"In the cold?"

Nickerson shrugged his massive shoulders. "He turned to talk—at least I thought it was to talk. He looked like he was going to say something. Then he just keeled over."

"But there's nothing really wrong with him?" Donna surprised herself with the question. It was the first time she'd spoken to Dr. Zeldenrust since he'd insisted she accompany Stone back to the hospital. What surprised her was the concern she heard in her voice. Genuine concern for the condition of Walker Stone. Until that moment, her thoughts had been wholly directed toward Paul. Her need to get back to him, back to Gunner's Field.

"Nothing wrong with Mr. Stone of a permanent nature, as far as I can tell," Zeldenrust said.

The chief snorted. Nickerson looked almost disappointed, Donna thought. She guessed he was looking forward to something to break the monotony of police work in this sleepy little town. She guessed, too, that he was looking for some way to disrupt Paul Trayne and his Miracle Show. Bitter resentment flared in her heart.

"My best guess, pure speculation," Dr. Zeldenrust continued, "is that his brain just, well, shut down for a moment. Shock, maybe. Extreme cold can do that to somebody, although it wasn't near cold enough last night." He shrugged. "Perhaps Mr. Stone is hypersensitive. Lot of things can cause shock. Not my field of expertise." He looked at Donna. "Perhaps I should be looking after you too, Miss Wojciechowski? You and Mr. Stone are . . . close. If you need a sedative . . ."

Donna felt the short hairs prickle on the back of her neck. "You . . . needn't worry. There's nothing wrong with me. Nothing at all." Donna looked away from him, at Nickerson.

"If you don't need me anymore, I'd like to go back out to Gunner's Field." She wanted to see Paul. And she was really beginning to feel the need of a smoke. And a drink. Several drinks.

"Then you don't want to wait and see what Mr. Stone has to say when he comes to?" Nickerson asked.

Zeldenrust added his professional agreement. "It could be of help to him to see a friendly face. He may be regaining consciousness at any time. It's hard to say."

Donna wondered if Walker would really consider her a "friendly face." Likely he would, even after all that had passed between them. His being here alone said as much. But she said, "I don't imagine it will make any difference if I'm here or not." She did not wait for their release. She turned and walked away from them as quickly as she could without actually breaking into a run.

Walker Stone drifted through a place that was not sleep, yet was not wakefulness. Largely it was a soft, dark place, warm and cozy. It was filled with vague, happy memories, good feelings that did not seem to come from any particular place, but wanted—yes, he was aware, the feelings seemed possessed of their own driving needs, their own wants—to fill up all the corners of his mind and make everything one great, smooth, soft, warm niceness. Anyone who had been in the room with him at just that point might have wondered what it was that caused the apparently unconscious man's lip to curl into a sneer beneath the cover of his thick moustache.

He let himself drift through the dark, warm place, finding here and there bright, sharp shards, like broken glass, scattered across the velvet void. These were infinitely more important to him than the warmth and solace promised by the darkness. These he tried to hang on to—a difficult task in the unphysical place, without hands, eyes, or any dimensions he was aware of. He concentrated on them, on the bright, sharp edges, and found they concerned themselves with Donna Wojciechowski.

Stone reviewed Donna. Her sheer physical presence was always the first thing that came to mind, when he thought of her. It amazed him that she'd abused herself so much, for so long, yet still possessed the ability to shake it off, to turn herself into an absolute, drop-dead stunner. Her height and her bones had a lot to do with it, he'd long ago decided. She was five feet ten, flat-footed, and her cheekbones . . . !

And of course—an observer would have seen now an ironic little smile—*those damnfinelegs don't hurt.*

Still, he'd seen her on enough mornings after—breath rank with stale old booze, eyes staring out of their sockets like frightened animals caught at the bottom of deep, black caves—to know just how far down she could go. To know that one of these days she would sink so low that she would not be able to come back up again. Walker Stone was a teetotaler, bar in car notwithstanding, but he'd known enough alcoholics to be able to read all the finer signs of Donna's disease. She was not one of those who were allergic to the booze, as the wise men of science now thought some alcoholics might be, poor souls doomed from their very first drink. Donna drank because she knew it was self-destructive. She carried—*used to carry?*—a deep and abiding self-hatred that had no foundations in any logic Stone had ever discovered.

His mind turned then to their last argument, in his office on Friday. That awful zap she'd thrown him about "the last time you had me on my back." He shuddered now—at least it *felt* as if he shuddered—thinking about it. In many respects the sexual aspect had been the worst element in the dissolution of their relationship. She'd seemed so willing and eager in his bed, from the very first time, that it had been a terrible blow to discover almost all of it had been a lie, faked.

Oh, Donna. My poor, poor Donna! If only I'd known sooner. If only I'd guessed, seen the signs, been psychic enough to know what kind of demons twisted your guts. I could have taken a whole different approach to our relationship. It might have all worked out very differently, then.

He'd absolutely hated the dissolution of their affair, seeing it as a personal failure; he'd convinced himself that he could save her from the booze, from the self-destructive bent. But mostly he simply missed Donna, sober Donna, real Donna. Missed her smiles, her laughter. Missed waking up next to her. Missed her crying unexpectedly over sentimental birthday cards.

Missed her sudden, surprising strengths. He even missed their fights, sometimes, when he was all alone in his apartment, high over Lakeshore Drive, the great waters of Lake Michigan. With Donna around there was something in his life beyond work. Walker Stone did not consider himself as a workaholic, but there was very little in his life not in and of the *Advocate*. He had his wall of videotapes, his massive knowledge of old TV, so he could argue quite effectively that he had a hobby. He took flying lessons, he hiked, he fished, he did "manly things."

But he always came back to the office, whatever the hour, when he needed to really feel the adrenaline surging again. "Citizen Stone," some of the staff called him—but never to his face. He knew about it, though, and when it started to get to him he would go and hunt and fish and do his manly things, and come back feeling frustrated and empty. More so than ever, now that Donna was no longer there.

Well, yes, she was there. There was a woman named Donna Wojciechowski who worked for the *Advocate*. She looked like the Donna he'd spent those many hours with, even sounded like her. But he could not reach out and touch her as she passed. Not any more. He could not talk to her, unburden himself when the world got too much and he wanted to punch a wall.

Like right now. But there were no walls, and no fist, in any case, to punch with.

More precisely, he wanted to punch the man or woman who had found Ben Carpenter's little piece in the *Observer* and forwarded it to Walker Stone's office. It seemed so harmless! Stone could not believe this insanity had grown from a simple nothing piece he'd assigned to Donna for exactly the reasons she'd accused him of: a rest cure. Make-work. Now, instead of turning in a quick, smash-and-grab debunking of this so-called Miracle Show, Donna had fallen under its spell, under the enchantment of the boy, Paul Trayne. But, then, was it really all that surprising? Alcoholics were dependent personalities, as Stone understood it. They looked for the solutions to life, at least shields against it, in a bottle. Donna looked for the justification for her own self-hatred. She found it. Each bout with the bottle drove her lower and lower, in turn sending her to the bottle again and again. Stone could chart the vicious cycle of it as easily as he could rattle off the stars of a hundred sitcoms. Drink, disgust, drink, disgust. Sometimes a little casual sex to add to the burden of guilt and shame, then back to drink and disgust. Until now. She was still drinking, but the disgust seemed to have evaporated. He could tell by the way she walked now. By the way she held her head, the way she refused to rise to his gibes. She was a woman transformed.

Yet, how can she be? he demanded of the emptiness, receiving no reply.

How could any part of what Paul Trayne offered be real? He'd neatly—or was that too cynical?—avoided Stone's questions. He would not, could not offer any real definition of what he did or how he did it. There was the sign on the gate, enough to satisfy all of Faulkner, but Biblical quotations carried little weight with Stone. He was a lapsed Catholic, happily so. Still, many in his family were very devout, and like Ben Carpenter, he was uncomfortable when the Bible was quoted as if its verses were more fodder for advertising jingles. His discomfort was broader than Ben's, however. Stone also disliked perfume companies that named their product for the founders of Far Eastern religions, or underarm deodorants that used the Statue of Liberty in their advertising. The Supreme Court's decision on flag burning troubled him deeply, until he put it into the proper political perspective the justices intended. He liked the world's symbols kept in their proper place. He'd abandoned the Bible, the faith it represented, but he did not like to see it used by others to their own ends.

It was this that brought his thoughts to his cousin, Father Tom Sylvestri.

Outside the hospital, a gray sky huddled low over Faulkner. Donna checked her watch again. It was 8:15. The sun was above the rooftops to the east, its light pushing in under the cloud cover just enough to dispel the cold of the night before. Donna trotted down the five broad steps from the hospital's main doors and turned right, toward Lafayette Street. The squat structure of Harrison District Hospital was on Grant

Street, the long avenue that defined the south edge of Faulkner. Only the grounds of the hospital lay beyond that line.

Donna judged she was twelve blocks from the center of town, if she walked along Randolph, which was parallel to Lafayette. Except for the fairly long stretch between Grant and Vermont—as she walked Donna checked her progress against the Faulkner map she'd just bought at the little newsstand kiosk in the hospital lobby—they were all short blocks. An easy walk.

From her map she learned at least part of the reason she'd had difficulty finding her way around at first: almost every byway in Faulkner was a named street; although the town was laid out in a traditional grid, almost everything was Something-or-other Street, whether it ran north–south or east–west. Only in one small neighborhood in the southwest corner, behind Ben Carpenter's street, was the grid departed from and terms like "Drive" and "Avenue" applied. There the streets also developed curious human names, like Madelyn and—strangest of all, to Donna—Bobby. She wondered if it was possible to put one's return address on a letter, keeping a straight face, if one lived on Bobby Street. It sounded to Donna like the name of a jazz musician.

She fished out her wallet from deep inside her purse and checked her cash. She had thirty-six dollars, mostly in singles, fattening the wallet and making it hard to refasten the clasp. She also had her credit cards. She decided to stop at a clothing store and pick up some warmer shoes and slacks. She increased her pace as she came at last to Carroll Street, intersecting Lafayette at the center of town. Faulkner was wide awake around her. There were people all over the streets. Some were faces she knew from Gunner's Field. One or two even smiled and nodded as she passed; she was becoming a familiar institution in the town.

As she started across Carroll, engines growled away to her left. She turned just in time to see two cars screeching down the street, one coming down the wrong lane, both barreling toward her at top speed. Donna stepped back, a quick jump that got her clear of the inside car just as it passed within inches of her. Slipstream tugged at her clothes, threatening to pull her after the speeding vehicles. They were both doing well over eighty miles per hour. Donna stared as they screamed down Carroll. No one else on the street seemed to be paying much attention. She looked at the passing people around her. Only a few heads were turned in the direction of the departed racers.

As she started across the street again, brakes squealed to her right. Donna heard the sickening crunch and rip of impact; the car tearing down the oncoming lane had met another coming the other way. Fire bloomed bright, just past the intersection two blocks away. Instinct started Donna in the direction of the sudden blaze, but the little voice stopped her.

Never mind. It can't be anyone you know. And even if it is, what would it matter?

Donna stood for a moment staring down the valley of Carroll Street toward the dark smoke curling up into the wintry sky. Bright firelight danced against the underside of the billowing plume. Someone was screaming, a terrible whooping sound, each cry more intense than the last. A few more of the faces around her turned toward the wreck. One or two people started drifting down Carroll in the direction of the mangled cars. None of them seemed particularly compelled to reach the screamer and help him. The fire burst up bright and hot as something even more incendiary than whatever was already burning caught and exploded. The screaming peaked, then stopped. Abruptly, Donna thought.

Never mind.

Donna turned away from the blaze and continued along her original path. An ambulance appeared ahead of her, racing past. The modified van wagon stopped a few yards short of the burning cars—Donna turned to watch—and two paramedics climbed out. There was no sign yet of a fire truck, and burning fuel and oil were spreading across the intersection. Something burst inside the flames, spraying gasoline up the side of a building. It caught and burned, like napalm, Donna thought. One of the paramedics pulled off his big winter coat and began swatting at the burning patch of brickwork. Donna lost interest and crossed the street.

Five doors beyond the corner Donna found a women's

clothing store. She went in, emerging twenty minutes later with more sensible boots, warmer slacks, and a snug winter jacket to replace the coat she'd borrowed from Stone. The cost was far less than it would have been in Chicago, though that did not interest Donna as much as the fact that she now felt warm for what was very easily the first time since her arrival in Faulkner. She was not at all bothered by the slovenly service she'd received in the store. The two clerks—middle-aged women with hard, colored hair—were far more concerned with talking to each other than with helping a customer. Donna found what she needed without them.

Carrying Stone's coat, boots, and slacks in a shopping bag tucked under one arm, Donna continued along Lafayette Street toward the *Observer* offices. She'd decided, while she shopped, that it might be a good idea to stop in and have a few words with Ben Carpenter. When Walker recovered fully— there was no doubt in her mind that he would—he'd want to talk to Ben again, in depth. Donna felt a need to prepare her new friend for that meeting.

She crossed the street, dodging traffic, and climbed the steep stairs to the door of the *Observer* offices. This time it was not locked. Donna stepped into a room that was at once very like and very unlike the city room of the *Chicago Advocate*. First of all, she noted, it smelled like a newspaper office—that peculiar odor of newsprint, sweat, and flesh. The offices of the *Faulkner Observer* were its original premises, Stone's researchers had determined. The *Observer* had been coming out of that large, single room every day since 1865. In fact, as the framed copy by the door testified, the front page of the very first edition declared the end of the Civil War—prematurely—with the surrender of Robert E. Lee on the day before, April 9 of that year. Donna crossed the room to the low oak railing in front of Ben Carpenter's enclosed office. Ben's secretary looked up as Donna approached. She was a small, round woman with oversize glasses and a great deal of reddish-brown hair piled in a loose bun that looked to Donna in imminent danger of toppling over the back of her head.

"Yes? Can I help you?" she asked, looking over her glasses with water gray eyes.

"I'm Donna Wojciechowski," Donna said. "I'd like to see Mr. Carpenter."

"Mr. Carpenter is . . . rather busy, Miss Wojciechowski."

Donna bobbed her head toward the small intercom unit on one corner of the woman's desk. "Why don't you ask him?"

The woman did so. After a heartbeat Ben appeared in the door of his little office. "Donna. Come in. Good to see you."

Donna pushed through the swinging gate on the rail and passed by Ben into his inner sanctum. She found an area that was a room only by popular agreement. Two glass-and-oak partitions set at right angles to the existing walls formed an enclosed space eight feet on a side, with a small desk dominated by a large typewriter. There were two worn old chairs, one looking rather more comfortable than the other. Framed front pages from the *Observer*'s years of publication hung on the two exterior walls, behind and to the right of the desk.

"Take a seat," Ben said, indicating the second chair. "Coffee? Tea?"

Donna shook her head. "Nothing, thanks." She sat. She crossed her long legs and set her shopping bag on the floor by the chair. "I wanted to talk to you about Paul."

"Delighted," Ben said. "Always delighted to talk about Paul. To anybody." He took his own chair.

Looking at him behind the little desk with the big typewriter, in front of the framed front pages, Donna decided she'd been wrong all these years in thinking Walker Stone looked like the editor of a small-town paper. Ben Carpenter looked that part, and he looked nothing like Walker Stone.

He smiled, a trifle sheepishly, Donna thought. "You know, it's funny," he said, "but I get real, well, excited talking about Paul. It's almost addictive."

"I'd say that's probably a good thing," Donna said. "We have to start talking about Paul. Spreading the word. Getting as many people as we can talking about him, thinking him. Knowing what he does."

Ben nodded slowly. He turned, looked up at the framed front pages for a moment. "Yes," he said. "This is too big for Faulkner alone. And too big for the *Observer,* glad as I am that the story started here." He looked back at Donna. "What do you think we should do?"

"I've got some contacts I think I can exploit in Chicago. I was thinking maybe we should try and get the network TV boys in on this. Call *Hard Copy* or something." Donna was surprised to hear her own words. It flashed briefly through her mind that there was a time—she remembered it, even if she no longer felt the same emotions—when she would have snorted in great derision at those she considered untalented pretty boys, the reporters of TV news.

Ben nodded again. "I'm surprised TV people aren't here already," he said.

Donna shrugged. "It was pure fluke that your article crossed Walker's desk and caught his attention. I'd be surprised if anyone else has even seen it. Now, right now, we have to make sure they see it. And understand what it means."

Ben smiled at her obvious enthusiasm. "I'm real glad to hear you talking like this, Donna. Especially after your reticence when you arrived."

"That was then, this is now. Can you get on it, Ben? Start the ball rolling?" Donna could also remember a time when she would have committed murder before letting another reporter near her story; now those feelings were trivial compared to the vital task of getting Paul Trayne's story out to the world. "I'm going out to talk to Paul about it. I'm sure he'll approve, but I want him prepared."

Ben rose as she did. "I'll come with you. I haven't seen . . ."

"No." Donna was surprised by the intensity of her reaction, a power of emotion she'd not felt in almost two days. She smiled disarmingly. "No. Get busy on this other thing first. We . . . can all go out and see Paul, after tonight's meeting."

Ben frowned, but his face cleared quickly. The brief anger he felt when Donna snapped at him faded. "All right, then." He thrust out a hand, which Donna shook.

"Good." Donna picked up her bag and Stone's coat and crossed to the door. "Oh, Walker's okay, by the way."

"Is he?" Ben's tone revealed his total lack of concern.

"Mmm." Donna paused. "Why did your secretary think you might be too busy to see me?"

"Oh . . . did she say that?" Ben's eyes unfocused for a moment. He reviewed in his mind things that had happened in the last twenty-four hours, seeking something that might be the cause of his secretary's reaction. "I guess it must be because of Mae," he said finally.

"Mae? What's happened?" Donna was aware of the emptiness in her tone. Her words were just words, automatic reactions. They carried no emotion, no concern.

Ben did not notice. "She's been arrested. Pete Hay came by last night with a warrant. They said she killed her mother."

Donna's eyebrows rose. This was almost interesting. "Killed?"

Ben spread his hands dismissingly. "Well, left her alone. Starved her to death, I guess. Seems Mae hadn't looked in on her in all the time she was staying at my place. Criminal negligence is the charge." Ben's voice had slipped into a dull monotone. It was clear to Donna he was not really interested in discussing the subject.

Donna shook her head. "Huh. Well . . . you will take care of our business?"

"Oh, sure." Ben reached for the telephone. "Go see Paul. I'll catch you later."

Donna walked out of Ben's office and promptly forgot everything he'd said. The only thing that mattered now was getting to Paul Trayne by the fastest means possible. She left the *Observer* office pleased to have accomplished something she saw as terribly important and doubly pleased Ben had not insisted on coming along with her out to Gunner's Field. She wanted to see Paul Trayne alone, if she could. She needed to talk to him about this beautiful plan to take his powers to Chicago, to the rest of the world. She thought about his distress last night, when Stone collapsed. Paul had been nearly frantic, Donna thought, as if this business with Stone was something of far greater concern to him than she would ever have thought. At the time, as now, she put it down to Paul's natural compassion for all his fellow humans. All the ills of the world, pressing down on his young shoulders. But without complaint.

The perfect whipping boy, Donna thought, remembering her earlier analogy. It was exactly true, she saw again. *Whipping boy to the world.*

She knew, again, that it did not really matter if Paul was recovered, either from last night's session or from his distress over Walker Stone. It mattered only that his power be brought out into the world. Exploited. She turned right coming out of the *Observer,* partly retracing her steps, then off Lafayette onto Washington, heading for her car.

Gunner's Field looked not at all like the calm, pastoral place Ben Carpenter described in his article. The grasses were flattened for four full acres around the tent. The ground was torn up, rutted, pools of dirty water turning into gray ice in the furrows carved by car tires and the smaller imprints of many, many feet. Donna pulled into the field and drove across the bumpy ground to the old Ford truck. She climbed out and tapped lightly on the side of the truck as she rounded to face the rear doors. There was a long moment of silence, of cold wind and a sensation of this place being far, far, far away from anything to do with the town of Faulkner and the state of Illinois. The world as Donna Wojciechowski knew it.

The door opened a crack, and Donna looked up into Robert Trayne's droopy-eyed face.

"Sister Wojciechowski." There was no surprise in his voice that Donna could hear. No emotion whatsoever. She had a sense, instead, of being cataloged, as if Trayne spoke her name aloud to summon from the depths of his memory the necessary information to create in his mind the full form of Donna Wojciechowski.

"Reverend Trayne. I know it's early, but I wondered if I might see Paul? It's very urgent."

Trayne opened the door wider and stepped down to Donna's level with one easy motion of his long legs. "It *is* early," he agreed. "Perhaps if you were to come back later?"

"Is Paul asleep? I know last night was hard on him, but he says he recovers faster each time . . ."

"He is resting, yes." Trayne had reached out to cup Donna's elbow, to turn her away from the truck. "Perhaps, later, as I said."

Donna resisted. "No. This can't wait. Paul!" She leaned to one side to shout past the tall man. "Paul, it's Donna! I need to talk to you!"

Trayne stiffened but said nothing. After a dozen of Donna's pounding heartbeats, the doors on the back of the truck opened again and Paul looked out. His face was dark-shadowed with great weariness. His body, as much as she could see through the narrow crack of the doors, was gaunt and hollow under his skimpy nightshirt.

"Donna? What is the matter?"

"I have to talk to you. Now. It's important." She freed her elbow from the older Trayne's grasp. "Very important. Supremely important."

Paul nodded. "All right. Father"—he looked at Trayne—"will you take Donna into the tent, please?" He looked back at Donna. "I will join you there directly."

Donna nodded and Paul closed the truck doors before she could say anything more. Trayne turned toward the front of the tent and Donna followed, letting him lead her into the warm, brown, womblike enclosure.

"Sit," Robert Trayne said, pointing at a nearby chair. Donna obeyed, and he departed. She sat quite still, content to do so, with no concerns disturbing her and scarcely any thought rippling the smooth, clear pond of her mind.

If Walker Stone could have seen her then, seen her glassy eyed expression, it would have been a dagger in his heart. He would have said Donna Wojciechowski looked blank, empty. Erased.

She sat in the dim silence, waiting. She knew it was Paul she waited for, even in the blankness of her mind; that was the reason for her utter contentment to sit and wait, sit and wait, as the light shifted on the walls of the tent, as the shadows tracked slowly across the floor.

"Hello, Donna."

She turned. The tent swam a little around her, liquid, elastic. She stood up. "Hello, Paul."

"Father says he thinks he knows why you are here. You've had time to think about what we discussed, he says." His young voice was full of hope. Donna felt tears in her eyes. "Are you here to . . . ?"

"I'm here to help you," she said. She felt as if she were listening to herself on a tape recorder, the words her own, but removed in time and space.

"To help me how, Donna?" He took a step closer.

"To help you reach the people."

"How, Donna? Father says it is very important that we understand how you can help."

"I have some friends. Powerful people, who know other powerful people."

"And what are you going to do about those friends, Donna?"

"I'm going to introduce them to you. So that you can help them."

"Help them. Yes. It is *help* I bring to people. And you are going to help me help more people." He was smiling. The smile of a child on Christmas morning, finding everything he'd asked for under the tree.

"Yes," she said. Her legs felt soft. She was leaning toward Paul Trayne. She was eight inches taller than he. His head tipped back to bring his eyes into line with hers. Fire was in his eyes. His pouting lips were full and red. Sensual. Desirable. She was focusing completely on the movement of his lips. His teeth flashed bright in the dim light.

He took her hand in his. His flesh felt hot against hers. For a moment she wanted to pull away. "You will give me your absolute devotion then, Donna?" Again the sensuous movement of lips and teeth as his mouth formed the shape of her name. "You will devote yourself to the cause. To my father's cause?"

"Yes. I will give you . . . everything." Donna could not take her eyes from Paul's. Only dimly, peripherally, she saw a movement that might have been Robert Trayne coming into the tent behind the boy.

Paul smiled, releasing her hand. "You will not fail me?"

"No. I . . . couldn't." *Fail Paul Trayne? Ridiculous! Impossible!*

"You must not," Paul said. "You must not fail me. If you do, you will fail the whole world!"

Donna felt the earth open beneath her feet. A mighty abyss yawned beneath her, cold and deep and empty. The abyss of her soul, suddenly robbed of the gift of Paul Trayne. The engulfing agony of a life without his sweet voice, his gentle touch. Dimly she was aware of Robert Trayne standing in the doorway of the tent. Looking at her. "N-no . . . Please . . ."

Paul put out a hand to touch her cheek. The abyss closed. The warmth of his peace returned. "You understand, then, Donna?" It seemed as though there were tears in his eyes, though in the darkness Donna could not be sure. "You understand what it would be like if I was suddenly taken from the world? If the world was denied what I can give it?"

"It would be . . . terrible." Such a pathetic little word. Nothing, compared to the infinite horror of a world stripped of Paul Trayne.

"Then you will help me spread my word," Paul said. "Help me build the new kingdom."

"A world without pain." Donna nodded, words coming to her clearly, easily. Thoughts springing to her mind as if they were her own. *But not my own. Not my own . . .* "A world without sorrow or guilt."

"Without guilt," said Paul Trayne. His smile was brighter than the light around it. "Without sorrow. Father says you are the chosen one, Donna."

"The chosen one?"

"Chosen long before you ever knew I even existed. Eons ago, perhaps. Chosen, shaped. Prepared for this moment. Prepared for the task that lies ahead. Tasks for both of us. You will be with me now for all eternity."

"All eternity . . ."

"All eternity." Paul laid his lips against hers. Gently. Not at all sexually. The world spun away from Donna Wojciechowski. She folded into an untidy pile on the dark ground at Paul Trayne's feet.

7

"Walker! I was trying to call you earlier today. How are you?"

"I've been better, Tommy." Stone's voice sounded thinner, more reedy to Father Tom Sylvestri than it normally did. The hollow whistle of long distance lines whined softly in Tom's ear.

"I wanted to ask your . . . professional advice," Stone said.

"Oh, really, Walker?" Tom frowned into the late afternoon darkness. It was almost four thirty by the grandfather clock standing across the hall outside his office, visible through the half-open door. Beyond the two tall windows at his back, the long gray shadows of late afternoon were turning to the deep purple of night. Tom had been drifting across troubling thoughts and had not noticed how dark it was getting until the jangle of the telephone pulled him back to the here and now. He leaned forward and flicked on the lamp on his desk. A puddle of ivory light spilled from beneath the jade glass shade. He wondered, as his thoughts turned from the path they'd followed all that afternoon, if he was really in the mood for the kind of "professional" conversation he almost always had with his cousin Walker.

"After all our years of sparring, however friendly, I would never have expected you to contact me in a professional vein," Tom said.

"Maybe not, Tommy," said Stone's cartoon voice from the earpiece, "but I've come up against something here—I'm in Faulkner, about sixty-five miles south—something that quite frankly has me a little spooked. And it's something that seems to intrude on your turf."

Tom smiled. "My 'turf,' yes. Would this be the young miracle worker your secretary told me about, Walker?"

"Oh, you know about that, do you? Yes, that's the nub of it." He described Paul Trayne and his Lincolnesque guardian in vaguely melodramatic terms Tom thought representative of modern journalism. Stone's description of Robert Johnston Trayne formed the clearest image in Tom's mind. The boy seemed almost a caricature, a Mark Twain creation of tan cheeks and gap-toothed grin. "He seems to have . . . well, he's snagged one of my people. Donna Wojciechowski. I think you met her a couple of times, about three, four years ago."

"Light brown hair? Five ten, eleven?"

"That's her. Not bad. You should be in my line of work, Tommy."

"Maybe we should trade." Tom heard Stone's snort and leaned back in his chair. The red leather squeaked. He cupped the end of the thick arm, rolling his palm around the smooth curve, enjoying as he always did the luxurious sensation, the sensuality of the wood. "How has Miss Wojciechowski been 'snagged' by this boy?" he asked.

Stone told him all that had been happening in Faulkner since the first of the year. Tom listened with increasing interest to the story his cousin related. Three or four times he interrupted Stone for the clarification of some detail. It all sounded fascinating and, if true, it might indeed be called miraculous.

"And this boy just popped up one day?" Tom asked at one point.

"Out of the proverbial blue," Stone said.

"No proverbs about blue, Walker. Did he begin right away with these—what did you call them?—these 'sessions' of his?"

"Seems like. Guess it took a bit for word of mouth to gather a real crowd—did I mention there were two, three thousand people out there the last time I was there?—but quite a few folks had wandered out by the second night."

"And they all got this miracle cure of his?"

"Yep. No dissatisfied customers, unless you count me."

"Oh? What happened to you?"

Stone related the details of his collapse. He'd placed the call to his cousin barely an hour after regaining consciousness—and over Dr. Zeldenrust's protestation.

"Really?" Tom pursed his lips in a doubtful expression Stone would have recognized had he been able to see it. "You think this was something to do with what Paul Trayne was doing?"

Tom heard a click; something had tapped lightly on the handset at the other end. He'd spoken to Walker enough in person and over the phone to be able to identify the sound: his cousin had removed his glasses and the sidebar had tapped against the plastic of the instrument in his hand. Next, Tom knew, would come the compulsive tightening of the tiny screws.

"If I thought Paul Trayne was behind my collapse somehow, that would mean I'd have to think he's for real, wouldn't it?" Stone said.

Tom could hear Stone's resistance to that thought. For all Stone's love of the fantasies of TV, Tom Sylvestri knew his cousin as a man who demanded a firmly grounded reality in his daily life.

"I mean," Stone continued, "to knock me for a loop when I wasn't even in the tent . . . But what else could it have been, Tommy? I'm as fit as a fiddle according to the doctor here."

"I think you may be looking for easy answers, Walker," Tom said, "and I'm afraid I don't have any. In fact, I seem to remember you telling me once you thought it was my *job* not to have any."

"Did I say that?" Stone laughed. "How profound of me. But, all right, yes. I am looking for something like an easy answer. I mean, hell, Tommy, I'd be just tickled pink if something like this was real. We all would. But how can it be?"

"Miracles do happen, Walker. Or is my opinion too biased?"

"Not entirely objective, let's say. And that's part of my problem here too. All the people who've been to see the Trayne kid . . . well, they're all so polite and happy and smiling and content you sometimes just want to strangle them. And even their friends and relatives are hard-pressed to say whether what's happened to them is really bad." He mentioned Chief Clarence Nickerson and his daughter, briefly describing Nickerson's attitude.

"Mmm." Tom nodded. "I guess it would be a bit of a problem. It sounds a lot like some of the people I've worked with in our drug and alcohol rehab programs. The hardest thing for some of them to realize is that they've changed. It's difficult to keep an accurate perspective on such things when you start messing with your mind. You lose your points of reference."

"Good analogy. I knew people in high school who seemed to go from absolutely straight to pushers, overnight. And not one of them could see in themselves the change the dope had caused. That's a lot like how it is in Faulkner. These people are so content being the way they are now, they can't imagine that it might be harmful."

"But all you really have to go on is a gut reaction, Walker. And you are resistant to the concept of miracles."

"So is the Catholic Church, as I recall, Tommy. The only reason your bosses avoided a major embarrassment when the Shroud of Turin turned out to be a fake was that they'd never really acknowledged it as a true relic in the first place." Tom Sylvestri smiled at his cousin's jab. He and Stone had been at this game for so long now that he knew Stone hardly even noticed anymore when he fired one of his barbs.

"True enough," Tom said. "We've had to become somewhat skeptical ourselves. But that's not new, especially. Do you remember enough of your Sunday School days to recall what it says in Second Thessalonians?"

He heard Stone sigh. "Remind me, Tommy."

"Chapter two, verse nine. It's a warning that the disciples of Satan will come 'with all powers and signs and lying wonders.' We're warned that the devil can use what appear to be good and holy works in order to accomplish his ends."

" 'The devil can quote Scripture . . .' " Stone remembered.

"Yes. Plus it's too easy in this modern world to fake the miracles. As I understand it, there are at least five different ways to make an icon cry, for instance."

"I would have thought that was a trade secret."

"Don't be snide." Tom paused a moment, considering. If even half of what Stone described was true, it would be worth investigating. He could use something to take his mind off the matters most vexing him at the moment.

No, that's not right, either, Tom Sylvestri thought. *I should attend to my own house. . . .*

"What would you like me to do, Walker? Are you asking me to come out to Faulkner and see this boy? Give you my professional opinion?"

"Well, that would be great, of course. But it's not really what I was after. To tell the truth, Tommy, I don't know what I was after. I just wanted, well, someone in your line of work to know about this."

"And now I know. But I'm not sure what I can offer in the way of sage counsel or whatever it is you want. Sorry."

"No need to apologize, Tommy. Your favorite atheist cousin calls you up out of a clear blue sky, with a cockamamy story. It's . . . Hang on a second, would you, Tommy?" Stone put his hand over the phone; the voices at his end became indecipherable mumbles in Tom's ear. Except for Stone's. He'd never been able to mask his high voice in that fashion, though for some reason he'd never realized that fact himself.

Quite clearly, Tom heard him say "Damn. When?" There was a mumbled response, then "Still there, Tommy?"

"Still here, Walker."

"Listen, ah, something just came up. Seems it would be a waste of time for you to come down to Faulkner now. Reverend Trayne and his wonder boy have done a fast fade into the night."

"Gone?"

"Without a trace. And nobody even saw them leave. I . . . think I'd better see what this is all about. Can I call you back?"

"All right, Walker. If you really think I have anything to add to all this."

"I don't know. Maybe. I almost hope so. Thanks, Tommy." The line went dead.

Tom dropped the handset back into its cradle. He leaned his elbows on the desk and rubbed his dark eyes with the heels of his hands. He watched the phosphors dance against the inside of his lids, then dropped his hands and stared into the flickering glow of the fire in the grate of the big fireplace on the wall opposite his desk. The fire was dying, the room growing cold as it did, but there were still occasional sparks and sudden crackles of flame. Some were bright enough to linger as afterimages. They mingled with the phantom sparks left from the rubbing.

Tom raised his head and looked at his reflection in the huge, grandly ornate mirror above the mantel. His head and shoulders were beyond the pool of light from the desk lamp. In the darkness of the room his face was deeply shadowed, the highlights that reflected in the pupils of his eyes tiny, fleeting. For the rest, because he knew it so well, the reflection showed him a long, angular face, a mass of wiry black hair shot through with silver, barely constrained by assiduous brushing. He was tall, which was not obvious in the mirror's image; broad shouldered, which was. He looked, he thought with a wry smile, as if he was in much better condition than he really was. As well he knew, he was twenty-five pounds overweight, and the cough that wracked him every morning told him he'd quit smoking too late. If he sat perfectly still he could see the light fading, watch himself blending into the dark of the wall behind his chair, the shadows beyond the puddle of light on his desk. Only his stiff white collar remained clearly visible, like a halo slipped down around his neck. But the reflected light was dimming there, too.

Dimming my fallen halo. How appropriate.

He pushed away that line of thought. Though he would be the first to confess he was not deserving of a respite, he was ready for one. The strange tale related by his cousin seemed to provide one—at least an alternative to the thoughts troubling and tormenting him since the suicide of Joseph Terranova. What was to be gleaned from Stone's story? How much of it was significant? This boy Paul was in the keeping of an older man who styled himself as "Reverend," yet made no claim to any church.

Could he be the real villain here, if villain there be?

Stone's description of the man did not suggest anyone corrupt enough to be using the boy to sinister ends. Indeed, as

Stone lamented, there seemed nothing sinister in the whole matter. Tom thought about the influence of men on boys, especially impressionable young boys. He thought about high school, before the priesthood beckoned. He thought about Billy Mitchell, his gym coach, the moment that sent Tom finally seeking God's House as his sanctuary against the darkness in his own soul.

Such unenlightened times. If it were today, if I were seventeen again, if that big, rough, handsome man said what he said, did what he did . . .

He leaned his chair back against the wall, his head against the high back, the soft cushion of the old leather upholstery. He closed his eyes.

So much confusion in youth! Much questing and questioning.

He remembered the conversations with Monsignor Cameron at the seminary. Kindly, understanding, but rigidly dogmatic Monsignor Cameron, understanding the weaknesses that could bring a young man to the Church, but not tolerating them once the call had been answered. Sometimes with him Tom Sylvestri found answers. Sometimes not.

All those young boys out there, facing just those same questions every day. Confused. Afraid. Especially in this age of AIDS and a swing of public sentiment back away from the enlightenment we—they, be honest—fought so hard to win. How do those young boys feel, when they find their hormones stirring for the very first time, and realize it is not the pretty girl with the long legs and budding breasts who excites them, but the boy with the red hair, the haunted eyes. . . .

He sighed. He'd summoned up an image from his past, quite without meaning to. It was painful, yet he found now that he could not easily banish it from his mind.

Malcolm Deerborne. Malcolm, I wonder what might have become of us, if we were young and innocent today? I wonder if you might have managed to resist Billy Mitchell, and I might have found the courage to reveal my own feelings, to share your pain instead of running from it? Would I have even come to the priesthood in today's world? Would I have sought my salvation here, swearing off the temptations of the flesh, if it were today that I had to face my true self?

I hope so.

But he did not know.

He wondered what had ever become of the red-haired, dark-eyed boy named Malcolm, but knew that there was no way he could ever—would ever—find out. Not now. Not after so many years. So instead of a might-have-been there was a here and now. Instead of one path acknowledged, there was another followed. And how proud had been his mother when he told her of his decision to enter the seminary!

Better for her than the other path. Better such pride than the shame that would surely have killed her.

But how surprising to find there, in those cloistered halls, so many who shared his secret nightmare, so many who had chosen that path for the same reason.

In the old days they put homosexuals in prison. Was it George Carlin who made a joke about that? The punishment for being a homosexual was to be locked away—with a lot of other men.

He rubbed his eyes again and reached for a cigarette. Then he remembered he'd quit smoking again; the pocket of his black jacket was empty. He swore softly, alone in his large, luxurious office. An office, he always thought, so much at odds with the neighborhood in which it was situated. St. Timothy's had been a rich man's dream; a way, he surely imagined, to buy himself the keys to the pearly gates. Tom sat up straight again, then rose and crossed to the window immediately behind his desk. He looked out. Streetlights were on, up and down West Addison. Snow swirled around them—spherical nimbuses, halos.

He thought about halos and the boy called Paul Trayne. The concepts were mixing in his head.

Am I already conferring sainthood on this boy? Tom frowned. *Am I so desperate to find some solace from my particular troubles that I seek it in the rumors of a young miracle maker? Living saints are hard to come by, nowadays. Those we think of as living saints so often have, well, toes of clay, if not actual feet.*

He smiled at the poor joke and pulled the dark, heavy velvet curtains across the windows. The room behind him retreated further into shadows and mystery. The flickering fire achieved a new, spasmodic plateau of brilliance in the darkened room. Was Paul Trayne a miracle, or something of far baser stock? And if the latter, how much did the boy know himself? How much of the deception was based on a misunderstanding of a native charisma, how much deliberate deception?

Tom returned to his desk, remembering a line from a book he'd read some years before. *Beware the charlatan who has forgotten he's a charlatan.* He frowned at the words.

Like me? But I'm not a charlatan. There is no crisis of faith here, no lack of belief. I'm a hypocrite. I am God's representative on Earth—one of them, at any rate—and the Book that is the transcribed Word of God condemns my innermost soul in no uncertain terms. Doesn't that make me a hypocrite, rather than a charlatan? And if it does, which is worse, I wonder?

He shook his head. If there was an answer to be had, he was not going to find it here, no matter how hard he pondered the point.

The clock in the hall chimed the hour. Tom pressed the ivory-topped button on the old intercom on the corner of the desk.

"Yes, Father?"

"I'd like a light supper in the sitting room, please Mrs. Buck," Tom said.

"That would be nothing at all after nothing all day," said the caring voice Tom knew so well, loved so well.

"Humor me. Tomorrow I'll let you feed me properly. Tonight I need an empty stomach to motivate my thoughts."

Mrs. Buck sighed loud enough for Tom to hear, then broke the connection. Tom left the big desk and crossed into the hall. He closed the office door behind him and stood for a moment with his hand still cupping the smooth, cool hemisphere of the brass knob. He remembered the first time he'd seen this hallway, the first time he'd been inside the residence beside St. Timothy's. It all seemed much too long ago to fit within the chronological compass of his years.

He let go of the knob and turned left, walking down the rich carpeted hall to the spacious sitting room. He crossed to the small writing desk under the window and looked out on the street. People passed. Somewhere out there, he knew, Joseph

Terranova's body would be lying in whatever state it was left in by the postmortem. Tom's heart went out to him, regretting their argument, regretting the weakness of his flesh that had led to it.

I'm sorry, Joseph, he thought, sending the thought out across the darkening face of Chicago, out into the unguessable distances of the universe. *For all the pain I caused you because of my weakness, I am eternally sorry. Maybe someday, some way, I will find a way to make amends to you, and to the God I have so thoroughly betrayed.*

With a sigh he realized he'd said nothing to Walker Stone of Joseph's writings.

"I didn't tell you the whole of it." Chief Clarence Nickerson leaned heavily on the footboard at the end of Stone's bed and squinted into Stone's eyes.

"What . . . more is there?" A squadron of vampire bats did slow rolls in Stone's belly. He knew from Dr. Zeldenrust that Donna had left sometime in the morning and had not been seen since. That she was away from the hospital—away from his much reduced circle of protection—when the Traynes departed . . .

"Ms. Wojciechowski," Nickerson said. "I think we've found her."

"Found . . . ? Where . . . what . . . ?" Stone did not like the way Nickerson said *think.*

Nickerson shook his bowling ball head and held up a freckled hand. "Understand, I only said we think we've found her. The woman we've found is . . ."

"Dead?" *No, please! No! No!*

"Yeah. We haven't moved the body yet." Nickerson shrugged. "I thought you might want to see. Maybe make a positive identification. The face is all mashed in, but the rest of her . . . Well, I thought you might be able to make a positive identification, like I said."

"Yes." Stone's mind raced. "You know Dr. Zeldenrust has forbidden me to leave until he's completely sure I'm not going to have some kind of relapse. He seems to see me as his responsibility, now."

Nickerson nodded. "Sounds like Mo." A vaguely conspiratorial gleam came into his narrow eyes as Stone watched. "Of course, he's at dinner now. And I'm parked by the back door . . ."

Stone was already swinging his short legs over the side of the bed. "Hand me my pants, would you, Chief?" He gestured toward the clothing draped over the back of the plain wooden chair by the single window. He jumped to the floor and grabbed hold of the bed as the room tipped. Nickerson seemed oblivious to his momentary distress. He thrust Stone's slacks at him and waited while Stone dressed. Then Nickerson led the way through the quiet evening of the hospital, down a short flight of fire stairs, and out into the cold night. Stone's breath clouded about his head as he followed Nickerson's broad back toward the big old car parked near the Dumpsters.

Stone pulled open the door of the Buick—it made a great wail worthy of the antediluvian beasts it resembled—and climbed into the passenger seat. The old car smelled of must and vast age. And something else, something Stone could not place. Nickerson climbed in next to him and gunned the big car away from the hospital. Acceleration pressed Walker Stone deep into his half of the wide seat. Nickerson drove like an Indy 500 finalist going for the checkered flag. Stone was frankly astounded by the older man's prowess at the wheel, until he realized Nickerson was driving on intuition rather than skill. From the way he hunched over the wheel, peering forward with eyes slitted, it was obvious that Nickerson had little idea of what lay ahead of him in the darting, weaving pools of his headlights.

By the time Stone became aware of this, however, they were through Faulkner and moving along Black Rock Highway toward the bridge over Pine Tree River. Stone's mind drifted to one snowy Christmas Eve three years ago. The first Christmas he and Donna spent together. He'd invited her to his apartment and wined and dined her in the very best holiday tradition; he'd hired a caterer for the evening at what now seemed a ridiculous expense, but the meal they shared was sumptuous and satisfying.

With the caterer dismissed with a heartfelt "Merry Christmas," Stone and Donna lay on the living room rug, a videotape of a burning yule log casting a golden light over them, the space heater providing the warmth the flickering flames could not. Stone remembered now how Donna balked at the ersatz fire when he'd suggested it, but after the glorious meal and mellowing of a fine vintage—he was not aware of her drinking problem then—she was enjoying the effect as much as he'd hoped.

"All we need is the smell of the wood," she'd said.

"I saw a spray can of something that professed to be just that," Stone answered, looking past Donna's recumbent form at the snow falling over the Lake beyond his broad windows. Away to the right he could see the glow of the big sign atop the Playboy Building, and next to that the lights of the *Advocate* tower. "I thought that might be pushing it."

"Bright boy." Donna smiled.

She was lying on her back. Her hair was spread on the ivory shag, and it caught the flames as occasional gold in bronze threads. Her eyes were bright and clear. Her lips most inviting. She'd put a hand behind his head, drawn his face, his mouth down to hers. Lips brushed, pressed, parted. Tongues explored. Stone drew her closer against him, well aware that his stock-inged toes reached only to her shins, not minding at all as her long right leg lifted up and over him, hooking, holding.

They'd undressed each other slowly, carefully, not wanting a rush to cause some garment to snag, damaging the mood. Stone had never known Donna so relaxed, so clearly ready for their lovemaking. She melted in his arms, rolling on top of him as the last of her clothes came away. She'd stretched luxuri-ously as he caressed her, arms above head, reaching for some unguessable prize beyond the ceiling, beyond the sky. Her fin-gers spread wide as she'd bent forward, digging her nails into the carpet above him.

They'd moved as a single organism, legs and arms entwined, flesh against flesh, until Stone found himself on top of her and, carefully again, slowly again, worked his mouth and tongue over the smooth expanses of her skin, lower and lower. With skill and patience he'd probed and manipulated, until she'd seized his hair in both her hands, fingers twisting deep into his dark curls, back arched so much her buttocks lifted clear of the carpet. Her whole body shuddered, and a low, low moan came from somewhere far below the floor to rumble up and out through Donna Wojciechowski. Stone moved up on top of her. Suddenly the mood was totally different. Donna was pushing him away. Her hands were against his shoulders, her legs pulling together, knees clamping tight.

"No. Walker, no," she'd said. He could hear the tears in her voice. He'd reached out a hand to turn her face into the light and seen moist tracks like streaks of silver down her cheeks.

"Chow . . . What?"

She'd pushed him off her and rolled away so that she lay for a moment with her back to him. He saw sobs run across her muscles in waves. He reached out a hand to touch her back, but she flinched away as if his fingers were red hot. She'd risen to her feet, gathering scraps of clothing as she rose. She pulled on her blouse, her slacks. She grabbed her bra and panties and, lacking pockets, shoved them down the front of her blouse. It made a curious bulge that, under another very different circumstance, Walker Stone would have found funny.

He scrambled to his feet, awkward and absurd, short and naked beside her. "Chow . . . Don . . . Donna . . ."

"I . . . gotta go." She could barely form the words. "Please, Walker. Don't . . . try to stop me."

He had been about to do exactly that. He let his hands drop. "Donna."

"No." She held up a hand. "I'll see you in the office. Monday."

She was gone. Stone walked across his living room in a daze, gathering his own discarded clothing without realizing what he was doing, coming at last to the big picture window that opened onto his balcony. Heedless of cold and snow he slid back the central glass panel—a sound like a huge firecracker, he remembered, as the ice caked against the outside of the track cracked with the motion of the sliding door—and stepped out, naked, into the snow.

He'd looked down. After a few minutes he'd seen Donna's Toyota come out of the parking structure beneath his apartment tower and speed away along Lakeshore Drive. He'd watched it out of sight, until the cold began to seep into his very bones. He'd stepped back into the apartment, pulling on clothes grown as cold as the night.

On Monday, as promised, Donna came to his office. She'd been contrite, apologetic, and, since his old office did not have picture windows facing into the city room, demonstrative. That night she'd come home with him and stayed for fifteen months. Stone never had a satisfactory explanation of what happened that Christmas Eve. He knew only that it had become simultaneously the worst, best, and ultimately worst again Christmas of his life.

A bump in the road jarred the base of Stone's spine, bringing him back to Nickerson's side. "What . . ." Stone could not quite bring his voice to form the question. It was too coldly professional to ask such a thing about a woman he'd once—still?—loved.

Nickerson guessed what Stone was trying to say. "She was shot three times at close range," he said. "Once in the throat, once in the stomach, once . . ." He paused. "Well, you can figure out the spacing, no? Then the face was mashed in. Not to kill her, by then. To delay identification. Smash up the teeth. And the fingertips were cut off."

"Damn. Damndamndamn." Stone's glasses had fogged. He took them off and reached without thinking for the penknife he'd slipped once again into the breast pocket of his shirt. He dearly wanted to ask Nickerson to stop, but he could not. No more than he could turn back the hands of his watch and undo the last forty-eight hours. "What else?"

"Raped. Zeldenrust thinks maybe four, five men. He can't be sure without an analysis of the semen. She was trussed up. Spread-eagled. Naked." Stone's anguish mounted with each word. Nickerson seemed almost to delight in the layering of detail.

"Ropes on her right leg were pulled so hard they'd dislocated her hip joint. Must've hurt like hell to have four, five men . . . Well, you know. Left breast was mutilated, too. Zeldenrust thinks the nipple was maybe bitten off. From the amount of bleeding he thinks she was still alive when it happened. Dead bodies mostly don't bleed, you know."

"No, I guess I didn't." Stone could not think straight. The pictures painted by Nickerson's words were so graphic he saw nothing else. Nothing but Donna Wojciechowski's final moments, how pointlessly terrible they must have been. He put his glasses back on. They fogged again. He left them alone this time. He looked out the side window, away from Nickerson.

Forgive me, Chow. I never would have sent you if I'd known.

They crested the bridge over the Pine Tree River. Nickerson turned the Buick to the left. "At the tent?" Stone asked. "In Gunner's Field?"

"Yah." They bounced over the edge of the shoulder onto Pine Tree Road. Ahead was only darkness, nothing Walker Stone could distinguish beyond the pale yellow cones of the headlights. No glow of the lights of the field.

"I thought the Traynes had packed up . . . ?" *Where are they headed that they won't need their tent?*

"No . . ." Was there the briefest hesitancy in Nickerson's voice? Stone could not be absolutely certain. "They're gone. Their truck is gone. But the tent is still there. All the chairs and the stage."

"Odd."

Nickerson shrugged, turning the car into the field, lights sweeping in a broad arc that confirmed his words: the tent was still there.

"Seems like they must've cut out in a hurry," Stone said.

After raping and murdering Donna.

Nickerson stopped the car. He leaned across Stone to retrieve a big, bulky old flashlight from the glove compartment. It was as much an anachronism as the man and the car.

Nickerson pushed open his door and climbed out. "Shall we have a look?"

For an awful moment he sounded to Stone for all the world like a real estate broker about to show a potential customer a new house. There was nothing in his tone to suggest the horror Walker Stone knew lay waiting for him in that stained, ragged old canvas box. Stone climbed out of the car, followed Nickerson to the front flaps, and stepped through ahead of the chief into darkness. Behind him Nickerson's flashlight flared, pushing back the shadows. The bright light bounced back dimly from the ocher walls, filling the tent enough that Stone could see the rows of old chairs, the stage.

But nothing else.

He turned. "Chief . . . What the hell . . . ?"

The cannon boom of Nickerson's huge Sturm Ruger drowned out whatever else Stone might have wanted to say.

PART
TWO

Convergence

8

When the telephone rang late at night, Clayton Garber knew it could only mean trouble.

He'd raised two daughters, been involved in the darker workings of Chicago all his adult life. He'd developed a sixth sense about such things. He put down his copy of *Newsweek* and reached over the curve of his wife's raised right shoulder for the cordless phone on her bedside table. She stirred.

He pecked her on the cheek, whispering "Go back to sleep, baby," before he raised the handset to his ear to say "Garber."

"Clay, this is Donna," said a voice.

"Oh, Donna, hello! Er . . . When I said call anytime . . ."

"This isn't about the Warner case. I need to see you, Commissioner. Right away."

Clay glanced at the clock, also on his wife's side of the bed; 11:56 glowed pale green on the digital face. "Certainly. I'll have my secretary make an appointment for you first thing in the . . ."

"No, now. Right away."

"Donna, it's nearly midnight."

"This is important. I'm about ten minutes away. Can I come? Please?"

"Donna . . ."

"Look, Clay, don't try to put me off, okay? I'm not kidding you when I say this is important. If . . . if Walker were here he'd tell you himself. This could easily be the most important thing that's ever happened to you. Maybe to all of Chicago."

Clay rubbed his eyes with the thumb and forefinger of his big right hand. Hyperbole did not usually work on him, but Donna's invoking of Walker Stone's name carried weight. If he was somehow involved in this . . . "All right. Come to the north side door and I'll let you in myself." The line went dead. He leaned back over his wife and cradled the phone.

"Who . . . ?" Marjorie asked.

"Donna Wojciechowski," Clay said. "You remember her. Friend of Walker Stone's. Works at the *Advocate*."

"Tall girl. All legs. Very bright. Drinks too much."

"That's the one. She's got some sort of flap on. She's coming here."

"Now? Tonight?" Marjorie sat up. The bedclothes fell away, revealing coffee-dark, smooth shoulders above her pale pink nightdress. Clay fixed his eyes on hers, managing as he always did to ignore the old sensations in his body. "Why didn't you . . . ?"

"I said I'd make her an appointment for tomorrow, but she wouldn't go for it."

Marjorie Garber flopped back onto her pillow and pulled the covers up under her chin. "You always were a sucker for a pretty face." She smiled. Her teeth were very white against the polished ebony of her face.

"I know," Clay said.

He kissed her on the mouth and climbed out of bed. He pulled on his winter robe and moved with the ease of familiarity through the darkness of the large bedroom. He did not turn on any lights as he moved through the house, waiting until he reached the side hall that passed between the kitchen and his at-home office. He turned on the light on his desk with the switch by the door and flipped on the hall light by the back door. Clay lifted aside the delicate lace curtain that hung over the top half of the door and peered out at the truck rolling up to his big house. His eyebrows rose high on the curve of his dark brow.

The battered old Ford was not at all the kind of conveyance in which he would have expected to see Donna Wojciechowski arriving. The truck stopped just past the door. The passenger side door opened and Donna hopped out. She climbed up the steps. Clay glanced at his image in the mirror by the door—big face, bright, smiling eyes, smooth brow rising up to the polished crown of his bald head—and opened the door without waiting for her to ring. He summoned his least committal smile to his full lips and thrust out a hand toward her.

"Donna." She accepted his hand and shook it, her grip strong. Clay thought she looked tired and said so.

"No, no," she replied, waving her hand dismissively. "Not much sleep since I saw you last is all. Nothing to worry about."

"Something brewing at the paper?" Clay gestured for Donna to precede him into his office. As she passed he looked again at the truck, sealed and unrevealing once again.

"No," Donna said, "this is more in the manner of a personal call." She walked into a large, warm, masculine room and crossed to sit in the right of two large chairs set in front of a big mahogany desk. Clay left the study door open and moved around her to sit behind the desk.

"I'd offer you some coffee or tea," Clay said, "but I'm afraid our cook is asleep, and she allows me access to the kitchen only to make an occasional sandwich, not to use any of the appliances."

Donna nodded. "If you have something stronger, I'd be glad of it."

Clay rose, crossing to the liquor cabinet against the wall to Donna's left. On the opposite wall a broad, tall window looked in on the room with many square glass eyes. Heavy drapes were pulled partially closed across it. Beyond, at some distance, Donna could see the house next door, and beyond that the lights of the residential lakeshore.

She looked back as Clay asked her to choose her drink. "Gin and tonic," she said. Clay fixed the drink, handed it to Donna.

"How many others in the house?" Donna asked. She crossed her legs. She was wearing one of the short skirts Clay remembered she'd begun to affect long before they returned to fashion. Dark leather boots reached to the knee and made her long legs even longer. Above the skirt was a dark red sweater, tight against her bosom. She was clearly not wearing a bra.

"Well, there's myself," Clay counted off in response to her query, "my wife, the cook, and the maid."

Donna nodded. "What about your daughters?" she asked.

"Still away at school, both of them." Garber was reminded of his brief meeting with Donna, in the lobby of the *Advocate* building. She'd asked then about his daughters, and he'd answered in much the same way.

"So, four in all," Donna said. She was very much in charge of herself, Clay thought, coming back to the situation at hand. In charge of the moment. She reminded him of the Donna Wojciechowski he'd met for the first time years ago. He'd seen her only infrequently since that first meeting, but he'd been aware—as a man with an eye for female beauty, he'd say almost painfully aware—of the changes her drinking was working in Donna.

"Now, if the third degree is over," he said, "perhaps you'd like to offer a few answers of your own?"

"Certainly." Donna leaned back. "I need your help. You're the highest placed official in the city government I can honestly say I know personally, and I want you to open the way for me to some of the loftier regions of City Hall."

"Surely you know Mannie Stuartson?"

"I . . . do." Clay caught the flicker of hesitancy in Donna's voice, but there was no chance to pursue it before she pushed on with what she had to say. "It's been a long time since I've spoken to him, even professionally. Red tape could get in the way. And I need to get all the way up, and fast. He's your friend. You've even been touted as his logical successor."

Clay shrugged. "That's not an office that intrigues me, especially. Besides, being the latest black mayor of Chicago is not going to ensure my place in the history books." He smiled. "Maybe being the first black governor . . ."

"That's all well and good," Donna said, "but right now I'm concerned with what you can do for me as police commissioner. And that's get me and my friends in to see Mayor Stuartson."

"Friends?"

Donna cocked her head back toward the open door of the study. "In the truck. A boy named Paul and his father, the Reverend Robert Johnston Trayne. May I bring them in?" She was out of her chair now, as she spoke.

"I suppose so. Donna . . ."

She stopped halfway to the door, turned to face him. "Yes?"

"What is this all about? Can't you tell me? Before you bring them in?"

"I'll tell you this," she said, her smile warm and bright in the lamplight. "You will absolutely never regret meeting them. Absolutely never." She rotated on one high heel and was gone. Clay felt a gust of cold air come under the front of his desk and strike his bare ankles as the side door opened and closed.

Marjorie Garber heard the truck growl up to the side of the house and debated getting out of bed. From the big window in the south corner of the bedroom she would be able to see the side door and driveway. She was curious about what brought Donna Wojciechowski to her house so late at night. It was troublesome to Marjorie that Donna should have called at this hour. It always troubled her when Clay had business with beautiful women.

So far as Marjorie knew, Clay had never, ever been unfaithful, but it had been nearly a decade since she and her husband shared this bed in any conjugal fashion. She loved Clay with all her heart, but the death of their son robbed the sex act of meaning for her. She did not know why. Certainly she and Clay never thought of sex as solely for making babies. Before Michael's death—drowned in the Lake, not thirty feet from the edge of their beach front property—she and her husband enjoyed a strong and constant sex life.

When she'd met Clayton Garber—introduced to her by Emmanuel Stuartson, when all three were at Northwestern—it seemed inevitable theirs should be a long, intense relationship. His body was then the most magnificent she'd ever seen, so broad and hard. His skill at manipulating her own young form had been unsurpassed. Eight years it had been now, since she'd known the touch of Clay's hands on her bare flesh. They still kissed, they still pressed together when they slept, and exchanged caresses when they passed each other, but something deep within Marjorie Garber's soul died in the cold waters of Lake Michigan, drowned with the eight-year-old boy who came in his short life to be so much the center of her universe. In all that time, for all his powerful masculinity, Clay had never strayed, never been unfaithful to her. She never questioned him on it, but she was sure she would know, in that painful empathic way a spouse always knows, if Clay were cheating.

I love you so much, my darling Clay, she thought. *Sometimes I dearly wish . . .*

She remembered the power of their lovemaking. Clay was enormously strong; although she was not a large woman, Marjorie was firm and athletic. Even now she kept herself in tip-top shape. Her once pert bosom, she would reluctantly grant, had lost some of its battle with the forces of gravity, but her hips were still trim, and her thighs were as smooth and firm as those of either of her daughters. It must be very difficult, she knew, for Clay Garber to live this strange, celibate life. Most especially as his oldest child came very much into awareness of her own sexuality.

Marjorie thought about DiAnne's parade of boyfriends, tall and short, bright and dull, and the looks she'd seen in Clay's eyes as his child went out to explore he knew not what new avenue of her sexual existence. Marjorie had not been surprised to learn of DiAnne's loss of virginity—learn obliquely, of course, as only a mother can—at the age of sixteen. She had been careful to shield Clay from the same discovery, and was, she thought, mostly successful. There was absolutely nothing incestuous in Clayton Garber's feelings for his daughters, but Marjorie knew from her experiences with her own father that there was a special kind of jealousy all male parents kept, unknowingly, in reserve, awaiting the moment of their daughters' initiation into womanhood. It was preposterous to suppose Clay had very long managed to maintain the myth of his daughter's chastity, even in his most naïve fantasy, especially after the unfortunate business with Gregory, their erstwhile chauffeur. That had managed to contain itself to an intense infatuation. Marjorie was reasonably sure no physical intimacy had occurred between DiAnne and the handsome, sharp-eyed young man who ferried the Garber clan from place to place on those occasions that Clay chose not to drive, or was unavailable.

Still, Marjorie knew there was a painful scar left in Gregory's heart; he had not been so invulnerable to DiAnne's charms as he professed. Even after Clay personally pleaded with him, Gregory had declined to remain in their employ. Not long afterward, DiAnne found the equally handsome—though not so darkly intense, Marjorie thought—Terry Munroe and, for DiAnne at least, the storm front passed.

All this going on around a man who was so vital, who had always viewed his sexuality as an important extension of himself, Marjorie knew must have been very difficult for Clay. Yet the fact that he tolerated it, and understood it, spoke much of the strength of their marriage, the bonding of their souls. Clay understood Marjorie's grief had destroyed something inside her. He understood that the physical act of love was anathema to her, a defiling of Michael's memory. Marjorie sat up, throwing back the covers and swinging her legs off the edge of the king-size bed. She dropped off the bed, her feet slipping with the ease of long familiarity into her slippers. It was cool in the room. The thermostat's timer was set to lower the temperature to sixty degrees while she and her husband slept.

Climbing out from under the warmth of the down comforter, Marjorie felt chilled. She took up her robe from the end of the bed and draped it around her shoulders. She crossed to the window and looked down. The truck looked ordinary enough. From her second-floor vantage Marjorie could not make out the state name on the license plate. The colors illuminated by the side door light meant nothing to her. She was not in time to see Donna leave the truck, only to see the storm door swinging closed on the side door. She turned away from the window for a moment, debating whether or not to go downstairs. Rose would be asleep at this hour, as would Anne, the maid. Marjorie could easily present herself under the pretense of offering tea or coffee; it would be a fair enough way to find out what was going on.

She did not believe this meeting was some kind of cover for a prearranged tryst, but Donna Wojciechowski was a remarkably attractive woman, and Marjorie had heard Clayton talking to Walker Stone in that god-awful men-talk-this-way fashion. It was, she sometimes thought, a little game Clay played in his own head. A pretense at being something his sexless marriage no longer allowed him to be, something his strong moral fiber would not permit him to be.

She caught a movement out of the corner of her eye and looked back down toward the driveway in time to see Donna opening the door of the truck. Through the windshield, she saw Donna extend a hand to a small form of indeterminate age and gender. The child wore a big parka that covered its head and buried its face in shadow. Its breath hung heavy in the air. The bundled head looked up, for a moment, seeming to see Marjorie high above, she thought. Still, she could not see a face in the darkness of the hood.

Marjorie could not stay in the bedroom any longer. She pulled the robe on properly and headed down the back stairs to the door.

As she came into the hall outside her husband's study she heard Clay's deep voice saying "Very pleased to meet you, Paul. Miss Wojciechowski seems most impressed with you and your father. Although"—and she heard him chuckle—"she doesn't seem to want to explain why just yet."

"You'll soon see for yourself," Donna said. "Paul, why don't you . . . Oh! Mrs. Garber."

Discovered, Marjorie stepped all the way into the room. "Ms. Wojciechowski. Clay? Are you going to introduce these gentlemen?" Clay did so. The older Trayne shook her hand with a firm, dry grip. His face was deeply weathered, she noticed, patterned with lines. Friendly lines. Smile lines. His eyes sparkled.

"This is indeed a pleasure, ma'am," he said. "Sister Wojciechowski has told Paul and me that your husband can be of great service to us, in our Cause." The capitalization was clear to hear.

But it was the boy Paul who seized all of Marjorie's attention, the moment she saw his young face. The shape and cast of it reached out to clutch at Marjorie's deep-rooted maternal instincts. First, there was a great weariness in the youthful features. A sorrow she would never have expected to see on a child's face. Plus, despite his narrow frame, Marjorie could tell Paul Trayne was well into his teens—about the age, in fact, that Michael would have been . . .

" 'Cause'?" Clay asked. Marjorie stepped closer to her husband, emotions jangling in her bosom.

"What cause is that, Reverend Trayne?" she asked.

"The Cause of Peace and Harmony," Trayne said, these capitalizations as clear as the first. "Tranquility. Freedom."

"Powerful sentiments," Clay said. He stepped back a pace to sit on the edge of his desk. He folded his big arms across his chest, well aware of the defensive attitude of his body language. "I wish there was something I could do to help."

Marjorie turned and frowned at her husband. "Of course there's something you can do. You must find something." She turned back to Paul. "Of course he'll find something."

Clay started to speak, then caught himself. Whatever these two were selling, Marjorie was buying it. And Clay could deny his wife nothing it was remotely within his power to give her. Still, he wanted *some* idea of what this was about. He said as much, his posture unchanged.

Paul turned toward Donna. He did not actually speak to her, but she nodded as if he had. "Yes," she said. "Paul would prefer to speak to everyone, your whole household, at the same time. Can you wake the staff?"

Two sleepy faces joined them in the living room of the Garber house. A big room, much as Donna remembered from one previous visit, high ceiling, a magnificent natural brick fireplace filling the north wall. To the east a huge picture window looked out across the Garber's deep, sloping property toward the expanse of the Lake, invisible now in the darkness. Donna stood by the window, watching the servants enter. Clayton Garber had come a long, long way, she thought, remembering his beginnings as a child of people much like his servants; people who'd struggled to make their way through the Great Depression, and succeeded because they were faster, stronger, and ultimately smarter than the thousands who fell by the wayside. Joshua Garber, Clayton's father, had been a butler in the household of Nathaniel Wentworth, whose money had sponsored much of the magnificent face of old Chicago. Garber's mother was Ceilia Standright, the cook in that same house, a granddaughter of slaves. Now Clayton Garber had servants of his own and a fortune that gave him a fine house and the time to play politics in what was, Donna always thought, surely the most political city in the nation, even the world.

The money was not entirely his own. He'd done well for himself in the private sector, but Marjorie brought a sizable inheritance to their union. Some five or six million, Donna heard, creating what Walker Stone always called Garber's *Upstairs Downstairs* life. Donna had not understood the analogy until Stone showed her a few episodes of that elegant British soap opera. Then she'd seen how Garber shared with the head of that fictional Victorian household his political aspirations and his wife's wealth to fuel them.

The cook and maid came in together, muttering to each other at the unseemly interruption of their sleep, with thick winter housecoats pulled around their shoulders. Clay motioned them to take seats and set about introducing Paul Trayne and his father. Paul sat in a high-backed chair beside the fireplace, his feet not quite reaching the floor, his hands resting palms up on his knees.

Donna studied each of the faces as they studied Paul. With an investigative reporter's eye she tried to read the subtle nuances she saw in their expression. Like so many things in her life of late, Donna found that skill now eluding her—found, too, that it did not matter as she watched Clayton Garber finish his introduction and heard Paul's pure, sweet voice begin to tell the assembly what it was he had to offer. She could read their faces easily enough when Paul was finished. Disbelief on the face of Rose, the cook, and Anne, the maid.

Garber is the one to watch, Donna thought. *He's come too far from his humble beginnings. Climbed too high. He won't want to risk his reputation on foolishness. . . .*

She caught herself. Such rebellious thoughts now seemed totally alien to her, almost as if another mind had spoken inside her head. A mind more like the Donna Wojciechowski who had not yet met Paul Trayne. The same mind, it now seemed, that had thought it was a good idea to contact Garber before the much more powerful Emmanuel Stuartson.

Is that why I've brought Paul here? Is that why we came to Garber, instead of going straight to the mayor? Clay was right . . . I know Mannie Stuartson at least as well as I know Clay. And that seemed the main reason she had chosen not to go to Stuartson, now that Donna looked at her thoughts and analyzed them. She knew Stuartson would not resist Paul, while Garber . . .

A flash of fear made her push the train of thought away. She looked at Paul. The boy was sitting quietly, staring into the creases across his palms. Trayne stood nearby, watching Garber, oblivious, for the moment, of Donna. Donna sighed. Trayne could not, so far as she knew, read minds. Her momentary transgression would pass unnoticed.

Garber did not notice the brief change in Donna's face, but he confirmed her impression of him with his words. "Look," he said, "I don't want to come off as some kind of unyielding bad guy in this"—he shot a glance at Marjorie, but her eyes were still on Paul—"but, well, dammit, if what you say is true, if what you suggest the boy can do is real, that's more than a little *frightening,* don't you agree? To have somebody reach inside your head, sift through your innermost feelings . . ." He shrugged. "I'm sorry, Reverend Trayne, but I just need . . . well, something more solid than a promise."

Paul listened to his statement with a small, sad smile on his all-American face.

"I can understand why you would not want to accept Paul's gift without question," Trayne said. "It is a difficult thing to believe, this wondrous talent he has."

"But I hope you will come to trust me, to accept my gift," Paul said. Anne smiled, her fear fading a little as she looked into the green eyes of the cherub-faced boy. Rose, too, warmed to the carelessly tousled hair, the mingled strength and weariness in the young face.

"I can tell," Paul went on, "that you are a strong man, Mr. Garber. A man who prefers to deal with life on his own terms. Certainly not on mine or anyone else's." Paul smiled. Donna felt the warmth of it suffuse her. Paul rose from his seat and crossed to stand before Marjorie Garber.

"Understand that I cannot take what you do not wish to give," Paul said, as he had said to Donna. "I am a vessel. Pour your sorrows into me." He paused. Marjorie appeared transfixed, Donna thought.

"Yes," said the Reverend Trayne. "But understand also that there are needings here. Not so many as Paul has had to take upon himself before, but still a great burden. You do understand this, don't you?"

Donna allowed herself to drift away as Trayne began the speech she'd heard before. The warning speech. The cautioning speech. Telling them the burden they would place on Paul. Making them understand what a terrible thing it was the boy offered them. How awful to burden this innocent with all the terrors and griefs of their lives. Terrible to know that he would feel those private pains as if they were his very own. Terrible, too, to be unable to resist the urge to go ahead, to ignore the pain they'd give him. To release their anguish, pour it into him, as he asked. Fill his vessel to overflowing with the burden of their pain. The gift Paul Trayne offered was almost impossible to resist; the underlying compulsion of Trayne's speech was, after all, that they should not resist.

Because it was Trayne, Donna understood now, the older Trayne, who was the real force at work here. Paul had the power, the miraculous power, but he was only a tool, an instrument for the world vision, the view of the future that rested entirely in Robert Johnston Trayne.

So many times, Donna remembered now, Paul had prefixed what he'd said with "my father says" or "my father thinks." It had seemed at first like nothing more than a son's loyalty or devotion to someone who was, after all, a powerful and dominating parental figure. But there was so much more. More, Donna thought, than she even guessed.

Than she *could* guess, if her mind kept slipping away, avoiding the details, saying *never mind, never mind.*

In a small place, buried deep below the growing control of Robert Trayne on her mind and body, Donna thought she might be beginning to understand why the gift had to be presented in just precisely this way, with the speech Trayne always made, with the emphasis on Paul's pain, on the terrible selfishness of the act of unburdening one's own soul at the expense of his.

The places Donna's mind wandered were strange: passages of unsurpassed darkness shot through at random intervals with light so pure, so blinding white that it seemed to pierce her soul. She moved across the unfamiliar landscape, drifting as might a toy balloon freed of the string that bound it to its earthly captivity. She rose and fell, carried on irresistible currents that were neither air nor water. The living room of the Garber house was far away, part of another world, another lifetime. She could not associate herself with that Donna Wojciechowski who stood to one side, watching Paul and Robert Trayne, hearing their words. She was another woman entirely. Her thoughts were only partially those of the original Donna. They came and went, peppering her thinking with phrases simultaneously strange and familiar, the way Walker Stone's speech was sometimes shot with snippets from the old TV shows he loved so dearly.

Donna thought about Walker Stone. She had been deeply troubled when Reverend Trayne finally revealed to her what he intended for Stone. Her reaction had surprised her, such a clear, sharp feeling to slice through the cotton wadding that surrounded her brain.

"Is . . . that really necessary?" she had asked, her voice trembling with fear of his anger. She remembered the moment in the tent, the edge of the terrible abyss. She knew now that it was Robert Trayne who had forced Paul to show her that chasm, that eternity of emptiness into which she could be so casually thrown, by the simple mechanism of denying her Paul's power. Paul could give, but he could also take. And when he took, when he removed the effect of his power—for which he clearly did not need the willing compliance of his subject—everything came back, all the old hurts and pains. Came back multiplied a thousandfold.

She was like a junkie, Donna thought, so dependent on her next hit, her next fix, that she would do anything, *anything,* to avoid losing her chance for it.

"All I do is necessary," Trayne had said. He'd been driving the truck north and east through the snow-swept darkness of rural Illinois. Paul sat between them on the bench seat of the old Ford, his head sunk on his breast, his weight against Donna. He dozed. She had begun to notice just how much the boy slept when Trayne was not pushing him. "Every moment of my days, every step I have taken, every thought, since the boy's gift first flowered, I have focused toward this time. Toward the great necessity of what lies ahead."

For a moment he looked away from the dark stain of the highway ahead, and the reflected lights bouncing through the old glass of the windshield made his face into something not at all like the kindly patrician features of Abraham Lincoln.

"The man Stone is one of the ones I have foreseen. One of the ones I have feared. It seemed only too likely"—he turned his gaze back to the highway—"that someone would appear one day who was immune to the boy's power. Immune, so that they went unaffected or, like the man Stone, were struck down before their minds could be opened and emptied of the things that burden them. When such are encountered, they must be eliminated. Killed." The words came in the singsong revival meeting rhythms. The incongruity of sound and content somehow gave Donna the strength to push on with her protest.

Donna said, "But . . . he could be useful to you."

Trayne slowed the truck, pulled over to the edge of the highway, and stopped. He shook his head. Shadows played across his craggy features. "He could not be of use," Trayne said. "His resistance endangered us. He had to be eliminated, in a manner that would not implicate us."

"But . . ."

"Sister Wojciechowski . . ." There was great weariness in Trayne's voice. Donna heard the sound of a parent, one who had tried and tried to be patient with a disobedient child, but who now saw at last that discipline—harsh discipline—would be necessary.

"I—" Donna's voice caught. She was suddenly very much afraid of the man in the frayed black coat. She felt the handle of the door pressing into her side. It would be awkward to reach from her present angle, with Paul heavy against her other side.

"Paul," Trayne said, his voice sharp.

The boy stirred, woke. He blinked, rubbed his small fists into the orbits of his eyes. "Father? Are we in Chicago."

"Paul," Trayne said, ignoring the question, "Sister Wojciechowski does not want to help us anymore."

Donna stiffened. "I didn't . . ."

"Donna?" Paul's eyes were wide with betrayal.

"Paul . . ."

"She must be taught a lesson," Trayne said, cutting Donna off. "You remember?"

Paul's eyes narrowed. "Like . . . Mother."

Trayne simply frowned, and Paul twitched, leaning back away from his father and more heavily against Donna.

"She must be taught a lesson. Only the first lesson."

Paul seemed to relax. "The first lesson."

Donna was totally confused. She looked from Paul to Trayne, then back to Paul. Back to Trayne.

The abyss opened beneath her. Everything Paul had done, all the wonder he had worked, shriveled and died in one searing instant that felt for all the world as if Donna Wojciechowski's soul had been suddenly torn from her body and hurled away. Donna gasped, doubling. Her head went into Paul's lap. A tiny part of her mind registered the slender legs, the bony knees. The rest of her, all the rest of her, was lost as every grief, every guilt, every sin she'd ever thought or dreamed of came tumbling back on her, crashing down on her like an unending rain of sharp, pointed stones.

Donna cried aloud, her scream filling the small cab of the truck and then, as suddenly as it had come, silencing itself. The scream continued, but only in Donna's mind, a mind now ringed with black fire that licked and hissed as Donna twisted slowly over its ebony tendrils.

"That is enough for now," she heard Robert Trayne say.

She felt Paul's hand on the back of her head, stroking. "Shh," said his voice, cool and soothing in the scalding darkness. His gift came back to her. It filled her. The darkness shrank. Her soul rose, refreshed, renewed, to its proper place.

Donna sat up. She drew a deep breath.

"Remember that," Trayne said. "The second lesson will be worse. The third worse than that."

Donna had stared into the darkness beyond the lights, rocking slowly side to side with the motion of the old truck, aware of the weight of Paul against her left arm. The boy's face was filled with emotions she could not recognize when she looked at him again.

"Don't make him do it again," Paul said.

She looked at Trayne. "I . . . won't," she said, hearing the words as if they came from somewhere else, from someone else's mind, into her own.

Trayne nodded, his face calm again. He shifted the Ford into gear and brought it back up to speed, back into the right-hand lane.

Now, hours later, she drifted away from Paul and Robert Trayne, away from the Garber house. She drifted over the life of Donna Wojciechowski and looked at each of the passing moments as if they were frames lifted out of context from some incomprehensible foreign film. The face of her mother. She felt no bond, no physical attachment to the shriveled, dried-apple features. Dark eyes no longer flashed pain into Donna's heart. Words falling with such uncaring ease from the wide mouth no longer stung her. When Donna tried to think of herself as a tiny cell, blossoming and growing in this stranger's womb, it was as if she tried to picture herself as born out of another species. Her connection to Viveca Wojciechowski had become so tenuous as to be nonexistent.

Yet this woman was my mother. She raised me. She made me much of what I was.

That was the key. Donna was no longer the woman Viveca shaped. She was created anew; if she had a parent now, it was Robert Trayne. He was the father of Donna Wojciechowski as surely as if his own hot seed had squirted into her mother's belly. He had reshaped her, as a sculptor does the clay; made a woman who could function as Donna Wojciechowski, think and act and sometimes even feel as Donna would, if the need arose. But who was not Donna. As her rambling thoughts came back again and again to that one solid truth in the shifting pattern of her new reality, Donna felt a pang, a longing, as if she'd remembered a great loss, the unexpected death of a close, dear friend. She seized the pain. It was real, it was true. More important, it was hers. It came from some small, shrinking part of Donna that was still all her own.

Despite what Paul Trayne's gift might have done to her, part of Donna's soul cried out for assurance that it was still a living, viable thing, could still touch her mind, her heart, and make her feel the things a human being is meant to feel. The intensity of the feeling shocked her, snapped her out of the drifting miasma of her thoughts, brought her lurching back into the reality of the Garber living room. With that sudden return the feeling vanished. The cry for freedom erupting from her deepest inner self shrank back into darkness. Paul was looking at her. His eyes were pained. Other eyes turned to her, Garber, Marjorie, the older Trayne. Donna realized with a shock that Paul had worked his magic on the Garber household in the time her mind drifted.

How long was I preoccupied? It seemed like only a few seconds.

However long, it had been long enough. Donna studied Clay Garber, stared openly, but could not read the expression on his face for good or ill. She felt a sudden sense of vertigo, as if a vital piece of her life had come unstuck. She trembled, knees weak.

Trayne took a step toward her, and the strength drained from Donna's legs. "Sister Wojciechowski?"

As Trayne reached out a hand for her, Donna started to topple forward. Of all in the room, Trayne alone was close enough to reach her before she fell.

Marjorie watched as the Reverend Trayne helped Donna to a chair. She looked up to Paul, still standing close by her chair. His young face was twisted with a terrible pain. Marjorie could almost feel his suffering, the way his heart and soul reached out to Donna Wojciechowski and embraced her pain. The lad seemed so small beside her. So helpless. So very much in need of the love Marjorie Garber could offer. If only the chance came.

Trayne lowered Donna into the big, soft easy chair by the

fireplace and placed a big hand against her brow. "I told you we should have waited," Trayne said, his voice soft, compassionate. "We could have come later this afternoon, or even tomorrow. You are so very tired."

The sweetness in his voice filled Marjorie's heart. Such a loving man. Such a perfect father. She looked again at Paul. He seemed relaxed, now. Content that Donna was in no immediate danger, his distress passing as quickly as it had come. He looked so worn himself, so tired and frail. Paul seemed to sense her mood. He turned and smiled. He looked happy, but his bright eyes were dull with fatigue. As he stepped away from Marjorie to take his place in the center of the room, Marjorie saw him tremble. She thought he might fall.

She moved to rise, but Clay put a hand on her arm. She turned to him, sitting on the arm of her chair. He shook his head, very slightly, side to side. His eyebrows were drawn close in a studied frown. Marjorie looked back at Paul. He was standing in the middle of the window. The lights of the room painted colors on the panes of glass.

He looks so small, she thought. *So much in need of care and love.*

She felt a swift stab of jealousy through her heart. Jealousy directed toward Donna Wojciechowski, who shared such perfect intimacy with the boy.

Paul was looking at Clay. "You have not given me your pain, Commissioner Garber," he said.

"You're right. I haven't. I don't intend to."

Paul sighed. His narrow chest shook, looking to Marjorie for all the world as if he were about to break into tears. The Reverend Trayne crossed to his son. He put a big, gnarled old hand on the boy's shoulder and spoke softly in his ear, words that Marjorie could not hear. Paul shook his head. "No, Father. Let me do this. Let me try to help him."

Marjorie guessed she was not supposed to hear the words either, but she did. She turned again to her husband. "What's wrong, Clay? If you could only feel what he can do . . ."

Clay drew in his lower lip and ran it back and forth along his upper incisors for a moment. Then he shook his head, looking at Paul. "I understand what you're offering," he said, his big voice soft and calm, a patient, abiding tone Marjorie recognized from talks he'd had with their children, "and I can tell already that you've worked some kind of change in Marjorie and the others." He paused, as if hearing his own words and suddenly doubting them. "I don't know how you do what you do, but I am aware that you do it." Clay rose. "I'm also aware that I cannot be so easily relieved of my responsibilities."

Paul stepped closer to Clay. "You misunderstand. It is not responsibility I take. Only fear. Only pain and grief."

Clay shook his head. "I do understand that. But I can't quite see how I could do my job if all the world suddenly seemed as perfect as you say you can make it."

"As he does make it," Donna said. Clay turned to look at her. She sat in the big chair, her long legs stretched out almost straight in front of her, crossed at the ankles. She looked odd in a way Clay could not quite put a name to. He decided he did not know her well enough to judge whether she was behaving uncharacteristically.

"I don't intend to dispute the fact of Paul's gift"—again the words sounded strange to Clay, the acceptance too easy, too pat—"only whether I should partake of it. I don't think I should."

"Clay . . ."

"No, Marjorie. My mind is made up on this."

"You . . . might want to reconsider, sir," said Rose. Donna looked at her for the first time since she'd come back from her mental meanderings. There was a definite change in the woman's face. A relaxing.

"It really is . . . quite wonderful," Rose said. "I'm all of a sudden aware of a whole lump of things I had buried down inside me, eating away at my insides. Only now I see how stupid and trivial and unimportant they really are. How easy it would be, will be, to solve them all." She smiled. "Like I said, sir, it's wonderful."

"Good," said Clay. "Enjoy it. All of you. And I don't mean that facetiously. Just don't ask me to join you. Please. Believe me, I know best in this." He turned to Paul. "And you will not try to take this from me, will you?"

"Father says I must not," said Paul Trayne. "I must only

receive, as I told you." He dropped his eyes. "This means you will not help us after all . . . ?"

"I didn't say that. I didn't say that at all. I've sat here and listened to what you had to say, Paul. I've watched the changes come over the faces of my wife and staff. I've seen your miracle."

Paul looked back into Clay's face. "Then . . . ?"

"I'll help you see Emmanuel Stuartson, as I promised. In fact, I'll stop by his office and set up an appointment today, first thing." He looked at the clock on the mantelpiece. Almost three A.M. "Right now, however, I need some sleep."

"Why didn't you want them to stay? We could have made them quite comfortable, with the guest room and both girls' rooms being empty." Marjorie Garber climbed back under the covers of the big bed.

"They'll be fine with Donna," Clay said. He took off his expensive velvet robe and hung it carefully in the closet. He would never be so accustomed to wealth that he would not appreciate luxuries and treat them accordingly.

"That's not an answer," Marjorie said as he climbed into bed next to her. Her mind was full of the face of Paul Trayne.

"I know it isn't." Clay sighed. "Will you just accept that I had a, well, a sort of uncomfortable feeling about it? Without knowing why?"

"If that's all you have to give me."

"That's all."

"But you are going to help him?"

"I said I was." Clay looked into his wife's face. Marjorie Garber was the kind of woman other people called handsome. Not delicate enough of feature to be pretty, not elegant enough to be glamorous. A comfortably beautiful face, a loving face. An ageless face. She was heavier than the day they'd met, but she did not look any older: face unlined, jet black hair straightened and smoothed back about her head. Clay reached up to touch his wife's cheek. The skin was soft against his palm. He ran the tip of his thumb across her full lips. She puckered slightly to kiss him.

"I'll help," he said. "For you. And because I think the world might be well served by somebody like Paul Trayne." He did not need a lifetime in the police force to know that.

"Then you believe in him, even without experiencing what he can do?" There was a note of rapture in her voice Clay had never heard, even when she was most happy in her life.

"Yes," he said. He took his hand away from her cheek, kissed her. Marjorie leaned into the kiss, caught his hand, and drew it to her bosom. Memories surged, and with them the heat of his blood.

"I love you, Clay," she said. Her arm went round the back of his neck and drew him down on top of her.

"And I love you."

"Will he have to die too?" Donna sat in the truck again, guiding Trayne as he wound through the sparse traffic toward her apartment. Paul sat between them, listening without comment.

"Perhaps," Trayne said, "if he cannot be brought to our purpose willingly."

"You could force him," Donna said. There was a knot of pain behind her right eye. She was beginning to associate it with Paul Trayne, with being in his presence. It was not a terrible pain. Not unbearable. But when he was there, it was there. Always now, it seemed. "He's not resistant, like Walker. You could make him give you his needing. Or you could turn him into a puppet, like Nickerson."

Trayne shook his head. "He cannot serve that way. It would be too complex a manipulation. Nickerson was easy. His life was small and without shading. But this man Garber is more complex. His emotions are more elaborate. I cannot do more unless he surrenders to Paul. And that must be of his own choosing. Everyone must give their pain of their own free will, or the plan fails."

Donna shook her own head. "I don't understand that part."

"It is not necessary that you understand," Trayne said. "It is necessary only that you serve." The abyss beckoned.

"Yes . . ."

Trayne heard hesitancy in her voice. "What?" His voice was a lash, a bolt of energy up her spine.

Donna shuddered. "No . . ." Her voice was very small. "It is nothing. Nothing. I swear."

Trayne shook his head. "Poor, foolish woman. Do you still have some germ of yourself, hiding in some dark corner of your soul? Some germ of who you were?" He slowed the truck and looked at her. "Have you so soon forgotten how your life was before we came? Is it time for your second lesson so soon? Paul . . ."

The abyss opened beneath her. Donna fell screaming into despair.

9

Walker Stone crawled through a world gone mad, just enough in possession of his faculties to know he must look like some bizarre three-legged beast, his right arm hanging useless, dragging, slowing him. He pushed through long grasses heavy with snow. In the darkness he could see less than a foot. The sharp edges of the grass raked his face, slicing like scalpels. Blood ran down his cheeks like scarlet tears. More ran hot down his arm, gushing in steaming torrents from the twisted ruin of his shoulder. Each time he slipped or the dragging arm caught, it was new agony, pain on top of pain. He bit his lip so hard to keep from crying out he tasted blood in his mouth. His hands were frozen with the cold; his gloves, deep in the right-hand pocket of his coat, were impossible to reach with his left hand. He was two hundred yards from the tent, he thought. If he had rightly judged the direction of his escape, he was now heading roughly parallel to Pine Tree Road, back toward the highway.

If only I could run! If only I didn't have to crawl, to keep my head down . . .

To stand now would be suicide. He could hear his pursuer crashing through the long grasses behind him. Every now and then a shot rang out, but none came near. Even in his agony he tried to force his mind into a logical sequence of thought. He would need to be in complete control if he had any hope of getting clear, making it to the highway, flagging down a car. Stone had turned to question Nickerson just in time to hear the discharge of Nickerson's big gun and see the flash of light. But Nickerson fired too quickly; his accuracy was off. His intent was to kill, but he only crippled. The bullet smashed through Stone's left shoulder, shattering the top of the humerus, shredding the complex joining of muscle and sinew that made the arm a useful part of his body. The impact hurled him back, spinning him to land flat-out on the muddy floor, across the ruined arm, experiencing in that moment the first of many agonies the night would hold. The impact of the bullet had been too much, too outrageous for his senses to assimilate, and had not hurt immediately. The impact and twist of the fall was another matter.

Nickerson's second shot went over him, coming so fast after the first. His speed was not the only thing impairing his aim. His bad eyesight had saved Stone's life, for the moment at least. He'd known his shot would hit only if he was extraordinarily lucky, but the moment did not lend itself to caution or precision. He needed Stone dead, and dead before he could react to what was happening. Stone had rolled off his damaged arm—more pain!—and scrambled for the side of the tent, out of the light from Nickerson's flashlight, his brain a blur of pain and fear, drowning clear thought. He moved as an animal moves, trapped, cornered. He knew there was a second door in the back of the tent, in the shadows thirty feet away. Even though he was not functioning in any fashion as a rational, thinking human, it was toward that hidden door his instincts drove him now.

Nickerson waved the light around inside the tent. He fired again. The bullet *thwacked* into the trampled grasses an inch from Stone's hand. A fragment of intelligence still functioning in Stone said *That's three.* He doubled his speed toward the back of the tent. He reached the far wall, slapping canvas with his good hand, searching for the flap. Nickerson's gun boomed again. The canvas tore ten inches to his right. Stone kept slapping. He could not find the hidden door. What if it wasn't there? What if he'd misread, misimagined his position in the tent's interior? Perhaps the impact of Nickerson's first shot had spun him more than he thought. Perhaps he was even moving away from his only avenue of escape.

Nickerson advanced into the tent, pointing his flashlight dead ahead. Suddenly the ball of light was all around Stone, pinning him. In the brilliance Stone could see something of the damage Nickerson's shot had done, the way his coat sleeve was spread out, the opening petals of some grotesque flower. Blood poured out of the top of the sleeve and ran down his arm. His hand was so covered with it that he looked as if he were wearing a red glove. Oddly, his pinkie finger remained dry, white, and bony in the light. Nickerson came within easy reach of him. Stone huddled back against the wall of the tent. The canvas, already torn by Nickerson's shot, ripped further under his weight. With a few seconds he could have made his own door in the fabric. But Nickerson had no intention of giving him that time.

"Hold still now, Stone," he said. "I'll make this quick."

Stone looked up the long barrel of the gun and thought of movies he'd seen where special effects wizards created the illusion of a bullet speeding out of that long black womb, hurtling directly at the viewer. He knew he'd have no time to really see the red-hot bolt of lead as it escaped its steel jacket. In final desperation Stone lashed out, kicking up toward the joining of Nickerson's thick thighs as hard as he could. His toe missed the soft and vulnerable target he hoped for, and struck into the fat overhang of belly above Nickerson's belt. It was not as completely disabling as Stone's original intent, but it was enough. Nickerson's breath whistled out of him and he staggered back. His finger tightened reflexively on the trigger, but the shot went wild. Stone took his last chance to dive sideways again, slapping, slapping. The canvas moved. The flap swung aside, catching him off-balance. Stone tumbled into the night air behind the tent. He fell full length again, but this time he managed to land on his left arm; there was no explosion of pain to jar his senses or slow his flight. He pushed up off the ground and ran, bolting hard right, the direction in which—he hoped, he prayed—the highway lay. Behind him he heard Nickerson swear, then a series of clicks before another shot shattered the silence. The grasses crackled over his head. Stone knew what it meant. He'd watched enough TV detective shows to know that Nickerson was using half-moons, fast loaders. He'd emptied the spent shells from his gun with a quick flick of the wrist and shot home two thin crescents of steel, each cradling three cartridges. He fired again.

Stone changed course, crawling sideways for a hundred feet before he angled back toward the highway. He wondered if he might be better off to break right and keep going that way, heading for Pine Tree Road. Would the going be any easier along that muddy, icy, furrowed strip? It might be, but there would be no cover. He decided to stay in Gunner's Field, pushing through the tall grasses, praying he was still heading for the highway. This plan had now brought Stone some four hundred yards from the tent, but the highway was still three times that distance beyond him. As the initial rush of adrenaline began to subside, his body's needs began to reassert themselves; he began to feel the dizzying effects of loss of blood. The ground became unsure beneath him. His body wanted to tilt in directions that had nothing to do with his flight. Then he heard it. Growling. Guttural. The stalking roar of some terrible beast.

The Buick's engine. Nickerson was taking a less subtle approach to his pursuit of Walker Stone. Stone heard a squeal and thump of metal as the big car bounced into the rough terrain of the field. The grasses behind were lit with the glare of the headlights. Shadows danced before him. Stone pushed to his feet—no point now in crawling. At least he could cradle his wounded arm. And he ran. That put his head above the grasses, but he was counting on Nickerson's poor vision. The pistol barked again behind him. He risked a quick glance over his shoulder. The Buick was coming fast, but not straight. If it continued in the direction it was now taking, it would pass thirty feet to his right. Stone decided to increase that distance. He kept going toward the highway, but angled left, away from the projected path of the car. Nickerson fired again, and the hard ground spat near Stone's right foot. Nickerson had seen him. Stone heard the Buick grunt as it turned to bear down on him directly. Stone's heart pounded faster. The blood running down his arm flowed faster. The ground beneath him passed faster, as his legs pumped.

But you can't outrun a car.

Even on this rough, plow-scored ground, he knew that. That was only in movies or on TV. In his apprentice days, he'd seen the mangled bodies of enough people who had tried that impossible adventure. He knew that his time was now numbered in seconds. Even if Nickerson was unable to hit him with his firing, he'd get him with the car. Stone wondered for a moment if he might be able to go under the Buick if he threw himself flat on the ground. But the ground itself was not flat, and corrugations of summer plowing ran the wrong way for Stone to make any use of them as cover. If he stretched himself out in one he'd be at right angles to the wheels of Nickerson's car. He needed to be parallel if such a plan had any hope of success. He abandoned further thought of it. He pushed on through the grass, praying now that no sudden change in the rhythmic pattern of the furrows would appear to throw him off his stride. He was better than halfway to the highway, he guessed. But it was too many years since he'd run like this, and that had been in junior high school, on a regulation track. Still, if there was no chance of his outrunning the Buick, as people did so easily in movies, there was something else he almost never saw in movies that he could try right now.

He broke right, stumbling, rolling as he went, sprawling full length into one of the furrows. The valley was full of ice-topped water. The ice was not thick enough to support his impact. Stone crashed through into brackish water. It was a long, narrow pond, barely eighteen inches wide and ten feet long, but it held enough water to drench his right side completely. The Buick roared by. Stone got up and ran on, still heading for the highway, watching over his shoulder as Nickerson swerved the big car. It fantailed and seemed to go out of his control.

Stone froze, transfixed by the new miracle in Gunner's Field. The Buick seemed for one long, liquid moment to be flowing sideways. It began to rise up on the right side, tipping over. It rolled, over and over, coming to rest on its roof, wheels spinning, engine screaming. Something Stone could not identify made a snapping sound, again and again, like a baseball card in the spokes of a child's bicycle. Stone tensed for an explosion, but that too was the stuff of movies. He heard the shriek of metal on metal as Nickerson forced the driver's side door open. But that removed some of the metal supporting the weight of the big car. Another sound added to the squeal and snap of the overturned vehicle. The roof of the Buick let out a mighty groan and folded like a Japanese lantern. Stone said a quick prayer of thanks for a car built before the days of Ralph Nader. It died in his throat as he saw Nickerson rise beyond the diminished bulk of the car. He seemed unsteady on his feet.

Wishful thinking.

An angry sob caught in Stone's throat. He started running again. Nickerson saw him and fired. Stone ran for all he was worth, lungs burning as he sucked frigid air. His heart pounded. His torn shoulder throbbed, and with it his head. Each time his foot came down it sent a shudder up his spine, threatening to dislodge his skull and send it bouncing back across the rutted ground of Gunner's Field, rolling to a bloody halt at Clarence Nickerson's feet.

Something for your trophy wall, Chief.

Stone forced the image out of his mind. It was enough to stay alive for the next five hundred yards—it had to be only that by now. It had to—to reach the highway, flag a passing motorist . . . Then the flaw in his plan hit him and unraveled everything so completely he almost stumbled, almost lost the drive to run. Any passing motorist on the road at this time of night would almost certainly be someone who lived in or near Faulkner. Anyone who lived in or near Faulkner might well have fallen under the thrall of the Trayne boy. Stone was convinced this mad hour of murder and pursuit was generated by Paul Trayne. Despite his protest to the contrary, Nickerson must have been one of the very first to fall. From almost the day the Traynes appeared, Stone now knew with absolute certainty, he'd been their pawn, their slave.

Nickerson pounded after him, his breathing heavy, gasping. Too many years smoking those unfiltered Pall Malls. Stone had not smoked since high school; his lungs, while burning from the exertion in the cold air, were much better suited to the task than Nickerson's. Stone heard a thump behind him, and again

Nickerson's gun boomed. Wherever the shot went, it was not near enough for Stone to hear its passage or its impact. He guessed Nickerson had fallen, stumbled over the rough ground or collapsed from exhaustion. He'd fired a shot in desperation as Stone continued to sprint away from him.

The—momentary?—termination of pursuit did not eliminate the problem Stone saw for himself: How could he be sure anyone he managed to stop on the highway was not one of Paul Trayne's slaves? Who were his friends? How far had the effect of Paul Trayne spread beyond Faulkner, beyond McLean County? There was no way to know, short of stopping a car. Stone feared that would be a test leading to destruction. Nevertheless he kept running. There was nothing else to do; for all the mystery the highway offered, it was better than the certain death presented by Nickerson and his big gun. The last three hundred yards of Gunner's Field passed beneath him. The edge of the field came into sight. A barbed wire fence stood at the rim of the plowed ground; beyond it was a drainage ditch and beyond that the road. Stone felt secure enough in Nickerson's distress—there was no sign of further pursuit yet—to take his time climbing through the fence. With his left arm useless he could not easily spread the strands of hooking wire. Ending his life strung out on the fence like a machine-gunned POW in an escape movie was not the picture Stone had of his death.

He managed to get through the wire, but as he started down the slope of the drainage ditch Nickerson's gun cracked again. The bullet smacked into the far side of the ditch. Three inches to the right and it would have hit Stone and ruined his left arm too. A foot to the right, it would have killed him. Stone ducked and scurried along the treacherous slope, heading left, north and away from Faulkner. He heard the rustle of the tall grasses, the thud of feet as Nickerson resumed his chase. Stone decided to risk Nickerson's poor eyesight against the darkness of the unlighted stretch of highway and make a break for the other side of the road. But that would mean jumping over the frozen bottom of the ditch, if he did not want to risk his feet becoming trapped in the sucking mud that might lie below the ice. Stone was not at all sure he could make the jump. He was dizzy. He was weak from loss of blood. The running and the pounding left no time for natural coagulants to seal the wound in his arm, even if they could with so massive an injury. Blood was still flowing. The useless arm was now just so much dead weight. Stone could not guarantee it would not throw him off, cause him to land awkwardly and topple back to the bottom of the ditch.

All this passed through his mind in an instant. He had no choice. He could not run along the steep incline on the field side of the ditch forever. Nickerson needed only to stay on the relatively level ground of Gunner's Field to overtake him. He had to make the jump. He forced himself into an extra sprint, a burst of speed to put between himself and Nickerson the tiny bit of distance that might make the difference. He turned and flung himself across the ditch. He landed hard and slid back until his boots crunched against the surface ice. But he did not break through, did not topple. He dug the fingers of his left hand into the frozen soil and pulled himself toward the top of the ditch. He rolled onto the shoulder of the highway, careful not to further aggravate his wound. Then he pushed himself to his feet and ran as fast as the level, solid tarmac could allow. Behind he heard the bark of Nickerson's gun; again the shot was wide. Stone risked a glance as he pounded down the middle of the highway. A dark mass that could only have been Clarence Nickerson was sliding down the field side of the drainage ditch to rise a few seconds later on the highway side. Stone looked back to the road ahead and ran on.

A truck would be very handy now. A nice big eighteen-wheeler coming barreling over the rise . . .

He could see it clearly. Nickerson hard on his heels. A nimbus of light behind the hill ahead of Stone telling him the behemoth was rolling up toward them. Waiting for the last possible instant before he hurled himself to one side as the truck plowed on over the hill and smeared Chief Clarence Nickerson a quarter mile along the blacktop. But that was something else that happened only in movies. If Stone was going to survive tonight, it would have to be by his own actions. He was going to have to find a way to stop Clarence Nickerson. Stop him permanently, stop him soon.

It was then that he saw the house. It was set back from the road, a dark cube that told nothing of itself save that it was, or had once been, a dwelling place. Stone ran up the path to the gate and rolled himself over the top. He thudded up the drive onto the porch. He did not have to knock to know there was no one at home; it was clear no one had been home for quite some time.

So the Munsters are out, he thought, amazing himself with his cold humor at such a time.

He huddled back in the inky blackness of the corner by the door, crouching down, peering back toward the road. He cupped his left hand over his nose and mouth, trying to warm his frozen flesh while heating the air he was drawing into his lungs. He forced himself to breath slowly. He was panting from the exhausting run; hyperventilation was a few short, sharp breaths away. Stone could not see the road clearly in the darkness. He wondered why the highway was so dark here and, lacking a local's knowledge of this section's unincorporated status, found no answer. He knew only that the darkness he'd prayed would hide him was now shielding Nickerson's approach.

Unless he didn't see me! The thought flamed in Stone's mind. Hope. Salvation. *If I really was lucky,* he thought, *if I managed to get across the road, up to this damn mausoleum without him spotting me, he may be jogging on his way to Peoria by now.*

Crouching in the darkness, Stone shook his head. Too much to hope for. The logic of the fleeing beast was to go to ground as soon as possible, and this old house was too obvious a hiding place for him to have passed it by.

Stone squinted up at the door to his left. It was a double door, the halves tall and slim, finely wrought in what might have been dark oak. There had been panels of glass in the upper part of each door, once upon a time, but those had been broken or removed, boards nailed to the inside of the doors filling the openings. Below the doors the porch had cracked and splintered. There was a large hole Stone had barely missed stepping into. Through the hole he saw the rotten, shadowy remains of a second flight of steps leading up to the front door. The porch was a later addition to the house, he reasoned, built right over the original steps. There were five windows, three of them to the right of the doors and two on the front of the rectangle that jutted out behind him and made the corner he crouched in. They were filthy, from what he could see. Maybe whitewashed. Stone pushed himself up onto his feet and moved carefully to the door again. He tried the knob of each panel and found that while both turned in his grip, neither door showed any inclination to open.

Stone looked back toward the darkness of the road. *Are you there?* he asked the darkness, mouthing the words, uttering no sound. He still could not see any sign of Nickerson. *Are you sneaking up on me, right this moment? Are you drawing a careful bead on me? Squinting down the barrel of your goddamn gun with your blind bat's eyes?*

It made his innards squirm to think it—involuntary trembles ran up and down the length of him. As if something cold and slimy had reached out and touched him, just where the bullet might strike.

I need a weapon.

It was completely against his philosophy to bear arms, but the situation seemed designed to override such finer sentiments.

I need a weapon. Something that I won't have to be too clever with. Something that will stop him cold with very little effort.

He'd learned a fair bit of self-defense and first aid over the years. He knew a dozen spots upon which he could render severe, even lethal damage, many of which a complete layman would not even guess. But he was not a fighter. If he was going to deal with Nickerson, pay him back in his own coin, he was going to need something considerably more deadly than his bare hands.

Hand.

For the first time Stone essayed a cautious, fingertip inspection of the wound in his shoulder. He found, as he feared, that "shoulder" was no longer entirely the appropriate word. A shoulder was a joint, a ball-and-socket connection of bone and muscle. What his probing fingers found under the shredded fabric of his sleeve lacked only a few minutes on a barbecue grill to render it quite passable hamburger. He managed a small smile at this further grim humor. He decided not to go back down the steps, but he needed to get away from the door, the obvious place to gain access to the house. He made his way to the end of the porch, placing his big boots carefully to avoid any sudden creaking of a board beneath them. He managed the distance, fifteen feet, in relative silence. He put out a hand to the old oak railing and steadied himself. He was going on pure will power, and he knew it. He should have fainted from loss of blood many minutes ago. If not that, the shock of the monstrous wound should have knocked him senseless.

Lucky boy.

He felt along the spindles supporting the rail. Several were loose; he pulled on them and found they slipped out easily. Stone hefted one of the spindles, thinking. If there was some way to sharpen the end of one of these things . . . He shook his head and set the slender, lathed rod to one side with its mates. Even with a real knife—his little penknife seemed not to count—to whittle the end of the spindle to a point, Stone doubted he had the strength—one-handed, weak from exhaustion and loss of blood—to drive the spike into Nickerson's vampire heart. The chief was wearing a bulky leather jacket, zipped to the neckline, the last time Stone saw him. There was no reason to assume that in this cold he'd pulled the zipper down to afford Stone convenient access to his soft flesh. Four of the spindles had come free altogether, creating the space Stone was needing. He hunkered down on the cold floor of the porch and slipped his legs through the gap. There were bushes around the porch, bare and skeletal, hugely overgrown without constant trimming. He twisted over onto his stomach, causing more pain as his useless left arm lolled free. He slid down between the side of the porch and the covering brambles. He crouched there, holding his breath, waiting for any sound of Nickerson's approach.

He heard it. Heavy breathing. Almost like some great animal, a huge dog or a bear. Coming up the sloping drive toward the house. Stone stared into the darkness. The moonlight was a uniform pearly glow behind the clouds, diffusing into a circular blur five times bigger than the moon would have been. The light it cast on the world below was ten times dimmer. Stone kept shifting his eyes, scanning from side to side. Shapes in darkness are seen better if they are slightly off center, he knew. He hoped this radarlike sweep would reveal . . .

There he is!

Hunched over, studying the broken ground. He looked alien, inhuman. His panting breath sounded as if he were sniffing at Stone's trail. The shadow of his arm moved against the larger darkness of his body, trailing his hand across the ground. The hand rose to his face, Stone heard a distinct sniff—no illusion at all.

Blood. I left a trail of blood all the way up here. He didn't have to see me come this way. He's been following the blood.

Stone frowned. *Then what took him so long to get here?*

As if in answer, Nickerson straightened and began limping toward the porch steps away to his right.

He's hurt. Stone did not try to suppress his grin. *He didn't walk away from that wreck unscathed after all.*

The porch steps creaked as Nickerson started up them. The chief was still following the blood. It led in a spattered line right to where Walker Stone crouched. Stone felt the urge to break cover, to run, but he knew he was too weak, too dizzy to get more than a few yards. Nickerson, limping or not, would be on top of him. He might not even bother to use his gun to finish Stone. He might be just angry enough to do it with his bare hands. The picture in Stone's mind pleased him not at all. Stone looked along the side of the house, to his left. There was no real way to get to open ground without making all kinds of racket getting out of the bushes. This brilliant hideout had become a place of entrapment.

Or had it? The porch stood four feet from the ground. Below the flooring, a foot-wide board ran around the perimeter. Beneath that, the rest of the way to the ground, a latticework of thin strips of wood fronted the sides of the porch. Within lay the dark, open underside. Stone remembered his deduction that the porch was new—newer than the house—and his mind raced. There were basement windows in the wall to his left, along the exposed side of the house. Might there be such windows under the porch? Old windows, from the days when this part of the house was open to daylight? Stone was desperate now. Nickerson was on the porch, moving surely toward him. Stone guessed he was checking each of the main-floor windows to make sure his quarry had not got into the house by any of them, leaving a faked trail of blood to mislead him.

Stone needed time. A few seconds. Anything that would put him out of Nickerson's reach, even for a moment. Under the porch he might be trapped, but he was trapped anyway, by his best reckoning. He put his back against the lattice and pushed. The dry wood snapped with a sound in his ears of a thousand firecrackers exploding in close order. He was unprepared for the sudden release. He toppled backward and discovered that the underside of the porch was excavated. He fell back and down two feet, landing hard. The back of his head cracked against the frozen ground. His teeth clacked together.

Nickerson's feet thumped on the porch above. Stone yanked his legs and feet out of the hole he'd made in the lattice and rolled into the darkness. More pain, but he didn't care anymore. He moved just in time. Nickerson's gun sounded three times; three bullets smashed through the porch floor and cracked into the hard ground where Stone had been lying. He heard Nickerson thump back along the length of the porch. As the chief reached the top of the steps something metallic clattered against the wood. He'd discarded one of his fast loaders, Stone knew as surely as if he'd watched him do it. The chambers of the big pistol were all full again.

Stone forced himself up onto his knees and crawled for the wall of the house. The way was not easy. Rotted timbers littered the ground and fragments of metal—*nails?*—dug into his knees. He reached the wall and began slapping at the facing stone, utterly blind, praying aloud for a window. He found one, a deep hole in the brick wall, with glass at the back. He pushed against the wood frame. It cracked under pressure. The glass snapped, firing blades into the darkness. Most fell inward, but one tiny sliver struck his left cheek, just below the orbit of the eye, and embedded itself there. Stone winced, ignoring that pain with all the others. He swung around, rotating on his buttocks, and kicked out the remaining fragments of window and frame. He rump-walked into the opening, feet first, and rolled over as his rear end reached the sill. Then he dropped through into the total darkness of the basement. Stone sank back against the cold flagstones of the wall. The surface was rough; uneven points poked at his back through his coat. He put out a hand and felt the texture of the floor. Rough concrete, more recent than the wall. It was cracked, probably from winter cold. There was a layering of dust and larger fragments he could not identify in the dark.

There was no sound but his own breathing, the pounding of his heart in his ears. He listened for Nickerson. Nothing. Stone wondered where he might be.

Has he gone? No. He's reloaded. He's not about to give up yet. I won't be free of his pursuit until I've killed him.

Stone was surprised by the easy way the concept crossed his brain. Walker Stone. The journalist. The pacifist. Ready to kill a man without so much as a second thought. If he only had the means. He leaned his head back against the wall. For the moment, the flow of hot, red blood from his shattered shoulder seemed to have stopped. He considered trying to shift the useless arm and slide the hand into his pocket to create a rough sling effect. It would keep the arm from swinging freely, as it had done while he ran, but it would also mean moving it. That would surely start the blood flowing again. Stone closed his eyes for a moment—dangerous, he knew, close as he was to lapsing into unconsciousness—and tried without success to make some sense out of the last hour and a half. Something creaked on the other side of the basement. Pale moonlight, very bright after total darkness, painted a widening rectangle across the floor. There must be a storm cellar door—open—there! Stone blinked automatically at the light. He saw the basement was a single huge, stone-walled room, broken only by thick trunks of old trees sawed into equal lengths, set vertically to support the floor above. There was a big, blockish furnace to Stone's left, and standing next to it a water heater, its pipes brown with rust.

A shadow moved across the rectangle of light. Yes, Nickerson had opened the storm cellar door. The illumination was not nearly so bright now as Stone's eyes adjusted to it, but he could still make out forms and distances in the basement. Wooden steps creaked as Nickerson began his cumbersome descent into the basement. Stone scanned the floor, the walls near him, searching for something he could use as a weapon. A pair of garden shears would have been welcome. Or a rake. A shovel. There was nothing. Nickerson was almost down the stairs. Stone's heart froze. No . . . It couldn't be . . . Could it? He'd thought of it once, and dismissed it . . . But it was all he had. His only chance, infinitesimal as it might be. Nickerson was at the bottom of the steps, breathing heavily. His head was shifting slowly side to side. Stone guessed Nickerson could not see him, thirty feet away on the other side of the basement. The light on the floor, pale as it was, would make his cloaking shadows that much darker. If Stone moved at all in this preternatural silence, it would tell Nickerson where he was, and Nickerson would act on that knowledge. But there was no choice. Not now.

Stone tensed his legs and pushed himself up the basement wall until he was standing. At the same time he groped under his coat for the pocket of his shirt, his left hand seeking the left breast pocket. He felt his heart rise as he touched the hard elliptical shape of the penknife under the cloth. He twisted his fingers inside the pocket and got two of them around the knife. He drew back, closing his fist around it just as Nickerson plowed into him. The old man came at him like a football tackle, slamming his free hand up under Stone, pressing in with his full weight. The wind whistled out of Stone's lungs. Bright stars burst inside his eyes. As a unit he and Nickerson toppled and crashed to the dusty basement floor. Nickerson kept his weight on top. He outmassed Stone by at least fifty pounds. His arms swung and the big gun struck against Stone. It caught the elbow of his good arm, and Stone's fist almost opened. Somehow he kept hold of the knife. He twisted around so that Nickerson would not see what he was doing and pulled open the short blade with his teeth. It felt so small against his lips. So ineffectual. He used it anyway, slashing across his arm, aiming for Nickerson's wrist, the bare skin above the cuff of his jacket. He connected, felt the knife bite, heard Nickerson's cry. The revolver clattered on the cold stone beneath them. Stone swung again, away from Nickerson. Sparks shot from the concrete where the knife blade scraped, but the back of his hand hit the gun as he'd hoped. It spun across the floor and vanished into the shadows under the basement steps.

Nickerson closed his short fingers around the back of Stone's neck, grinding his face into the rough, broken floor. Stone twisted under Nickerson's weight and struck out again with the knife, back up and over his shoulder, aiming for where he thought Nickerson's head would be. He hit something. A glancing blow, but it almost pulled the penknife out of his grip. Nickerson yowled. Stone stabbed again. And again and again.

Nickerson swung at him, but Stone rolled back at the same time. Stone was out from under him. The world was whirling, spinning down into his feet. He lunged, driving the little blade in a hard backswing, and felt heat and wet against his hand. The blade sank into Nickerson's throat just below the right ear. Stone pulled back and down, hoping to slit the throat. The angle was wrong. The back of the blade was facing the way he was pulling. It began to fold closed again. Stone felt the cutting edge bite into the flesh of his little finger. Nickerson tried to pull away, and his motion straightened the blade. Stone pushed forward. Again the knife almost came out of his hand. He pushed again, and his balance shifted. He realized he was going to fall sideways, Nickerson on top of him once more. The knife stayed in Nickerson's flesh. It cut with the efficiency of a scalpel if not the finesse. Stone felt the hard line of Nickerson's jawbone against the back of his hand and recognized the loose flap of wet flesh he felt over his fingers as Nickerson's ear, cut loose by the path the little blade scored under the chief's chin. He'd had to keep the short blade sharp, to keep it fine enough to manipulate those tiny screws in his glasses. With his last ounce of strength Stone pushed hard into the bundled ganglia under the place Nickerson's ear should have been.

10

Mae Faber absolutely could not understand what was happening to her. It was a nightmare. A terrible, terrible dream from which she could find no awakening. What was the matter with these people? With Ben? With Pete Hay? With all the police force of Faulkner? It was as if, overnight, something had transformed them from the friendly young men —and women—she'd known for years into insane storm troopers.

It was not as if she'd done anything—*anything!*—deserving the kind of treatment she'd received since Pete Hay had shown up at Ben's door. Pete had been very stiff and formal, as if he was someone other than the snotty brat Mae used to baby-sit years and years ago. As if the shiny badge on his dark blue winter jacket transformed him into someone who was actually as important as he seemed to think he was.

She could not stop thinking about the way Pete Hay had treated her. So rude, she thought. So cruel and harsh. And when he'd called in that policewoman and ordered Mae to strip . . . !

Mae shuddered. She was dressed again, but her clothes felt wrong, soiled. They seemed to crawl on her like living things, slimy, despicable. As Mae stood naked and shivering in the little back room into which she'd been led, the policewoman felt through each article of her clothing as if seeking hidden

pockets or concealed devices. Then the policewoman had gone
to the door and opened it wide, stepping out a pace to address
Pete Hay, just beyond. Pete stared at Mae, at her nakedness.
Once, she well knew, she would have cowered, turned her
back, tried as best she could to cover herself behind her small,
small hands. Now that seemed unimportant. There was nothing wrong with her body. Ben said so and proved it by his
actions. Mae stood with her feet slightly apart, her left leg bent,
her hips cocked a little, and stared back at Pete Hay, her face
saying, "What in the world are you looking at?"

Pete reddened and looked away.

"Her clothes are clean," the policewoman had said to Hay.
She was short and broad shouldered. She had large hands, Mae
observed, with bitten fingernails.

"Not just the clothes," Mae heard Pete say. She heard anger
in his voice that made absolutely no sense. "Check her."

The woman had balked. "You can't mean . . . What in hell
do you think she'd be hiding?" She'd closed the door behind
her. Mae forgot all about Pete Hay and his staring. She leaned
back on the edge of the heavy old wooden table that left no
space for other furniture in the room. She wondered about
getting dressed again—her clothes lay on the tabletop—but it
did not hold her thoughts for long. She could wait until the
woman officer came back and told her to dress. Her thoughts
had drifted, Paul Trayne at the center of them. Every time she
turned her mind one way, it would immediately find its way
back to Paul. It felt good to have such a solid center in her life,
especially now that Ben Carpenter had deserted her. She
thought that might be something important, the way Ben had
been so disinterested in her fate. The way he'd argued with
Pete Hay about accompanying them down to the station. But
like everything else, Mae could not find a reason to be particularly upset about Ben or his actions. She was perfectly content
to lean, naked, alone, against the table in the small room. She
heard raised voices beyond the door; it opened, and the policewoman came back in. She carried a pen-size flashlight in her
right hand and a pair of rubber gloves in her left. She looked
very angry, Mae thought. It seemed such an alien expression to
find its way onto a person's face.

"Turn around," the woman said. "Put your hands on the table. Move your feet apart."

Mae saw instantly the position that would put her in. Now the flashlight made sense. She frowned, not in distress, particularly, but in a vague sense of wonder. "Why? I'm not hiding anything."

The woman scowled. "Do it, or I'll have one of the other officers come in and hold you."

Mae took the ordered position.

"Further apart," the woman barked, and as Mae shifted, the woman actually pushed against the inside of Mae's calves with her foot.

"Wider." There was the elastic snap of a rubber glove being pulled into place.

In her cell, twelve hours after that moment, Mae was still completely unable to understand what it had all been about. Her mother was dead—that much she understood—and Pete Hay seemed in some way to blame Mae for the death. Mae thought about that and decided he was probably right. As she'd said when Pete came to the door of Ben's apartment, it had been some time since she'd looked in on Edna. But what difference could that possibly make? Her mother was dead. That did not mean she loved her any less. How could she? The gift of Paul Trayne made it impossible for Mae Faber to feel anything but peace and tranquillity. It was most welcome after the frustration Mae had experienced on her return home the night of her first meeting with Paul. She'd tried to tell her mother how she felt. Edna Faber was nearly eighty and never strayed beyond her bed in the little room Mae had fashioned for her out of an alcove off the living room of her small apartment. She lay in bed, growing thinner each day, fading from a world she could no longer understand or tolerate.

Mae Ellen remembered coming home from the Miracle Show and tapping lightly on the painted wood trim that edged the mouth of the alcove. Behind the heavy curtains across the opening she'd heard her mother stir and say "Yes?" It occurred to Mae Ellen then that it had been more than a year, perhaps as many as two, since her mother had called her by name or used any old endearments. Mae Ellen might as well have been a hired nurse, and not a very popular one at that. As she'd pushed aside the curtain and stepped into her mother's "room" that Monday night, Mae realized she was no longer bothered by it. She loved her mother, and knew she always would. Her feelings about the poor, sick old lady were basically unaltered.

But Paul Trayne had taken all the pain away. She would not have expressed her feelings as "I'm happy." Like so many people burdened with constant, daily misery, Mae Ellen had survived nineteen years of her mother's incapacity by a constant and conscious denial of unhappiness. And if Edna Faber had done nothing else in Mae Ellen's thirty-eight years, she'd instilled in her the conviction that a child's duty was to its parent, that devoting half one's life to the care of an invalid mother was no more than due payment for services rendered through infancy, childhood, and beyond. Mae Ellen was still aware of the bitterness bristling around her feelings for her mother, particularly nasty thorns upon an otherwise splendid rose bush, but as she looked at her mother's tiny, withered face, she felt none of the old longings for the life denied her.

"You look different," Edna said.

"I want to tell you about something, Mother." Mae put out a hand to cover the spindly sack of finger bones lying on the coverlet at her mother's side. "Something that happened tonight." Mae stopped. She realized with a sudden piquant sensation that she could not describe what had happened to her. It was not simply that she was unable to say to the woman who'd raised her, "Mother, I don't begrudge you this care anymore. Mother, I don't sometimes hate you anymore." It was that there were no words in her experience, perhaps in any human experience, she'd thought, that could describe the lifting, the freeing of her soul. The beautiful boy was a vessel, the kindly faced Reverend Trayne had told the twenty or so citizens of Faulkner gathered in the big tent. "Come pour your sadness into him."

"He hath borne our griefs . . ." Mae Ellen thought.

She tried the simplest approach. She described, one by one, the events of the hours before. How she'd stood before the boy. How standing on the low stage he'd smiled at her, his smooth, perfect face just above hers. She'd had to tip her head back just a bit to meet his open, honest gaze.

He'd said, "What is your needing, Sister?"

She had not understood his use of the word, but before she could say anything she felt a sensation rising through her that was totally unlike anything she'd ever experienced. Her knees went weak; if the Reverend Trayne had not stepped quickly from his place at the side of the stage, she might have folded like a rag doll onto the flattened grasses beneath her feet. Trayne supported her, helped her walk to his own chair by the side of the stage. The tent had buzzed around her. Others had risen from their seats. Mae Ellen looked into the faces of those in the row nearest to her. She saw them no longer as faces of people she'd known all her life, people whose words and actions had left their marks on her. She saw them not as classmates who'd teased her, pretty girls who'd mocked her plain, ordinary looks. Not as boys who'd tricked her and, as her mother's illness consumed and finally dominated her life, shunned her.

They were new to her. Not strangers. She knew each by sight, many by name. Knew the place of each one in the community. But she saw them now reborn. The injuries, great or small, layered on Mae Ellen Faber's vulnerable mind dissolved; she could begin anew, taking each one as he came to her, bearing no grudges, remembering no past offenses.

No, that's not right, Mae had thought, as she sat at her mother's bedside, seeking words to describe what had happened.

She had not forgotten what these people might have done to her, what she might have done to herself for fear of what they might do. But it no longer seemed important. She could summon from the well of memory each detail of ancient hurt; she could turn it in her slender hands, but there was no longer any feeling attached to it.

On that Monday night, home from the Miracle Show, wanting desperately to tell her mother what had happened, Mae Ellen could not find the words that would open up for Edna the true miracle of it all. She'd pressed her mother's hand, risen, and leaned over to kiss the old woman on her dry, lined forehead.

Edna frowned but said nothing. She was used to her daughter's shifting moods.

Mae then left her mother's side and crossed the living room to the small bathroom. She removed her clothes, bathed, and put on her nicest, prettiest nightdress. She stood for a little while before her dressing table mirror.

In front of the mirror, on the polished oak tabletop, stood a small oval frame containing a portrait of Marie Antoinette. Mae Ellen had clipped it from a copy of *Arts and Antiques*. For years that picture had been Mae Ellen's only conceit. She did not think of herself as a pretty woman, but Mae knew Marie Antoinette was reputed to be one of the most beautiful women of her Age. When she'd seen a charcoal sketch of the famous French queen on her way to the guillotine, she'd had seen her own face in the pinched features. The portrait on the dressing table was of Louis's queen in her full royal finery. It had pleased Mae Ellen to think she might, somehow, look like that. But since meeting Paul Trayne, she no longer needed the fantasy of the beheaded courtesan. She took the little frame from the table and placed it facedown in the bottom drawer of her dresser. That done, she smiled, climbed into bed, and slipped almost at once into the soundest sleep she'd known since childhood.

Sitting in her prison cell, Mae Ellen frowned for a moment. She had been thinking it was impossible for her to feel anything but love, yet she saw now that was not entirely true. It was more that she simply did not care, that she had lost all the anger and hatred, as Paul had promised, and in its place remained . . .

Nothing.

As Ben Carpenter observed, Pete Hay avoided responsibility whenever possible. Being Clarence Nickerson's chief deputy represented to Pete the perfect screen for wandering around Faulkner looking very proper and deputylike, but actually having nothing to do and preferring it that way. A deputy, he reasoned, was one of the few people in Faulkner who could be seen sitting behind the wheel of his car, parked at some out-of-the-way junction, hat down across his eyes and apparently dozing, without people thinking he was shirking. After all, who knew what a deputy might be doing, as part of his ever-vigilant job of guarding the community? As long as Clarence Nickerson himself did not find out, Pete knew he was reasonably safe to cruise, loaf, and generally avoid entanglement in the life and times of Faulkner.

Now he was driving his patrol car—one of the four official black-and-white police vehicles in Faulkner—up and down the silent streets, searching for some sign of Nickerson's Buick. It was too much like work. Pete would rather have been rolling about with Marcy Kavelhoff in her big, soft bed, but Nickerson had not answered his radio or his home phone, and it was hours since he'd been seen at the hospital. It was seven thirty in the morning; around Pete, Faulkner was beginning to wake and stir. He turned right onto Yeiser Street and guided the car down the quiet residential block. The houses were a mixture of lighted and dark, the morning sky still dark enough that one or two front porch lights cast a saffron glow over the white of the snow. Cars parked along both sides of the road were smoothed and rounded by a thick layer of the fluffy flakes that had begun building up just after midnight. Pete's headlights were expanding cones of swirling white. The road ahead was virgin snow, his tires the first to score their parallel tracks. Halfway down the block he passed a sexless human form, bundled up in heavy parka, scarf, and cap, sweeping the piled snow from a ten-year-old Pontiac. The figure waved as Pete passed. Pete waved back automatically, wondering who might be wrapped up in that disguise.

He turned off Yeiser onto the curve of Memorial Drive, following that to the intersection of Madelyn Avenue without sighting Nickerson's car. To Pete's right, over the low roofs of the little houses, he saw the lights of Harrison District Hospital, one block over on Grant. Ahead the sky was pink with the broad bands of the first light of day, muted by the dark mass of snow clouds that appeared to Pete to stretch well past the eastern horizon. He thought about the craziness blossoming so relentlessly all about him, the family fights, the sudden, unexpected acts of violence. The drag racing Donna had seen was only a part of the amazing disregard for life and limb—their own and anyone else's—that Pete was seeing around him.

There was the nastiness with Edna and Mae Ellen Faber, night before last. He'd been the one to answer the call after a nosy neighbor found Edna Faber's body. She was the first human corpse Pete Hay had ever seen. Her face was twisted in a nasty, pained rictus. She lay on her left side, and he'd made the mistake of pushing her over. As she settled back onto the pillow Pete turned away, but not before the purple, splotchy marks of lividity etched themselves into his mind. The way her lips fell back from teeth made big by shrunken gums . . . the way she moved as a piece, locked in rigor . . .

Then the added frustration and anger boiling up as he'd tried to deal with Mae and Ben Carpenter. It had taken Pete a while to deduce Mae's probable location, that late at night. It was after midnight when he rang the bell at Ben Carpenter's apartment. Pete rang ten times, finally leaning on the buzzer until Ben opened the door.

"Oh, it's you, Pete." The blank complacency in Ben's face astonished Pete Hay. Pete asked if Mae was there. She was. She was wearing an old bathrobe—as was Ben—and was obviously naked under it. There was a sheen of sweat on her face and bare legs Pete Hay could attribute to only one cause. He told Mae in the bluntest fashion he could that her mother was dead. The whole evening was driving him to distraction. He saw no reason to be gentle with Mae Ellen Faber.

"Oh?" No recognizable emotion appeared on May's face. "That's a pity."

Ben started to close the door. "Well, thanks for coming by, Pete . . ."

Pete blocked the door with his booted foot. "Now hold on!"

Even now, nearly eight hours later, Pete could not force the scene to make sense. He remembered how he'd reacted when he'd learned of his own mother's death six years ago. He could not believe Mae Ellen's reaction. Nor could he understand the objections from Ben Carpenter when Pete suggested he accompany Mae down to the station. Mae was under arrest, as far as Pete was concerned. He wanted Ben to answer some questions. Ben flat-out refused. It was as if the circle of events that had now enveloped his girl friend was utterly unimportant to him. As unimportant as Edna Faber's death seemed to Mae Ellen.

Pete frowned. He concluded for the fiftieth time that the roots of this madness lay in Gunner's Field and congratulated himself again for having forbidden Marcy to take her kids to see Paul Trayne. Pete enjoyed ordering Marcy about. She'd been pretty docile by Pete's standards since that first time, some twenty months ago, when he'd gotten so angry he'd actually pulled her over his knees and paddled her broad behind with the flat of his hand. Not exactly modern twentieth-century theory at work there, Pete thought, smiling at the memory, but it seemed to him that Marcy actually enjoyed it. The procedure had been repeated four times since. Pete suggested she stay away from Paul Trayne in a manner that he felt sure would make her understand the degree of ire she would risk if she went. Pete smiled as he turned the patrol car back onto Lafayette toward the underpass and Black Rock Highway beyond. He'd had quite enough of this search for Nickerson, thank you. What he wanted now was that big bed and Marcy. She'd have got her two kids off to school by now, he knew. They'd have the old house completely to themselves.

Pete gunned the car onto the highway. His mind was so focused on thoughts of lush, soft Marcy Kavelhoff that he almost failed to see the odd light behind the grasses of Gunner's Field.

Clay Garber arrived in his office at twenty minutes after nine on the morning of Thursday, the thirteenth of February. Thirty-three days had gone by since Paul Trayne's Miracle Show first appeared near Faulkner. Only three since Donna Wojciechowski began to lose her soul to Paul Trayne. Clay left his car and crossed the parking structure to the elevator without seeing anyone. He rose in silence to the third floor, his mind still full of the memory of that morning, in his big bed with Marjorie after Paul Trayne left.

They had made love. For the first time in eight years, limbs bent and locked around each other, seeking the half-forgotten formations. At first it had been strange; memories of their last night together as a fully active married couple collided with the reality of the present. Clay was eight years older. Marjorie was eight years older. Her flesh still felt like velvet to his touch, but things were . . . different. She was heavier. Thighs fuller, belly rounder. His own girth was greater. It was very much like making love for the first time. Testing, experimenting. *Is this motion all right? Does this bring pleasure? Pain?*

They explored each other, pathfinders seeking new trails through virgin wilderness. As they searched they found familiar landmarks in their mutual sensuality. *Yes, this is something she always liked. This place has a special sensitivity.*

Smiling, Clay left the elevator and walked the length of the corridor that was the last area of free movement for the people of Chicago who came seeking city officials. Beyond these tall, heavy doors lay the reception offices, and beyond that no man or woman passed without first undergoing the most minute scrutiny by the squadron of efficient secretaries who waited within, incorruptible bulkheads between the masses and their bosses. Clay stepped through the outer door to his own office. He hung his hat and coat on the old brass hat rack Marjorie had found in a consignment shop in Skokie and paused by his secretary's desk. Sally Pini smiled up into her boss's face with eyes bright and beaming. As if, Clay thought, she sensed something different, something changed in his life. Luckily, she was sensitive enough to realize the change was not something he was interested in discussing.

"No messages yet, Commissioner," she said. "Looking to be a quiet day."

She sorted a loose sheaf of papers into a neat stack with her tiny, short-fingered hands. Mother Nature had dealt Sally Pini an unfair hand. Her round, pretty head sat atop a squashed and stunted body barely three feet tall. Her short legs bowed in a manner that always looked to Clay to be excruciatingly painful. Her arms were barely long enough to bring her fingertips together across her bosom. Nevertheless, she was the most ruthlessly efficient executive assistant Clay Garber had ever had.

"See if Hizzoner is in yet, would you, Sal?" he asked.

She nodded, and he passed her desk and went into his office. He shut the thick walnut door behind him and crossed to his desk. Through the windows behind the desk he looked out on the southern half of Chicago. To his right, rising dark and hard against the clear blue sky loomed the extraordinary stepped obelisk of the building all Chicago still called the Sears Tower. To his left, obscured by the cluster of buildings spread before him, lay Grant Park, the Art Institute, the glorious Buckingham Fountain. Beyond, the Lake. Clay seated himself in the big chair behind his desk and reached for the telephone. For a moment his eyes lingered on the little plaque set beyond the phone. In slender script on a square brass plate were the words of Rudyard Kipling: I HAVE STRUCK A CITY . . . A REAL CITY . . . AND THEY CALL IT CHICAGO. THE OTHER PLACES DO NOT COUNT.

Once Clay dreamed of seeing that plaque sitting on the mayor's desk. Now he wondered if there would be a place for it in the governor's house, in Springfield. Donna Wojciechowski had been right in her assessment. To a man like Clayton Garber, the office of police commissioner was just one more step. The top of the ladder lay . . . even Garber was not sure. The world was changing. Who knew what doors might be opening?

The door of his office opened. "He's in," Sally Pini said. Her head was just higher than the knob of the door.

"Thanks, Sal." Clay rose and crossed to the side door of his office. It opened into the private corridor that ran behind all the offices on this floor. The "underground railway," some called it. It ended at an elevator that rose to a small foyer outside the back door of the mayor's office. Clay walked along the plush carpet, feeling safe and secure in the muted lighting, as he always did. He pushed the elevator button and waited for it to come. It took only a few seconds, then he was inside and rising toward the mayor's office. He stepped out and nodded to the uniformed officer who sat behind the small desk adjacent to the mayor's secret door.

"He's expecting me," Garber said.

"Yessir, Commissioner." The officer rose and tapped lightly at the mayor's door. Emmanuel Stuartson opened it from within.

"Clay." Stuartson nodded. "Only got a couple of minutes before I have to go beard the zoning pashas in their den." He stood aside, waving a hand for Clay to enter. Clay stepped past his old friend and longtime political ally. He was immediately aware of how much his bulk diminished the room. It was not a small room by any means, but Stuartson crammed it with over-sized, overstuffed furnishings, quite at odds with his own narrow frame.

"Couple of minutes is all I need," Clay said. "This is only slightly official, at the moment."

"Yes? How's Marjorie, by the way?" Stuartson never missed a chance to inquire after Garber's wife.

"She's fine. She's always fine." Mannie Stuartson was the one man in all Chicago with whom Garber might share the intimate secrets of that morning, but he did not. He'd not told Stuartson about the situation as it existed between Marjorie and himself; he was not about to tell him of the change. He dropped into one of the big chairs in front of the mayor's desk. Stuartson pushed a flat, unadorned box of Havana cigars across his desk top. Clay took one, snipped the end with the offered clippers, and accepted a light from Stuartson's ornate desk lighter. The room began to fill with the rich smoke.

"There's someone I'd like you to meet," Commissioner Garber said.

There were moments of crystalline clarity. Moments when Donna seemed to remember who she was, what she once believed in. Moments when she wondered how much despair a human soul could endure before death came. But in those moments she realized there would be no release in death. No escape from the agonies that tore at her soul, that made her scream and sob until there was no breath left in her body. All the while there was Paul. Paul who had become the center of her universe, who could undo her pain with a word, a touch, when his father commanded.

"You must serve us in all ways," Trayne had said, in one of the moments when he allowed Paul to return the joy his gift brought her, and the world reshaped itself into a more familiar form.

"Serve, if you hope to keep the peace the boy brings." His smile was a hideous thing on the face so like the beloved President Lincoln. Not a smile that belonged on such a face.

"Yes," Donna said around her sobs, and in that moment the tranquillity returned. She clung to it, drew on it as she once had—still did—strong drink.

I've become a machine, she thought. The voice was distant, not entirely her own. *I've become a robot, marching to the orders of this man, this monster. I'm not Donna anymore. Not the Donna I was before Faulkner.*

Paul and Robert Trayne were not there. She was alone. She did not know when they'd left her. She was in her apartment, she thought, though her mind was still drifting, still floating in the serenity Paul had left with her. She wondered, for a moment, what Walker Stone would have thought of her in this state. It was so much worse—yet how could she think of it as worse?—than anything the booze had ever done to her.

Walker. She remembered the tone she'd heard in his voice that night so many lifetimes gone, when she'd called him. *I miss you, Walker. I wish I could have died instead of you. I need you here. I need you to yell at me. To make me face myself and not be such a helpless little robot.*

She tried to form the image of Walker Stone more clearly in her mind, make him real. Make the shape and substance of Walker Stone complete and true within the framework of her imagination. She very nearly succeeded. It helped her if she concentrated on their more physical intimacies. Then she could almost feel his skin beneath her fingertips. The way his beard sometimes tickled when he kissed her. The way his moustache spiked her upper lip when he trimmed it too close. The way the hairs went up her nose if he left it too long. She summoned all the details of Walker Stone. The sounds of him. The smells. The tastes. She delved into her memory and brought out each detail of the Christmas Eve when he'd brought her to her first true orgasm, and she'd hated him for it.

She did not hate him now. She loved him. She loved Walker Stone with a special part of her heart, very small and vulnerable. A dwindling part, that would not last too long against the pains inflicted on it by Paul Trayne.

The rest of her heart was Paul's. The rest of her loved Paul Trayne and longed for the touch of his small, soft hand. It was her only oasis from the pain, the piercing anguish Trayne could compel the boy to bring to her with a word, a gesture. She craved the sweet, consuming peace that came afterward, as he allowed her to experience again the serenity his son's gift first delivered to her. More and more she recognized it as an addictive sensation, as she knew booze to be, as she imagined drugs were. All the pains flowed away, leaving only a cool and beautiful place in which she floated, free and happy, until the agony began again. Each time it began again the subsequent peace was better, sweeter, so that she found herself longing for the pain because of the joy that followed. Yet hating the joy. Hating the freedom. Hating the voice that told her everything was unimportant, every old and cherished pain inconsequential.

A small part of her still longed for Walker Stone. It cried out for him to come, to save her from Paul Trayne, from herself. Each time her body writhed in agony or ecstasy, pain or pleasure, that fragment of her lost reality screamed at her to free it, embrace it, cherish it for the shriveling particle of hope and truth it was.

But in the rest of her mind a small, soft voice said, *Never mind. He's dead now, and it doesn't matter. Nothing matters. Nothing but serving Paul Trayne. Serving him in every way he wishes.*

"In every way he wishes." Donna heard her own voice say aloud. She opened her eyes and looked up. Robert Trayne was standing over her, infinitely tall, infinitely broad, a darkness that stretched across the full horizon of Donna's universe.

"You must tell me more about the way this city works," Trayne said. He reached down with his big hand and pulled Donna into a sitting position. She came to a dim awareness of being on the couch in her living room.

"How . . . ?"

"How the city works. Who the powerful men are. Who we should ask the mayor to arrange for us to see. We must not waste time, as in Faulkner." His eyes burned. Wrong in the Lincoln face. Wrong. Wrong.

"Must not waste time," Donna parroted.

"We must spread the power from the top down this time," Trayne said. "We must begin with the most corrupt. Those who have sold their souls to worldly power. We will purge this city from the halls of its government. We will loose the light which Satan stole. The light that festers in the souls of men."

"Release the light," Donna said, understanding nothing.

"And you must help."

"I must help."

Clarence Nickerson was lying atop Walker Stone, his body stiffening with rigor mortis. His dried blood mingled with Stone's in the stains spattered across the filthy floor of the cellar, in the mangled remains of Stone's shoulder. Inside Stone's body natural defenses rallied as best they could against this alien intruder, white blood cells already on the site of the wound attacking the foreign cells of Nickerson's blood. It was close to a losing battle. Stone was as near to death as any human being could get without actually crossing the line. His breathing was virtually nonexistent. Stone's head was tipped back, the skin at his throat purple. Nickerson's big, bare hands lay to either side of his neck, where they had dropped when the life finally oozed out of Nickerson's body.

Stone's clumsy incision had severed the chief's jugular, that big, thick vein through which so much of the body's life flows on its return journey to the heart. Nickerson's blood had splashed over Stone, choking him, blinding him. As Nickerson flailed in panic, his big hands had found Stone's throat and closed about it. The right hand had not been functioning well at that point, the wrist slashed and bleeding heavily. But Nickerson had pushed down and in with the left, with sufficient force to crush Stone's larynx before dying. Now the only sound in the darkness was the tiny rasp of air as it made its way past Stone's broken airway, drawing in and out to the slow, uneven rhythm of his lungs.

If Stone could have somehow absented himself from his body at that point and stood to one side as an impartial spirit observer, he would have given himself no chance of survival beyond the next half hour or so, and that was a generous esti-mate. He'd lost too much blood, pushed himself far, far beyond the body's natural tolerances. The weight of Nickerson's empty husk made breathing almost impossible, even without the partially crushed throat. Since Stone could not remove himself from his broken shell of flesh, he was no more able to make this phantom assessment than he was able to see the sun rising beyond the rectangle of the open basement door, see the shadow that filled that lighted space, or hear the creak of the old boards in the basement steps as Pete Hay made his way down into the basement.

Pete blinked as he came down, his eyes adjusting slowly to the black oblivion of the basement. The first thing he saw looked for all the world like old Clarence Nickerson humping someone on the cold stone floor. Then Pete saw the pool of blood and took an involuntary step away. The back of his calf hit the bottom step and he lost his balance, sat down hard. Tears welled up in his eyes and the blurring effect almost made it seem as if Nickerson really was moving, really was having sexual intercourse with the body beneath him. Pete belched, bent over, and added the Faulkner Diner's Early-Riser Breakfast Special to the variety of liquids drying on the basement floor.

Ben Carpenter heard the banshee wail of sirens down Lafayette Street and looked at his watch. It was just coming up on eight in the morning. Outside the tall windows of the *Observer* offices a bleak, gray day was lying low over Faulkner. He leaned forward on the sofa, pushing aside the slats of the venetian blind. A police car and an ambulance squealed past, heading up Lafayette toward Black Rock. Ben let the venetian blinds drop back over the window. He looked around the office. At first glance it appeared every surface was strewn with Chinese takeout cartons. Ben burped at the memory of the feeding frenzy that had seized him the night before. Without Mae Ellen to go home to he'd stayed late at the office—the *Observer* was still his mistress, after all—and when the hour got late and he'd had no dinner . . .

He rose, stretched, scratched, and crossed to the small office toilet. He emptied his bladder and splashed some cold water on his face. He wondered what it might be that sent the cars screeching by at such an early hour. They were headed north.

Toward Gunner's field? That was the only interest he could summon, a concern that this might be something to do with Paul. *If Paul is in some kind of trouble, some kind of danger . . .*

He crossed to the office door, grabbing his jacket and coat along the way, and hurried down to the street. He retrieved his car from the lot and drove the four blocks to the police station. He pushed in through the front doors, and found the outer offices deserted. He crossed to Nickerson's desk, calling out:

"Clarence? Pete? Anybody?"

There was the sound of a flushing toilet from around the corner. A few moments later Arnie Steadman rolled into view. Steadman was the police dispatcher, a coarse-faced man with wiry brown hair and legs that had been sliced off above the knee by a Vietcong booby trap.

"Oh, Mr. Carpenter, it's you. What can I do for you, sir?"

"I saw the cars and the ambulance heading up Lafayette," Ben said. "I wondered . . . Is it something out at Gunner's Field? Paul . . . ?"

"Oh, no. Nothing about him." Steadman debated for a moment telling Ben of Pete Hay's discovery, but Pete had cautioned silence in a tone that made Steadman think it best to obey. He opted for something Pete had not specifically forbidden him to talk about. "Say, did you hear about the body in th' Dumpster over by Keene's Hardware?"

"No." Ben's tone was indifferent. He felt a passing surprise that something like that could have happened almost under his nose, across the street from the *Observer,* without his knowing about it, but it did not stay with him. He was feeling a strong need now to go out to Gunner's Field and make sure everything was all right with Paul.

"Damndest thing," Steadman said. He described the find in graphic and embroidered detail. "Near as anyone could tell, it was what was left of Ollie Twine. Seems like somebody'd carved him up. Like you'd carve a spring buck."

"Huh," said Ben Carpenter, thoroughly disinterested. "I'm

. . . going out for a while. If Pete gets back before I do, tell him I've gone out to Gunner's Field."

"Maybe you shouldn't do that, Mr. Carpenter . . ."

"Oh? Why?"

Steadman groped for a way to keep Ben away from Gunner's Field without telling him what Pete had found in the cellar of the old Tempest place. If Ben went out to the field he would see the cars and the ambulance . . . Steadman opted for the closest he could come to the truth: "The Traynes are gone."

Ben felt his feet begin to sink into a floor gone soft beneath them. "Gone . . ."

"Yeah. Pete discovered it." That was too close to the truth. Steadman summoned up a reason for Pete to be out by Gunner's Field so early in the day. A reason more accurate than Steadman knew. "Guess he was on his way out t'see Marcy, huh?"

Ben's mind was whirling. An anchor had been taken from his life; he was adrift in a hostile cosmos. He slapped the pockets of his jacket, searching for his car keys.

"I . . . I think I'll go out there anyway," he said.

"Er . . . you sure you don't want to look in on Miss Faber, long as you're here? She's . . ."

But Ben was already heading for the door, and Steadman knew from experience there was no way he could stop a man once he reached the steps in front of the courthouse.

"Hello, Donna. Clay Garber."

"Commissioner, hi. What's the good word?"

"I've made an appointment for you with Stuartson. Next Tuesday, the twenty-first."

"That's too long to wait. Can't we see him today?"

"I'm afraid that's out of the question. He's booked solid, today and all this week."

"But we have to see him. Today. Tomorrow at the latest."

"Surely there's no rush, Donna. I mean, Paul isn't on some kind of time limit, is he?"

"You don't understand. It hurts him when people are in distress. When they're being all chewed up by their grief. Hurts him physically. And in a city the size of Chicago, he's picking up all kinds of things out of the air. All kinds of grief and guilt and pain."

"That's . . . very touching, Donna. But I'm afraid it won't have any effect on the mayor's schedule. He's booked until next Tuesday. And I'm afraid that's pretty much the end of the discussion."

"No. It can't be. There must be something you can do, Clay. There must be."

"Donna, I have done all I can."

"I can't believe that. You're his friend. Did you explain it to him? How important this is?"

"I told him what Paul can do, and what Paul wants to do."

"You told him what Paul did for your wife? For your staff?"

"Yes. Everything. I was . . . most eloquent, if I do say so myself. Almost as if I was speaking from a prepared speech."

"Then he must see Paul. Today. Tomorrow at the latest."

"Tuesday, Donna. At ten. That's the best I can do. Now . . ."

"No. No, wait. Please, Clay. You've got to help me. If I go to Trayne and tell him this . . ."

"Yes?"

"No. Never mind. Look, please. You've got to do more."

"I can't. Now please, Donna . . ."

"A cancellation. Suppose there was a cancellation in the mayor's appointments."

"That seems highly unlikely."

"But suppose there was. If there was a cancellation, for tomorrow, would he see us? Would you make sure he sees us?"

"Yes. I could do that. But you're building castles in the air, Donna. Everyone who wants to see the mayor has been waiting weeks themselves to do it. You're fortunate to be able to see him this soon."

"But if there's a cancellation you'll make sure he sees us then. You'll make sure."

"Yes, yes. But don't count on it, Donna. Now, I really must go."

* * *

"Nothing we can do for Clarence," Dr. Zeldenrust said, kneeling by the tangled bodies of Stone and Clarence Nickerson. "Somebody help me get him off from this man."

To Pete Hay's right a flash burst like bright lightning in the dark cellar. Shadows like black holes sprang up and just as quickly vanished as the police photographer captured the details of the grisly scene. He was the staff photographer from the *Register,* like so many professionals in Faulkner, doing double duty. The nearer of the two paramedics who'd come with Dr. Zeldenrust stepped forward and began pulling Nickerson's corpse away. As it rolled onto its back, the wound in its neck gaped, a second mouth. A mouth smeared, it appeared to the young para, with an injudicious application of lip rouge.

Dr. Zeldenrust brought his ear down close to Stone's mouth and listened for a moment. "I think his lungs are filling with blood," he said, guessing from the faint gurgling sound that followed the rasp of each breath. "We'd better get a move on. From the condition of the bodies he's been here quite some time."

The paramedic pulled his eyes from Nickerson's ruined throat and turned to his partner. Together they unfolded the stretcher they'd brought into the cellar of the old Tempest place. They laid it on the floor and lifted Stone onto the canvas rectangle. Bursts from the flash picked out moments of their actions. Not a few of these "official" pictures, Pete knew, would end up on the front page of the *Register* and, if the photographer could make the sale, the *Observer*.

"Gonna be a bitch getting him up them steps," said the younger of the two paramedics. The doctor scowled. This was the first time since his youth in Germany that he'd had to face this kind of calculated bloodshed; he was in no mood for additional problems, especially of what he considered an imaginary kind.

"Lash him down," he said. He stepped past to where Pete Hay crouched by Nickerson's body. Dr. Zeldenrust shook his head. "I didn't even know Stone was gone!" He made a mental note to severely chastise his night staff for leaving a patient unattended so long, especially a patient in a private room. Since Stone was not on instruments, with no fellow patients to monitor him as there would have been in a public ward, any change in his condition could have been determined only by periodic checks.

"I didn't ask how you came to find them," Dr. Zeldenrust said as Pete rose from his crouch, knees popping loudly in the basement. Pete had said no more than a dozen words since discovering Nickerson's body.

"I was looking for the chief," Pete lied. "I thought maybe I'd take a look out in Gunner's Field. As I came up I saw a funny light. I hiked over and found the chief's car overturned and wrecked. The light was from the headlights. They were still on. I would've expected the car to burn or something . . ." He shook his head, forcing his thoughts back on track. "I couldn't tell if he was inside, but there were tracks in the snow, so I followed them. When I lost 'em on the highway, I checked here 'cause this seemed like the direction they was goin'."

Dr. Zeldenrust turned away, saw that the paramedics had got Stone almost to the top of the steps. "I'd better get after them," he said. "Got a lot of work to do."

The old Tempest place was awash with whirling blue light as Ben approached. He felt just enough of a prick to his professional curiosity that he drove past Pine Tree Road and turned into the driveway of the old manse. The squad car and ambulance he'd seen from the *Observer* were pulled around back, with another car Ben recognized as Pete Hay's. Ben drove up next to the ambulance, stopped the car, and got out. He heard voices coming from the open storm doors of the basement, crossed, and started down the steps. He only got one foot over the sill. Two paramedics were halfway up with Walker Stone lashed to the stretcher between them. Ben took a step back to let them pass, then went down, almost bumping into Dr. Zeldenrust this time.

"Mr. Carpenter!" It was Pete, away to Ben's left. "What are you doing here?"

"I heard the Traynes had left," Ben said. The thought flashed across his mind that Stu Gillis, the *Observer* photographer, should be there as well as the *Register*'s man. *Never mind,* said his own voice, a whisper in his ear.

"Is that right?" he asked. "Have they left? The Traynes?"

Pete blinked. "Aren't you gonna ask what happened here?"

Ben looked down at the body of Clarence Nickerson. "Why? Is it important?"

Dr. Zeldenrust heard the total lack of interest in Ben's voice. He rose. "This is a killing, Ben. Murder."

"Really?" Ben looked around the basement, his head dodging from side to side to peer into the shadows behind the other men.

"For fuck's sake, Carpenter . . ." Pete Hay began.

Ben turned and climbed back out of the basement. A moment later Dr. Zeldenrust and Pete heard the sound of his Mazda speeding away.

They stared at each other in disbelief.

11

"I say he's lucky to be alive." Dr. Maurice Zeldenrust lowered his glasses onto his nose and looked up from the report in his hand. Stone lay in the same bed he'd so recently departed to search for Donna Wojciechowski with Clarence Nickerson. The doctor was pleased to note Stone's condition as stable. "Something of a miracle. He should have been dead hours before he was found."

Pete Hay shuddered. Long hours after pulling away from the grisly find in the cellar of the old Tempest house, his mind was still there, trapped in the shadows, hovering over the body of Clarence Nickerson. In truth, Nickerson's body had been removed at the same time as Stone's. It now lay in the morgue, awaiting autopsy, something Pete found appalling when Dr. Zeldenrust brought it up.

"You know the rules, Petey," the old doctor had said, riding back into Faulkner in Hay's patrol car. "This is a murder. I must determine the cause of death."

Pete had blinked, hot tears in his eyes. "For Chrissake, Doc! His *throat* was slit open!"

"Yes. But did that kill him? We must know." Zeldenrust sighed, staring out at the bleak sameness of the winter country-side. "It's something I never thought I'd have to do, Petey. I've known Clarence since before you were born. Never thought I'd have to . . ." He shook his head.

"Goddamn weird, Doc," Pete said. "This whole town is goin' apeshit on us."

Dr. Zeldenrust nodded, itemizing the carnage of the past two days. "Body in Dumpster. Fire. Beatings. Children and animals being tortured. Car crashes. Girl's leg in the park. I would never have thought this could happen here. Not here. In Chicago maybe. In a place that could breed a man like . . . What was the name? That killer they just had on trial?"

"Warner. Errol Keane Warner." Pete had read all the stories. He was fascinated and disgusted.

"Shouldn't happen here."

"Too much time on their hands," Pete said.

"What?"

The door behind Pete opened and a pretty young nurse came in with a small tray lined with a brilliant white cloth. The crystalline cylinder of a hypodermic glittered against the starched background. "Dr. Zeldenrust? Mrs. DeForrest said you needed a hypo administered . . . ?"

"Yah." Zeldenrust held his hand out in front of him and it trembled in midair. "I'm too damn tired to do it myself."

"Yes, sir." She crossed to the bed. Pete watched her, her trim figure and easy professional manner enough to distract him for a moment from the nightmares boiling around his skull.

But only for a moment. He tipped his head at Stone. "When's he goin' to be able to talk?"

"Not for quite some time, I should think. Days. Maybe weeks."

"That's not half good enough, Doc. He's a murder suspect." Pete stretched, joints popping loudly. By his reckoning it was going on twenty hours since he'd had any real rest, and Pete Hay was not one who liked to miss a moment of sleep.

Dr. Zeldenrust cleared his throat; stifling a yawn would be ill timed here and now. He'd spent the last few hours on preparatory postmortems, dealing with the remains of Ollie Twine, the severed leg, and the other fatalities of Faulkner's new and busy day. He frowned. "A murder suspect? Stone? You're not really going to cling to that ridiculous theory, are you, Petey? I was there, in the cellar. I saw the bodies, I saw how they were positioned. I don't think Stone was involved in some plot to kill Clarence. Quite the contrary, in fact. I think he killed in self-defense."

"Your opinion is noted, Doc," Pete said, fuming as he saw the nurse's eyebrows rise at Zeldenrust's words. It was going to be impossible to keep this under wraps for long, even assuming Arnie Steadman had not already disobeyed Pete's orders and broadcast the details of Nickerson's killing all over Faulkner. Along with the body in the Dumpster and the crudely amputated leg, it was all far too much to expect a natural gossip like Steadman to keep to himself for long, even under direct orders.

"But, I'm afraid your opinion don't mean diddly," Pete added. "Clarence wouldn't do that, kill like that. Not the Clarence Nickerson I've known all my life."

The doctor said, "I've known Clarence a long time too, Petey. But he shot Stone in the shoulder at point-blank range. You can tell that from the powder burns. How does that fit into your reading of this?"

It didn't. In fact, it stuck in Pete Hay's craw. But he was not about to let it shatter his lifetime picture of Clarence Nickerson. "The chief's gun hasn't turned up yet," he said. "My bet is Stone got it away from him. Planned to use it on the chief."

"When did Stone get shot, then? Before he got the gun from Nickerson? So he was able to grab that weapon from a man half again his size, and Stone with only one arm?"

Pete scowled at the man in the bed. Stone's right arm was held at a forty-five-degree angle from the side of his body, his shoulder swathed in bandages. Zeldenrust was still being noncommittal on whether or not the arm could be saved. Tubes snaked into the tracheotomy that restored breathing. Stone's breath was an intermittent whistle, loud in the small room. Pete tried to imagine Stone, even in the best of shape, getting that huge Sturm Ruger out of Nickerson's big, red freckled fist. The picture refused to gel.

But that has to be what happened, Pete Hay told himself, over and over. *It has to be what happened.*

But even if that particular package could be forced to remain as neat and tidy as Pete's mind needed it to be, it did not clear up any of the other insanities percolating around him.

"Son of a bitch," Pete said. "I'm gonna go see Alice Nickerson. She doesn't know yet that her father's dead."

He sighed. He was not going to be able to avoid his responsibilities now. He no longer wanted to. Not, at least, until he knew exactly what had happened in that old tent in Gunner's Field.

Knew, and had meted out such vengeance as the situation required.

Ben came back to the *Observer* late in the afternoon. Shadows were long across Lafayette, the rooftops of the buildings across the street painting a jagged line between darkness and light across the front of the *Observer* building. He paused outside the ground floor door to the newspaper office. Up and down the street it was cold and quiet. The snow had stopped, and the tracks of two or three cars weaved around each other on the road. A few people moved here and there, none close to where Ben stood. To his right a yellow ribbon of plastic stretched across the opening of the service alley next to Keene's Hardware. Dark lettering along the yellow read POLICE LINE—DO NOT CROSS, repeating and repeating until the ribbon ran out.

Not quite knowing why, since nothing held his interest now but the disappearance of Paul Trayne, Ben leaned in close to the plate glass of Keene's front window and, shading his eyes with the flat of his left hand, peered in. The store looked closed, silent, and empty. Yet there was something. Something that nibbled ever so slightly at whatever reporter's instincts remained in Ben's soul. He stepped away from the window and crossed to the front door. He tried it and found it unlocked. He pushed it open, not fully entering yet.

The plastic bird did not squawk as the door opened. Ben looked up and saw it was gone, snapped off its hanging stand, only its white feet and part of one leg remaining. Ben stepped inside, closing the door behind him. It was very warm in the store—too warm, he thought. He'd known Ralph Keene for twenty years, as long as he'd owned this store beneath the *Observer*, and in those two decades Ben had never known

Keene to allow the thermostat in his store to be set above sixty-eight degrees, even on the coldest day.

"Ralph? Trina?" Ben called.

Over the years he'd known Ralph, he'd watched Trina Keene grow up from an awkward schoolgirl, all knees and elbows, to an attractive young woman. Or one who would have been attractive, Ben thought, had she not always looked so tired. There was an indefinable tension between father and daughter—he'd seen the way Ralph looked at the boys who came round the store on the pretense of shopping for hardware needs but really to talk to Trina—and sometimes Ben wondered if it was only his small-town prudery that kept that tension undefinable. Ralph's wife, Ellen, died when Trina was six, and the little girl assumed most of the roles traditionally belonging to a wife and mother.

But not all the roles.

Ben walked farther into the darkened store. He was not prepared to think that of either Ralph or Trina, whatever veiled looks he might have seen pass between them. Ben crossed through the store to the office door in the back wall. He knocked and the door swung in from the pressure of his first tap. He pushed it farther, and it swung back until it stopped against something lying on the other side, on the floor.

Ralph was sitting behind the desk, head slumped forward, lower lip vibrating in a rubbery way that made Ben's own lip curl. Ralph was asleep and snoring, but he made no sound. He looked a mess, his usually plastered-down hair disheveled, his shirt rumpled and stained. Ben looked around the door. It was Trina. She was sitting on the floor, braced against the boxes stacked against the left wall. She was naked, and her slow and steady breathing indicated that she too was asleep. Her hair was also matted and askew. Dust from the floor adhered to her arms and legs, the top of her chest. Ben frowned and put out a hand to touch her cheek.

"Get your goddamn hands off of her!"

Ben turned. Ralph Keene was awake and on his feet. Ben's brain balked at the image it was receiving. Keene was not wearing any pants. His naked flesh was pale and pasty, spotted with fine black hairs like wire against his flabby thighs. His exposed genitals were dark red-brown against the whiteness of the rest of his flesh. Ben straightened up, away from Trina. "Ralph . . . ? What the hell . . . ?"

He did not have the opportunity to finish his query. Ralph grabbed one of the packing cartons from the top of his desk and hurled it. Ben ducked to one side, and the box exploded against the wall behind him, spilling hundreds of mismatched screws across the floor. Some landed on Trina, lodging in her hair and the cleft of her thighs. They made strange little *tok-tok-tok* sounds as they bounced off the top of her head.

"Get *away* from her!" Keene grabbed another box and raised it for the throw. "She's mine! Mine!"

Ben danced back through the office door and pulled it shut behind him. The box smashed against the inside of the door, cracking the thin two-ply and buckling the door outward. Ben staggered back three paces and came up against a freestanding steel shelving unit loaded with boxes of light switches and coils of insulated wiring. The shelf unit wobbled under Ben's collision and started to topple backward. Ben broke around the falling shelf and bolted for the front door. He allowed himself one glance over his shoulder as the shelf crashed into the next, the domino effect toppling half the shelves in the store.

The office door was still closed. As he reached the front door, Ben paused. He could not hear anything from the little room in the back. He pulled the front door open and stepped back into the cold street. As he did something crunched under his feet. It was the plastic bird from above the door. It emitted a feeble croak, a poor imitation of its trilling, as it broke under Ben's foot.

Ben left the door to swing shut and hurried to the *Observer* entrance. He stepped through, twisting the deadbolt lock behind him. On impulse he ran down the narrow hall to the right of the stairs and turned the lock in the back door, even though that was almost always left open. He returned to the front and pounded up the stairs. He entered the *Observer* office and forgot what he'd seen downstairs.

Donna watched the gray afternoon surrender swiftly to twilight, the sky blackening above the city to the east. She watched the lights come on in the little houses crouched around her apartment complex, in the windows of the apartments in the twin tower across the way. It was Thursday evening, she told herself. Tomorrow was Friday, Valentine's Day. All around her the people of Des Plaines, the people of Chicago, Illinois, and the world were going about their daily lives, knowing only that it was a Thursday much like any other Thursday, with a light snow falling outside, the regular Thursday prime-time lineup beginning in a few hours on TV.

Thinking of television made her think of Walker Stone. Immediately the voice in her head said, *Never mind,* but as she stood before her picture window, looking out over the darkening town, Donna's eyebrows drew close above her nose and she tried to push aside the voice, the message, the gift of Paul Trayne.

She *wanted* to think about Walker. She wanted the pain his memory brought. She did not know why. There had been more than enough pain in the past few hours. There would be more, if she could not dissuade Trayne from his plans for later that evening.

It's murder. Plain and simple. Murder. No way to talk around it, no way to justify it.

The voice tried instantly to disagree: *It is for Paul; all things are justified when they are for Paul.*

Donna shook her head, a movement too fine for any human eye to detect. At that moment there were no eyes to see. *No, that's Trayne's logic. It's murder. Cold-blooded. Premeditated. An innocent life ended to push forward a plan . . .*

She thought about the plan, Trayne's plan. Trayne's Plan. She was an integral part of it, yet did not understand it. She did not understand why some people—Clarence Nickerson for instance—could be enthralled, possessed, turned into puppets of Robert Trayne, yet others—the people of Faulkner, Garber's staff—must act of their own free will, must come to Paul, unburden themselves, pour their pain and grief and guilt into him willingly, by their own choice.

"Have I not said it is not really necessary that you understand?" Trayne had said, not more than an hour ago, as Donna found herself in sufficient possession of her faculties to ask the question once again. Oddly, masochistically, she thought, the times with Paul and his father seemed worst when the gift made everything seem good, sweet, and wonderful.

"But surely I can serve you better if I understand . . ."

"You serve me well enough as it is," Trayne said. "If you understood the fullness of the plan, it might only confuse you. It is enough that you know the people must come of their own free will, by their own choice."

"Like Clay Garber?" Donna felt emboldened. The ghost of Walker Stone stood by her side, egging her on.

Trayne frowned. "Garber has strengths. You did not warn me of them." He seized Donna's chin in his big hand. The tips of his fingers bit into her cheeks—they were steel talons now instead of fingernails.

"Strengths? I didn't know . . ." It was a lie, but Donna found the lie came more easily than she might have expected.

"No." Trayne released his grip on her face. "I suppose you did not. In this you failed me. Failed Paul." He might as well have raised her from the ground and impaled her on a steel spike. Donna felt his words go through her heart, through the center of her being.

"No . . ."

"Yes. In this you have failed us—although there were others in that house I will find use for, I expect." Trayne stepped away from her. He opened the curtains over her broad living room windows. Donna saw the afternoon light over Des Plaines. She'd lost all track of time in the darkness. She thought as much as a week might have passed since last she'd seen the sun.

"The wife will be of use, certainly," Trayne said. "She was quite taken with my son. It is difficult, using the sons of Cain like this, but nothing is made easy in this work. The wife will be useful. Useful to Paul."

Donna felt a stab of jealousy, mirroring exactly the one Marjorie Garber had felt. Wasn't Donna alone enough for Paul? Didn't she serve him, as she had promised, in every way?

Except that I didn't tell him about Garber. About his strengths.

"How will Marjorie be of use?" Donna asked.

Trayne turned from his surveillance of the town outside Donna's windows. "You question me?" There was genuine surprise in his voice. "And in that tone?"

Donna's lower lip trembled. Her jaw followed. A shudder ran through her whole body as Trayne crossed the room to her. "I'm sorry."

Trayne shook his head. "Paul!"

The boy emerged from the bathroom at the end of the short hall. He came down the hall pushing his white shirt into the tops of his dark green corduroys. He zipped his fly as he came into the room. "Father?"

"Another lesson is necessary, Paul," Trayne said.

Paul frowned as he looked at Donna. Again she could not read the expression on his face. It was not, she thought, so much that it was really an unreadable expression. It was more that she could not make it fit on that face, could not make it belong to the sweet mouth, the big, bright eyes.

Paul shook his head. "Why, Donna? Why?"

"You don't have to do this, Paul," Donna said. Or, rather, it was what she'd meant to say. What had emerged was nothing like language. It was an ululating moan of unendurable anguish.

Remembering, hours later, Donna sank to the floor before her windows. Trayne and his son were gone. Gone on their mission of murder. It might already have been accomplished. There, in the heart of Chicago, a man's life might already have been taken to make way for the plan—the Plan—of Robert Johnston Trayne.

If only Paul could be freed from his father's hold, Donna thought, not for the first time. If only there was some way she could get through to the boy, open his mind, find out what it was that gave Trayne his power over Paul. It had to be something more than a son's devotion, surely. Even the most devoted child could not be forced to do the terrible things Paul had done to Donna just out of obedience to parental authority.

Although, why not? As she thought about it, Donna realized the power of parent over child. As much as she had been twisted by her own parental authority figure, dear, dear Viveca, Donna knew there was little she would not have done had her mother commanded it. She'd been so full of the need to recapture her mother's love. To regain the feelings that, in all honesty, had perhaps never been there in the first place.

It would be easy enough for Trayne to manipulate Paul, of course. As easy as it had been for uncounted generations of parents, consciously and unconsciously, to manipulate their children.

Donna sat on the couch and stared out the window at the dark sky. Thinking of Trayne. Of the things Trayne would be doing tonight. Murder.

Call him, the last shade of Donna's free self shouted, a faint voice in a hurricane wind. *Call the hotel. You know the number. You weaseled it out of Stuartson's secretary. You told Trayne where it is. If you called, you could warn the poor, unwitting victim. Warn—*

But that would not please Paul, said the other voice, the stronger voice. *If Paul is to see the mayor, this must be done. For Paul.*

Not for Paul, Donna frowned. *Paul's just a kid. An innocent kid.*

Innocent? She saw again that look on his young face. That look she could not comprehend, could not make belong there.

Never mind, said the other voice, the strong one. *Let it go. It doesn't matter. Only serving Paul matters.*

Only serving Paul. But Donna shook her head. She pushed herself up on shaky legs, steadying herself with a hand against the cold glass table in front of the couch. She stood erect, breathing deeply, trying to cling to the feeling of release coursing through her. But there was something else there, something lurking, a highwayman at the roadside. Waiting for Donna to be once more in control of herself, so that this old and so familiar evil could assert itself again. Donna swallowed. Her throat felt as though she had not had a drink—any kind of drink—in days, weeks. She knew now that the long passages of time in Paul's infinity of darkness were illusory, but the thirst was not.

She forgot about making the call. She crossed to the kitchen-ette and opened the cupboard above the refrigerator. She took down a half-empty bottle of Gordon's dry gin and took a glass from the dish rack by the sink. She poured a full glass and drank it in two gulps. By the time Paul returned, she decided as she refilled the glass, she would be very, very drunk, and he could do whatever he wanted with her.

It occurred to her as she downed the second drink that she did not really care what Robert Johnston Trayne thought or did anymore, and that seemed a victory of a kind.

Halfway through her fourth drink she remembered the call she'd meant to make.

"Now don't you go saying such things against Father Tom," Mrs. Buck said. Her normally soft voice was cold steel, her pale gray eyes a storm-tossed sky.

"Now, you know I'd normally say nothing at all," Bert Whipple said, nursing the half mug of Sanka on the kitchen table in front of him, "but it's two days now he's been . . . well, I don't know. Some kind of robot, my Lisa said, and that comes as close to saying what needs to be said as anything."

Mrs. Buck topped off Bert's coffee from the pot she kept going all the daylight hours. There was never a soul, she was proud to say, who'd knock on the vestry door and not go away with a good, hot cup of coffee inside them.

"He's got a lot on his mind," she said. "You heard about young Mr. Terranova?"

Bert nodded. "Terrible, terrible. To kill himself like that. And him being a special favorite of Father Tom's."

"Father Tom has no special favorites," Mrs. Buck said. There were no shadings to Bert's remark, she knew, but Mrs. Buck had been around Tom Sylvestri long enough to read him far more closely than he might have wished. She knew there was more to his relationship with the strange young writer than what might be considered usual between a parishioner and his priest. How much more, Mrs. Buck was not prepared to consider.

"The thing of it is," Bert said, "he's not paying any attention. He took the confession this afternoon and . . . well, I'll swear I could've said I was Satan himself and I'd just come from barbecuing babies, and he'd have done no more than give me three Hail Marys and an Our Father."

Mrs. Buck poured a small cup of coffee for herself and sat across the table from Bert. "He *has* been distracted. But it's the Terranova suicide. Father Tom's all filled up with praying for the poor damned soul of that young man, you see."

Bert shook his old head. "I've seen a lot of hard times come and go for Father Tom. I remember when his poor mother passed on, not ten days after he came to take over for Father Percival. I would never have known such a thing had struck him, if you hadn't told me. Now you ask me to think this is all for Joseph Terranova?"

Mrs. Buck sipped her coffee and said nothing for a long time. Shadows were dark in the corners of the tall, stone-walled kitchen. A heavy sky crowded low outside the tall windows over the sink, blotting out the moon, the stars. "I'll talk to him," she said at last. "I know he's distressed about young Mr. Terranova, but you're right. He should not let it affect his work with the people of this parish. He should not let it stand between them and the Lord."

Bert smiled, finished his coffee. "There's nothing more any of us could ask, Mrs. B."

Pete Hay sat in the patrol car, watching windblown snow drift gently across the front of Clarence Nickerson's house. It was a house he'd been in at least two dozen times, Pete reckoned; twice for Thanksgiving dinner, the rest for various football and baseball games. The house seemed completely appropriate for Clarence Nickerson, broad and squat and solid, with a wide, slow-sloping roof that suggested in Pete's mind the way Clarence's head and shoulders seemed to be all of a piece. Even the siding reminded him of Clarence Nickerson; old and tough, stained but durable.

Pete blinked back tears, then snorted. He'd been sitting staring at the house for half an hour. He did not want to go in, did not want to face Alice Nickerson. But what else was he to do? He was Clarence's number two man. His friend. In any case, he could not reasonably postpone the visit any longer. A night had passed without Alice knowing where her father was. It struck Pete as odd, as he thought of it, that Alice had not called the station house to find out where Clarence was. Pete let the thought go. He recognized it as the avoidance of duty it could easily become—*If she doesn't care enough to call in, why should I?*—and forced himself to face the fact that this was not a situation in which he could justifiably shirk his responsibilities, whatever counter-programming a lifetime of habit might have produced.

You coulda let Arnie call her, Pete reminded himself, but he could not really accept the idea.

Pete felt he owed at least this much to Clarence, that his daughter should not have to hear of her father's death over the telephone. Pete pushed open the car door. The day was cold, but not as cold as yesterday. Pete's breath streamed in the air, but he did not feel the need to pull up his collar or put on his gloves. He leaned his chest against the door to close it, then climbed over the drifted snow to Clarence's front door.

Not "Clarence's" anymore. Alice's now. At least it looks like her, too. He snorted at the ill-timed jest.

Memory assailed him. It seemed every moment he'd spent in this house wanted to crowd into his brain, all at once. He remembered the fabulous cooking smells of those two wonderful Thanksgivings—Alice was plain as an old bucket by anyone's standards, but she was one terrific cook—and the even more fabulous flavors. He remembered whooping and cheering in Nickerson's basement rumpus room as their designated favorite team scored another touchdown on fields far from Faulkner. He remembered how he and Nickerson had sworn a hundred times that one day they would actually go to a Rose Bowl Game. They would be one of those colorful dots waving and cheering when the TV cameras panned across the impossibly huge crowds. Or they'd go to Chicago and see the Cubs under the bright lights of Wrigley Field.

Never do that now. Not with Clarence, anyway.

He remembered the few times, feeling good and with perhaps a couple too many beers behind his cowboy belt buckle, when he'd wondered why Alice had never married. Yes, she looked like her father in drag, but she was *such* a great cook, *such* a terrific housekeeper, it seemed there should be somebody, somewhere who would want her for a wife.

Pete considered himself mature and intelligent enough to

know that not all a wife's duties were confined to the bedroom, whatever his relationship with Marcy Kavelhoff was. Alice kept her father's house absolutely spotless, kept him well fed, kept his clothes neat. Pete mounted the steps, pressed the doorbell. Inside, he heard the tinny chime mimic the tolling of Big Ben and waited for Alice to peek through the curtains covering the three little rectangular windows in the top of the door. Peek and wave, a familiar ritual.

Alice's face did not appear at the window. Pete rang the bell again. He went to the edge of the formed concrete steps and leaned over the wrought iron railing to look into the living room window. He blinked, trying to dispel the vision of what he saw. If the whole house had been lifted from its foundations and tipped on end, the effect could not have been more dramatic than what he saw. Chairs were turned over, fabric slashed, the stuffing looking like grotesque vomit strewn across the room. The knickknack shelf Clarence had so arduously assembled and hung was torn from its corner and smashed in the fireplace grate. Its tiny glass and china ornaments were bright, sharp memories on the worn pile of the living room rug.

Pete stepped back, pulled open the storm door, and reached for the inner knob. The door was locked. He sprinted down the steps and around the side of the house, almost slipping on the patch of ice that always formed where the path turned the corner. He ran to the back door and repeated his manipulation of doorknobs with no greater success.

Pete pounded on the door. "Alice?"

He leaned in close to the door, shouting against the glass. Through the lacy curtain on the inside he could see Nickerson's kitchen in disarray that matched the living room. Pete pushed the storm door all the way open and adjusted the spring-loaded closer to keep the aluminum panel back out of his way. He pressed the side of his head flat against the glass and squinted around the edge of the curtain. The key was in the deadbolt on the inside.

Pete unhooked the flap on his holster and drew his service model .45. He made sure the safety was firmly in place, grabbed the gun by the barrel, and swung the butt against the glass. The glass *thunged* and bounced the weapon back. He'd aimed his blow too close to the supporting upright of the wood frame. Pete braced himself and swung harder, striking more toward the center of the pane. The glass shattered. Pete jumped back as the lower half of the big pane disintegrated and the upper half dropped like a guillotine blade. It smashed itself against the bottom of the frame, spilling jagged triangles of glass around Pete's feet. Pete holstered his automatic. He reached around the torn curtain, which had been ripped by glass falling inward, and turned the key in the lock. He pushed open the kitchen door and stepped inside.

The house was hot. Pete unzipped his winter jacket and took off his hat. He moved from old habit to put the hat on the counter by the door, then stopped himself. Sugar and flour were spilled all over the counter. What looked to Pete like the crumbled remains of a dozen different kinds of cookies were scattered across the spillage. On the floor strips of uncooked, defrosting bacon were starting to curl and go bad. At least a dozen eggs were splattered against the walls and cabinets, against the face of the refrigerator. It looked to Pete as if someone had stood in the middle of the room and swung an egg carton like a jai alai racket.

"Alice?" He almost screamed the name, his nasal voice cracking. "Alice!"

He moved on into the house. He found each of the ground-floor rooms in comparable disarray. As he passed the basement door he heard the TV. He leaned against the doorjamb and looked down. There were no lights on in the basement, but around the turn into the rec room he could see the flicker of Nickerson's big console color TV.

"I'd like to buy a vowel," said a female voice he did not recognize.

"Alice?"

He started down the steps. He pulled the .45 out again and held it at the ready as he rounded the corner into the familiar room. *Wheel of Fortune* was on TV, Nickerson's favorite chair, his huge BarcaLounger, was pulled too close to the screen. Over the back Pete could see the top of Alice's muddy blond hair. On the floor all around were torn, emptied boxes—*boxes!*

—of Twinkies, Hi-Hos, Oreos, Cheez Doodles. Every junk food known, it seemed.

"Alice?"

Pete stepped around the chair and looked at her.

12

Alice Nickerson sat naked, Red Indian style, fat white legs drawn up and crossed on the cushion. Her eyes were vacant, fixed on the TV screen. Her right hand was at her lips, the fingers pantomiming the motion of forcing food into her mouth. Bright orange drool ran from the corners of her mouth, dripping onto her bare chest. Her left hand lay between her legs, fingers twitching occasionally.

Pete turned around as if spun by an unseen hand and bolted for the small bathroom just off the rec room. He managed to keep his stomach where it belonged by splashing cold water on his face. He reached for a hand towel and rubbed vigorously at his face with it. His reflection in the mirror was wan and panicky. It took him several heartbeats to realize he could not see Alice in the mirror. Her father's big chair was nearly centered in the doorway over his left shoulder, but Alice was no longer in it. The skin on his back prickled as Pete turned slowly to look at the chair instead of its reflection. An illogical fragment of his brain was trying to convince him the mirror was at fault. That Alice—the awful apparition of Alice—had not really moved from the chair.

Pete tried to swallow in a throat gone bone-dry. He stepped out of the narrow, confining bathroom into the TV room again. He felt he was going wall-eyed, so desperately was he striving to see in all directions at once. Even with that he did not see

Alice until it was too late. She was crouched by the bathroom door, hunkered down low on Pete's left. As he stepped out she threw herself at his legs, a football tackle that hurled him sideways. With a startled yelp he landed with a painful thud as Alice came down on top of him.

She began grabbing at him. Grabbing at his clothes. She pulled his shirt up out of his pants and pushed her hand up under it. Her flesh felt cold and clammy against his, as if she'd been soaking in a tub of ice water for hours. Pete tried to push her off him, but Alice shifted her angle of attack. In the moment he bucked, she got her left arm around his neck. She pulled his face up into the dangling sacks of her breasts while her other hand pushed backward, under his belt, groping. Pete struggled, outmassed and—amazingly—outmuscled by Alice Nickerson, until her questing fingers closed over their target. In that moment Pete found new strength. He pushed hard, kicking over with his right leg. They rose and rolled as a unit, he and Alice. He came up on top of her and kept going, rolling away as far as he could.

The Barcalounger stopped him, his back slamming into it. Alice was already rolling onto her hands and knees as Pete jerked himself to his feet. From a kneeling position she made a grab at him. She missed, falling full length again, facedown. Pete's instinctive backward step brought his thighs against the TV table by the chair. Empty junk food boxes went flying. Jumping to one side as Alice made another grab, he ducked and seized her flailing right arm. He pinned her forearm, pulled his handcuffs off his belt, and snapped one stainless steel loop around her wrist. Before Alice could regain any part of her balance, Pete yanked hard on the other end of the manacle chain, dragging her across the TV room and out into the unfinished part of the basement. He knew the layout well enough to remember the two adjustable metal poles supporting some of the weight of the floor above, each about ten feet from the TV room. Ignoring the effect the rough concrete floor might be having on Alice's bare flesh, Pete hauled her to the nearest pole and snapped the other wrist band around the screw fitting at the base of the pole.

The action delayed him just enough that Alice was able to

make another grab. She got him round the knees and pulled him down again. She pushed herself on top and began smothering him with big, wet, orange-stained kisses. But it was almost impossible for her to hold him with one arm shackled as it was. Pete pushed out from under her and rolled away again. He stood up. He wiped his jacket sleeve over his face, again and again, trying to scrape away the feeling of Alice Nickerson's mouth against his. Alice pulled herself into a semirecumbent position on the cold stone floor. She reached up to him with her free hand.

"Petey," she whimpered. "Don't leave me like this Petey. I love you, Petey."

Pete resisted a sudden urge to kick Alice squarely in the face. Instead he crossed by her to the phone on the small wet bar by the TV room door. He picked it up and dialed the Harrison District Hospital number from memory. The reception desk nurse patched him through to Dr. Zeldenrust in the morgue. After speaking to the doctor and telling him what he had found, Pete went back up to the kitchen. He wished dearly that there was a door at the top of the basement steps. He wanted to close himself off from Alice Nickerson. All through the phone call to Dr. Zeldenrust she'd lain whimpering in the other room, occasionally muttering "I love you Petey."

Ten minutes after Pete Hay hung up the phone in Clarence Nickerson's house, Maurice Zeldenrust buzzed the front doorbell. Pete crossed through the wreckage of the living room and let him in.

"That's cab fare the city owes me, Petey," the doctor said. Now his use of the name made Pete Hay's skin crawl. "Where is she?"

"In the basement." Pete breathed deeply of the cold air coming through the open door. "Listen, if you don't need me . . ."

Dr. Zeldenrust frowned. "I didn't say I didn't need you. I'll need a car, if we're to get her back to hospital. You seemed to think she might need hospitalization, I thought."

"Yeah. No. I don't know." Pete took a deep breath. "Look, I gotta get outta here, okay? Here's the key to my cuffs. Call me with your report." Before Dr. Zeldenrust could protest further, Pete bounded down the front steps and across the snow-covered lawn to his car. He needed something to clear his head of the memory of Alice Nickerson, and the best thing he could think of to do that was Marcy Kavelhoff's smooth and plentiful flesh. He'd started out for Marcy's that morning, before the terrible discoveries of the day. Now he could not imagine a more compelling contrast than the naked bodies of those two women, Alice and Marcy.

Besides, it was three days since he'd last seen her, when they'd caught a movie on the previous Monday night. Afterward she'd come back to his one-room apartment for a few hours, but the relief, as Pete thought of it, had not been so great as could have been achieved by a more prolonged stay. Anticipation of what lay ahead successfully exorcising the phantoms of Alice Nickerson from his mind's eye, Pete guided the patrol car along Black Rock Highway and let the cold air from the open window blow the cobwebs from his brain.

It occurred to him that he might be overtired for any really good sex, but there were alternatives. If nothing else he knew, under the right circumstance, he could goad Marcy into a humdinger of a fight, and that was sometimes as satisfying as sex, for Pete. Especially if it meant putting her over his knee again. Pete frowned briefly at the thought, wondering if such thoughts were a proper memorial for the very proper Clarence Nickerson.

Hey, Pete thought, addressing Faulkner in general and the ghost of Nickerson in particular, *at least I ain't never tied her up or nothin'.*

Then, too, thought Pete, if he was not too tired there was the potential of immediate reconciliation, so two birds might well be slain at once this early evening. He'd once before had sex with Marcy right after he'd spanked her, and he'd loved her moans of mingled pain and pleasure. He scratched the front of his slacks as he drove, smiling despite the clouds gathered around his personal horizons. He didn't radio in to Arnie Steadman to report his destination. Pete knew all of Faulkner was aware of his extracurricular activities with Marcy—"the pretty widow" everyone called her, and she hated it—and he wasn't about to provide them with any new fodder. Anything he told Steadman that Steadman might be able to interpret as outside official business would be all over town inside twenty minutes. Plus he did not want Steadman calling him, as he almost certainly would. In the two years Pete had been seeing Marcy Kavelhoff he could think of at least a dozen times when he'd made the mistake of telling Steadman he was heading out to her place. The telephone had rung each time, Steadman needing desperately to contact Nickerson's chief deputy, usually over something completely inconsequential—by Pete Hay's way of thinking, anyway.

He turned off the highway onto the gravel track to Marcy's house, a mile and a half west of the main road. To his back the sky was dark, snow clouds piling up again across the moon. The radio had warned ten to fifteen inches might be on the way through this area, and Pete Hay thought the idea of being snowbound at Marcy's particularly appealing. He looked at his watch. Just about five, sky dark as midnight. Her kids might not be home from school yet, hers being the last house the school bus would come to. Marcy often complained how late the kids sometimes got home—it seemed to Pete as if she blamed them—especially in the dark winter evenings.

Pete smiled at the thought of the two Kavelhoff kids sitting forlornly in the bus as one by one their schoolmates were dropped off, themselves still miles from home. Perhaps, if the snow was properly timed, they would be caught in town and he would have Marcy all to himself until the snowplow came through and "freed" him. He turned into the driveway in front of Marcy's big two-story house and tooted the horn of the patrol car. He climbed out, turning off the engine but leaving the keys in the ignition as he always did. Marcy appeared at the side door. She smiled and waved.

"Hello, stranger," she called, and Pete found a smile somewhere.

He strode up the uneven path alongside the house and up the side steps two at a time. He swung an arm around Marcy's waist and pulled her against him, planting his lips firmly against hers. Her arms went round his neck, her right hand pushing up against the back of his head, partly dislodging his broad-brimmed hat. As they broke apart again, Pete Hay grinned, the warmth and familiarity of Marcy's body pushing back the horrors crowding around his life.

"Man, I needed that," he said, pulling Marcy closer. He liked the way she felt against him. He was reed thin—all bone and gristle, Nickerson used to say—but Marcy Kavelhoff was a full-fleshed young woman, round of face and big of bosom.

"I'm cold," she said. She pulled out of his grip to step back into the kitchen, just inside the door. Pete followed, slapping her ample behind with his broad, long-fingered hands.

"Kids in school?" he asked confidently, feeling his heart sink a good three feet when Marcy said "No."

"They sick?" Pete asked, his whiny nasal voice ill suited to disguising the displeasure he felt.

Marcy turned to face him. "Oh, don't worry about them. They're down in the playroom."

Pete knew one of the last acts of Jake Kavelhoff's life had been to complete a rosewood-paneled playroom in the basement, finished only ten days before his tractor rolled over backward and ground Marcy's husband of five years into the mud of spring thaw. Marcy smiled and pressed herself up against Pete Hay in just that way she knew he liked. Her eyes flashed mischief. "We could go upstairs."

Pete frowned. "What if they come up for somethin' t'eat or t'watch TV or somethin'?"

"They won't." Marcy took hold of Pete Hay's hand and pulled him toward the stairs. Obediently he went with her, but he looked at the door to the basement as they passed it. There was something wrong with it, but he couldn't place what it was. He shrugged the feeling off and went on up the stairs behind Marcy.

At the top of the stairs he paused. "I could use a shower first," he said.

Marcy drew her lower lip into an irresistible pout. "More than you could use me?" She leaned in close to him, and Pete felt the tiredness battling mightily with his feelings of arousal.

"Just a quick shower," he said. He smacked her once on the behind, short and sharp. Marcy squeaked and trotted off toward the bedroom. "Don't be too long," she said over her shoulder from the door, "or I'll start without you!"

It made him think of Alice, and he shuddered. He tried to concentrate on the things that were different about Alice Nickerson and Marcy Kavelhoff. He turned on the shower and peeled off his clothes. He climbed up into the big old clawfoot tub and began to lather himself, skin and hair as well. It took several goes before he felt really, finally clean. Then he turned off the shower and pulled the curtain back. He was clean now, but nowhere near as refreshed as he'd hoped. His eyelids felt as if carefully crafted lead shutters were fitted over them, and sometime when he was not paying attention it seemed as if somebody might have attached ton weights to each of his legs.

Marcy was in the bathroom. He knew she must have come in when the water was so loud that it masked the sound of the door opening and closing. She'd already removed her dress and stood, back pressed against the bathroom door, in bra and panties. She had a habit of wearing a bra that was half a size too small. Her big breasts bulged over the white fabric of the cups.

She took a step forward and caught Pete's dangling penis like a bellpull. She squeezed, gently but firmly, like milking a cow. Pete felt himself harden in her grip. He stepped carefully out of the tub and embraced her, pinning her grasping arm between their bodies. Marcy let go of his rising organ and wrapped her arms around his neck, pulling his face to hers, kissing him all over. Pete fought back a piercingly sharp memory of Alice Nickerson, but he was too tired to stop the shudder that came with it.

"What's the matter, hon?" Marcy's round face was a mixture of concern and hurt.

"Nothing," Pete lied. He caught a finger in the upper edge of her right bra cup and ran his nail back and forth over her flesh. "Nothing," he repeated.

Marcy caught his hand. "Then let's get out of this steamy old bathroom and go somewhere we can make our own steam."

Pete picked up his pants from the seat of the commode and pulled them on. The last thing he needed was Jeremy or Kelly coming bounding up the stairs to find their mom half naked with a stark-naked policeman. He followed Marcy to the bedroom. For any number of reasons it was his favorite room in the house, a big, white-walled room with bare floors, blond wood cut in large, uneven planks and buffed to a deep shine. Marcy stopped immediately through the door and turned into his arms again. Pete clasped his hands under her buttocks and lifted her bodily from the floor. She wrapped her legs around him. He pushed his face deep into the valley of her bosom.

Blind, he kicked the door shut behind him and strode across the bedroom. He toppled onto the big, soft bed, landing on top of Marcy. Marcy squealed her delight, pushing down on the top of his head. Pete let his face slide across her round belly until his pointy chin caught in the waistband of her panties and his moustache tickled her navel.

"Maybe I should lock th' door . . ."

Marcy frowned. "You stop now, Pete Hay, and there'll be no reason for you to start up again." She increased the pressure on the top of his head.

Pete felt uncomfortable with the idea of Marcy's kids suddenly appearing in the doorway to the master bedroom, but the urgent pressure against the front of his pants gave him good reason to trust in her insistence that the kids were nothing to worry about. He caught the elastic waist of her panties in his teeth and pulled downward.

Donna was drunk, but it was not like any other time she could remember being drunk. It was, she decided, as if a part of her had split away and hovered now, a few feet above her, watching her. A piece that was stone sober, and not in the least forgiving of Donna's present state.

A lot of thoughts were slip-sliding their way through Donna's brain, and she realized too that it was probably only because of that phantom floating above her that she was able to make any sense out of even the least of them. She remembered her intent was to anger Reverend Trayne. That was why she had got drunk. That much she was reasonably sure she had achieved. When Trayne returned from his unholy mission, he would rage at her, scream at her, strip the flesh from her bones in slender ribbons of absolute agony. She wanted that. Not out of any growing masochism, but because, as she had already realized, somehow there was freedom in the pain. It sharpened the tiny piece of her—the floating, phantom self?—that was still Donna Wojciechowski, and not a sycophant in the thrall of Paul and Robert Trayne.

Then, too, there was Walker. The memory of him was a pain in and of itself. Another thing to focus her mind, collect, and refine the dwindling particles of her former self. Much as Donna loathed the woman she used to be, that version seemed a shining paragon in her eyes now, set against the Donna who slumped on the kitchen floor, her back against the refrigerator, spittle dripping from the point of her chin.

The phantom Donna looked down and sneered and asked in her otherworldly voice what the real Donna thought Walker Stone would say if he could see her now.

"Can't see me," Donna said, lips loose, tongue not altogether successful in shaping the words. "Dead. Nickerson killed him."

She raised the fingers of her right hand in a child's imitation of a gun. "Bang," she said. The hand dropped to the floor, cracking her knuckles hard against the linoleum.

"Ow," Donna said, but part of her seized the small pain and drove it as a tiny wedge into the fog alcohol and Paul Trayne had made about her mind.

You could have escaped if you really wanted to, the phantom Donna said. *You had the strength to cheat Paul of an easy victory by taking him to Clay Garber.*

"Hurrah for Clay Garber," Donna said. "I knew he'd come through for me. I knew he wouldn't let Paul bulldoze him. Top cop. Too tough. Don't get to be top cop by being a wuss."

But he's made an appointment with the mayor, hasn't he? Top cop or no . . .

"Not till next week. Lot can happen before then." Donna could only too well imagine what. But so long as Clay Garber was still his own man, there was some kind of hope for the world.

"I wish Walker was here," she said.

"Stone is dead." It was Trayne. He stood in the doorway of the little kitchenette, tall, dark. Donna looked up. She could not see Paul, but she felt the dull throb centered behind her eyes, the pain of his presence. She'd made herself so drunk she did not notice it without conscious effort.

"Stone is dead . . . and you are drunk." Donna felt herself yanked to her feet. She'd not registered that Trayne had moved the two steps to where she lay.

"Done your dirty deed, have you?" The booze made her reckless. "Come back to roost, like a bad ol' vulture after a fat feed." She breathed heavily the fumes of her intoxication. The dark man's nostril's flared, his lip curled.

"I should rip you in two and throw the pieces off your balcony," Trayne snarled. Donna felt her spine twist as if he was about to do just that. "Worthless female! Like all worthless females! Like the boy's own mother, damn her soul."

He was holding Donna's face very close to his own. His stale breath was hot against her cheek. But he was not talking directly to her, she could tell. He was raving, as she had seen him rave before. This was the madness, Donna thought, that controlled Paul Trayne. That controlled, quite possibly, the greatest power ever unleashed on the earth.

"She never understood," Trayne said, and Donna, having slipped away for just a moment, had to grope for his meaning. Trayne was talking about his wife. "When the boy showed his power, she fled. She ran from me, as you have tried to run from me. But while you chose a bottle, she chose the arms of another man. A boy. She ran to his arms, to his bed. And they fled together. As if she thought I could not find them. As if she thought she could take my son from me!" Donna tensed; she had not known this part, though the rest was increasingly familiar. "And thought I would not track her to the ends of the earth to take him back," he finished.

Trayne turned suddenly, slamming Donna back against the door of the refrigerator. One hand was clamped about the front of her shirt so tight as to almost choke her. The other began to roam about her body, probing, pinching, twisting in obscene emphasis of his words. "And how did I find them, when I found them? In fornication! Rolling about naked and unashamed, like wild animals. I had known the pleasures of that young body myself, to be sure, but always in the proper way. Always as the good Lord intended. Controlling my pleasure, focusing it. But when I found them they were rutting like pigs in heat. She was kneeling! Kneeling! And he mounted her as a dog mounts his bitch. And she wailed and tossed her head and carried on as if a thousand hellions were inside her, driving her deeper into her sin of flesh!"

He was tearing Donna's clothes from her now. His big hands, the ragged nails, bit into the soft flesh of her breasts, her thighs. Weakly, for his strength was great, Donna began to fight him.

"I killed them," Trayne said, his mouth almost on hers, his spittle spraying on her lips. "Quickly for him, for he was just a poor tool of her sin. But slowly for her. So slowly." Donna felt the blackness pierce her, even as his hands continued to work their physical anguish. "I took a week," Trayne snarled, his eyes blazing, his body pressed against hers. Dimly Donna wondered if he was going to extend his physical assault to rape. It seemed a small thing, somehow, against what he had already shown himself capable of doing to her soul.

"I killed her," Trayne repeated. "I turned her soul inside out, over the space of a week. And she screamed. Oh, how she screamed and screamed. You think you have screamed, Sister Wojciechowski?" The phrase rang silly and preposterous against Donna's burning brain. Over Trayne's shoulder she saw Paul now. Saw him standing in the kitchen door. Watching. His eyes were large, the way she might expect the eyes of a fifteen-year-old boy to look, confronted with the nakedness of a grown woman.

"Paul . . ." She was barely able to choke it out. Trayne slammed his fist across her mouth. Donna felt pain, tasted blood.

"You have known nothing," Trayne said. He was continuing his tirade unabated. "Nothing. I turned her soul inside out. And I made the boy help me. I made him learn the lesson of disobedience. I made him understand his power. As I will now make you understand."

The pain in her brain was gone. The assault on her soul diminished, vanished. Trayne's big hands closed around Donna's throat.

"But I will pleasure myself," Trayne said, "by watching you die as a chicken would die, when I twist your neck . . ."

"You need me," Donna gasped around the blood filling her mouth. Pink froth sprayed against Trayne's chin. "You still need me." She could no longer move her head, but she turned her eyes to Paul. If the pain was gone, the anguish, he was no longer drawing the power of his gift out of her. "Paul. Tell him. Tell him you still need me."

Paul was frowning. His eyes continued wide, continue to stare at what he could see of her naked, pink flesh. "Father . . ."

Trayne's hands tightened on Donna's throat. She tried to find the strength to resist him, to kick, scratch, anything. The combination of booze and the ferocity of his assault robbed her of what little strength she had. Darkness began to crowd in around the edges of her world. The kitchen receded. She did not have much longer.

"You need me." She choked the words out. It took the last gasp of breath in her lungs. The world was bright red. Trayne's face was vermilion shadow.

"We do, Father," Paul said. He'd crossed the small space between them. His hand was on Trayne's arm. "We do still need her."

Trayne hesitated.

He looked at Paul.

His hands relaxed.

He nodded. "Yes. We need her. For a while longer, at least." He looked back at Donna. "But, unfortunately for you, there are many things I can do to you before I kill you. Time for your fourth lesson."

This time Donna welcomed the abyss.

It seemed to Mae Faber that she'd been running for days, for weeks, although the small part of her mind that still concerned itself with practical matters told her it could not be more than minutes. The police station was on Jefferson, half a block east of Lafayette, and only three and a half blocks south of the *Observer*. Under any normal circumstances Mae knew she could have walked the distance in five minutes or less. But these were far from normal circumstances.

For one thing, Mae was not used to traveling through the narrow service alleys snaking through the center of Faulkner. At most she might have looked down one or two of them, wrinkling her nose at the garbage piled up behind the stores and offices, at the smell that came from the dumpsters behind some of the restaurants. She'd never stepped off the proper sidewalk onto the cracked cement and macadam of one of the alleys. Now she was running down them, pressing herself flat against the rough stone walls as she reached each junction with the street, and looking up and down before she risked the quick sprint to the next dark valley between the old buildings.

Pictures flashed again and again across her mind. The terrible pictures of Arnie Steadman, his wheelchair upended, his skull cracked open on the smooth porcelain lip of the commode in her cell. She had not really meant to kill him. It seemed inconsequential now that she had, in fact, yet the image was so sharp in her mind it sometimes seemed as if it floated in the air before her. She could still hear the sound of his head striking the bowl, the awful clatter of the wheelchair finishing its trip to the floor. Almost, if she thought about it—she did not want to, but it seemed inescapable—she could feel the fabric of his shirt, the give of his soft pectoral flesh beneath as she pushed against him. She'd meant only to push him back, out of the way, out of her line of flight to the door of her cell. But somehow the wheels of the chair locked, or caught; instead of moving back, the chair tipped over.

Mae came to the end of the alley opening onto Carroll Street, one block south of the *Observer*. She flattened against the west wall again and looked out into the street. There were people everywhere, but they were not the people Mae knew. Not anymore.

Some ran, pursuing or pursued. Some raced by in their cars, tires screeching. Several cars were crashed along the street, one right through the window of the shop where Mae bought all her plain, simple dresses. Smoke billowed around the jagged glass teeth of the broken window.

Closer, a group of five or six boys—teenagers—had captured

a woman Mae thought to be in her mid-twenties. Captured was the only word to fit what Mae saw. They'd stripped the woman nearly naked—one stocking still hung on her leg—and tied her across the front of a car like a hunting trophy on her face, her arms pulled up high above her head. They were raping her. Raping and beating, it seemed, for Mae could see the cruel red welts across the woman's back and, as the boy who was sodomizing her stepped back, laughing, another stepped up to begin flailing at her skin again with his belt. The woman hung limp. She did not scream as the leather thong bit into her flesh. Mae thought she might be dead. Clearly it did not matter to her captors either way.

Or to the clutch of a dozen or so onlookers who sat on the hoods and trunks of parked cars, laughing and cheering. Breath steamed in the cold air. Somewhere a shot rang out.

That was why she hid, why she ran. Everything around her frightened her. As she ran, she began to realize that the wondrous gift of Paul Trayne did not function when one was completely alone. At least, it did not function for Mae Faber. She needed the faces, the eyes, the looks of the others in Faulkner, so that her spirit could rise up against them and dismiss them. But she could not face these people, these transformed creatures who were no longer the same ones she'd known all her life. With nothing, no one to dismiss, Mae could only run, fearful of the emptiness of the streets, fearful of the images in her mind.

She darted across the street into the last stretch of alley and in a moment was at the back door beneath the *Observer*. She tried the latch and found it would not move. That surprised her. Part of her plan—if that was not too grandiose a word for these spontaneous bursts of activity—depended upon that door being unlocked. She knew from experience that it usually was; she could not imagine why it would be locked now. Mae stepped to the right and tried the back door of Keene's Hardware. It was locked, but that did not surprise her. When she was working in the *Observer* office, she'd heard the bell ringing downstairs many times. She knew Ralph Keene kept the door locked and opened it only for deliveries.

Mae was stymied, confused by the sudden derailing of her

plan. She looked around the alley. There were some old crates pushed up against the wall to the right of the hardware store's door. Mae realized that from the top of these she could reach the window of the *Observer* storeroom. It would be a tricky climb, she judged, especially with her hands as cold as they felt —she'd not taken time at the police station to search for her coat and gloves—and her slim cotton dress would provide poor protection for her legs and knees against the rough wood. She looked back along the alley for anything that might be stacked against the lower crate to provide a more easy climb. There was a small packing barrel against the wall some fifteen feet to her right. To her left was a flat rectangular wooden box that looked to Mae as if it might have held a harp. She made the deduction because it leaned outside Prunkl's Music Shoppe, which backed onto this same alley from Randolph Street.

She dragged this, first, toward the crates. It made a terrible screeching sound as a protruding nail found the concrete of the alley floor. Mae's heart almost stopped. She looked up and down, but no faces appeared at the few windows that faced the alley, and no one was passing on the street. She shifted the box slightly and dragged it the rest of the way. Then she picked up the empty barrel—thick, hard cardboard with a metal rim— and set it, bottom up, against the harp box. This made an uneven three-tier effect to the level of the first crate. Mae put a hand against the top of the tallest tier, just above the level of her shoulder and raised a cautious foot to the inverted bottom of the barrel. It seemed prepared to take her weight.

She pulled herself up and raised her foot to the edge of the harp box. The wood cracked with a sound like cannon fire in the echoing alleyway. Mae's foot dropped into the narrow box, her ankle bending suddenly, unnaturally. She felt the joint pop. Pain shot up her leg. She cried out, and her balance was gone. She toppled back.

Her right leg was too far down into the box to let her fall easily. Bones snapped. The jagged end of her shinbone tore through the thin layer of flesh around it. Mae's leg bent double four inches below her knee. A spurt of bright blood drew a plume of scarlet up the sides of the crates still above her. She screamed, a single shrill sound that bounced against the alley walls. Mae did not hear the echo. Her head cracked hard against the floor of the alley. She hung there, inverted, supported by the grotesque bend in her leg, hot blood steaming in the cold air as it gushed from the wound and ran down, following the force of gravity, flowing past her knee and on down the exposed length of her thigh. The world swam around her and pain dissolved into darkness.

Pete Hay lay across Marcy's king-size bed, his left foot on the pillows, his right sticking out into empty space past the edge of the mattress. Marcy lay curled at his left side, her head still nuzzled against his lap, his hand stroking slowly across the smooth expanse of her right thigh and buttock. All he could think was that Arnie Steadman had not called him. Not five minutes after he arrived at Marcy's. Not while he was in the shower. Not while he was asleep. Not while they had been making love. Not at all.

Pete lifted his head and looked past Marcy at the phone. It was the tenth time he'd done so in the equal number of minutes since he'd exploded into the most satisfying climax he'd ever had with Marcy. In the two years of their relationship he'd come to think of her as *a good, solid roll in the ol' hay*— his words, thought though never spoken—but this had been different. This was a Marcy who had not hesitated to release herself completely to the explorations of his hands and mouth, whose own had been equally adventurous.

She stirred now, as if sensing his thoughts. Her eyes opened, sleepily. Pete moved his hand from her bum to her face and stroked.

"Go back t'sleep, baby," he said, slipping himself out from under her and reaching over her shoulder to pull a pillow from beneath the rumpled bedspread and slip it under her head in lieu of his thigh.

"Where are you going?" A mumbled sound, all in one short, soft breath, *"Wr-u-gn?"*

"T'get a glass of water," Pete said with some honesty. His mouth was dry, as it always was after sex. But he also wanted to get to the kitchen, where he could use the phone without disturbing Marcy. Or insulting her, with this intrusion of thoughts of business on the warm afterglow of their sex.

"Don't be long," she said into the pillow.

Almost before the words were out, Pete could tell she was asleep again. He picked up his trousers from the floor where they had fallen forty minutes earlier and pulled them on. Barefoot and bare chested he padded down the stairs. The house was warm, the small rooms he passed dark. It struck him as odd, now, that Marcy's kids had made no sound, no move to make their presence known. As he came to the bottom of the stairs he looked at the door to the basement playroom, and again it looked wrong in a way he could not define.

His mind preoccupied with unfamiliar thoughts of duty, Pete moved past the basement door into the kitchen. He dialed the station and let the phone ring twenty times before hanging up. Sometimes, if Arnie was in the can, it would take at least that long for him to get to a phone. Pete crossed to the refrigerator and pushed his hand between the milk cartons and plastic bottles of diet Coke, questing for the last can of beer he hoped would still be there. He found it, opened it, and drained half its contents while leaning against the closed refrigerator. Then he tried the phone again, and let the other end ring forty times. Still Steadman did not answer.

Where the fuck is he? If Clarence finds out . . .

Pete stopped his thoughts. He'd forgotten Clarence Nickerson was dead. Only for a fraction of a second, a heartbeat, but it left him feeling he'd betrayed his friend and mentor.

I'll get the bastards, Chief. Whoever did this to you, I'll find them, and I'll blow their fucking heads off.

He headed back toward the master bedroom and the rest of his clothes. As he mounted the bottom step on his way up, he looked once more at the dark brown basement door.

This time the penny dropped. He saw what was wrong with it.

The door was nailed shut.

13

It was a sign of Trayne's contempt for her, his certainty of his control over Donna, that he could leave her alone. There was nothing she would do, could do, to damage his scheme. She knew he was sure of that. She knew she had given him no reason, not the least suggestion of a reason, not to be sure. But the part of her that could still concern itself with such things clung yet to the notion that there might be some chance, some way to escape. A way, she knew, would not be of her own engineering. That was past her, outside the scope of her abilities. But something might come. A miracle, maybe.

Even thinking about it brought her pain now. The abyss beckoned when her mind turned to disobedience. Would there ever be words to describe the way she felt when Paul took away the sweetness of his gift and she fell into that place? She was trained to use words, to express herself perfectly through the language she had been born to, but in this the power failed her. No one could ever understand what it was like out there, in the infinity of the universe, knowing you were alone, knowing no one cared, no one even knew you existed. Alone with pains that came up from the darkest part of the soul, pains that jangled down the nerves, setting them aflame, making them ring like a chorus of chimes blown on the gust of wind burning up from hell.

But it was not her nerves that rang. It was something real.

Something of the world Donna could still connect to, if she worked very hard at it and concentrated.

A telephone.

The pain abated, dwindled, passed. Donna shuddered and looked up. Twilight outside the windows. The ringing of the telephone grew louder as the pain drew back. Donna pushed herself to her feet. Naked, she now discovered. Her skin burned as if she'd been lashed by ten thousand whips for ten thousand hours. But the only marks were those left by Trayne's fingernails—and her own.

She crossed to the end of the couch and picked up the phone. She had to struggle to find her voice. She coughed, her mouth dry. "Donna Wojciechowski."

"Hello? Is that the Ms. Wojciechowski who works for Walker Stone?" A voice Donna did not recognize. She hesitated a fraction of a second before answering. The lashings of Robert Trayne's "lesson" filled her with fear, lest she misspeak so much as a single word. Yet the rebellious side was still there, dwindling, dying, but there.

"Yes," Donna said cautiously. "Who's this?"

"This is Tom Sylvestri. Father Tom Sylvestri. I don't know if you remember me, Miss Wojciechowski. I'm Walker Stone's cousin. We met a couple of times when you and Walker were dating."

"Yes," she said. "I remember you, Father. What can I do for you?"

"Walker called me a few days ago. He was concerned about your well-being and some other things. I tried to call back down to the hospital in Faulkner this afternoon but all the lines into town seem to be busy. It's as if everyone in Faulkner is calling out, long distance, the operator said. Anyway, on the off chance you'd come back to Chicago I thought I'd call. I remembered you lived in Des Plaines, and I sort of assumed there wouldn't be more than one Donna Wojciechowski in the book."

"It's not the most common name in the world, no." The twilight was fading fast into night. The apartment grew visibly darker as she hunched at the end of the couch. Donna turned on the lamp at the end of the couch, then turned her attention back to the telephone. "What can I do for you, Father?"

"I thought I should offer whatever help you might need."

"I don't need any help, Father." While inside a voice cried just the opposite.

"Walker seemed to think otherwise. Look, this isn't a professional call, Ms. Wojciechowski—do you mind if I call you Donna?"

"Go ahead."

"Thanks. This isn't a professional call, Donna. Walker and I are friends. The fact that he called me makes whatever it is that concerns him kind of a concern of mine. As a friend."

"I . . . appreciate the thought," Donna said. "But I'm all right. Really."

She heard Tom sigh. "Look, do you mind if we meet somewhere?" He sounded very tired, she thought. "I know you're probably wishing I would just butt out and mind my own business, but . . . well, something happened to me yesterday that makes me want to help. Whatever this is."

"I don't understand," Donna said.

"I wouldn't expect you to. Just . . . please? Can we meet? I'll come there, if it would be more convenient."

Donna frowned. There was a war waging full blast inside her soul, and she knew she would need to act quickly, if there was any hope at all of Donna Wojciechowski—the real Donna, the one fading down deep inside her—surviving that war. "Father Sylvestri . . . ?"

"Yes?"

"Would you care to come to my apartment? Tonight?" She flinched as she spoke, drawing up her knees, folding herself, waiting for the lash of Robert Trayne's wrath. It did not come. Not immediately. The instinct to recant, to change her mind, to tell the priest "no" surged up. But it was too late for that.

"That would be fine," Tom said. "I think I know the way, from your address in the phone book. What time is good for you?"

"I . . . What time is it now?"

"Just gone six thirty." She could tell by his tone he found it odd she should ask.

"Eight, then," she said. "Give me time to . . . to clean up a bit." She hung up without saying good-bye. She clung hard to the moment of revolution she sensed stirring around her.

Walker? Is that you? It feels like you. Give me your strength, Walker. I need your strength.

No one answered. Donna pulled herself from the couch and staggered to the bathroom. She turned on the taps in the tub, waited while the water flowed into the enameled hollow, then lowered herself into it. The water was too hot, but she welcomed the pain. It was of this world, a real thing. A thing she could control.

As she had controlled the decision to accept Tom Sylvestri's offer of help. She did not believe there was any sort of help he could truly bring, of course. He would fall into Paul Trayne's thrall, fall under Robert Trayne's power as quickly and as easily as any man. But the moment of rebellion meant much to her.

How much, she could not then begin to guess.

Dr. Zeldenrust closed his black bag and turned away from the still, small forms lying on the kitchen table. Pete Hay leaned back against the kitchen counter, the edge of the Formica top a sharp line across his buttocks even through his heavy trousers. He was fully dressed. He'd had to get all his clothes on before he could drive back into town to get Zeldenrust. All the way in to Faulkner Pete kept trying to raise Arnie Steadman at the station house. He'd tried on the phone again before calling Zeldenrust to let him know what had happened.

Zeldenrust immediately called him back at Marcy's to say there was no response to his call to the police station. Also it seemed all the hospital drivers were out somewhere. And he couldn't get through to either of the local cab companies. If Pete wanted him out there beyond Gunner's Field, Zeldenrust finally told him, Pete was going to have to come fetch him. He told Pete to leave the Kavelhoff children exactly as he'd found them. An inexperienced hand might do more damage than good attempting to move them. Pete, with one year of Boy Scout medical training twenty years behind him, was not about to debate the point.

He found Zeldenrust in his office in the strangely silent hospital. Pete's booted feet echoed as he walked down the long, empty halls. He'd looked up and down several corridors as he passed, but saw no one moving. He'd almost begun to wonder if he'd find Zeldenrust, or if he'd stepped through the Looking Glass and was now the only living thing in the world. In the face of everything else that had happened in the past few days, Pete would not have been totally surprised by this. They'd raced back to the Kavelhoff farm at speeds Pete knew—and Zeldenrust did not hesitate to remind him—were insane on the snow and ice-slicked streets and highway. At least there was no other traffic. The streets of Faulkner were silent, darkening. Lights that should have been on by now were dark. Stores were closed, locked, empty. Twice Pete stopped to check, to confirm what he was seeing. Zeldenrust argued against such stops—if the children were as badly off as Pete reported, every second could count—but Pete sensed with growing certainty that they were in the midst of something greater than the lives of two children, however precious those individual lives might be.

Both the children were dead when Zeldenrust examined them. They lay broken and bloodied on the floor of the basement. Zeldenrust estimated they'd been dead at least two days. The men moved the bodies up to the kitchen and laid them on the table. Zeldenrust completed his examination, cursing under his breath the whole time. Pete stared at Marcy's kitchen floor.

Zeldenrust slowly stripped away the children's soiled clothes, examining the sores and welts he found beneath. Both had been severely beaten before they were locked in the basement to starve. The boy had lost an eye from the lashing. The girl's back and upper left arm were torn to shreds, shards of chipped bone mixed with the ripped flesh, scarcely human. Strips of dried skin had come away with the remains of her dress as Zeldenrust examined the wounds.

"This is all part of the pattern, you see, Petey? This is all part of what has been going wrong in this town since that damn tent show arrived."

Pete shook his head. "It can't be. Marcy didn't go to the show. I told her not to."

Zeldenrust raised a spiky eyebrow. "And she obeys you, this young woman who's been in charge of her own life for, what, three years now? She does what you tell her to?"

Pete frowned. "Why wouldn't she? She'd have no interest in what the Traynes were selling anyway." He did not mention to Zeldenrust what Marcy would be risking if she did not obey him.

Zeldenrust stroked his chin. "I wonder. I wonder. Do you know how many people went out to Gunner's Field over the last two weeks? Thousands, Pete. Just about everybody in Faulkner, at one time or another."

"The crowds *were* getting pretty big."

"How many times were you there?"

"Four, I think. Crowd control. Not that they much needed controlling."

"But you did not partake of this so-called 'gift' from the boy?"

"Shit, no."

"Why not?"

Pete started to answer, a reflexive, smart-alecky reply, but stopped himself, considering. Zeldenrust's question deserved a well-thought-out answer.

Why not?

From everything he'd heard, the gift of Paul Trayne was just the sort of thing Pete Hay should have gone after for himself: freedom from guilt and grief, and therefore, by anybody's definition, freedom from responsibility. That did not seem so appealing now, as he looked at the shredded flesh on the children's bodies and tried to imagine what Marcy could have used to inflict such wounds. The only thing that came to mind was a length of barbed wire. Pete knew there were several bales of it in back of the house, waiting to be turned into a fence in a coming spring that seemed a long way away to Pete Hay.

"Guess I . . . just wasn't interest in what he was selling," Pete said, seeking an answer to Zeldenrust's question, but feeling unhappy with the one he now offered.

Zeldenrust sensed Pete's dissatisfaction. "I don't think so. I think that maybe there was something more to it than that."

"What?" For a moment Pete was fearful the old doctor might be reading something out of Pete's personality that the deputy himself was not aware of—or at least chose to overlook.

"I don't know you well enough to guess. But I know a number of people—myself included—who did not go out to Gunner's Field, even when friends and relatives insisted. My chief nurse was virtually threatening to kidnap me to get me to go with her. I think she must have been out there almost every night, and every time she took a group of people with her."

"And they took people, and they took people . . ." Pete shook his head, frowning. "I guess maybe it's possible somebody persuaded Marcy to go." He thought about their recent lovemaking, and the time on Monday last when she had come back to his apartment, however briefly. A heavy, sick feeling settled in the pit of his stomach as he realized her kids would probably have been sealed in the basement even then.

"I'm . . . gonna go have a little chat with Marcy," he said. His hands had balled into tight fists. He forced them to relax. He walked away, leaving Zeldenrust in the kitchen, without waiting for an answer. He passed the basement door on the way up. It hung crooked on its hinges, broken away by Pete's shoulder pounding against the grip of the nails. They still stuck in the frame with uneven chunks of wood clinging to them.

Pete stared for a moment in fascination; the nails, the wood, were all painted over so that no one would immediately notice the door had been nailed shut. That was why he'd taken three passes to register what was different about the door. From the basement, a stench of urine and feces rose on a sudden updraft of air. Pete wrinkled his nose and went on up the stairs. At the door to the master bedroom he paused. Down the hall, to his left, the doors to the kids' rooms stood open. He could see the Rainbow Brite poster over Kelly's bed and the pile of comic books against the far wall of Jeremy's room. Gaudy colors. Bright. Full of life.

He turned the old key in the lock of Marcy's room and stepped through the doorway. She was sitting on the edge of the bed, still naked. In the darkening room she'd turned on one of the bedside lamps. The light of the bulb picked out soft yellow highlights on her full flesh. She sat with her knees together, her feet not quite reaching the floor. She looked up and smiled as he entered.

"Where you been, lover?" Nothing in her tone or expression indicated that she was aware of anything being wrong in that cozy little house.

Pete closed the door behind him and stayed by it, as far from the bed as he could be with the layout of the room. "Why don't you put on some clothes," he said. He did not like the distracting signals her nakedness sent through his body.

"Why?" Her hands were resting on her knees. As she spoke she pushed her elbows into her sides. Her breasts mountained between her arms in that way she knew Pete especially liked. "Don't you like looking at me?"

Pete swallowed, crossed to the closet—passing closer than he wanted to the bed—and pulled out Marcy's floral print robe. He tossed it at her. "Put that on."

She shrugged and rose, pulling the robe around her shoulders without fastening it. Shadows moved in interesting ways in the division between the two halves of the front of her robe.

Pete locked his eyes on hers and forced his mind to fill with what he'd found in the basement. "Don't come any closer, Marcy."

She tipped her head in that way he'd seen so many times before when something was said that she did not entirely understand.

"What's wrong, lover?" She raised a hand toward his shoulder. Pete caught her wrist before the hand made contact. He bent her arm back and down, pushing against it to lock the elbow. Marcy took three clumsy steps backward, Pete following to retain his grip. The backs of her legs hit the side of the bed and she sat down again. "Pete . . . ?"

"I want some answers, Marcy," he said. He twisted her arm and saw pain flash across her big eyes. "I want to know what the hell has been going on around here."

"Where? When?"

"The tent show." He saw no reason not to go straight to the

heart of the matter. "You went out to that goddamn tent show, didn't you? Even though I told you not to."

Marcy looked genuinely puzzled. "Yes. Why not? There was no reason for you to tell me not to."

Pete let his breath escape his nose in a long, loud sigh. Anger boiled into rage. He released his grip on her wrist. He brought his right hand up and across the side of her face, knuckles first, as hard as he could. Marcy was actually lifted slightly off the mattress. She fell backward and sideways. She lay on her right side, looking up at Pete with the eyes of a frightened beast. Her robe was wide open; her big breasts shook with her frantic breathing.

"What . . . ?"

Pete did not let her finish. He grabbed the closest lapel of her robe and pulled her back into a sitting position. He heard the seam rip open down the back. He let go of the robe and grabbed Marcy by the shoulders, digging his bony thumbs into her soft flesh.

"Tell me what happened, goddammit," he shouted. His voice cracked on the peak of the shout. Color rose in his neck. He slapped Marcy again, sending her sprawling the other way. Her head hit hard against the dark oak headboard.

"Ow!" She pushed herself to her feet and sprang at him, fingernails first like the claws of a striking cat.

Pete caught her before her leap was complete and pushed her back onto the bed. It slid back under the impact of her body, its wooden feet screeching on the bare floor. Marcy pushed up on her hands and knees, crawling across the mattress for the other side of the bed. Pete reached out and caught her ankle. He dragged her back. The robe rode up around her, baring her broad, pink cheeks to him. Pete drew her closer, still pinning her ankle, and began slapping madly at her behind with his free hand. Marcy squealed, and this time it was not from delight.

She kicked at him, twisting wildly in his grip. Pete continued slapping at her as hard as he could with the flat of his hand. He didn't care what he was hitting. His world was suddenly full of soft flesh and the machine-gun staccato of his slaps. He released Marcy's ankle and began swinging at her with the tightly balled fists of both hands. One swing brought his knuckles into the middle of her face, full force. He heard and felt the bone snap in her nose. She screamed.

In the midst of his rage he felt strong hands on his biceps, pulling him back. He let go of Marcy's ankle, twisted his head as far around as his neck would allow, trying to focus on the face of the man behind him. Zeldenrust. Pete let the scarlet fog drift from around his eyes and mind. He pulled on the hands that restrained him.

" 'M'okay," he said around gasping breath.

Zeldenrust released him. Pete leaned forward, resting his hands on his knees, gulping air. He felt the heat fading from his cheeks and neck. Dimly he was aware of Marcy cowering against the headboard, pulling her torn robe to cover herself. Her right hand was over her face. Blood gushed through her fingers, splattering across her chest. Her bosom heaved with labored breaths. There were bruises already starting to show all over her exposed flesh. Pete straightened.

"Sorry you had to see that," he said to Zeldenrust. "I was tryin' to find out what happened."

"Of course you were." Zeldenrust's voice was cold steel. He stepped back a pace. Pete could see uneasiness in his leathery face, and fear. He must be afraid Pete might suddenly lash out at him. When Pete put out a hand to assure him there was nothing to worry about, Zeldenrust flinched visibly.

"Don't worry, Doc," Pete said. "I'm all done." He looked at Marcy and felt heat return to his neck. "For now."

Marjorie Garber pulled her robe tight around her nightdress, bracing against the anticipated cold, and opened the front door. She was mildly annoyed to have to answer the door herself—where *was* Anne?—but when she saw who was on the snowy step, her annoyance faded at once into joy. She beamed her delight. "Paul! I didn't expect you."

"Is this a bad time, Mrs. Garber?" Robert Trayne's voice was soft, gentle. "We could come back . . ."

"No, no. Come in. Come in."

Paul and his father stepped into the spacious front hall, the boy looking very small and vulnerable, Marjorie thought, in that big, open place. She was suddenly aware of all the sharp corners, the hard edges on the table in the center of the hall, the tall armoire by the door to the living room, the two Chippendale chairs at either side of the front door. Even the gently curving dark oak bannister grew threatening, filling her mind with the image of flying shards of wood, sharp as needles, lethal as daggers.

"Come into the living room, why don't you?" Marjorie said, leading them. There was no sign of the Wojciechowski woman. Good. Marjorie did not like sharing Paul, even with the woman who "found" him first.

"Your husband is not home, Mrs. Garber?" There was something odd in the way Reverend Trayne said "your husband," or in the way she heard it. Something that made her want to take an immediate defensive stance, to protect Clay from . . . what? When she turned to look into Trayne's eyes the feeling passed at once, and in its place was something almost the exact opposite; if there was anyone in need of protecting here, she thought, it was Paul.

"Clay's still at City Hall, I guess," Marjorie said. "Sometimes he's quite late getting home. There can be so much to do in a city this size. So much crime. And he has to deal with all of it. That's his job." Marjorie caught herself, aware she was on the verge of babbling. "But then," she finished quickly, "you don't know anything about that, do you?"

"Enough," Trayne nodded. "Enough to know my son's gift is needed sorely here." He'd been walking a slow circuit of the big living room, looking at the furnishings, the pictures on the walls, the odds and ends that comprised this portion of the lives of Clay and Marjorie Garber.

Wednesday morning seemed a very long time ago now to Marjorie. She could not, if she turned her thoughts to it, remember a time when Paul Trayne did not fill all the important places in her universe. She reached for the call button hidden behind the antique—and nonfunctional—bellpull by the door.

"Would you like something, Paul? Reverend? I can call Anne and have her bring you a snack. Have you had dinner?"

"Yes, we have eaten, thank you," Trayne said.

"I would not mind having some cookies, though." Paul

smiled. They were the first words he'd spoken. He still stood close by Marjorie at the entrance to the big living room. "If you have any."

"I'm sure we do," Marjorie said. "Do you . . . have a favorite kind?" She felt a momentary fear pass through her, as she spoke the last words. There was, she realized, a tremendous need in her, now, for Paul to name a specific kind of cookie. "We have some . . . honey grahams . . . chocolate covered . . ."

Paul beamed. "Those would be wonderful." He paused, and Marjorie felt something brush across her mind. Something that made her think of Michael. Almost, she thought, it was as if Paul himself was thinking of Michael. Donna Wojciechowski had explained that all the pains that went into Paul took memories with them. It seemed now almost as if Paul was deliberately setting out to manipulate Marjorie's memories of her lost child.

Never mind, said the voice in her head. The now familiar voice.

"They *are* my favorite," Paul said.

Marjorie pressed the button. "Some cookies and milk for our guests," she said, when Anne appeared at the door. "Some of the chocolate grahams."

"Yes'm." Anne nodded, essaying a quick, coy look at Paul, before she headed back toward the kitchen.

"Is she the only servant here tonight?" Trayne asked as he looked after Anne's departing form.

"Why, yes," Marjorie said, puzzled by the question. "It's Rose's regular night off."

Paul said, "I like this house." Marjorie's puzzlement evaporated.

"Won't you sit down, dear?" She crossed to the big couch facing the picture window, the darkness of the Lake beyond. She patted the cushion at her side. "Here. By me."

Paul sat near her, his hands resting on his thighs, palms up. She put out a hand and rested it on top of one of his. "I'm very glad you came, Paul," she said. "Very glad. But . . ."

". . . Why?" Trayne finished for her.

Marjorie smiled, turning her eyes in his direction. "Yes, why."

"Paul wanted to see you."

Marjorie looked back at Paul. He smiled, filling her heart with joy beyond measure. "Really? You asked specifically to see me?"

"I . . ." Paul hesitated, his eyes drifting away in the same way Marjorie remembered Michael's would, when he had some great and terrible secret to tell her, and was not quite sure what her reaction would be. "I knew Commissioner Garber would not be home tonight," Paul said, admitting the untruth with a quiver in his voice that suggested to Marjorie a fear of punishment. "We called his office to make sure he was still there." He sighed. "I wanted to see you."

"I'm so glad," Marjorie said. "But is there some special reason?" Marjorie shifted on the couch. Her thigh came against Paul's. He did not pull back, and neither did she.

Paul turned his face back toward her. His big, sea-green eyes were bright with tears. "You . . . When I was here yesterday . . ." He shook his head. Marjorie's impression was that he was trying to form into words concepts beyond his young vocabulary.

"That was a very special moment," she said, trying as best she could to ease things for the boy. Feelings were rippling through her. Odd feelings. Maternal, yes. But also sexual. Oddly incestuous.

He smiled. "Yes, it was a special moment." His eyes drifted away again. Marjorie was conscious of how very pale his skin was, contrasted against her own dark chocolate hue.

"I'm very glad we met," she said.

Paul's fingers curled around the hand resting on his. "I don't really remember my mother," he said, and Marjorie's heart grew heavy with the weight of the grief she heard in his words. "Not what she looked like or sounded like. Father has taken me to see some specialists in such things, and they say it is something to do with the . . . trauma?" He looked at Trayne as if for confirmation that this was the right word.

Trayne nodded. "Trauma."

"They say that it is something to do with the trauma caused by her death."

"You and your mother were very close?" Marjorie remembered the bond between herself and her lost son. Clay's attention had been focused on his career in the first few years of Michael's life. With the girls growing into young ladies, discovering boys and all the wonders of the world around them, Marjorie had spent many hours alone with Michael.

"We were." Paul nodded. "Very close. Very, very close. That's why it hurts so much when I can't remember her." He turned, met Marjorie's gaze. "That's why it was so wonderful when Sister Wojciechowski brought us here." His grip tightened on Marjorie's hand. "When I saw you . . . suddenly I remembered all there was to remember about my mother. How she looked, how she smelled, how she sounded. Because it was all you."

"I . . . remind you of your mother?" Marjorie's heart raced. It seemed absurd, but there was little use denying it was exactly what she wanted to hear, needed to hear. But there was potential for pain, if she was misreading his words, unlikely as that seemed to her now.

"It's more than just reminding me," Paul said. "When I went away with Sister Wojciechowski and Father, it was like the . . . trauma came back. All the memories went again. But when I thought about you, I could almost see her again, because I could see you. I could hear her, if I thought about how you sounded. That's why I had to come back here tonight. To ask you something. Something very important."

"Paul . . ."

"No, let me finish. I want you to come with me. Come and live with Father and me."

"Paul . . ."

"Please. I need you, Mrs. Garber. I need you to come. To be my mother . . ."

"Where would you like this, ma'am?" Anne's voice was soft as a whisper, but it sliced through the moment.

Marjorie started, turning. The room shifted in and out of focus around her. Anne seemed simultaneously to be standing almost on top of her, yet far away, much farther than the diameter of the room should allow.

"Here, Anne," Marjorie said, indicating the walnut coffee table in front of the couch. Anne crossed to the table, set the big kitchen tray on it. There were two glasses of milk—cold enough for moisture to have condensed into slippery trails along their outsides, Marjorie noticed—and a plate piled high with the chocolate-coated honey graham squares. Marjorie blinked at the number of cookies; Rose must have emptied the whole package, she thought. Then she remembered again it was Rose's night off, and Anne was alone in the kitchen.

"Thank you, Anne," Marjorie said, gesturing for the maid to depart. The look that flashed in Anne's hazel eyes told Marjorie the wave of her hand had been every bit as curt as it felt. Marjorie turned back.

"These are very good." Without waiting, Paul had helped himself to the cookies. He had a small pile of six or so nestled between the fingers of his left hand, Marjorie saw, neatly sorted into something like a deck of cards; with his thumb he lifted off the top cookie and took it with his right hand. His mouth was already at work on what looked to Marjorie to be at least three other cookies.

"You shouldn't stuff yourself like that," Marjorie said, at the same time delighting in this further similarity to Michael. She'd scolded him so many times about his piggishness with sweets that she had once tried banning them from the house entirely. That had not lasted long, and as Paul now smiled at her around his mouthful of spit-softened cookie crumbs, she found she could not maintain even the fleeting annoyance she had felt at his behavior.

Paul shrugged at her mild reproof. "They *are* very good."

Marjorie smiled. "Yes, I know they are." She took one of the cookies herself, biting it in half and chewing very much as Paul did, as a child would. She picked up her glass of milk and drew deeply. The white liquid filled her mouth and trickled over her lower lip, bearing tiny, dark cookie crumbs like logs on a wide, white river. Marjorie giggled—dimly aware of the foolishness of the sound—and wiped her chin with a napkin. "You're sure you wouldn't like something, Reverend?"

"Nothing. Thank you."

Paul was smiling at her, beaming at her. He lifted his hand and placed a cookie against her mouth. Although she had not finished with the first bite Marjorie took another. She felt the touch of Paul's fingertips against her lips as she bit the dark square of the honey graham. She let her lips stretch out a little, to make the contact more direct, more intentional. Paul kept his hand by her face, his fingers against her lips. With his other hand he raised her glass and guided it to her mouth. She drank. She sank down on the couch, slipping into a languorous recline. She stretched, cautiously, feeling very sensuous, feeling a delicious softening in her limbs, as though she were suddenly very, very tired and stretching out in her big, soft bed.

Paul's slender hand was stroking her cheek, caressing the dark curve. His little finger was extended away from the rest, downward, and now and again, as his hand reached the line of her jaw, the small digit drew across her throat, across the subtle pulse of her jugular.

"Mother . . ." he said. In the sleepy haze filling Marjorie's world, his voice was every bit Michael's voice, his face every bit Michael's face.

"Michael . . ." Her voice was slow and slurred; in her own ears it sounded very distant. She looked into Michael's face—such a young face now, such a baby face—and reached up a heavy hand to touch his cheek as he touched hers. She knew, as she had begun to know before that moment, that she was Paul's slave, his property; that she would, now and forever, do anything she could to serve him. Very dimly, as the Paul/Michael face expanded to fill her whole being, Marjorie was aware that the telephone in the front hall was ringing.

Father Tom Sylvestri was every bit as handsome as Donna remembered. As she opened the door to her apartment, he filled the space beyond, tall and broad shouldered. His dark hair was dusted with gray, and the lines around his mouth and eyes told her his smiles would be bright and wide. But there was pain too, she saw. Pain in the friendly eyes—deep, but not completely hidden.

She stepped back, gesturing for him to walk past her into the apartment. "Come in, Father." She was launching a campaign that made no sense to her, though she had thought it through a dozen times. It had come to her, suddenly, when she was alone, that this could all be part of some scheme of Trayne's, some trick to test her loyalty. This man looked as she remembered, sounded as she remembered, but that did not mean he was not a pawn of Trayne's. Until she was sure, one way or the other, she could not come right out and tell this man what was wrong, what kind of hell she'd fallen into. But there were ways she could send signals, ways to test him, and, if he was as he claimed, alert him all was not as it should be.

That he was a priest suggested one way, one obvious, clumsy way immediately. To that end she'd dressed in a suitably enticing outfit, experiencing a small flash of disappointment when Tom Sylvestri did not react immediately to the effect, and she moved to work it to its best advantage.

"Something to drink, Father?" Donna asked as Tom seated himself on her low leather couch. She paused by the door to the kitchenette.

"I could use a brandy, if you have any." He watched as she nodded and entered the narrow room, stretching to open a high cupboard and retrieve the bottle. She was as tall as he'd remembered, legs just as long. She wore a tiny beige suede skirt that was most unseasonal and a pale pink blouse with padded shoulders. The front of the blouse clung to her breasts as she stretched, the effect calculated, deliberate. She was plainly not wearing a brassiere. She seemed to be wearing more makeup than Tom remembered. Her lower lip and jaw seemed puffy, as if she were using blush to cover a bruise.

Tom cocked his head slightly to one side and wondered about Donna Wojciechowski. She came back to the living room and set the brandy bottle and two glasses on the small coffee table in front of the couch. She sat next to Tom, poured two drinks, and handed one to him. She leaned back, crossing her legs and presenting him with a length of smooth white thigh that, he knew, would have a devastating effect on almost any other male. Her behavior seemed to him so outlandish, so exaggerated, that he began at once to think there was—must be—something going on here, something he should put himself on guard against.

He told himself not to let her slightest word pass without scrutiny.

But why? he asked himself. *Is all this because of Walker's uncertainty, his concern over the apparent powers of this Trayne boy? Or are you looking for a scapegoat? Someone you can dump your own emotions onto, your own feelings of guilt and anger? And isn't that supposed to be just what this Paul Trayne offers?*

"It's a great pleasure to see you again, Donna," Tom said. "I've been reading your articles on Errol Warner. A fascinating piece of work. You seemed to see right into his soul."

"That's just what Clay Garber said." Donna smiled, shrugged. "I doubt it. I don't think anyone has ever seen into his soul. Although I like to think I came closest. He did seem very open with me." She sipped her drink. "So you and Walker go back a long way, I guess." She blinked, as if against tears. Almost too fast for Tom to notice.

"To childhood. Our mothers were sisters. Walker was about as close to a black sheep as our family ever got."

"I've never thought of him as being anyone's black sheep," Donna said. Tom could read the layering in her words. Was there something she was not telling him?

"How was he the last time you saw him?" he asked.

"Fine," Donna said, instinctively. She paused and thought it through. For Stone to have called Tom Sylvestri *after* seeing the change in Donna, it would have to have been while he was in the hospital, before Nickerson took him away to kill him. "I mean, fine, all things considered. That was . . . strange, that attack. He told you about it?"

"Only that he'd had some kind of breakdown. His own welfare seemed a great deal less important to him than yours."

How like Walker, Donna thought. She blinked again against her tears. They were very close. They were part of the pain that strengthened her now. Gave her the resolve she needed to carry out this stupid, mad charade. If only Tom Sylvestri was keen enough of wit to pick up on what she was sending him. If only he didn't dismiss her as a silly tramp trying her wiles as part of some foolish need to prove something to herself.

"Is there something . . . ?" Tom was miles beyond his depth. He'd come to offer some support to Donna, as one friend of a friend to another, out of consideration for Walker Stone. While driving to Des Plaines in the church's Oldsmobile he'd considered a few different scenarios that the conversation might follow. This was none of them.

"I don't know exactly what happened," Donna said. Her voice was empty of any emotion Tom could identify. "I'd never known Walker to have a sick day in all the years we worked together. It was . . . sort of mysterious. Like something out of one of those damn TV shows he loved so much." As she said the words, Donna remembered Walker's apartment, his huge videotape collection, his fruitless efforts to interest her in the things that fascinated him. Strongest, at that moment, was the time he tried to get her to see the finer points of *Gilligan's Island.*

"Most people will tell you it's just a stupid sitcom," he'd said. "But what you need to remember is that most of these episodes"—he lifted a VHS tape from the shelf and fed it into one of his machines—"come across as if they were directed by Salvador Dali."

Their romance was new enough then that Donna was prepared to tolerate quite a bit. She watched three episodes in a row before begging for mercy. Stone sighed and shrugged, removing the tape from the machine without rewinding it.

"I guess it's a cumulative effect. After you've watched about a hundred . . ." He'd seen the horror in her eyes. "No. Don't worry. I'm not going to inflict that on you. But . . . would you try *Green Acres*?" She'd agreed, and that particular brand of lunacy she had found completely inspired.

To Donna's small delight the memory was quite poignant. She clung to that too. Something was building, she thought. She could not say or guess what, but it seemed vitally important now that she let it come, let it happen, whatever it might be.

"Who was the doctor there?" Tom Sylvestri asked.

"Zeldenrust, a local guy . . ."

"Was he good, do you think? Is Walker in good hands?"
And if he isn't, why are you here? Why did you leave him?

"Yes," Donna said, considering. "He seemed very professional. Real no-nonsense kind of guy."

Donna's grip on the moment was failing her. She shifted on the couch, draped an arm behind Tom Sylvestri, then recrossed her legs to present them at their best advantage.

"What happened down there?" Tom asked, visibly perplexing Donna as her charms failed to work on him.

"Is that important?" She leaned forward and set her glass back on the table beside the brandy bottle. As she drew her hand back, she brought it to his right knee and left it there. "I'd much rather talk about you, Father. It's been quite some time since we last met, but I *do* remember you."

Tom lifted her hand, placed it on the seat between them. "Ms. Wojciechowski . . ."

" 'Donna,' remember? You asked if you could call me 'Donna.' And I said 'yes.' "

"Ms. Wojciechowski," he repeated, "I don't know what this is all about, but Walker was concerned about you. He thought something happened to you that upset the balance of your mind." He tried to fix her gaze, but her eyes slid away from his. "Your behavior is making me think he was right."

Donna frowned. "Why?" She leaned back. "Don't you find me attractive, Father?" She hated saying it, the artificial coyness in her voice, but she had a mission to perform, and this was her only way to get it done.

"I'm a priest, Ms. Wojciechowski," said Tom Sylvestri.

" 'Donna.' " Her voice took on a petulance that seemed to him utterly out of place. A childlike pretend-hurt that did not match the sophistication he read in her face and posture. "Isn't a priest a man, Father?" She put her hand back on his knee. "Doesn't a priest have needs?"

Father Tom sighed. It was all suddenly so insane it bordered on the grotesque. *I've come to talk to this woman about my cousin, her former lover, and the concern he had for her emotional well-being—and she's trying to seduce me!*

"I could fill those needs," Donna said. She slid her hand

along his leg until her extended little finger touched the fold of cloth that covered his zipper.

Tom lifted her hand away again. "I think you should explain this, Ms. Wojciechowski. What kind of game are you playing here?"

Donna shook her head. "No game. Unless it's the oldest game." She smiled. "The game all men and women play."

Not all. The memory of Joseph Terranova was a sharp pain under Tom's heart. "Ms. Wojciechowski . . ."

" 'Donna.' "

"Donna," he said, relenting, "can you tell me what happened? Walker said something about a boy named Paul Trayne." He saw a definite shift in her eyes at the mention of the name.

This is significant. He is at the center of everything, this boy Paul. And I am right to feel uneasy about him. There is an evil there. I do not know what kind yet, but it's something to do with the way Donna is behaving now. And much to do with all that is odd in Faulkner.

"Walker thinks this Paul Trayne had done something to you," Tom said. "Affected you in some negative way."

"Affected . . ." Donna was having difficulty focusing. She blinked again.

"Walker thinks you've been *altered* somehow."

Donna shook her head. "No. No, that's not what Paul does." Her face twitched. "I know that's what Walker thought . . . thinks . . . doesn't matter . . ."

Tom thought she might be remembering old pain, perhaps pain not quite so old.

"Tell me," he said. Her use of the past tense in referring to Stone had not gone unnoticed. There was much he needed to know. And soon. "Tell me what happened."

Donna was trembling. She pushed herself off the couch and crossed the room to the big sliding glass doors to her balcony. Beyond, snow swirled across Des Plaines, and above the city lights the night was black.

Altered, she thought, and again the small voice said, *Never mind.*

But the ghost of Donna Wojciechowski pushed in against the

muffling cotton wadding around her brain and her heart. It made a tiny rip, a microscopic slit. Something like the light of reason stabbed through the hole, bright as a laser beam through Donna's mind. She twitched.

"Are you all right, Donna?" .

"Yes . . ." She opened the latch on the sliding glass door. She stood for a moment with her hand resting on the handle, not opening the door, not moving at all.

Tell him! screamed the ghost of Donna Wojciechowski. *Tell him! He's Walker's cousin, his friend. And he's a priest. He may be able to do something!*

She could not speak. She looked at the reflection of Father Tom Sylvestri in the glass, clear as a mirror against the dark sky. She saw in his reversed countenance all the concern, all the genuine depth of feeling she would have expected from someone who'd found his particular calling. And she saw something more. Something that stirred painful memories, reminded her of the way Walker Stone looked at her, cared about her.

Walker. You came to Faulkner because you were worried about me. You even sent me there because you were worried about me. You've always been worried about me. And now you've died for your troubles. Died for my sins.

She pushed against the latch and slid back the door. A blast of cold air hit Tom as Donna stepped onto the balcony.

That's not much of a basis for a relationship, is it, Walker? You were always worried about me—I gave you plenty of reason to be, I know—and I always hated you for it. I always hated you for seeing the weakness inside me, for trying to help me overcome that weakness.

Tom went to the glass door and stood just inside. He looked down through the railing into the lights of the residential neighborhood spread around the apartment complex. Donna was staring to the right, to the east, to the glow of Chicago against the low, slow clouds.

"Donna . . ."

"Do you believe there's really such a thing as a soul, Father?"

The question, like everything else about the evening, caught

Tom off guard, but not without an answer. "I do," he said without hesitation.

Donna turned to look at him. "I never used to," she said. "I never used to. But I do believe there is a deep, inner part of a person. Maybe not the way they teach it in Sunday School, but something real. Something very special and private. Something that can be hurt, if the way is known."

"Yes," said Tom. She spoke with such conviction, such a haunting devoutness in her voice he felt himself a novitiate before her. He was not the priest, the guardian of the faith. That mantle had passed to Donna Wojciechowski.

"And . . . and maybe that soul is something that survives death," Donna said. "Not like with heaven and hell and all that, but just . . ." She made an expansive sweep with her right arm, encompassing the universe. "All this has to have meaning, doesn't it, Father?"

Tom saw the muscles in her long legs tense as her weight shifted. He set his glass down on the top shelf of the cinder-block-and-board bookcase by the window. "Yes," he said. "I have never doubted that there was a reason, a plan behind the falling of a single leaf."

"Yes. A meaning. A meaning that goes beyond all the stupid, senseless, god-awful things we do to each other all the time." She rose on tiptoe.

Tom tensed. "Yes," he said. In his softest, most reasonable voice he added, "Why don't you come back inside, Donna? You must be cold out there. I know I am."

There were tears drawing bright lines down her cheeks. Her mascara was ruined. "I wish Walker were here," she said. Her voice cracked on the name. Tom sensed Walker Stone at the hub of all this, a talisman binding Donna to her train of thought.

"I wish he were, too, Donna. He's a good friend."

"Yes, he was."

The past tense again. Tom sensed more in Donna's choice of words than a reference to a dissolved romance.

"We used to fight like hell all the time," she said, "but he could make me laugh, and make me feel good about myself.

. . . I guess, in the end, that's what drove us apart, though. People like me don't want to feel good about themselves."

Don't want what Paul gives.

"People like you?" Tom did not like what he was reading in her posture. He measured the distance between them, calculating. "Why don't you come back . . ."

"No." Donna's hair moved in a single coppery wave as she shook her head. She looked back over the twinkling lights of Des Plaines. "No, I can't. I can't come back in. Not after all that's happened. Not after what happened to Walker. I think I must have loved him after all. Maybe I should tell him that."

She leaned forward and toppled over the railing, nineteen floors above the ground.

Tom moved. With all the speed he could summon, he dived after Donna. He threw himself nearly horizontally across the balcony. He knew he was going to hit hard, and he steeled himself for the pain of impact. He would not let it make him loose his grip on her—always assuming he was able to get a grip, any grip, as she toppled over the railing.

He slammed against the hard cement of the balcony rail, but his hands closed around Donna's ankles and he pulled back, throwing himself to the left, using his weight against hers, gravity against gravity. She was not more than halfway over the railing when he connected. She cried out as his flying tackle pulled her back and down, scraping her belly and chest, ill protected by the thin blouse, across the cold, rough metal rail that ran along the top of the balcony wall. The blouse tore, a loud, harsh sound.

Donna came down on her feet, frozen there for a fraction of a second before losing her balance and tipping back. Her knees bent. She sat down hard, her weight coming down across Tom's shoulders. His head was between her feet, his forehead a fraction of an inch from the balcony railing. The back of Donna's right thigh struck him a glancing blow to the side of the head as she came down. It drove his chin down into the concrete floor, snapped his teeth together. Pain shot through his inner cheek, and he tasted blood.

Donna rolled to the side. She kicked her legs free of his grip and grabbed for the metal rail. She hauled herself to her feet as if contemplating a second attempt. Tom was not about to allow it. He pushed up, threw his arms around her waist, and clasped his hands tight. He pulled her back. The movement carried them halfway into the living room again. Donna came down on top of him again, her weight driving the hard edges of the track of the sliding door into Tom's side. He yelped despite himself.

Donna kicked at him. She twisted madly in his grip, driving her elbows into his ribs with all the force the difficult angle would allow. Tom spit a mouthful of blood and used the oldest trick he knew to disable an opponent pinned as Donna was. A trick he'd learned in handling the more violent cases in St. Timothy's drug rehab program. He pulled hard with his clasped hands, driving the heels of his palms up into Donna's belly, just below the sternum. Air exploded from Donna's lungs, making her lips flap involuntarily and forcing something very like a Bronx cheer out of her.

She went limp, the fight forced out with the air from her lungs. Tom relaxed his grip, carefully, ready to tense again in less than a heartbeat. Donna did not move to take advantage of the relaxation of constraint. Tom pulled himself out from under her and pushed himself up on hands and knees. There was blood on his hands. He realized Donna's blouse was not the only thing that had torn. The flesh of her belly was raked raw in several places.

Donna was moving, but slowly, nonviolently. She was beginning to curl into a fetal position, her body closing around itself in the instinctive, prehuman response to danger and distress. Tom grabbed her under the armpits and pulled her up. Her legs were jelly, unable to take any weight. He shifted his grip and half carried, half dragged her to the couch. He dropped her onto the seat, then poured more brandy into her glass and placed the glass against her lips. Donna sipped slowly, an automatic, undirected action.

Tom stepped quickly away from Donna, to the small kitchen. He found a clean towel, wet it thoroughly with lukewarm water, and returned to Donna. He wiped the dark blood from her belly. He ran an unbloodied portion of the towel across her face and saw the dark bruises emerge from the camouflage of her makeup.

"You should have let me die." Her lips hardly moved. She did not raise her head. Tom cupped her chin and raised it so their eyes met. Donna's were half closed, bleary. "You should have let me die," she said again.

"I couldn't do that."

She looked up at him from beneath her heavy blond eyebrows. The shadows around her eyes seemed almost black in the angled light from the lamp at the end of the couch. "Professional commitment," she said.

Tom felt her head bob slightly against his hand, a small nod. "Only in part," he said. "Mostly I don't think people should throw their lives away." He stepped past her and sat.

Donna seemed aware of this return of their positions to that of the abortive seduction. She shrank back visibly. "Why shouldn't people throw their lives away?" she asked.

There was a quality in her voice Tom was ill put to define. Bitterness, perhaps, though the way she slurred her words now made it hard to be sure.

"It's their life, after all," she went on. "Who has the better right?"

"Ignoring the obvious answer"—Tom smiled, putting all the warmth and sympathy he could command into his own tone—"I'd say no one really has that right. It's a bit too final, after all. No chance to change your mind."

Donna raised her head and looked at him directly. "What if you don't want to change your mind? What if you want to be dead? What if that's become a real, viable alternative to the misery your life has become? What if anything, *anything* would be preferable to the place you're in?"

Tom opened his mouth to speak, but no words would come. Donna's eyes were no longer half closed. They were wide open, and what Tom saw in them sent a searing ache through the deepest part of his being, through his soul. Walker Stone spoke of his concern for the woman he loved—still loved. That was what had brought Tom here. But Tom had come without the slightest inkling of what he might be facing, what might be waiting for him here, in Donna Wojciechowski's apartment. He was not entirely sure even now, looking at Donna, looking into her eyes.

But he would be sure. He promised himself that much. There was something of vast significance, perhaps vast evil unfolding around him. He would fathom it completely and, if necessary, he would place himself directly in contention with it. He would bring the strength of his unshakable faith in opposition to the darkness he felt lying so thick about Donna's heart.

14

In the kitchen of the Garber house Anne Salicrup, the maid, stood in puzzled contemplation, her work forgotten, her mistress forgotten. All thought focused on an attempt to grasp a fleeting fragment of memory, of something that touched a distant part of her brain. Something that prodded at a piece of Anne's brain that seemed to have sealed itself off from the rest. Anne tested her memory, a sensation oddly like touching a loose tooth with the tip of her tongue. There was something there, most assuredly, but the more she probed, the more it seemed to retreat from her. And as it retreated, something else came to take its place. Something darker that flowed like squid's ink around the place she was trying to reach, the memory she was trying to evoke.

The harder she tried to sort out that element, the more the darkness spread through her mind, infiltrating every corner, until there was nothing left but darkness. Darkness and a shadowed, cloaked desire that had lain deep in Anne's troubled breast for many, so many lonely, empty years. A desire that now seemed more and more the focus of her every thought, her every attempt at thought.

As she turned away the phone rang. She thought to ignore it, but reflex beat conscious reaction. Anne picked up the receiver before she even realized she had done so. "Garber residence."

"That you, Anne?"

"Oh, Commissioner. Hello, sir."

"Is my wife there?"

"No, sir. She went out for the evening with some friends." A lie, coming to Anne's mind as quickly and completely as the truth would. All that mattered, her every sense told her, was that Madam and her guest remain undisturbed. But when had she remembered Madame had guests? *Never mind.*

"I thought you knew, sir," Anne said.

"No, she didn't say . . . which friends?"

"She didn't say, sir."

There was a long pause at the other end. Anne tried to picture Garber in his office at City Hall. She always tried to imagine the surroundings of people she spoke to on the telephone, but in this case she could only guess. She had seen no more of Garber's office than one corner, and that in a grainy photograph in the *Sun-Times*. She had extrapolated that into a huge, sumptuous chamber she considered the least her employer deserved, though logic told her there was probably no such extravagant office anywhere in City Hall, even for the mayor.

"She didn't leave a number where she could be reached?" Garber's voice brought Anne back to the kitchen and the phone in her hand.

"No, sir," she said.

"Damn. All right, Anne, just have her call me when she gets home."

"Yes, sir." Anne hung up the phone. Around her all the once familiar objects of the kitchen were indistinct and strange. She could not ascribe any form or function to anything she saw. No thought could find proper purchase in her mind. There was nothing in her mind now but utter, unrelenting despair. Despair she somehow knew had come from Paul Trayne—how could that be, when only good came from Paul?—placed in her, hurled at her when . . .

What? Again there was a flickering memory. Paul. Mrs. Garber. The living room. Something Anne had seen. Something she was not meant to see, to know. But the images were lost beyond the blackness that consumed Anne Salicrup's soul.

She strode through the kitchen into the side hall, the same

hall through which Paul Trayne had made his first entrance into the Garber house. She opened the side door and walked out onto the steps. They descended to right and left, a wrought iron railing between Anne and a fairly long fall. She turned right, toward the back of the house. As she went down the steps a sudden suck of wind closed the door behind her with a slam. The glass rattled.

Anne did not hear. She passed around the side of the house, between the rear corner and the front corner of the garage, and walked across the back lawn. Light from the living room window spilled across the deep snow.

Anne kept walking, the going far from easy. The snow was deep. In many places across the broad expanse of the Garber property it had risen in fluted drifts, like the waves of sand across a desert, forcing Anne to lift her knees high and plunge her nylon-stockinged legs deep into the freezing cold.

On she walked, until the smooth snow was broken into jagged, jutting angles, looking, she thought, like a miniaturized representation of a great mountain range, the Rockies or the Alps. She mounted the slope of one wide, sharp-edged stone, six feet across its broken base. The going was treacherous, a slim layer of ice coating the face of the rock under the dusting of snow. She was forced, eventually, to proceed on all fours, crawling across the granite, tearing the flesh of her right knee at one point, and from then on leaving a widening dot of blood each time the knee took weight, a scarlet period to the end of each swing of leg. At last she cleared the rocks and stood at the edge of Lake Michigan. The blood running down her leg was hot against the cold of her flesh. She looked out across the flat, black surface of the lake. Away to her right the sky was turned to mother-of-pearl by the lights of Chicago, to the left the dimmer colorings of Evanston. Ahead, out on the waters, lighted buoys rose and fell in the inky blackness: stars, she thought, fallen from the dome of a sky obscured by heavy clouds.

Anne stood looking into the darkness for some time before her right hand rose to the Velcro fastener across the top of her apron, around the back of her neck. With a sound like tearing cloth Anne pulled the fastening apart and took off the apron.

She folded it neatly and set it on a taller spur of rock to her left. She unfastened her skirt, pulling down the zipper on her right hip and stepping out of the tapering cylinder of dark cloth. The wind was cold against the bare flesh above the tops of her stockings. She unhooked her delicate lace garter belt and set it atop the folded skirt. Balancing precariously on each foot in turn, she took off her plain black pumps and rolled down her stockings. She stripped off the rest of her clothes, goose pimples rising to march across exposed flesh, her nipples tightening in the chill. She stood naked, shivering.

It was the only time Anne had ever been naked outside her own quarters, the only time she had ever placed herself in such a position that anyone else could have seen what she was so ashamed for even her mirror to see. She looked down at her spare, bony form, the sad, slack breasts that hung like dry sacks over the exaggerated xylophone of her ribs. The hollow, fruitless belly. The narrow, boyish hips. The gaunt thighs, the big, bony knees. She hated what she saw, and hated the world that made her hate it, made her long for a full-fleshed body, with high, proud breasts and long, full-fleshed legs. The kind of body, Anne knew, Donna Wojciechowski had.

In fact, there was nothing nearly so wrong with Anne Salicrup's body as her imagination painted. She was slender, and the joints of her bones were large, but it was more her own repressive upbringing—not so very different in the broadest detail from that of the woman she envied—that drove Anne to loathe a body that many a man would have found as much and more than he could ever desire. And it was that loathing that was fanned to a consuming flame now as Anne stood shivering on the spur of cold, hard rock, white and frightened in the darkness.

She looked back over her shoulder toward the house, her feet facing the lake and planted firmly on the stone beneath her. The stone didn't feel so cold now; it drew heat from the soles of her feet. She turned back to the lake, stepped to the edge of the rock, and looked down into the icy lake waters. Small pieces of drifting ice washed back and forth in the ebb and flow of the waters, brushing against the rocks, leaving shards of themselves in the water. She stepped down from the

rock. She was not sure, not altogether clear in her mind, as to
what she might expect from this action. Her descending foot
pierced the black surface of the lake. A water demon with ten
thousand icy fangs clamped its jaws around her leg. Anne had
never experienced such sudden, jolting pain. She cried out and
tried to pull her foot back, thoughts suddenly clear, suddenly
her own, but it was too late. The jerking movement combined
with the slick surface of her platform sent her supporting left
foot slipping to the side, out from under her. She flailed her
arms, but balance was not to be regained. She fell full length
into the waters of the lake. The ice demon drove its muzzle
through the walls of her chest and sank its teeth into her heart.
She screamed once, swallowing, choking, and vanished beneath the waters.

A while later, seen by no one, dark in the darkness, a tall,
lanky form separated itself from the shadows by the side of the
Garber house. The figure crossed the deep snows easily with its
long legs and moved with a spider's agility across the tumble of
rock at the water's edge. Big hands, thick-skinned and heavily
veined, gathered up Anne's abandoned garments and tucked
them inside a worn, frayed-edged black morning coat that
hung loosely about the figure's broad, bony frame. Robert
Johnston Trayne turned his dark, Abe Lincoln eyes toward the
Garber house. For a moment the drooping lids drew back
fully, and anyone looking into those eyes would not have mis-
taken the madness that gleamed in the shadows of his brows.
He looked back toward the lake. Something white and glistening was drifting away on the gentle pull of the waters. As the
elder Trayne watched, it turned over, slowly, revealing small,
fleshless breasts and a dark triangle of pubic hair.

It sank. Trayne smiled, his face not at all old Abe Lincoln's.
He moved with spidery ease into the shadows under the trees,
making his way toward the street. His job here, his mission
with Marjorie Garber, was done. It was time to get back to the
Wojciechowski woman's apartment. It had been an unfortunate but necessary expedient that she be left alone to deal with
this meddlesome priest. It was time to get back, to add Paul's
powers to Donna's feminine wiles.

There was no doubt in Trayne's mind that Donna would, by

now, have seduced the priest and brought him to their side. His mind filled momentarily with the image of the two of them, Donna and the priest, locked in the throes of carnal ecstasy, her long legs wrapped about the priest's naked body as he pounded his manhood into her welcoming flesh. It was the power of all women that they could strip a man of his senses, ensnare and enthrall even the strongest. And it was Robert Trayne's firm opinion that priests by their very nature were far from the strongest of men. The vow of chastity that they believed strengthened them, he was sure, created a cancer in the center of their souls. A man was not meant to deny himself the pleasures of the female flesh. Only to deny them, the women, the power that pleasure might bring.

"Father . . . ?" Paul stood by the side door, the door through which they had first entered the Garber house.

"Done," Trayne said. "She will not be telling anyone we were here." He smiled. "Time to get back to Sister Wojcie-chowski."

"Yes . . ." The pause hung between them.

"Paul?"

"Will she . . ." Paul seemed not quite able to find the words. "Will she need punishing again, Father? Will she need another lesson?"

Trayne nodded. "Almost certainly. She will have to be punished for what she has done tonight in your service. She must be made to understand that such things are not done by her free will. That she is your slave."

Paul nodded. "Yes," he said, and the smile he smiled was very like his father's.

The latest in what was beginning to seem an unending stream of grim discoveries awaited Pete Hay back at the station house. As he carried the heavily sedated Marcy Kavelhoff up the steps and into the outer offices, Pete was already shouting Arnie Steadman's name at the top of his lungs. When he crossed into the back, where the cells were, he learned why Steadman was not answering.

The door to cell 4 stood open. Arnie Steadman lay on the floor, still sitting in his overturned wheelchair, his head at a terribly wrong angle on his neck. Pete wanted to scream, wanted to hurl Marcy's limp body against a wall and start smashing things. Chairs. Desks. Anything he could lay hands on. He wanted to smash and scream and rage against the madness consuming the town he'd grown up in. But he couldn't. Duty, devotion to the memory of Clarence Nickerson, crouched all around his brain and made him stop and breathe slowly and evenly, eyes closed, until the need to go insane backed off a few paces and he could look again at poor Arnie and his twisted neck. Pete hauled Marcy into the cell opposite, number 3, dumped her on the cot, and slammed the door. Then he turned back to face cell 4. Mae Ellen Faber, not at all surprisingly, was nowhere in sight.

"Hell and damnation," said Pete.

He jogged back through the front of the station, out the doors, and down the steps to his car. He climbed behind the wheel and, less than five minutes later, pulled up in front of Harrison District Hospital. He'd dropped Zeldenrust and Alice Nickerson off there not fifteen minutes before. The bodies of the Kavelhoff children remained where they lay, on Marcy's kitchen table.

Pete left his engine running and ran up the steps to the big glass doors of the central lobby. He pushed through. The wide, high lobby area was still, silent. He saw no one at the reception desk and went on through into the hospital proper. The silence followed him.

Where's the goddamn staff?

He looked through the round porthole windows of a couple of the public wards as he passed. He saw only a few patients in their beds, but no nurses or doctors.

It started to get to him. When he reached a junction of four main corridors, Pete stopped and turned. There was no one as far as he could see in any direction. His heart pounded. He took a deep breath and yelled Zeldenrust's name at the top of his lungs. He yelled again. After a few thunderous heartbeats the old doctor poked his head out of one of the private rooms down at the end of the hall to Pete's right.

"Pete? What the hell . . . ?"

"You gotta come to the station house, Doc," Pete said, walking quickly toward Zeldenrust. The hairs were prickling on the back of Pete's neck. He was tensed, and he realized it was for an anticipated assault from one of the doorways between his position and Zeldenrust's. The silence and the emptiness were so wrong in Pete's mind that he was beginning to feel certain people were hiding from him, just waiting to pounce.

Zeldenrust sighed and sagged. "Petey, I am very tired. All this craziness, these deaths . . ."

"Yeah, well, we got another one, Doc." Pete told Zeldenrust what he had found. It was hard to judge Zeldenrust's reaction. The enormous weariness in his thick features overlaid everything else.

"All right," Zeldenrust said. "Is your car out front? Go wait there. I'll be right out." He stepped back into the private room. The *very* private room, Pete saw as the door closed. SECURITY WARD—NO ADMITTANCE was emblazoned on the door. Pete looked through the round window and saw Zeldenrust approaching Alice Nickerson. She was lying on a bed against the far wall, under a tall window covered with a thick steel mesh. Alice was lashed to the bed and seemed to Pete to be sleeping peacefully.

He turned and jogged back to the front doors. The night air was bitterly cold. When he inhaled his nostrils closed with a click. Pete walked down to the patrol car, climbed in, and slid down low in the seat. He tried very hard not to think of anything at all that had happened in the last twenty-four hours. He tried to concentrate on his one-room apartment and how soon he might be able to climb into bed and let the exhaustion poisoning his blood and his thoughts finally overwhelm him.

The passenger door opened. "All right, Petey," said Maurice Zeldenrust through the scarf he'd wrapped around the lower half of his face. "Let's go."

Pete gunned the car away from the curb, intending to take the first right, Albert Street, and circle back to the station. He didn't get very far. As he rounded the end of the block onto Albert, he hit the brakes hard. The patrol car slid sideways and did not stop before the crunch of metal on the outboard fender told Pete his tail had slammed into one of the cars parked along the curb.

Zeldenrust was leaning forward in his seat, peering through the windshield with wide eyes. "What in name of . . . ?"

Pete was already out of the car. His headlights lit the scene in stark relief. Half a block ahead a crude barricade had been thrown up across the street. Sofas and tables and even an old freestanding bathtub had been piled across the narrow pass between the parked cars. Pete was out in front of the patrol car. His shadow stretched down the street. Along the top of the barricade sat three men. Pete knew two of them. He knew all three of the rifles they held.

"Hold it right there, Pete," said the middle man, sliding down the front of the barrier and advancing to a few paces from Pete Hay. His long-barreled hunting rifle was slung casually over his right shoulder by a leather strap fastened to barrel and stock. Pete could see how easily it could be whipped up into firing position.

"What the hell is this, Frank?" Pete demanded. He kept his right hand hanging loosely near the holster of his service issue .45. He was excruciatingly aware of how long it would take him to unfasten the clasp securing the leather flap across the top of the holster and free the weapon. And how very little time it would take for Frank Parady to level that rifle and put a shot through Pete's head.

"We're staking a claim," Parady said. He was tall and dark. In the light from the patrol car his eyes glinted and seemed to Pete to be not altogether human. "Me and Ted and Howie have lived on this street nearly twenty-five years, each and every one of us. We've decided we don't want people makin' such free and easy use of our property anymore."

"Your property?" Pete was having real trouble following the sense of what he was hearing.

"This street," said Howie Manson, maintaining his position on top of the crude barricade.

"This street isn't your property," Pete said. In a different context he knew he would have laughed. The way the other two men shifted their grips on their rifles told Pete this was not the time.

"Your houses, maybe," Pete said, "but the street belongs to . . ."

"Us," said Parady, a steel edge to his voice.

"Don't be stupid, Frank. I have to take Doc Zeldenrust to the station house. I'll circle back and take the next block over, but after I drop him I'm coming back." He gestured at the precarious mound of old furniture. "When I get back I want this street cleared." He turned and started back toward the patrol car. Behind him Parady's rifle boomed. Six inches to the left of Pete's booted foot the pavement flashed and *pinged*.

Pete froze and turned slowly, using his body to cover the motion of his hand to his holster. He unlatched the flap and tucked it back behind the butt of the .45. Parady, rifle raised to shooting position, still had the advantage, but Pete felt a hundred percent better with his gun that much more accessible.

"You stupid idiot," Pete said. "Now I'm gonna have to take you in."

Parady shook his head slowly from side to side. Pete's peripheral vision picked up the movement of the others, shifting along the top of the barrier, placing themselves wider apart. Even if he could somehow manage to get his pistol clear and squeeze off a shot at Parady—Pete was a crack shot, but it would take a lot of luck to hit Parady anywhere that would prevent him from returning fire, even at this range—there was no way he could fire on either of the others before they would have drawn a bead on him. "You're not taking any of us anywhere, Pete," Parady said. "We've put up long enough with people driving and walking all up and down our street. Dogs crapping on our lawns. Kids playing. Teenagers with their goddamn radios blaring at all hours of the day and night. D'you know I caught young Cassie Ellis in the backseat of her father's Dodge last week with her boyfriend? She was suckin' him off! Right there in the car, right on the street. Where any of our kids could walk up and look!" Parady's face twisted at the memory. "Now we're putting a stop to it."

Pete looked from Parady to the other two, back again. "And what about the other people on this block? What do they have to say about this?"

"They're with us," said the man Parady had identified as Ted.

"Then where are they?" Pete kept his eyes on Parady, measuring distances, wondering if he might be able to get close enough to use Parady's body as a shield against the return fire of the other men. Unlikely. And given that Frank Parady was bone thin, it seemed a good bet to Pete the rifles the others carried would be able to pierce his body and hit Pete anyway.

"The others are minding the other end of the block, watching TV, or sleeping," said Parady. "This is our watch. We've been taking turns all day."

Pete sighed, his breath a white cloud to either side of his face, the shadow of his head a dark tunnel through the steam. It occurred to him that Parady might be at something of a disadvantage, with Pete standing as he was with his back to the lights of the patrol car. Not enough of a disadvantage, though.

"All right, Frank," Pete said. "I'm not going to stand here freezing my ass off arguing. You can keep your damn barricade, if it makes you feel like real men." Pete saw the muscles twitch along Parady's jaw. "I'm going to turn around and walk back to my car and drive away. But you better know this is damn stupid and it ain't gonna last long."

Parady raised the rifle until the end of the barrel was level with the tip of Pete's nose. "I'd have to say you're wrong on that one, Pete." He smiled. "I give you free passage to leave, but don't think you can come back making trouble. This is our street now. We mean to keep it that way."

"Petey . . ." It was Zeldenrust, suddenly opening his door and sticking his head out into the cold night. Pete turned and dived as a shot rang out. He hit the hood of the patrol car rolling, pulling out the .45, pulling back the slide and firing blind. He saw Parady reel back, his shoulder spraying pink froth into the headlights. Pete hit the pavement on the other side of the car. Another shot boomed. He heard the glass shatter in the passenger side door.

Pete landed awkwardly, but on his feet. He scampered like a jackrabbit around the back of the car. He stuck his head and arm around the passenger side—Zeldenrust had pulled the door shut again—and squeezed off two shots in succession. He heard one clang against the enameled cast iron of the old bathtub. The second elicited a sharp bark of pain from somewhere behind the barricade. "Doc!" Pete's voice was a harsh stage whisper. "Can you hear me? Are you hit?"

"I'm okay," came the reply through the shattered passenger side window.

"Slide over behind the wheel," Pete said. "Start backing away. Slowly. I'm gonna be right behind you."

"Petey . . ."

"Just do it, for Christ's sake, Doc. And be careful! If I have to duck to one side to keep from getting run over, these idiots will have a clear shot at me."

"Petey, I haven't driven a car in thirty years . . ."

"Would you please just do it? We gotta get our tails outta here before the rest of these lunatics come crawling out of their houses."

The car bounced on its springs as Zeldenrust complied. Pete put a hand against the cold metal and tried to guess just how ready the old doctor was. The brake lights brightened as Zeldenrust put his foot on the pedal. The amber backup lights lit up. Still hunkered down, Pete began backing away. The car followed, as if the hand Pete leaned against it was drawing the vehicle along with him. The back of the car wobbled from side to side. Pete kept his balance, kept the .45 leveled at the barricade. Something round and headlike popped up as soon as the car started moving. Pete fired his fourth shot and the head dropped. The bullet *thucked* into a big armchair, toppling it down the far side of the wall of junk. They reached the end of the block.

"Turn the wheel to the right," Pete whispered, and the back of the car swung around to his right a moment later. Pete crawled to the driver's side door and opened it. "Slide over," he said.

Zeldenrust moved immediately. He did not shift the automatic transmission out of reverse and the car started to roll back with Pete only halfway in. Pete's left boot dragged along the pavement and his shin hit the base of the open door. For a moment it threatened to bend, to snap halfway up the calf. He grabbed the wheel-mounted shift and pushed it up into neutral. The transmission howled, but the car lurched to a stop, then rolled forward on the slight incline of the street. The pressure against Pete's leg was gone. Pete pulled himself all the way in and slammed the door. He shifted into drive and shoved his foot down against the gas pedal. "Get your head down," he snapped. The doctor ducked, banging his forehead against the glove compartment door.

Pete leveled his pistol across Zeldenrust's back and fired three of his remaining shots at the barricade. There was no return fire as the car raced away. Pete pulled over hard right, bounced over the corner, and sped away from the seceded street. "Damnation," he said, and again.

Zeldenrust straightened, rubbing his forehead gently with his mittened fingers. "What was that all about?"

"You tell me, Doc." Pete swung the car onto Randolph. The houses were quiet, the glow of TV sets flickering in most of the windows. "I've never had to deal with a whole goddamn street that didn't want to be part of a town before."

Zeldenrust said nothing. He stared ahead, and the silence stretched until Pete turned onto Jefferson and the lights of the police station came into sight. "This is all very bad," he said at last. "Very bad."

Pete stopped the patrol car in front of the police station and turned to stare at Zeldenrust.

Brilliant, he thought, but he said nothing.

15

 Clayton Garber turned off the radio by the window of the breakfast nook and turned to face his cook. "I'm sorry, Rose. What were you saying?"

"I said I don't know where she could 'ave got off to, Commissioner. None of her clothes is gone, and the suitcase she always uses is still in the back of her closet, but 'er bed wasn't slept in, and she didn't leave no note for me. She always does, you know, if she's called away unexpected."

Clay looked at Rose over the top of his glasses. His mind was full of other things—not the least of which being Marjorie's vagueness about where and with whom she'd been the night before—and had Rose not brought it to his attention, he wouldn't have noticed Anne was missing, if "missing" was not too strong a word.

"It wasn't her night off, last night? No, of course. She was here to answer the phone." He could never seem to keep straight in his mind the various days off of the staff. Luckily Marjorie always knew who was where, and when. "She seemed fine then . . ."

Didn't she?

"Last night were my night off, not 'ers. But she weren't 'ere when I got 'ome."

"And that was around midnight, you said?"

"Yes, sir. I went to the late show at the Gem. They were

showing *No Love for Johnnie.* I've ever such a fondness for Peter Finch, as you know, sir." Rose's Cockney accent, usually carefully controlled, was quite pronounced this morning. Garber had learned to recognize that sign of extreme agitation in the cook.

"No, I didn't know. Could she be with . . . a boy-friend . . . ?" The words brought Anne to Clay's mind, and he found it immediately impossible to place her into any kind of romantic situation.

"No, sir," Rose said; Clay heard a dismissing tone in her voice that matched his thoughts.

"Well . . ." Clay shrugged. It all seemed odd, but unimportant. Anne was in her late thirties—he thought—and she could surely take care of herself. "Perhaps she got a call from a friend or something. Some kind of emergency."

"But no *note,* Commissioner." Clay sensed her use of his title was this time intended to demonstrate the degree to which she'd applied proper police procedure, collecting her clues.

"Mmm." Clay shrugged again. "If she doesn't turn up, or if we don't hear from her by, oh, this afternoon, I suppose I can find somebody to put on it. Or my wife can call . . ."

"Madame will be out all day today, sir."

Clay frowned, trying to remember what he knew Marjorie must have told him. "Oh, yes. One of her lunches." He unfolded his copy of the *Advocate* into reading position and rustled the crisp pages in a punctuating fashion. "You call then, Rose. I'll trust your judgment. If you really decide it's a police matter, call me at downtown."

"Yes, Commissioner. Thank you, sir." She returned to the stove, and his breakfast.

Clay started reading the front page. Rose finished preparing his bacon and eggs and turned to find him staring at the smudgy black newsprint as if, she thought, he was trying to force the letters to rearrange themselves on the page. She tipped her head to follow the line of his gaze and read the first few words of the piece that so gripped his attention. Finding nothing of interest she turned away to dish up his breakfast.

Clay continued to stare at the newspaper. It was a short

article. He'd almost missed it, down at the bottom of page four of the *Advocate*.

CHARLES ADDISON KILGORE DEAD AT 57, said the headline. The article devoted most of its space to the bizarre details of Kilgore's death. He'd been found in bed by one of the maids at the Waterbury Hotel. When no one answered her knock she'd used her pass key, intending to make up the beds and change the linens. Her scream had awakened the entire seventeenth floor. Kilgore was lying on the bed, fully dressed, his face twisted in such an expression of absolute horror that none of the people who saw it would ever be able to drive it from their minds. The reporter, who had evidently not seen the body himself, spent considerable column space on vivid first-person descriptions from those who had. Clay shuddered at the clarity of imagery. The man should have been writing horror fiction. He would have made Stephen King sound like a novice.

Garber scanned the rest of the article. Kilgore's wife—*widow*, Clay corrected the usage automatically—was flying in that afternoon to claim the body. There was nothing else of significance.

But Clay knew one thing the paper did not mention. Charles Addison Kilgore, financier, real estate developer, self-made billionaire, had an appointment with Mayor Emmanuel Stuartson at eleven A.M. this very day, Friday, the fourteenth of February. Valentine's Day. It seemed incongruous at best.

He asked Rose to bring him the cordless phone from its place by the door. She did, then went back to her cooking. He flipped up the call button and dialed. He waited as the lines buzzed and clicked before his MCI service connected. His mind was full of the terribly clear picture the paper created of the remains of Charles Addison Kilgore. It was not at all difficult to believe the reporter's assertion that Kilgore had been literally frightened to death. The question was, by what?

"Stanislavski."

"Garber. What do we have on the Kilgore case?"

"Oh, morning, Commissioner. Looks like just a coronary." Jacob Stanislavski was Garber's second-in-command. If there was anything to know, he would know it. If there was any

reason to suspect foul play, Stanislavski had an almost preternatural way of sensing it.

"Then, nothing to get involved with at this point?"

"I shouldn't think so, Commissioner."

"All right, Jake. Thanks."

Garber broke the connection and sat tapping the phone
against his chin for a moment. He reached up to the ledge by
the window over the table and extricated the Near North Suburban phone book from the magazines that had accumulated
there. He flipped to the W's and paged through until he found
the number he wanted, then dialed.

The phone rang at the other end. A familiar male voice
answered. "Ah, hello, Reverend Trayne? Good morning, sir.
Clay Garber. Is Donna there? No? Well, er, I have some . . .
well, some rather odd news . . ."

For the second time in as many days, Ben Carpenter woke on
the sofa in the big main office of the *Faulkner Observer.* His
head pounded. His stomach churned. His eyelids were lined
with grit, and at his first move his muscles screamed at him. He
rolled his legs off the sofa, pushing himself into something ap-
proximating a sitting position. In and around the barbed wire
wrapping his brain, Ben found scraps of thought that seemed
as though they should be commanding his attention. He
looked around the office. It was as he'd left it when he sank
onto the couch, exhausted. He pushed himself up off the sofa.
Something in the back of his mind told him there had been a
sound of some kind, somewhere. His thoughts steadfastly refused to be any more lucid on the subject. His thinking processes were muddled, he knew. He was still out of kilter from
the flurry of the day's discoveries. The disappearance of Paul
Trayne, the bizarre scene in Keene's Hardware, and, of course,
the condition in which he'd found the *Observer* office when he
entered.

The whole room was a shambles. Desks had been overturned, drawers pulled out, and contents scattered. The railing
surrounding his secretary's desk was broken, part of it smashed
flat, the oaken spindles snapped. Pictures had been thrown
from the walls, and broken glass crunched under his feet as he

entered. Ben had stood for a long time, shaking his head slowly
from side to side, struggling to comprehend what had happened to this safe harbor of his life. He'd left the office door
unlocked, of course, when he raced out to the police station.
That much he remembered, and with the memory he felt a
terrible pang of guilt and grief—alien sensations now, after the
effects of Paul Trayne's gift. This vandalism was his fault. Whoever had done it could not have got in, had he not left the door
unlocked. The steel mesh on the inside of the frosted glass
would have stopped them, unless they had brought the tools
necessary to force the lock. That seemed unlikely, since the big
bolt shot a full six inches into the steel-braced door frame—a
concession to what Ben always dismissed as his predecessor's
wartime paranoia. The mesh and bolt had been installed during World War II, a defense, Ben had been told, against any
German or Japanese invaders. Finding the destruction, he'd
closed the office door behind him, locking it this time, and
crossed to his office.

Everything was in a shambles there, too. His desk stood on
one end. His framed newspapers were destroyed, the glass broken, the fragile newsprint shredded, so much confetti on the
floor. He pulled the desk back into its proper position and
lifted his typewriter back onto the desk top. He tapped a few
keys at random, and the strikers responded with their usual
satisfying *thunk* against the hard rubber of the roller. He
straightened his chair and sat, looking across the desk to the
office door and the carnage of the newsroom beyond.

Who could have done this? His first thought was a disgruntled employee, and he wondered why that seemed a natural
thing to think. He leaned back in his chair and kneaded the
bridge of his nose with the thumb and forefinger of his right
hand, eyes closed, thoughts wandering. It seemed logical that a
disgruntled staffer would have come here and done all this.
That fit with the pattern evolving in Faulkner, a pattern even
Ben, in his clouded state, could not fail to notice. A pattern of
violence, of . . . release. He felt a part of it, as he sat and
surveyed the ruins of the *Observer* office. He'd straightened his
desk and chair, but only because they were his, his things, his

property. His inclination was to leave the rest of the office as he found it.

It doesn't matter, said the voice in his head, back again, coaxing Ben to consider his own needs, his own wants, and ignore what the world might consider his responsibilities.

Ben sat up. "No," he'd said aloud to the empty room. "No, that's not right."

He'd stood up and walked out into the newsroom. Slowly, very slowly at first, he'd begun to straighten and restore what he could. He squatted on the floor and sorted through the papers strewn like leaves on autumn grass. He made educated guesses as to which belonged with which, and which drawer of which desk was their home.

It was about twenty minutes into this reconstruction that he thought he heard a noise in the alley behind the office. A *sequence* of sounds, really. A loud, teeth-gritting squeal of metal on stone, followed a few minutes later by what sounded like the crack of dry wood, followed in turn, almost immediately, by another sort of crack. Wet. Unpleasant. He'd ignored the sounds then. There would be time enough to investigate the curious sounds when he was done with the task he'd set himself.

Halfway through the cleanup he began to feel hungry. He reentered his office cubicle, dialed the Panda Pavilion, and placed an order for delivery. It arrived, enough food for three people, and Ben sat behind his desk to eat—to gorge again—for a full hour before he returned to the task of restoring the *Observer* offices. Two hours later he swung back the gate on what was left of the railing around Hannah Clark's enclosure and crossed to the main door. He jiggled the latch, determined that the door was still locked, and flipped up the three switches that worked the overhead lights. He made a slow circuit of the office, part of his brain still wondering what the noise might have been—if it was a noise; he still wasn't sure—the rest wondering what in the world he was bothering for.

He felt vaguely pleased that this latter part seemed smaller than it had been. The golden glow of Paul Trayne's influence had dimmed, if only slightly. He returned to his private cubicle. He closed the door, so as not to have to look at what ruin

remained, which was too much for him to fix. He sat behind
the desk and threaded a sheet of blank paper into his old manual Smith-Corona. He leaned back, cracked his knuckles, and
stared into the white infinity of the empty page. He was still
staring at that virgin sheet when he thought again of the
sounds. He would have gone to investigate then, but the words
that had been swirling around inside his head suddenly began
their orderly march to his fingertips, and he leaned forward to
type. He forgot all about the sound again, for a while.

After half an hour of typing, Ben remembered where he
thought the sounds had come from. He left his inner office,
went into the storeroom, and stepped across to the tiny window. He looked down into the alley. Someone, a woman, was
lying—hanging—at what seemed a particularly awkward and
uncomfortable angle, one leg bent oddly over the rim of a tall,
flat box leaning on end against the crates against the stone
wall. He registered that the woman in the alley was Mae Ellen.
That struck him as odd, in and of itself, but he wasn't sure why.
He tapped at the glass to catch her attention. She did not respond. He shrugged and walked away from the window. He
crossed back to his office and picked up the phone. He dialed
the number of the Panda Pavilion and placed another order for
Chinese food. He turned, swept the dozen or so piled cartons
off his desk to make room for the new ones when they came,
and sat back down in front of the typewriter.

He cracked his knuckles again and started typing.

"She's resting more comfortably now, Father, but she's still
running a bit of a fever. I think we should call a doctor."

Tom Sylvestri looked up from his reading and set the Bible
facedown over his knee. He was sitting in the big wing chair by
the fireplace in his study. His housekeeper stood over him, lit
in front by flickering yellow light from the fire and behind by
cold, white outdoor light. Beyond the tall windows the snow
was falling heavily, as he'd thought it would. The room, beyond the glow of the fire, was quite chill.

"I don't think a doctor would be a very good idea just now,"
Tom said. He did not mention that his reticence came from the
knowledge that, given the circumstances, a doctor might want

to inform the police. He wanted more concrete information, a more solid base from which to act, before he allowed the authorities to be brought in on all this. He wasn't sure why. Instinct, he thought. The same instinct that had told him to carry Donna out of her apartment last night after his flying tackle caught her and pulled her back from the precipice. Carry her away from whatever caused her strange behavior. He was convinced it was strange for her, even though he did not really know her.

"I think," he added, "that Miss Wojciechowski would be best served by being left to . . . shall we say, her own resources?"

So far Mrs. Buck was being very good about this decidedly odd business, Tom thought. He'd awakened her at close to midnight, rousing her from her little room, her cozy bed, to help him tend to Donna Wojciechowski. As housekeeper at St. Timothy's, Mrs. Buck had served John Percival for most of his tenure at the church. Now she cared for Tom Sylvestri, cooking and cleaning and generally giving the church residence the look of a proper Christian house—as she put it—and not the domicile of a confirmed bachelor.

After all, Father Tom was quick to agree, that was as good a description of a priest as was anything else; while it would be generally acknowledged a priest could have his spiritual life well in hand, he was as likely to drop his dirty socks in the middle of the bedroom floor as any man.

So Mrs. Buck came to see the strange woman Tom installed in the guest room next to his own bedroom. She asked no questions and, clearly, expected no explanations. She'd bustled Tom out of the room—she did everything in something of a bustle, he thought—then stripped and bathed Donna, cleaned off her makeup—yes, there were bruises under the blush on her jaw—dried her, and somehow managed to get her into one of Father Percival's old flannel nightshirts she'd retrieved from a trunk in the vestry attic. This last act impressed Tom most of all, given that Donna was almost twice as tall as Mrs. Buck, if only half her weight.

It had been eleven and a half hours since Tom had roused Mrs. Buck. In that time Donna had been asleep, except for one brief session of twisting and wailing, which caused Mrs. Buck to bustle Tom from the room again. He'd come down to his office, lit a fire, and opened the old Bible Monsignor Cameron had given him when he left the seminary. In the years since he'd last seen his mentor, it had been a source of great inspiration and comfort, but he sought neither at that moment. Rather he was looking for armor, a weapon against the insidious presence of Robert Trayne.

"It's your decision of course, Father," Mrs. Buck said, though her tone did not agree with her words. "I've done as much for her as I can."

"I'm sure that's plenty, Mrs. B. Perhaps if you could prepare some lunch now? I'm afraid I haven't eaten since yesterday."

Mrs. Buck clucked at this dereliction and bustled herself out the door of Tom's study, bound for the kitchen. Tom set the Bible on the small side table and went to the window. Beyond the convoluted rooftops of the old sandstone buildings huddled around St. Timothy's, the tops of the tall buildings of Chicago rose, glass giants. After five minutes, during which time his thoughts ranged far, his brain ill equipped to the task of marshaling them, he turned from the window to discover the small fire had gone out.

Tom adjusted the rotating thermostat to bring some heat to the room, then walked briskly down the tall, narrow hall bisecting the vestry. Two hundred black-and-white photographs looked down on him as he passed. A tunnel, he thought, composed of the whole history of St. Timothy's, captured in moments of grainy two-tone: forgotten faces, faded, brown, and indistinct. He felt the eyes of those faces watching him as he passed. A hundred years of priests and churchmen—even a pope—looking down on Tom Sylvestri, their frozen expressions neither accusing nor forgiving.

How many of you came to your calling for the same reasons I did?

Father Tom paused at the foot of the stairs, looking back along the hall. There were always whispers about the number of homosexuals in the priesthood. Lately, it seemed to Tom, it had become much more than whispers. Joseph Terranova professed—*had professed*—to have one gay friend who swore he'd had more men of the cloth than, in his words, a Vatican Council.

The temptations of the flesh are always strong. How many priests have surrendered to the lure of a woman's charms? At least three of the men I was with at seminary are married now. One even asked me to be godfather to his son!

He looked at the pictures again.

So many faces. So many servants of God. And yet, from the more cynical viewpoint of a vanishing twentieth century, how many of you would be in defiance of one of God's first laws, in spirit if not in fact? I am not the first priest to have fallen from the path. I shall not be the last.

He climbed the stairs, remembering the first time he'd broached the subject of his homosexuality, obliquely, to Monsignor Cameron at the seminary.

"The Bible is quite specific, my son," Cameron said. "I should not have to quote any passages for you. Not with your memory." He'd inclined his head and looked deep into the eyes of young Tom Sylvestri. "I don't think there's a great deal of room for interpretation, do you?"

"But," Tom had protested feebly, "if there is no physical act? If it's only in the . . . the heart? The mind?"

Monsignor Cameron steepled his hands, resting the tips of his index fingers against his chin. "Our Savior said that to lust in the heart was every bit as evil as the physical deed."

"You think homosexuals are evil, Father?" Tom had felt his soul shrivel.

"I think the fires that burn in their souls are evil," Monsignor Cameron said. He'd looked over the slim, dark rims of his perfectly circular spectacles, eyes pale and old but missing absolutely nothing.

"The Good Lord put us here on earth for many reasons, Thomas, and not the least of them was the propagation of the species. Yet, even in that Our Savior preached against the weaknesses of the flesh. Recall that He praised those who had made themselves eunuchs for the sake of the Kingdom of Heaven. In any case, it was not God's intent that men find love with other men, or women with other women. Look to Romans, chapter one, twenty-six through thirty-two. Or Leviticus, chapter eighteen, verse twenty-two. Or First Corinthians, chapter six, verse nine. Can you quote those for me, Thomas? Or has your wonderful memory found itself a few selective holes?"

Tom had chewed his lower lip and wondered if he should speak of some of the things he'd heard, beyond the walls of the seminary, about the young nuns and how they were welcomed by their older sisters. It seemed a sacrilege even to have such thoughts, yet it was obvious that those who spread the tales were excited by the concept. In those days, still confused and frightened by his own sexuality, Tom had not seen anything erotic in the notion. Nevertheless, he quoted the Scriptures, in the order his mentor had named them.

"But surely some of that proves the point," he'd said to Monsignor Cameron. "Romans, chapter one, verse twenty-six says that it is God Himself who 'gave them up unto vile affectations.' So, surely it is the Lord who makes a homosexual what he is? Does He not create each of us, specially, to be who and what we are?"

And are we "vile"? he did not want to ask. It would be years before he would decide in his own heart that the answer to that question was "no."

"Some think God makes men twisted and evil as part of His plan. Consider Proverbs, chapter sixteen, verse four," Monsignor Cameron said. "But that implies predestination, and I do not believe in predestination." He'd shaken his head. "Recall that last verse of Romans, chapter one: '. . . they which commit such things are worthy of death. . . .' I believe in the concepts of heaven and hell, Thomas, and I cannot bring myself to accept anything but free will if I am to remain firm in that belief. God would not make us sinners. He would not create us to burn. That is contradictory, an insult to the Creator to make Him so spiteful and petty."

Tom struggled a moment with the inherent contradictions he heard in the old man's words. Monsignor Cameron was quick to quote Scripture, to enforce the exact letter and deny interpretation. Yet when he found something he could not entirely accept . . .

"God is often spiteful and petty." It was one of the boldest statements Tom Sylvestri dared utter in the presence of an older priest. He waited for lightning to strike, to leap directly from Monsignor Cameron's eyes. When it did not, he said, "Was it not petty to turn Lot's wife into a pillar of salt? Or spiteful to torment Job?"

Cameron had rocked his head from side to side, eyebrows raised. "I might agree with you, if I agreed that God could be measured by mortal precepts. There is much in the Bible that seems cruel and petty, and indeed would be cruel and petty, were it not the Lord who was behind it. God does not answer to us, after all. It is we who answer to Him. It touches on faith. God refuses to prove He exists. I think He does not have to."

Monsignor Cameron looked from side to side, seeming to see beyond the tall walls of the seminary garden where they sat, a summer breeze rustling the green canopy above them. "The devil is so active in proving his existence, and, of course, one implies the other."

"One implies the other . . ." said Tom Sylvestri, twenty years later, his hand on the knob to the door of Donna Wojcie-chowski's room. With his other hand he rapped lightly against the door.

"Won't you be seated, Reverend Trayne?" Emmanuel Stuart-son gestured to the second chair set in front of his big desk. "And Paul, why don't you sit here?"

"Thank you, Your Worship," said Paul Trayne.

" 'Your Honor,' " Clay Garber corrected. He smiled into the boy's big green eyes.

"Your Honor," Paul said. He colored behind his freckles.

Stuartson smiled too, his ebony face splitting wide to show the huge, tombstone teeth that were his bane and the delight of Chicago's editorial cartoonists. " 'Mr. Stuartson' will do just fine, Paul," he said.

Stuartson settled himself into his own chair. He studied the Traynes. He was amazed at how much the old man resembled Abraham Lincoln, just as Garber had reported; it was a face that could not fail to inspire trust and confidence. Black man or white, there were few who did not admire the man who was, in Stuartson's considered opinion, every bit as much the father of his country as had been George Washington before him.

"Now then," Stuartson said, "my police commissioner here has told me something of what happened at his house the other morning, but I'm not altogether sure how I can help you any more than Donna Wojciechowski. She has the ear of all Chicago, through her newspaper." He smiled a politician's smile, looked at Garber. "I have only the ear of the few who support my policies. The dwindling few."

"Sister Wojciechowski has left us," Robert Trayne said. "Temporarily."

From his position by the door Clay watched this exchange with his mind racing. He was not at all satisfied with Trayne's tale that Donna had been called away on a story. Trayne had no details of the nature of the story and it seemed to Clay that Donna must surely think she was already covering the biggest story going right here, in Paul Trayne. Why else would she have expended so much energy and effort on the boy's behalf? But Trayne had sidestepped Clay's questions, and now, here in the mayor's office, there seemed no chance to pursue the matter further.

Stuartson pulled the flat cigar box toward him and opened it, selecting one of his cherished Havanas without, Clay noted, offering them round this time. The mayor lit the cigar and leaned back in his chair. His head disappeared from Clay's view for a moment, hidden within a nimbus of blue-gray smoke.

"It must have been terrible for Mr. Kilgore to die like that, away from his family and friends," Paul said.

"I'm sure it was," Stuartson nodded. "But I wouldn't distress myself over it if I were you, son."

"No," said Robert Trayne, "best not to dwell on it, Paul. What's done is done, remember?"

"Yes."

Was there a quaver in Paul's voice? Something more than his distress over the death of a complete stranger? Garber could not be sure.

"Now then," Stuartson said as the whirring air conditioner behind his chair sucked the smoke away from him. He stabbed the cigar at Garber. "Clay here tells me some amazing things about you, Paul."

Paul bowed his head. "I only do what God has given me the power to do." He raised his head, smiled. "I'm glad Commissioner Garber has told you about it, though."

"He said you worked some kind of minor miracle at his house yesterday morning," Stuartson said. "And that you've been doing much the same thing for thousands of people down in Faulkner."

"That was the place we chose for our beginnings," Reverend Trayne said, leaning in his chair to place a big, gnarled hand on Paul's shoulder. "I have waited a long time, since Paul first showed his power to heal. Testing him very carefully, on small things, here and there, until I felt he was ready. Ten years it took, to be sure. Then I selected Faulkner simply because the fates had chanced to bring us there at a time I felt the boy was ready. It was big enough to be a true test of his power without overreaching his strength."

"What made you think that?" Stuartson asked.

Clay sensed the subtle shift in the mayor's mode of speech. He was no longer the friendly "city father." He had become the famous lawyer he'd been before politics beckoned. *The famous prosecutor,* Clay reminded himself. How many times had they worked together to bring some reprobate to justice, in those days?

Stuartson was letting the Traynes know, in no uncertain terms, that his guard was very firmly in place and he was not going to tolerate any nonsense.

Reverend Trayne smiled. "Faulkner is a small town," he said. "I'd hoped the pains and griefs we might find there would also be small."

Stuartson blew a perfect smoke ring, speared it with his cigar. "That seems a bit like Pollyanna, Reverend," he said. "People are pretty much people, no matter where you go."

Trayne bowed his head slightly in the suggestion of a nod. "Nevertheless, that was my hope."

"And were you successful?"

"I believe so," Trayne said. He looked into Paul's eyes, back to Stuartson. "If you could see it for yourself . . ."

"I don't think I want to trek all the way down to Faulkner," said Stuartson around a slow dribble of rising cigar smoke. He tapped off the ash in a large gilt ashtray and changed his tack a trifle. "These 'needings.' Just how are you able to detect them?"

"That is what Father does," Paul said. "He can tell who has a needing and who does not."

"Almost everyone does," Reverend Trayne said, face and voice sad. Both rang false to Garber. He wondered why, wondered if the mayor saw it.

"And all this needing," Stuartson said, "you just, what, suck it into yourself? Like taking a deep breath?"

"I am but a vessel," Paul said.

"Can you describe the sensation?" Stuartson asked. "Can you tell me precisely how it feels to take these 'needings' into yourself?"

Clay was struck by the manner of Stuartson's speech. It sounded as if he already believed in Paul Trayne and his gift, or more correctly, *wanted* to believe, if the evidence was strong enough. It was very much what Clay himself had felt that first night. He hoped Mannie Stuartson was on guard against it, as he had been.

"There is a sense of emptiness at first," Paul said. His eyes had gone very far away, and as Clay watched he seemed to sway a little. Trayne's hand was still on his shoulder; Clay saw the fingers tighten, steadying the boy. "There is a sense of emptiness," Paul repeated. "As if I am standing on the edge of a great precipice. But that precipice is somehow inside me. Inside my soul. Then I open the barriers around my soul and all the grief comes in."

"And how does that feel, Paul?" Stuartson's voice was even, but Clay noticed the stenographer leaning forward in her chair, a child at a scary movie. She was still scribbling madly on her pad, but her eyes were riveted on Paul Trayne.

"It feels terrible," said Paul. His lower lip trembled. "As if my soul is being torn to shreds by wild animals. And then, after, there is great sorrow. A darkness over everything. I cry a lot." It was a pitiful image; Clay could tell all in the room were touched by it, moved by it. Even the elder Trayne seemed touched, Clay thought, as if he had not heard these words before.

Or am I reading too much into that face? That damned, dearly beloved face.

"Yet you wish to go on doing this?" Stuartson asked. "You would voluntarily perform this . . . service here, in this city, even knowing the kinds of grief and evil you might have to confront?" The brief hesitation before the word "service" was the first and only indication Clay had that Stuartson might not be buying Paul Trayne's story lock, stock and barrel after all.

"Yes," said Paul, simply and eloquently.

Stuartson leaned back in his chair, swiveling it slightly from side to side as he spoke again. "Could you tell me about the first time? Do you remember clearly when you discovered you had this talent?"

Paul frowned. Only slightly, but Clay saw a swift pain in the boy's eyes. Paul glanced up at his father before he went on. Clay tried to read the look that passed between them, but it was too subtle.

"A girl I knew," Paul said. "Her name was Abigail Dehner. She was twelve years old. Her uncle raped her, made her pregnant. She came to me because she knew I was someone she could trust." He looked from one pair of eyes to the next, slowly. "She'd had an abortion. An illegal abortion. I didn't know what that meant. I was only five. But I could tell it was something very bad."

Paul hesitated. Clay saw Trayne's hand tighten on the boy's shoulder. "Go on, Paul."

"That was a terrible thing she did," Paul said. Bright tears welled in his eyes. One large droplet freed itself and drew a wavering line down his right cheek. He wiped it away with the back of his hand. "She understood how terrible it was. To murder an unborn child like that, no matter what the reason for its existence. So she came to me because she knew I would not condemn her. I was known around Three Forks then as someone who was a good listener. Everyone said I was wise beyond my years."

"Everyone," Reverend Trayne nodded. Garber saw something he took to be pride in the man's face. It wasn't easy to be sure.

Paul said, "As we talked—as she talked, really—I began to feel the pain she felt. The grief and the guilt. As if the feelings were my own. And after a while she stopped talking and just sort of sat quiet for a moment. Then she looked at me, and she smiled, and she kissed me on the mouth and said 'Thank you, Paul.' I didn't really understand what she meant. I just knew that I felt terrible. As if I'd done something really, really horrible. But I knew I hadn't. She had. Only now I felt it."

Listening, Clay was struck again by the two separate voices that seemed to come, at different times, from Paul Trayne. Right now, talking to Stuartson, sitting in the high-backed chair, Paul sounded very much like what he was, a young boy from a very, very small town. Yet the night before last, at Clay's house, he'd spoken with an adult's timbre, a sureness, a sense of purpose that seemed missing now.

"What did you do then?" Stuartson asked.

"I told Father what had happened. He understood."

"Understood?"

"I recognized the boy's power for what it was," Trayne said.

Stuartson retreated for a moment behind a wall of cigar smoke. When it cleared he said, "Recognized? Just like that?"

Trayne drew a deep, slow breath. Clay sensed a shift, a change in the dynamics of the room, the tensions. "I have," Trayne said very slowly, "a small gift of my own. A small power, along these lines. It is this which allows me to recognize the needings in others."

"Oh, really?" Stuartson shot a look at Clay, who shrugged. It was the first time he'd heard anything about Robert Trayne's having a gift of his own. "Tell me more," Stuartson said to Trayne.

"It is nothing. I am the crude clay compared to Paul. He is the completion." He smiled. "My greatest work."

"But your power . . . I'm not sure I understand how you can have the same power and yet never have been heard of before now."

"Because my power is so much less," Trayne said. Garber sensed the impatience in the man's voice. "My power is as nothing. It was not until Paul that I saw what great potential could truly be achieved."

"How does it work, then, your own power?"

"I cannot define it."

Stuartson touched the end of the cigar against his pursed lips, rolled it between his long fingers so the tip turned in his mouth. "Try."

Trayne sighed. "Please, Mr. Mayor, I do not wish to continue this. I am nothing. I have a small—a very small—power to read the emotions of others. To sense what they feel, what they need. But Paul has so much more. He can do so much more."

"What do you say, Paul?" Stuartson leveled his coolest gaze at the boy. "Are you better at this than your dad?"

"Father says so, sir." Paul looked at Trayne. "I believe everything Father tells me."

Stuartson nodded. "Yes. I think I do too." He smiled. "A pity your power is so much less than your son's, Reverend. There were a lot of times in the last sixty years we could have used someone like Paul."

"Yes," Trayne nodded. "Many times."

Clay was almost certain Trayne was thinking along lines quite different from those the mayor might mean. Certain enough to make, at that moment, an important decision. Perhaps—and he knew even as he thought it that he was probably being overly dramatic—the most important decision of his career.

16

Pete Hay woke up screaming. He'd been dreaming. In the dreams he stood again at the barricade across Albert Street. But the scene was different from the night before, the barricade higher, more intimidating. Great iron spikes thrust into the air, quills of some outrageously huge porcupine, human arms and legs dangling from the bloodied tips. And all around, filling the air, filling his ears, the terrible, terrible scream, the inhuman scream that had haunted Pete Hay for fifteen years, lying deep down in his darkest dreams, waiting for him.

The tiers and crannies created by the barrier's lethal spears were full of quivering, dough-skinned women who were Alice Nickerson and Marcy Kavelhoff combined into one shuddering, obscene image. In the dream the air was hot and prickly. Pete looked down to see himself naked before the hideous women. No sooner had he recognized that fact than they began to move, climbing down from their perches, inching toward him, dozens of them, unending in their approach, each ponderous step sending waves shuddering up through their bloated, chalk-white flesh. Gigantic, pendulous breasts moved of their own accord, flowing and floating, reaching out toward Pete Hay the same way the women's grotesquely fat and flabby arms did. Nipples were too long and pale; in the worst moments of the dream there were as many of them clustered around each other in the centers of the bulbous breasts as there were groping fingers on the pasty white hands. The hands that reached out and grabbed Pete Hay and pulled him toward them. Pulled him into the infinite, suffocating embrace of those massive breasts. The white flesh enfolded him, engulfed him, more liquid glue than skin. Where it touched him it stuck. Where his nostrils and ears were open to it, it flowed up inside him. It forced itself into every orifice of his body. It pressed past his lips, no matter how tight he drew them closed; it filled his mouth, forcing it wider and wider until it seemed as if his jaws must surely rip apart.

When they did, he woke up screaming. He was sitting up. He dropped back onto the narrow cot in cell 2. He put out his hands to find the edges of the cot and hung on for dear life, fearful that any moment the cot would tip and he would be thrown off, thrown down through a viscous floor into the embrace of the horrible Alice/Marcy creature. When the cot showed no indication of tipping Pete released his grip and sat up again. He swung his legs off the edge. He tested the floor and found it solid beneath his boots. He was fully dressed; he'd fallen on the cot without even removing his jacket. He'd come back to the station house after escorting Zeldenrust and Arnie Steadman's body back to the morgue at Harrison Hospital. Zeldenrust was in a deep, deep funk, silent and brooding. When Pete finally managed to pry a reason out of him it was simple enough: the Kavelhoff children and Arnie Steadman represented three more corpses than the hospital morgue could hold. The six drawers were already full, a condition Zeldenrust had never before experienced.

Leaning over the washbasin Pete thought about his own problems. None of the other Faulkner police had responded to his call. Mae Ellen Faber was loose, somewhere in the city, and he had no way of tracking her down without the rest of the force to call on; there were just too many places she could hide from one man, searching alone. When he thought about it, Pete realized he was not even particularly inclined to search. Mae Ellen's crime, awful as it was, slipped lower and lower on his list of priorities as the horror left behind by Paul Trayne continued to reveal itself.

Pete was firmly committed to the belief that Paul Trayne was behind everything that had gone wrong in Faulkner. The town had been perfectly normal, peaceful, and quiet before the Miracle Show arrived in Gunner's Field. Pete wondered for a moment if anything might have turned out differently if he'd gone to check on the new arrivals himself, instead of driving into town to tell Clarence Nickerson.

Could I have prevented any of this? Would Clarence still be alive? Marcy still herself? Everything the way it's supposed to be, if I'd just done my job properly in the first place?

And, he asked himself, was that why he was suddenly acting the way a police officer was supposed to act? Was guilt the driving force in Pete Hay's transformation?

He shook his head. No point in pursuing that line of thought. He pulled off his jacket and rolled up his shirtsleeves. He ran cold water into the little sink in the corner of cell 2 and splashed his face. His cheeks were rough against his hands, and when he ran his fingers through his curly hair, it stood up in greasy loops. He turned off the water and dried his hands on the scrap of towel by the sink. He unzipped his pants, lifted the lid on the small commode, and emptied his bladder into it. He flushed and left the cell without washing his hands again.

He walked over to cell 3. Marcy was asleep. She was in the same position she'd landed in when Pete tossed her onto the cot: on one side, her head curled down against her chest. Her nose was covered with a bright white square of bandage— Zeldenrust had done what he could, but she would never look quite as she had before—and her lips moved as she breathed. Pete stared at her and tried to connect the picture his eyes transmitted to the woman whose bed he'd shared three hundred times in the past two years. It was still Marcy. The same hair, same round face, same big bust, big butt. Pete knew that if he were to open the cell door now and cross to the bunk, she would feel the same and, if she woke to his touch, sound the same—taking into account the new nasal quality brought on by the broken nose. He dropped his hand onto the lock of the door. The keys were in his back pocket. It would be easy enough to open to cage and step inside. But why would he want to?

Pete thought about continuing his questioning of his erstwhile lover, but he remembered how it had felt questioning her
at home, how very much out of control he'd found himself. He
decided it was for the best to leave the cell door locked, with
himself on the outside.

Marcy stirred. A long, blubbery snore escaped her lips. She
rolled onto her back, shifting herself into a more comfortable
position without coming fully awake. Pete watched the undulations flowing through her soft flesh. He and Zeldenrust had
managed to manhandle her into a big, shapeless shift they'd
found in her closet. Pete felt memory stir in the palms of his
hands. Once that memory might have been for the way her
flesh moved as his hands stroked her. Now it was for the sharp
crack of his hand against her flanks, her exposed, vulnerable
flesh. He shuddered and stepped out into the front office. Cold.
He crossed to the thermostat and turned the heat up to eighty
degrees. He heard the thump and whoosh of the furnace in the
cellar responding to the command. He looked at the big clock
over the front door. It was just gone noon. He'd been asleep
for half the day, but he was still bone weary. He crossed to
Arnie Steadman's command station, flicked up the toggles, and
sent power into the radio transceiver. He picked up the big,
old-fashioned desktop mike.

"This is Central to all cars," he said. "Come in, all cars."

He listened to the birth crackle of the universe—Arnie had
told him that was the origin of static on any unoccupied radio
channel—and heard nothing else. He had not expected to. He
shivered—the furnace was pumping hot air into the big room,
but it was not having much effect yet. Pete ran his hands up
and down his arms and jogged up and down a little, in place, to
accelerate his circulation. He thought about breakfast—*lunch?*
Normally Alice Nickerson took care of the meals, as she took
care of all mundane matters for her father. Like Aunt Bea on
the old *Andy Griffith Show,* Pete thought, she would prepare a
picnic basket breakfast, which Nickerson would bring in, if
there were prisoners. Usually there was at least one occupied
cell. Seventeen thousand people produced a minimum of one
drunken row, one overactive family argument, per night.
Somebody would need to be fed, and Nickerson would bring in

the basket and, if the prisoner was not released by noon—most of them were "overnight guests"—Alice would come by with lunch and later dinner. That would not happen today.

Pete set the microphone back on the desk and flicked the toggles to *off*. The return to silence was oppressive. Pete wanted to be far, far away from Faulkner, but he could not imagine where. He'd come to the awful realization that his newfound sense of responsibility would not let him escape these problems even if he were to travel to the far side of the world. For the first time in his professional life, Pete Hay thought he might have an idea of what Clarence Nickerson went through virtually every day that he lived.

"Who is it?"

"Father Sylvestri. May I . . . ?"

"Come in, Father."

He opened the door. Donna was sitting up in bed, three pillows fluffed up behind her, cool light spilling across her from the window above the left side of the narrow single bed. It filled the pale-cream-colored room with a soft white light. The sheets on her bed looked white as the snow falling outside, the green blanket very dark. On the nightstand to her right was a tray with one large mug from which steam still rose. Tom could smell Mrs. Buck's wonderful bouillon as he stepped into the room. Donna closed the magazine she'd been reading and set it on the comforter beside her.

"Hello," Tom said.

Donna blinked. Something like a smile began across her face. The expression died unborn. "Hello," she said.

"A problem, Donna?"

"I don't know whether to thank you or run like . . . or run out of here."

Tom picked up the plain old walnut chair resting to the left of the door, alongside the equally old and equally plain five-drawer dresser. He placed it by the end of the bed and sat, crossing his legs, angling himself slightly away from his guest. She looked deathly tired, he thought, as if she was only now beginning to recover from a long illness. He was not prepared to let Donna know, just yet, how much he knew, or how much he was prepared to believe of what she might tell him. There was always the danger—*the very real danger,* he reminded himself, emphasizing, trying to set it so clearly in his mind that nothing could shake it free—that Donna was still a slave to Robert Trayne.

"Why would you want to run away?" he asked, his voice soft, his manner easy, calming. "Are you afraid of me?"

"I . . . have some rather confused memories of last night." She paused.

"Last night." He nodded. "What do you remember?"

"I seem to recall doing a rather heavy-handed . . . I mean . . ." She sighed. "I tried to seduce you, didn't I? I mean, that's what I was supposed to do."

"You tried, yes. You didn't succeed." He smiled. "I don't think your heart was really in it."

Donna sighed again. "I'm surprised to find I still have a heart to be in anything." She met his gaze. Her shadowed eyes were bright and steady. "Why did you bring me here? And where is here, for that matter? I don't have a very clear memory of arriving . . ."

" 'Here' is the rectory of St. Timothy's, my church. And as to why I brought you . . ." Tom shrugged. "Something told me it might be for the best."

"Something?"

"Something. Intuition." He was deliberately noncommittal.

"I . . . tried to commit suicide too, didn't I?"

Tom nodded again, slowly. "It certainly looked like that, yes."

"You stopped me."

"I stopped you."

"You must've been pretty fast, if I remember . . ."

"I was just fast enough," Tom said. "I caught you, pulled you back. Scraped you up rather badly, I'm afraid."

Donna raised two fingertips to the tenderness on the side of her face. "I was wondering where that came from. Hit my cheek on the cement of the balcony?" That fit her limited recollection of the previous night. "I must be starting to look a sight."

"Yes. The other . . ."

Donna touched her lip, only slightly swollen now. "Reverend Trayne. When he got a little carried away. But . . ."

Donna drew herself up taller against the pillows. Her hair fell about her shoulders in natural waves, catching dark gold out of the gray morning light. Scrubbed of makeup, her face looked tired, Tom thought, even haggard, but there was still a strength there he found he could admire. He saw her shoulders stiffen and lock, as if she was bracing for a physical blow.

"Why?" she asked.

"Sorry?" He was taken quite by surprise by that particular question.

"Why did you stop me? From killing myself."

"I believe we covered that last night. 'Professional commitment,' you called it."

"Yes, I did. And you said that was only part of it. I remember that." Donna reached for the mug of bouillon and sipped it slowly. "This is very good," she said over the rim, hoping her voice would not reveal how much of a lie that was. What she really needed was a stiff drink. Many stiff drinks. She decided to see if such a thing were possible. "Although I wouldn't turn down something stronger . . . ?"

"I'm not sure that would be a good idea, at this point." He saw the flash of pain in her eyes and wondered if there might be some need in her greater than the simple, bracing effect of a quick drink.

"How about a cigarette, then?" Donna asked. It seemed like weeks since she'd had her last.

Tom reached for his inside pocket. His hand stopped halfway. "Sorry. I'm afraid I've given it up."

"For Lent? Oh, well." Donna sighed, sipped her bouillon again, and tried to make it feel and taste like something much stronger.

Watching her, Tom was taken by the notion that she was cataloging sensations. Building—or rebuilding—in her mind the shape and texture of the world. He sucked in his lower lip, considering.

"Did I disgust you?" Donna said through the cloud of steam above the mug.

Tom hesitated, not wanting his instinctive "Yes" to be the

first thing from his lips. "You were in pretty bad shape," he said.

Donna smiled, weakly but with warmth.

Tom was struck again by how beautiful she could be, with the proper care.

She sipped the bouillon. "You're a diplomat, Father."

"It goes with the collar." Tom leaned forward. "And I think you should probably call me 'Tom,' all things considered. What can you tell me, Donna? Last night you started to say some things, after I pulled you back and during the drive here. But you weren't really in control of yourself. What can you tell me now?"

"You ask a lot, Tom." She showed no hesitancy in using his given name, and Tom was pleased. The fewer the barriers between them, the easier it might be to learn what there was to learn.

Especially since it is no longer knowledge I seek here. Only confirmation of what I already suspect.

"I ask a lot because I think a lot is at stake," he said. "Certainly Walker thought so."

Tom saw the mug tremble. Donna set it down quickly, barely managing to get it to the table before a terrible wrenching sob shook her whole body. She collapsed forward. Tom had to put out his hands to stop her going off the edge of the narrow bed. He pushed her, gently, back against the pillows. Her head lolled on the top of the pile. Tears were streaming down her face.

"Walker," she said around sobs. "He's dead. They killed him." She let out a long, gurgling moan, a soulful thing with all the agonies of the damned wrapped up in it.

It seemed heartless, but Tom realized his best and fastest avenue to the truth was to pursue this particular line while Donna's defenses were down. "You told me all about that, after I pulled you back from the balcony. There were times last night when it didn't seem to bother you so much."

"Last night I was in hell."

"And now?"

"Now . . . I'm not so sure." She leaned back on her own, so that he did not need to support her. She looked up and out of the tall window by the bed. Tom saw her eyes move, tracking snowflakes.

More cataloging, he thought.

"I feel as if I'm . . . I'm my own self again," Donna said. "I feel as if what I say is what I want to say. What I do is what I want to do."

"And you didn't feel that way last night?"

"Not for all of it. Not when I was trying to . . ." Again she had trouble saying the words. "When I tried to kill myself, that was my idea."

Tom wondered if he should be bothered by the fact that Donna apparently found it easier to discuss her failed suicide than her failed seduction.

That she should put less value on her life than on her sexual skill—or am I misreading this? Perhaps it is that the seduction revolted her more than the suicide. Maybe there's something to be built from there . . .

"It was Trayne's idea to seduce me? He's behind all this, isn't he? Behind Walker's death, and the rest?" His tone told her that he already knew the answers, but it told her too that he had to hear it from her own lips.

He still doesn't trust me entirely, Donna thought. She sensed there was more. As if he already knew about Paul, about his power. As if he already believed . . . There was a brief whiplash moment of sudden fear. If he believed in the power of Paul Trayne, could he be a slave of Robert Trayne? Could this all be some kind of horrible, elaborate hoax?

"Yes, it was all Trayne's idea," she said, cautious in her words, her phrasing, needing to sound him out, to know who this man in the dark suit really was. "I . . . don't think I'd have come up with something like that on my own. I hope I wouldn't."

"Because I'm a priest? Or is there something more than that?"

She smiled, weakly. "You ask some pretty ruthless questions, Padre. Considering that we've barely gotten to know each other yet."

"This is a pretty ruthless situation," Tom said. "I've seen

only the tip of it, but I have a pretty clear idea of what I'm—of what we're up against."

"You see Trayne as some kind of . . . enemy? Why? I mean, why especially, why you? Because you're a priest?"

"Maybe. Does that seem likely to you?"

She felt the closing of the trap—if trap it was—would surely be triggered by her next words. Choose them carefully, then? Select a lie that, if possible, would please Robert Trayne and yet, if Tom Sylvestri were not enslaved, also somehow reveal to him that she was free herself?

If I am free. A sob rose to shake the tip of her chin.

"Donna? What's wrong? Or is that a foolish question?" His smile was warm, real. Wonderful.

Donna sighed. "I've been worrying that you might be under their spell," she said. Lightning did not flash. Thunder did not roll. She pressed on: "I've been trying to think how I could find out, without getting killed . . . or worse."

"Take your time, Donna," Tom said. "You've been through a terrible ordeal."

"You say that as if it's in the past tense," Donna said, raising her head. "It's not, you know," she went on. "Not in the past tense. Not over."

"No. Nor will it be for some time yet."

"I wonder," she said at last in a very small voice, "why I was able to, well, you know, get out from under."

Tom shook his head. What he was learning—had begun to learn, in pieces, first from Donna's night of delirium, and now more as she spoke from a clear mind—stunned Tom Sylvestri. It was as if a doorway into the deepest pit of hell had opened before him. He did not doubt the existence of hell—not the hell of Dante, but a place where sinners met their just punishment—but he had never expected in all his life to come face to face with something that seemed so clearly a manifestation of that ancient horror. There could be no doubt that there was a demonic force here, and he had theories, several, about the way this power worked, but he was not about to impart them to Donna. There was a danger of her being Robert Trayne's pawn even now, her dependency on the "gift" of Paul Trayne not diminished enough to truly free her from the old man's grasp.

And, he reminded himself, there was a greater danger that he might cause her, inadvertently, to lower her defenses if he told her the wrong thing, the wrong assumption as to the source of her present liberation.

"I can only guess what happened," he said. "You had quite a bit to say, as I drove you here and as Mrs. Buck took care of you. I told her you were just raving, but I was listening carefully for the core of truth that might be in your words. I'm still groping in shadows, you understand, but I'd say it's possible—remotely possible—the effect of what Paul Trayne does is temporary. That it varies in the length of its hold from one individual to another. I can't begin to be sure. That's why I want you to tell me about the first night. Everything."

Donna sighed, ordering her thoughts. When she began to speak, the words came at a carefully measured pace, one after the other, reminding Tom that this young woman was, after all, a professional writer. When she told a story, when she was not delirious, she told it carefully, logically.

He listened for the better part of an hour, asking questions only once or twice, for clarification. In the end he found no additional details that could explain how she was able to escape—*temporarily?*—the power of these imps.

That was how Tom found himself thinking of Paul and Robert Trayne. Not as cute little cartoon creatures, however. When a priest, this priest, used the word it meant something darker than the homogenized, Hollywood image of a cloven-hoofed satyr prancing about with a pitchfork. Far, far darker.

But perhaps not dark enough. Tom was deeply disturbed by the implications of Paul Trayne's power. *Can it really be as far-reaching as Donna seems to think? Can it really be able to reach into the souls of all those men and women and suck from them the very thing that makes them human? Without guilt, without grief we are no better than the beasts. There would be nothing to keep our baser nature in check. Nothing to stop us stealing, killing, raping . . .*

"I don't think there's anything there," Tom said as Donna completed her story, "that could really explain your present emancipation. Walker resisted Paul Trayne too, in a different way. Perhaps it was something you learned from him, or learned from each other. Or, perhaps, it is something Robert Trayne intended all along."

Donna's heart sank. "Why . . . why would you think that?"

"I don't know. Maybe he just wanted you to think it was your own idea." Tom was not sure yet if Paul and his father were separate entities, or avatars of the same central evil.

"You think I might go back, don't you? You think I might fall under their control again." She resisted the next thought, but it came out anyway. "You think I might *still* be under Trayne's control. I guess that's only fair. I doubted you . . ."

Tom nodded, slowly. "Yes. You might be working under some kind of . . . I don't know. Call it posthypnotic suggestion, for lack of a better term. There is always that possibility. Even your abortive seduction could have been part of a plan." Tom drew a deep breath and steeled himself to the reaction that might come from what he was going to say next. "This could be a part of that. This image you are so strongly projecting, the damsel in distress."

Donna snorted and met his gaze directly. "Is there . . . some way to test me?" she asked. "Is there some way to be sure?"

"I don't know. If this were all part of some master plan, I'd really have no way of knowing, would I? It's not as if I can brandish a crucifix and see if you react. You're not possessed. Paul Trayne is not a vampire. Not literally, anyway."

He might be something like an incubus. That drains the life force from its victims, supposedly. And what Paul Trayne seems to do . . .

He shook his head. *Wrong path. Wrong path.*

"I . . . tried to kill myself last night." The moments of the attempt were very clear in Donna's mind now. Very important. She found herself clinging to them as the only proof she had that she could still act of her own volition. That some of the strings binding her to the Traynes were frayed and broken.

Tom shrugged. "Assume for a moment that you are still under Trayne's thrall. I know that's the last thing you want to be thinking about, but we might as well consider it now, Donna, as long as it's come up anyway. If you are still working out part of some master scheme of Trayne's, your attempted suicide could have been a part of the seduction. When your more direct approach failed, it might have seemed logical to try presenting yourself in another light."

"Your damsel in distress, you mean? 'Damsel' is not a word I've ever thought to apply to myself. Or 'distress,' for that matter."

"And yet you clearly were in distress, last night," Tom pressed. "And you seem very much to think you still are. I saw the fear in your eyes when I suggested you might slip back under Trayne's control."

"Then you do believe I'm free right now?"

"Cautiously, yes." He smiled warmly, encouragingly. "You'll forgive me if I don't turn my back to you just yet, if there are any blunt instruments in the room, but yes, I do think you're probably free. What I don't understand is *how* you're free. What happened yesterday, or maybe even earlier, that set you on a path toward this freedom."

"I was playing some pretty outrageous mind games with myself," Donna said, "testing my limitations. Probing for loopholes." She frowned, as an errant thought crossed her mind. "I was kind of curious . . ."

"Yes?"

"Well, I know about the vow of chastity and all that, but . . ." She shrugged, realizing there was nothing to do now but plow on ahead with her stupid, vain question. "I was sort of wondering . . . If my memory is clear, I laid on my very best vamp for you last night. But you didn't seem at all, well, aroused by it. Am I losing my touch?"

Tom frowned. "Does it seem important to you that you should have been able to seduce a priest?" He leaned forward, uncrossing his legs, listening for the slightest nuance in Donna's voice, the tiniest suggestion that she was slipping back under the spell of Robert Trayne.

It could happen so easily, he thought.

"I don't know," Donna said, honestly. "I've always had a pretty low opinion of myself. Sex has never been what you'd call my favorite thing." *I can't believe I told him that!* "This all seems sort of part of the same thing. I guess there's some part of me that wants to know I didn't fail simply because you were completely turned off by me." She met his eyes again, and Tom saw the great pain lying immediately behind the dismissing smile she tried to offer him.

"It wasn't that, exactly," he said. "Not in the way you mean, anyway."

"What then? I . . . I know this is just nuts, but I really need to know."

"All right. I guess I'll tell you. It might turn out to be very important, later, that we have no secrets from each other. Nothing Trayne might use." Tom reached over to take the empty glass from Donna's hand. He set it on the little folding table, next to the remains of her lunch.

He told her.

Emmanuel Stuartson had loved only one woman in his life, and she was the wife of his best friend.

It was not a triangle. Not in anything like the classic sense. Clay Garber and Mannie Stuartson had known each other for most of their lives, and when Marjorie appeared on the scene they had both been taken by her beauty, her intelligence, her sheer physicality.

"The most female female I've ever known," Stuartson said, not long after they met.

In fact, it had been he who first made contact with Marjorie, and it was he who, to this day, sometimes regretted introducing her to his big, loud, thoroughly lovable friend. It sometimes seemed in Stuartson's mind that Clay and Marjorie had been tearing off each other's clothes and climbing all over each other's bodies before he'd got past the first syllable of the introduction.

Still, when the best man won—his love for Marjorie Garber was such that Mannie Stuartson would never allow himself to believe she had settled for anything less than the best man, whatever that belief might cost him in ego—Stuartson played the game by the kind of rules he believed and understood to be correct. He was warmly congratulatory. He was best man at their wedding. He was godfather to their oldest child.

But he still loved Marjorie Garber, still yearned for her—when he allowed himself such luxuries—and when anyone asked why a man so rich and powerful, so much in the public eye as the mayor of Chicago had never married, Stuartson would flash his tombstone teeth and say, "Married to the city. What woman could take second place to that and like it?"

But, of course, there was such a woman. And she was married to Clayton Garber.

For this reason, the subtle but undeniable frustration of his unrequited love, Stuartson was amazed to see Marjorie's car parked in front of his tall brownstone when the city limousine pulled up at his door that evening. In the darkness of the backseat, lost in rumination over the amazing discovery Clay had brought into his office that morning, Stuartson did not see Marjorie's car until the limo stopped and the driver, aware that Stuartson was at some distance from the mortal plane, said "We're here, sir."

Stuartson started to say thank you, saw Marjorie's car, stopped. It was her car, all right. He'd seen it in the driveway of the Garber house. He'd seen Marjorie behind the wheel. But he'd never seen it here, for it was strictly Marjorie's car, and Marjorie Garber never came to the mayor's house without her husband.

Stuartson climbed stiffly from the limo. His heart was pounding. His breath was short. He felt all those foolish sensations he associated in his memory with a first date. Apprehension. Anticipation. Even, yes, sudden sexual arousal.

He closed the limo door without a word to the driver and walked up the steps to his house and through the front door. Raschid, the dark Arabian butler, materialized at Stuartson's side, slipping the coat from Stuartson's bony shoulders as the mayor came into the entrance foyer.

"Good evening, Your Honor," Raschid said. "Mrs. Commissioner Garber is waiting in the study."

Stuartson swallowed, his throat dry. His brain was full of images he'd tried to keep pushed down and away for all the years he'd known Marjorie Garber. Images of dark brown skin, smooth, rich, supple to the touch. Images of a lush, warm mouth, red lips moist and inviting.

He walked to the foot of the massive circular staircase that corkscrewed through the center of his broad, shallow brownstone. He knew there were questions he should be asking—when did Marjorie arrive? Did she give any indication of why she was here?—but nothing would come from his mouth but his own panting breath. He went up the stairs to the study on the second floor and stepped inside.

It was a large, warm room, all four walls covered with floor-to-ceiling book cases, punctuated here and there by tall windows, doors, and a large mahogany-fronted fireplace. A big desk of hand-carved ebony, stood to the left as he entered, two high-backed chairs facing away from it toward the fireplace. For a moment it seemed the room was empty, until Stuartson saw Marjorie's hand on the arm of the nearer chair.

He cleared his throat.

Marjorie leaned around the side of the chair and flashed her most devastating smile. She stood, crossed, and took both his hands in hers. Her flesh was cool against his—or was it that his was burning?

"You saw Paul today, didn't you?" Her voice was the same soft music it had been in college. She seemed almost unchanged from the day of their first meeting.

"Yes," Stuartson said. Somehow the mention of Paul Trayne gave power to his voice at last.

"Did he . . . do anything for you?"

Stuartson could not quite understand what she was saying. "Do anything?"

"Did he help you?"

Stuartson shook his head. "I don't . . ."

Marjorie smiled. "Yes, he did. I can see he did. Isn't it wonderful?"

"Marjorie . . ." The English language was rapidly becoming a poorly understood second tongue to Stuartson. The room had shrunk behind Marjorie. There was nothing in his field of vision but her eyes, her mouth, the liquid silk of her skin.

"He can help even if you don't want him to. Even if you don't know he's doing it." Marjorie's smiled broadened, brightened. "I understand that now. That's why I have to come to you. Because Clay was able to resist him, so Clay is useless."

"Clay is useless." Stuartson did not know what she meant, but he was thrilled to hear her say it. Emboldened, he reached out one of his big hands to cup her cheek. Her flesh was cool there too. "Marjorie . . ."

"I know," Marjorie said. "I've always known. But, of course, I was married to Clay. I loved Clay. I still do, I suppose, even though he's of no use to Paul. And all that really matters is who is of use to Paul." She raised her hand to his, lifted it from her cheek, and carried it down to the outer curve of her left breast. Stuartson felt the stiffness of her bra under the softness of her blouse. She pressed the hand close. "We must help Paul, Emmanuel," Marjorie said.

All he could comprehend was the weight of her breast in his hand. He lifted his other hand to the other side of her chest and pushed his hands together, seeing the fabric of her blouse pleat itself, seeing the shadows deepen in the V of her neck-line.

She kicked off her shoes, dropping half a head in height. Her face was barely level with his chest. She looked up into his eyes. "You will help, won't you? You'll do anything for Paul now."

"Anything . . . for . . . Paul . . ."

Marjorie's hands were on his belt, the clasp of his trousers, the zipper of his fly. She slipped her hands inside his trousers, inside his boxer shorts. The coolness closed around his blazing, engorged flesh.

"Marjorie . . ."

Marjorie was not at home when Clay returned to his big house by the Lake that afternoon. With her many interest groups, Marjorie was often later than Clay in getting home from a day in the city, so he was not surprised. But he was disappointed. He wanted to see her, to be with her, before he left for Faulkner. That was the decision that had come finally to his mind as he sat in his own office once more, the meeting with Stuartson and the Traynes ended. He sat looking at the framed pictures on the wall, thinking about Paul Trayne, Walker Stone, Donna Wojciechowski.

I have to go to Faulkner, he'd finally said to himself. *Mannie must not know I'm going. Marjorie. Donna. No one but me.*

As he bounced the car over the low curb at the beginning of his driveway, he looked at the Seiko on the inside of his left wrist. Just gone two. Clay parked the BMW in front of the big, stable-style garage and walked to the side door. He let himself in quietly and walked through to the kitchen. He glanced automatically at the answering machine on the counter. The little red message light was not lit. When Clay looked more closely, he saw the machine was not on. He pressed his lips together in a passing annoyance. Marjorie knew she was never supposed to leave the house without turning on the machine, even if the servants were still there.

Rose appeared to be elsewhere—*still looking for Anne?*—so he crossed to the refrigerator and opened it. He squatted down to dig through the crowded shelves, finding at last the half-empty package of processed turkey breast he was looking for. He pulled a loaf of whole wheat bread from a lower shelf, found the head lettuce in the big drawer at the bottom of the refrigerator, and rose to build himself a sandwich. His mind drifted as his hands went through the mechanical motions.

He wondered about Donna Wojciechowski—what had happened to her. "Busy" was all the Traynes would say, but Clay wondered now what could possibly have kept her so busy she missed the meeting. It had been so much the focus of her entire existence, he'd thought. All that seemed to matter to Donna was getting Paul to see Stuartson.

And yet she didn't take him directly to Hizzoner's office.

Clay was not sure why that still buzzed in the back of his head. Stuartson would have been much more inclined to accept what Paul was offering. Much less resistant than Clay himself was.

Could that be it?

The thought slipped away from him before Clay was sure of it. Why would Donna want Paul to meet someone who'd resist him? Clay raised his completed sandwich and took a huge bite. He chewed slowly as he walked through the kitchen to the adjacent dining room, leaving the sandwich makings forgotten on the counter for Rose to clear away.

The matter of Charles Addison Kilgore's death was also on his mind, a sore spot since he'd read of it in the *Advocate* that morning. Kilgore's death had to be a coincidence, he told himself. Perfectly timed, but a coincidence. He considered the bizarre circumstances of Kilgore's death, a most unlikely way for anyone to die. And in all those years on the force, Clay Garber thought he'd seen as many permutations of death, unnatural death, as there were. But this, after all, was supposed to be a natural death, wasn't it? A massive coronary.

He walked on into the living room and paused just inside the door, looking at the room and remembering it as it had been two mornings past, remembering it with a policeman's mind, looking now for the details a policeman looked for.

Marjorie sat just there. Rose and Anne there.

Clay frowned. When he thought about it like this, it all seemed absurd. Had he really opened his home to strangers at that ungodly hour? Donna Wojciechowski was not a total stranger, but she was hardly someone Clay would have imagined himself welcoming into his house at midnight, especially under such unusual circumstances.

He crossed to the big picture window and looked out at the gray, choppy surface of the Lake. White breakers were foaming against the rocks that edged his property and spewing bright droplets high into the cold air. The green grass of the big lawn was lost under a blanket of snow. There were footprints, crossing the lawn. They were away to the left, by the garage. At first he thought them only shadows, but there was nothing by which a shadow might be cast. He followed the line of steps. They were close together, suggesting to his mind a woman's stride or a child's. They led past the garage, across the lawn and down to the rocks at the shore. Or did they come up from the shore? There was no way to be sure, from his angle of view. They could just as easily represent the tracks of someone coming toward the house, from the Lake. Closely spaced.

Like a child's stride . . .

Clay shuddered. Michael's body had been recovered and interred in the family plot, but Clay could not keep his mind

from creating ghastly images of a bloated, bleached form—
how could skin so dark have become so pale?—plodding up
from the freezing waters, dragging heavy, lifeless feet across
the lawn, knees lifting high to clear the drifted snow. An unnatural walk, like some grotesque puppet. He stared into the
froth of the Lake's edge.

His mind slid back, across the years. It had been so different
the day Michael died, so calm the Lake looked like sheet glass,
the sun a perfect yellow-white ball in a cloudless sky. They'd
been splashing and laughing, Michael six years old, then, the
girls seven and fourteen. DiAnne was already looking very
much the beauty, tall and straight with cheekbones high under
skin the color of dark coffee. The graceful curve of her hips in
subtle evidence, breasts just beginning to push out against her
halter top.

Were we paying too much attention to her, that day?

Clay had played this scene through his head many times
before. He and Marjorie had been sitting on a blanket on the
edge of the grass, just where it turned into the tumbled rock
and gravel of the beach, DiAnne parading—that was the only
word—before them in her first bikini. A very demure bikini, at
Clay's insistence, but brief enough to show off an awful lot of
that smooth, brown skin. Skin very much like her mother's.
Their attention strayed from Michael for, what? Three minutes?

Two minutes too long, with an adventurous boy like that.
Clay shook his head, alone in the living room. He wiped away
hot tears, took another big bite of his sandwich, and guided his
mind back to thoughts of Paul Trayne.

Why did I let them in?

Clay considered hypnotism, then abandoned the thought immediately. He was not about to allow himself to drift off into
that kind of comic book stuff. The situation was potentially
strange enough all by itself without embellishing. He knew
there was no way Donna—or the Traynes—could have worked
any kind of hypnotism on him. He thought about Mannie
Stuartson, his intensity. It was unusual to find such neediness
in Stuartson's face and voice. He really wanted the gift of Paul
Trayne to be true.

And why not? I'd like it too, if it were. So why do I suddenly find myself doubting it? I saw the magic it worked in my staff and my wife.

The change in Marjorie: so subtle he doubted anyone but himself would really have noticed. Paul Trayne had touched her soul, and in doing so had unlocked the sorrows she'd kept there since her son died. But that had not brought a torrent of pent-up grief, anguish, tears, as Clay might have expected. Instead, peace. Tranquillity.

Clay finished his sandwich in two more bites and breathed out hard, nostrils flared, twin pools of condensation forming on the cool glass of the picture window. Something was not right in all this. As much as he felt comfortable in trusting Paul Trayne and his father, there was about this whole business a wrongness. A penny that would not drop. He sorted through the details, searching for the thing that made the bump in the otherwise perfectly smooth plane of his thoughts.

Walker Stone. Donna Wojciechowski. Faulkner. Paul Trayne. Reverend Trayne. The boy's amazing gift. I was willing enough to accept the idea yesterday. Even today, listening to Paul in Mannie's office. Am I all of a sudden going to start questioning what Paul is capable of? Start doubting this gift of his? Start thinking like a cop?

That was it, of course. That was what was happening here. What should have happened from the first moment, Clay chided himself. He was thinking like a cop. *Finally* thinking like a cop.

He thought hard about Paul Trayne's gift. It was preposterous. Ludicrous that a boy—that anyone—could pop out of the woodwork one day with this—what?—mutant power to make all people feel good in themselves. The power to take their guilt into himself.

He thought about the phrase Donna Wojciechowski had used, when they'd found a moment to talk after Paul had worked his magic with Clay's wife and staff. "Whipping boy," she'd called Paul. With the gift of Paul Trayne there would be no suffering. A young boy simply looked into the eyes of a man or a woman—or a whole crowd—and, if they were willing, drew out of them all the pain and suffering of a lifetime and made them whole human beings again.

If they were willing. Clay turned the phrase in his mind. *How could anyone not be willing?*

He'd declined Paul's gift, for his own reasons, but the average man on the street, miserable in his life without really knowing why—how could he refuse the gift? How could he hesitate to pour his grief and anger and guilt into the bottomless receptacle that was Paul Trayne.

Bottomless? The cop in Clay Garber studied that word, what it implied.

Is he really? According to Reverend Trayne, all the guilt and grief Paul takes into himself he feels as his own. How much of that, how many hundreds or thousands of lifetimes of bitterness and anger can he draw into himself and experience as his own, without its destroying him?

Clay crossed the living room to the foot of the center stairs and walked up slowly, his mind still wandering these undirected pathways as his feet carried him to the master bedroom.

Reverend Trayne made it very clear with his little preamble that it was terribly painful and tiring for Paul to take all this shit into himself. It seemed damned important to Trayne that we all understand what Paul was doing, how much it would grieve the boy—and yet how very much Paul wanted, even needed to do it, to take our pain. He certainly seemed hurt, deeply hurt, when he realized I had not participated, not let him have my slice of sorrow.

Clay started stripping off the clothes he'd worn all day. His slacks he folded neatly and draped over the silent butler in the corner. Shirt, socks, and underwear he dropped in the big hamper at the foot of the bed. He started water running into the tub and sat on the commode to wait while the tub filled. It would have been quicker to take a shower, but he was in no real hurry; he wanted to relax and think some more. For as long as he could remember, the best place to do that was in the tub. On impulse he dumped some of Marjorie's bubble bath into the water and watched as the pink-tinged foam rose up the edge of the dark tub.

After five minutes the water was high enough to get in, and

Clay slipped down into the steaming pool. He left the taps running, an old habit, and sank down as low as the length of the tub would allow. The bubbles, tickling his nose smelled faintly of violets. Clay clasped his hands behind his neck and started to think about the trip to Faulkner. Uneasiness about Paul was melting away into the warmth of the tub. He found it difficult to focus, now, on the things that had perplexed him only a few minutes ago. A slight frown creased his brow as he sent his thoughts hunting for the reasons for his worries.

"Want your back scrubbed, big fella?"

Clay opened his eyes and looked back over his left shoulder. Marjorie was standing in the open door of the bathroom. She'd come into the bedroom without Clay hearing and evidently had been there for some time as she'd stripped off her outer garments. She stood now in her slip. Her flesh looked dark and rich as coffee against the pale pink of the satiny fabric.

"Anytime." Clay smiled. He grabbed the brass handhold on the wall-mounted soap dish and pulled himself up into a sitting position. Sudsy water sloshed back and forth along the length of the tub, around his belly, his bent knees. Marjorie crossed the bathroom, rolling up the sleeves of her blouse as she came. She lifted the big sponge from the caddy and knelt beside the tub. She scooped up water and bubbles on the sponge and began rubbing Clay's back.

"Mmm." He grinned. "That feels good. Have a good day?"

"Pretty good. Out with the ladies. You know." She hesitated, and for a moment Clay thought there might be something else, something she did not want to say.

"Oh, no," she said, when he asked. "I was just thinking about . . . well, I had a long chat with Velma today."

The name did not click at first in Clay's mind. "Velma?"

"Fantuccio."

He raised an eyebrow as the memory kicked in. "What on earth for?"

Marjorie shrugged. "I just called her. Out of the blue, really."

"But you can't stand her. You said the happiest day of your life was when Frank Fantuccio retired from public office and took away the last time you'd ever have to see or talk to Velma

Fantuccio." He smiled. "Although I think you were a bit more choice in your language."

Marjorie laughed. "I called her 'that bitch Velma Fantuccio,' as I recall. I may even have used the *F* word."

"So?"

"I wanted to tell her about Paul. I've spent the whole day talking about Paul. I thought Velma might be of use to him."

"How?" Clay did not like the sound of this, though, as with all his feelings today, he had no real, solid reason he could pull out and show for his uneasiness.

"Oh just, you know, helpful. She knows a lot of people. And Joe is still chairman of Willowbrook. Paul might have use of the auditorium there." She changed the subject, abruptly. "You're home early, aren't you?"

"Mmm." She was pushing hard against the set of his muscles. It was difficult to care about Velma and Frank Fantuccio —whom Clay liked no more than Marjorie—with this going on. Clay felt tensions dissolving into the sudsy water and pulled her close to kiss her. Marjorie leaned back as the kiss finished, Clay's wet handprint clearly defined on the front of her slip.

"Well, this won't do." She smiled.

She stripped off the slip in an easy, flowing motion. Rising, she unhooked her bra. She slipped out of it and the rest of her underthings and climbed into the tub. She straddled Clay, sitting in his lap. She smiled at the pressure she felt beneath the water. "I didn't realize I was that talented a back scrubber."

"I . . ." All at once Clay felt embarrassed by his tumescence.

Marjorie put a hand to his mouth, two fingers across his lips, silencing him. With her other hand she reached down between them, under the bubbles. She shifted, rising up, then lowering herself again.

"Mmm," she said, mimicking his own sounds of pleasure as she had rubbed his back.

Clay let his hands roam over his wife's body as she rocked slowly back and forth in his lap. The water sloshed against the side of the tub and gurgled down the overflow. It did not take long for him to reach climax. Not long after that Marjorie followed. She leaned into him, the length of her body against his as he slid down into the tub. The water lapped at his chin. It swirled around the mounds of her breasts, pressed out into lush, dark curves by the weight of her body on his chest. As she shuddered into her own deep, full orgasm, the motion squeezed their bodies together and three short jets of soapy water squirted out of the passage between her breasts. Spent, she settled down on him, her chin against his shoulder, her mouth close to his ear.

"Clay . . ."

"Mmm?"

"All those years . . . after Michael . . ."

He stroked her back. "Don't talk about that now," he said. "We'll have lots of occasions to make up for lost time."

She lifted her head and kissed him. Something was in her eyes when she met his gaze again. Something Clay Garber could not evaluate, could not remember ever having seen there before.

"What I wanted to say, though," Marjorie said, "it's about all those years. I used to feel . . . not guilty, exactly. You were so wonderful, so understanding that I never felt like I had to feel guilty."

"And you didn't." He kissed her again. "Because I love you."

"But now . . ." Marjorie shook her head. "Clay, there's something . . . I don't know, odd about the way I feel now. I mean, I like the way I feel now . . ." She moved her pelvis to emphasize her words. "But . . . but it seems strange that I can't find any trace of the way I used to feel. The not-exactly-guilty feeling."

"That's good, isn't it?"

"Is it? I don't know." She frowned. "It's like I have this little voice in my head. Really, just like a little voice. And every time I start to think about something that used to bother me, it says 'Never mind. It doesn't matter.' "

"That bothers you?"

"No." Marjorie rose up so that she was sitting on Clay's lap again. The foamy water rolled down her front, pinkish-white bubbles catching the overhead lights like diamonds against her dark skin.

"You see?" she said. "That was one of those times. You asked me if it bothered me and I said 'no,' right away. But it wasn't me that was saying 'no.' It was that voice inside my head. And yet . . ."

"Yes?" Clay tried to coax all the words out of his wife. He wished they were in some other place, some less distracting situation. Marjorie's body was difficult to ignore, and Clay felt that he was bound to miss something vitally important if he could not keep his attention on the proper track.

"Nothing," Marjorie said.

"Honey . . ." Clay sat up straighter in the tub. His buttocks squealed against the enameled base and he felt heat rising in his chest and neck. If only he and Marjorie were somewhere else, in some other, any other room in the big house . . . Marjorie rose, lifting herself carefully from the water, stepping out of the tub. She pulled one of the big, plush bath towels from the rail by the sink and began drying herself. Clay looked up at her, feeling his mind drift away from the questions he wanted to ask. He was mesmerized by the movement of the towel, the long swing and sway of the soft cloth against Marjorie's softer skin.

"Honey . . ."

"I'm hungry," she said, reminding Clay that throughout their married life, sex had been followed by food, in what to him always seemed a perfect combination. Marjorie finished drying herself and took down her robe from the hook behind the bathroom door. "Meet you in the kitchen," she said, and there was something devilish in her smile.

Clay pulled himself out of the tub. He turned off the taps and flipped the big chrome toggle to open the plug. The water level began to drop. He stood, dripping and naked, staring at the water and the remaining bubbles as they began their spiraling dive toward the drain and oblivion.

Like my thoughts. He felt chilled, and it had nothing to do with his wetness and the open bathroom door. He snatched up the other big bath towel and began drying himself. He stepped out of the bathroom and crossed to the intercom on the wall by the bedroom door. He was aware of the big wet footprints he was leaving across the dark carpeting, but he did not care.

He pressed the button by the neatly typed label that said KITCHEN on the plastic face of the intercom. From the little speaker he heard Marjorie's voice in song. The distortion made him think of Walker Stone's voice on his answering machine. Walker Stone made him think of Paul Trayne and the trip to Faulkner.

He crossed back to the bathroom and finished drying himself. He dressed in fresh socks, underwear, fresh shirt. He pulled on the same slacks he'd worn earlier, then paused. He opened the sock drawer of his dresser and reached into the back. A small canvas satchel was there. He pulled open the drawstring and slipped the contents into his hand: a police .38 in a dark leather holster, a clip on the side to fasten it to his belt.

Clay clipped the holster in place, against the small of his back, took out the pistol, and checked the load. There was a cartridge in all but the first chamber. He slipped the pistol back into the holster, picked up his jacket, and pulled it on. The gun felt strange. It had been a long time since Clay Garber had felt the need to carry ordnance of any kind. He felt the need now. He did not know why. But he felt the need.

He was not going to ignore his feelings. Not anymore. Not ever again.

17

The study was still quite cold, though Tom had turned up the heat over an hour before. As he stood by the window, looking out over the eastern rooftops, he could almost see his breath in the air before him.

"Tell me again about the first night," he said, not turning to face Donna Wojciechowski where she sat in the big wing chair by the newly built fire. He'd brought her down to the less intimate setting of his study; the line of questioning he felt he needed now to pursue seemed completely inappropriate to a bedroom.

Donna's portion of the dinner Mrs. Buck had cooked sat on a tray beside her, largely untouched. "Tell me again about the first time you slipped under his spell," Tom said.

" 'Slipped under his spell.' " Donna leaned back in the big chair, folding her long legs under herself, snuggling deeper into Tom's loaned dressing gown. It was a comfortable old thing, touching Donna's nostrils with his scent, subtle and masculine. She reached for the small glass of brandy Tom had poured her. He could see she was forcing herself to sip at it, instead of dashing it back in one gulp. He tried to remember if Walker Stone had ever said anything about Donna having an alcohol dependency. Certainly there were strong indications.

"It's difficult, still, to think of it that way," Donna said. "I've never been a big believer in fairy tales, ghosts, witches, that sort of thing. There's this part of my mind that doesn't want to think or speak of it as a 'spell,' even though . . ." When she paused Tom turned and looked at her. She was sitting with her head down, her chin resting on her chest. She was shaking her head, a slow rocking motion from side to side. "Maybe this is something they implanted, I don't know, but I still think Paul Trayne is just a kid. A well-meaning kid who just happens to have an amazing power. And a total psychotic for a father." She paused. "You know, I just had a weird thought . . ."

"Mmm?"

"Well, if Paul really *is* just a kid, a kid with some kind of mutant power . . . No, don't look like that. Go along with this for a minute. What if he's just a kid. He's sucking all this guilt and grief and crap out of people, and he knows where it came from. I mean, the knowledge of whatever caused the guilt and anger that comes with it."

"Yes? So?"

"So, what's that doing to him? To Paul? What effect could it have on a fifteen-year-old kid to suddenly have all these grown-up psychoses bubbling around in his brain? Fifteen is like, nothing, after all. It's a time when you start to believe you know everything, but I've really thought—well, Walker said once that until you're about thirty, every year is a process of realizing how stupid you were last year. So here's this fifteen-year-old kid, and a kid from some tiny little boondoggle town, on top of that. What is it doing to him? What effect is all this shit having on his own psyche—or soul, if you want?"

In her mind's eye Donna was seeing quite clearly as she spoke, the face of Paul Trayne. And it was his face shaped—twisted, she now thought—by that odd, indecipherable expression. An expression that suddenly made a terrible kind of sense to her.

"What if . . ." She shuddered, realizing the full import of what she wanted to say. "What if he's starting to *like* it? He helped his father torture me, and I thought all the time it was because he was under his father's spell, his domination. But what if he was *liking* it? Getting off on it. All those thousands of souls he cleansed in Faulkner. How many sickos and per-verts and, well, just plain nasty people, just plain nasty thoughts that even nice people have—how many of those are all mixed up in Paul's psyche now? Part of his psyche."

Tom nodded. "That's a good question. A very good question. And it's something we'll have to keep in mind as we make our plans."

Donna drew a deep breath. "Something else comes to mind. Something that puts an even weirder slant on this."

"And that is?"

"Reverend Trayne. The way he acts, the way he seems to think. Like nothing stands in his way. Nothing stops him from doing whatever he wants, making Paul do whatever he wants. As if there are no checks and balances in his brain anymore."

Tom saw the direction she was going. "As if he himself has been a recipient of Paul's gift."

Donna nodded. "Wouldn't that be something? It makes a crazy kind of sense. Who else would have been there when the power first appeared? His mother and his father. And Paul's mom ran off when the power appeared. What if it wasn't fear, like Trayne thought? What if it was . . . well, what if she just didn't care about Paul and Trayne anymore?"

"Or care what Trayne might do to her?" Tom wondered about it for a moment, balancing Donna's scenario against the one that had grown so quickly in his mind. "I don't know," he said. "Perhaps a mutation could produce something like this. And perhaps it could all happen in just the sequence you describe. But . . ."

"But you still think Trayne is some kind of demon."

"Yes. Granted his behavior is as one would expect from someone who has been touched by Paul Trayne's gift. But there's more. There's the—well, I hedged around the word before, but there's the vampirelike nature of it all. The way Trayne seems to operate. It's weaknesses that he feeds on, you see. Moral weaknesses. It's why he prefers not to compel people to surrender their guilt and grief to him. They must do it voluntarily, knowing how great a burden it will be for the 'poor boy.' "

"So that they'll be weakened somehow?" Donna was still not certain she understood this part.

"Yes. To dump all that—call it 'bad karma'—into a poor,

helpless boy is a particularly selfish thing to do, you see? They get all the benefits of Paul's gift, while he gets only pain and suffering. Their souls are cleansed, while his accumulates more and more spiritual detritus. At least, that's the myth he's selling."

"Say he *is* some kind of demon," Donna said. "Just for the sake of argument. Do you think you can handle him? I mean, with what you told me, aren't you something of a—well, a fallen angel?"

Tom shook his head, but he felt his heart sink, his resolution dwindle. There was something to be considered in Donna's words.

Is this pride? Sinful pride? Shouldn't I be seeking out the assistance of my superiors? Shouldn't I call the archdiocese . . . ? My faith is rock solid, but am I a worthy vessel for that faith? I have fallen far from the proper path. I have transgressed the laws of God, and at least one poor soul has suffered and died because of my transgression. But I refuse to believe God would have turned His face from me. I feel His strength, His power in this house, in me. I am His servant. He will not let me fall. "The Lord is my light and my salvation; whom shall I fear? The Lord is the strength of my life; of whom shall I be afraid?"

But, even as he drew strength from those words, Father Tom Sylvestri felt an emptiness at the center of his being. A cold, dark hollow carved out by the pointless death of a wonderfully talented artist. A death easily avoided, if Father Tom Sylvestri had been as strong as he knew he would need to be now. Did his weakness in this one thing mean he was weak in all things? *How powerful are these creatures? Am I risking the world—yes, potentially the whole world!—to seize this as an opportunity to make amends for my weakness of spirit?*

"My name's Garber. Clayton Garber." The big black man paused, as if expecting Pete Hay to respond to the name. When the deputy did not, he went on, "I'm from Chicago. I came to find out about Paul Trayne. Do you know—"

"Paul Trayne." Pete was immediately on his guard.

He was naturally defensive in the presence of a stranger.

And this stranger knew about the devil boy. And he was from Chicago, the same place as that nosy lady reporter and her boss.

"What do you want to know about Paul Trayne?" Pete was sitting in the broad, tall chair behind Nickerson's old desk. He had the chief's Sturm Ruger—recovered finally from the cellar of the old Tempest place—spread out in pieces on the blotter. He'd been cleaning it, carefully, using the slow, precise, mechanical motions to focus his mind.

"I want to know everything there is to know," Clay said. He leaned forward, hands as big as two of Pete's together balled into fists, resting his knuckles down on the edge of the desk.

If there was ever anyone who could truly be said to loom, Pete thought, it was this dark stranger from Chicago.

"You with a newspaper or something?" Pete asked. He wasn't about to tell anything of what he knew until he understood exactly who Garber was. The fact the man seemed to feel his name alone carried weight was not enough for Pete Hay.

"I'm the police commissioner," Clay said. He resisted adding *and I'm used to having weasels like you jump when I speak.* He did not know who this young man might be, but he did not like him. There was an edge to his nasal voice and a pinched quality in his narrow face that put Garber on guard. He'd driven down to Faulkner right after making what now felt like a lame excuse to Marjorie. He did not want her to know where he was going—there was still the risk she'd tell Paul, still the risk Paul might do something to stop him—so he'd invented an evening meeting he'd "forgotten" to tell her about. Marjorie accepted the falsehood without question, something that tickled uneasily at the back of Garber's mind as he drove. She could usually see through him pretty well. She had not even reacted to the presence of his pistol under his jacket. He was sure she must have felt it when she hugged him good-bye. But . . .

He'd left the house with the distinct impression there was something else occupying Marjorie's thoughts. No—not her thoughts, exactly. Clay could not define the feeling, but there was an invisible wall of *something* between himself and his wife. Something she knew. Something she'd done. Something she was not telling him. With his own deception so fragile a thing, Clay had not pressed. In the two hours it took to get to Faulkner, he began to wish he had.

Something to do with Paul Trayne?

"And why would you care about Paul Trayne, Commissioner?" Pete used the title in the hopes Garber would realize he put no great stock in it.

"Because he's in Chicago, right now." Clay saw the flicker in the deputy's eyes, and knew he'd struck a nerve. "I fear he may be working some kind of mischief. Has there been anything, well, unusual going on around here since the Traynes arrived? The town looks kind of, well, beat-up, but . . ."

Pete barked a bitter laugh. "You might say that, Garber." He started reassembling Nickerson's pistol, the oiled parts sliding perfectly against their mates with satisfying clicks.

"Take a seat, Commissioner," Pete said, nodding to the bench against the near wall. "Let me tell you a little story."

Emmanuel Stuartson sat on the big bed in the master bedroom of his tall town house, naked and dark against the peach-colored sheets, staring at his image in the full-length mirror that hung on the dressing room door directly opposite the foot of the bed. He looked amazingly emaciated to himself, as he always did, his brown skin hanging in sharp points at the juncture of bones in his long, lean form. The soles of his feet, crossed at the ankles, were as pink as the sheets he rested upon, and loomed large in his reflection.

He ran his hand over the crumpled sheet at his side, watching his mirror self-duplicate the action, remembering—trying to will forth—the images that mirror would have caught ninety minutes earlier. He'd looked past Marjorie, looked past her deep umber nakedness rising and falling slowly atop his recumbent form, and seen a scene he'd only dared dream reflected in the silvered glass of the mirror.

Marjorie Garber, astride and impaled upon Emmanuel Stuartson. Marjorie Garber shining with the sweat of sex, with subdued lamplight casting highlights that rose and fell, undulating across her gleaming form as she moved up and down, up and down.

Stuartson raised the long cigar, set it to his lips, and drew deeply on the fragrant smoke. It had been better than he could ever have imagined. Marjorie was everything he'd thought she would be and more. And she was not so changed, he thought, from their school days. She might be fifty, but to his eyes she could pass for nineteen, easily.

And the best part about it was the complete absence of any guilt, any shame, any sense at all that what they were doing was wrong, was a betrayal of his lifelong friend and her loving and devoted husband. He had wanted Marjorie Garber for thirty years. Longed for her—he had not realized until tonight just how much—and now that she was his, there was nothing, no consideration of Clay, no contemplation of immorality, that was going to take the pleasure of this divine consummation from him.

The telephone rang on the bedside table, his private line. He reached over and lifted the headset from its base. "Yes?"

"I couldn't tell him." It was Marjorie. Stuartson felt an ice pick go through his heart.

"You mean, you're not . . ."

"No! Oh, no! I'm coming. I'll be there in twenty minutes. I just . . . couldn't tell Clay about us. There was something . . ." She paused for a moment. "He was in the tub when I got home. He was miles away. I don't think he knew I was there for a couple of minutes."

Stuartson found nothing of consequence in Marjorie's words. All that mattered was that she was still coming. Coming here. Coming back to him. He looked in the mirror, imagining the things it would see over the next nights, weeks, months. He imagined it would take him quite some time to tire of Marjorie Garber. Quite some time.

"It doesn't matter if you didn't tell him," Stuartson said. "He'll figure it out soon enough when he finds you gone and starts seeing you with me."

"I suppose. But . . ."

"What?"

Marjorie paused a long time. Stuartson could see her, standing in the master bedroom of the Garber house, still wearing the clothes she'd had on when she left, shaking her head in that way he'd seen so many times when she had something to say but the words would not quite come together. "Thirty years," she said at last.

"Does that really matter?"

"No, but . . ."

"Can Clay help Paul?"

"No."

"Then get back here. Now. I can help Paul. That's all you need to know."

"He was manipulating your own negative psychology, your lack of self-esteem." Tom Sylvestri leaned his elbows on his knees and looked into Donna's shrouded eyes. "My best guess is that he simply overplayed his hand, pushed you too far."

"I wouldn't have thought he'd be inclined to make a mistake like that, Father," she said, "if he's really who you seem to think he is." She was still not convinced, but he'd listened to her ideas, and now she listened to his.

Tom shook his head. In the hall the old grandfather clock chimed the half hour, ten thirty. It had been a long day, even with her sleeping late. And it was not over yet.

"I'm not suggesting he's anybody in particular," Tom said, his voice devoid of any emotion to her ears. "Not Satan, if that's what you mean. Possibly one of his servants. Possibly something else. We of the Universal Church do not generally acknowledge such things in public, but there are other forces in the world. Evil forces. Some of them—many of them—are far, far older than Christianity, or even the Judeo-Christian synthesis."

Donna shook her head, feeling her hair move on the back of her neck, repressing a shudder. It felt like cobwebs brushing across her flesh, and like everything else that made her feel uneasy or uncomfortable, this now reminded her of Robert Johnston Trayne. She leaned back, finishing her brandy with one quick swallow. She looked at the empty glass. "Oops."

"How long have you been an alcoholic, Donna?"

She blinked. "Walker . . ." The name caught in her throat

this time. A jumble of memories came along with it. She coughed. "Walker used to say I'd been a confirmed alcoholic for three years. The . . . honest self-appraisal I got as part of Paul Trayne's 'gift' makes me think it's probably been a lot longer. Why? D'you think the booze might be part of it? Might be the reason I'm free at the moment?"

Tom shook his head. "I've always been inclined to think of hard drink as a pathway to damnation, not a ward against it. Still, it's worth pursuing, I suppose. It is an element of your personality. You had been drinking when you first encountered Paul Trayne."

"Yes." Before her meeting with Paul Trayne her instinct would have been denial. Now, it did not seem so important that she prevent the world—prevent herself—from knowing of her addiction. "I'd had a few the night before. At Ben Carpenter's place."

"And by the time you met him he was himself under the Trayne's control."

"I don't know if 'control' is quite the right word. But, yes, he'd been to one of the 'sessions.' He'd come away a full-fledged Trayne acolyte."

"Do you think he might have got you drinking to lower your resistance?" Tom shook his head, staring into the invisible infinity above and beyond Donna's dark blond hair. "This is the wrong track. I can feel it. There's something else at work here. Some other reason you were able to escape Paul Trayne."

Donna drummed the backs of her nails against the side of her empty glass. The sound was soft and mellow in the small, paneled room.

Almost like church chimes, she thought.

They reminded her that the glass was empty, and that sent her mind sliding along worn, familiar paths. She fought against the pattern, seeking something to deflect the flow. It was very hard. The residual—she prayed it was only residual—effects of Paul Trayne's "gift" made her want to get herself a drink, a real drink, and damn the consequences.

Almost as if sensing her thoughts, Tom rose and crossed to the sideboard liquor cabinet. He closed the walnut-laminated door, turned the little brass key in the lock, and removed it, slipping it into an inner pocket of his jacket. With Donna's confessed alcoholism out in the open Tom would not allow himself to be used to feed her problem. Donna's nerves were tightly wound, and he had no doubt a drink would help her, right at that moment.

But only for a moment, and if she was as far gone as she now readily admitted, one drink could only lead to another. He berated himself for having let her have the two brandies, reading in her as he had the all-too-familiar signs.

Shaking that thought from his mind, he turned to pick up the threads of their interrupted debate. "I think we are talking about a legitimate—if that's the appropriate word—servant of darkness," he said, hoping his last word would not capitalize itself melodramatically as he spoke it.

"Now the serpent was more subtle than any beast of the field . . ." *Subtle enough to have created this whole mad scheme? And the "beautiful boy"? Why not? Lucifer himself was the most beautiful of God's servants. Beauty and evil are often intertwined.*

He turned back toward Donna. The fire was low in the grate. Tom crossed to the fireplace and stabbed at the burning logs with an ornate poker. "I wonder what would have happened last night," he said, turning his head to meet her eyes again, "if I had succumbed to your beauty. I've known priests who might have."

He thinks I'm beautiful, Donna thought. *After all I've told him, all he knows about what happened between me and Paul Trayne. He thinks I'm beautiful.*

She sighed. *Of course he has to be a priest. And gay. What a perfect combination!*

"I'd as soon not think about what might have happened if . . . if you'd been . . . weaker," she said. "Go on with what you started to say. About thinking Trayne pushed me too far."

" 'Took you too high' might almost be a better way to phrase it," Tom said. He returned to his seat. "From what you've told me, it is not difficult to see you have an extraordinarily low opinion of yourself, Donna. I won't ask you to tell me the story of your life so I can try to figure out its origins, but I'll almost bet you had a pretty miserable childhood, and Walker mentioned once that you were unhappily married, and quite young."

"I had no idea you and Walker"—again her voice threatened to catch on the name—"had discussed me at such length." She was surprised to hear no anger in her voice.

A vestige of Paul Trayne's "gift"?

"We didn't really discuss you 'at length,' " Tom said. "I just have this trick memory. Everything stays with me. Walker was even a little surprised that I remembered what you looked like, when he called from Faulkner. But that's just the way my mind works." He smiled. "Came in very handy in catechism class."

Donna returned the smile, but without much warmth. She was still considering her lack of annoyance at Walker's discussion of her, in whatever depth, with someone who was, after all, essentially a stranger to her.

Please don't let me still have any remnants of Paul Trayne in me. It was so like a prayer she found herself blushing.

"Something . . . ?"

"Nothing. You are very astute, Padre," she said, hoping it might cover her blush. "My mother was a world-class bitch, and my husband's picture is in the dictionary under 'bastard.' " They both smiled at the old joke. "Together—well, with my help, yes—they managed to create a pretty miserable creature out of the clay I gave 'em. So why didn't Trayne know this?"

"He can't read minds," Tom said. "You're certain of that. But he can read the subtlest indication of a person's spirit, psychology, soul. Call it what you will. But if he is an agent of the forces I believe him to be, he may not have had much choice in how he treated you once you fell under his thrall. Evil must always *be* evil, after all. And subtlety tends to fall quickly by the wayside when an opportunity to twist a mortal soul occurs."

"And I must've looked like a great chance. I was already doing some pretty good twisting on my own." She looked at the empty glass still on the table. "That's why I didn't stop being an alcoholic"—it still came so easily to the lips!—"under Trayne's spell. It was part of the degradation process."

"Yes. Everything he did to you seems to have been intended to shrivel your soul, make you feel less and less worthy."

"But . . . I mean, there was his gift. I hate to call it that, but what else is there? Paul's gift made everyone feel so good about themselves. Even me."

Tom shook his head. "That's the key element of the trap, I think. Don't confuse what Paul created with 'feeling good about yourself.' If anything, I suspect he was setting up exactly the opposite of that. Reverend Trayne's introductory speech—you said he delivered it at every meeting, even at the Garber house? Well, I see that as a kind of preconditioning effect. He offers you this wonderful gift, but he makes sure you understand what a terrible burden it will be for Paul. He makes you understand what a basically rotten thing you're doing to this poor kid, in order that he can free you of all the problems in your life."

Donna thought about it for a moment. "Yes . . . that fits with what Trayne himself said about not wanting to compel people to accept his gift. How it was part of the plan, his plan, that they come to Paul willingly, and take the gift willingly."

"Precisely. And he gave it to you, and then Trayne sent you off down this road of grief and degradation so that each time he let you return to the real world the power of his gift would be reinforced."

"He drove me down," Donna frowned, trying to assimilate the concept, "so that I would be more uplifted?"

"More or less. The gift functions very much like a drug." Tom paused, realizing there was a more immediate metaphor, and wondering if he should use it. He decided to risk it. "Like alcohol. The more you have, the more you need. And the deeper down he drove you, the more you should have needed the gift. Vicious circle."

" 'Should have,' you said?"

"Should have. That's the point I'm getting to. Your whole life seems to have been one of self-denigration, self-destruction. By offering you the freedom of his gift, Paul Trayne was actually offering you something your whole psyche was created to reject."

"So I pulled out of it all . . . because he made me feel good, not because of the pain and humiliation?"

Saved by my own lack of self-esteem. She sighed. *If I really am saved. Maybe that's one I owe you, Mother.*

"He was inverting the conditioning of your personality. Remember what you told me, about your mother calling you 'slut' just before she died? That was the capper, the icing on the destruction of your personality she'd inadvertently—yes, give her the benefit of the doubt—inadvertently created in trying to prevent you from turning into what she felt she'd become herself. So your poor, ragged personality accepted that condemnation, and for the rest of your life you've been doing everything possible to prove your mother right."

Donna tipped her head, not following the thought. "Prove her wrong, you mean, don't you?"

"No. That's the key. Your mother defined you, planted an image in your mind. An image you could not escape. And it perverted everything good in your life, made you seek out the worst for yourself, made you flee the good." He slipped from his seat, dropped to one knee in front of her. He took her hand in both of his.

"That's what you've got to be on guard against now. That way lies exactly the method by which Trayne ensnared you in the first place. He was playing off your lack of self-esteem. Feeding it. Stoking it."

"Maybe." She drew herself up straight in the chair. She looked toward the window; the flickering streetlight painted a pale blue-white glow down the front of her face, the firelight catching her hair with golden memories.

I can see where Walker would have fallen very hard for her, Tom thought. *She must have seemed like something unattainable at first to him with his squeaky voice and short stature. Not hard to understand why he was so devastated when he couldn't make her as happy as she made him.*

He sighed. *Poor Walker. I must save this woman, if only as a memorial to you.*

Donna let go of his hand and went over to the window. The snow was coming down very fast. Against the whiteness of the window she looked like a black hole to Tom, like the mouth of a tunnel. If Robert Trayne had stepped through that hole, the abyss at just that moment, stepped through Donna as he might a door, Tom would not have been surprised. He rose himself, dusting off his knee and crossing to stand an arm's length behind her.

"He drove you down, then tantalized you with the freedoms of his supposed gift," Tom said. "Where he miscalculated was in judging you to be someone who would welcome his gift, who would see it as a boon."

"So . . ." Donna turned slowly to face Tom. "It was my need to feel like dirt that saved me? I got out because he was making me feel too good, not . . ."

"Essentially. An oversimplification, of course. But, essentially, that is it."

"Do you think . . . do you think Walker guessed any of this?"

Tom shrugged. "I don't know. He was worried about you, about the change he saw in you."

"But . . . supposedly he saw only the 'positive' effect of Paul Trayne. The sweetness-and-light effect."

"Walker was a pretty perceptive guy. I think he would have spotted something amiss, something wrong in you—wrong for the structure of your personality—without really guessing why."

"Walker . . . was probably the best think that ever happened to me," Donna said. She threw her arms around Tom's neck and buried her head in his chest, sobbing.

"Yes, I suspect he was."

"Promise me we'll get him," she said after the first round of sobs abated a little. She lifted her head from his breast and met his gaze with a cold fire in her eyes. "Promise me we'll crucify Reverend Robert Johnston Trayne."

Tom nodded. "We'll make a good try, I promise you that. But you must know that will not bring Walker back."

"I know. I know. Walker is gone, and it's as much my fault as if I'd pulled the trigger myself. No, don't try to deny it. I . . . well, I sort of need that one, to give me a focus."

"All right. I won't try to convince you . . . for now. But we'd better start formulating some kind of plan, Donna. There are millions of people in Chicago, and unless something is done soon they are likely to fall under Trayne's spell as quickly and completely as the people of Faulkner."

Donna nodded. "He was going to start at the top this time, he said." She took a deep breath, stepped back from Tom. "I wonder what he thinks that means? I got him to Clay Garber, and by now Garber will surely have gotten him to the mayor. Plus there's Marjorie . . ."

"We must try to get in touch with Stuartson. He should be warned. You said Trayne could compel people to believe him, believe in Paul?"

Donna nodded. "Yes."

"It might do us well to catalog the extent of Paul Trayne's powers." Tom frowned, thinking. "I wonder just how much he can do, really?"

Donna shook her head. "I'm not so sure. Is there anything we could use as a defense?" she asked, bringing him back to the study and the situation at hand. "Any . . . I don't know, any charms or verses or . . ."

"Trust in prayer," he said, finding immediate confidence in the dogma. "The power of prayer will protect you."

"Even though I don't believe in it?"

"Yes." Tom was smiling now. A small smile, but full of a warmth Donna could feel flowing across the room to her. "It doesn't really matter what you believe," Tom said. "It's what Trayne believes."

"And . . . some people can resist him, anyway. Walker, though it cost him physically. And I'm pretty sure Clay Garber was genuinely untouched."

"And how did Paul react to that?"

"He was very unhappy. It hurts him when he can't . . ." Donna's eyes went very wide. "Oh, Jesus."

Tom crossed to her in two long strides. He caught her arms, she seemed so near to tumbling out of her chair onto the carpet. "Donna . . . ?"

"I was going to say . . . It was all there again. Just a flash, but everything. As soon as you asked how Paul Trayne reacted, I was ready to go into the whole spiel. How it hurts him not to be able to take the grief and pain out of another person. But how he can't do it unless they let him. Oh, Jesus. Jesus! It was all there!"

"Don't worry about it right now," Tom said, and meant it. It was important that Donna not dwell on her experiences in the Traynes' thrall.

She could slip back at any moment, he thought, *if she isn't on guard. She is free now, quite free of the snares created around her by Trayne, but she could be drawn back into those snares by a misplaced word, a thought gone off along the wrong tangent. And if that happens, will I be able to tell? Will I know if she's once more a slave to Paul Trayne?*

He realized he was experiencing the same insidious doubt that Donna had felt about him.

He robs us of trust, this monster. And without trust, we cannot survive as human beings.

"You were thoroughly conditioned by Trayne," he said aloud, seeking anything that might comfort Donna without allowing her to drop her guard completely. "You will have to watch out for that kind of Pavlovian reaction. Watch out for it, but don't dwell on it."

Her eyes were still wide, terrible fear in them. "For how long? How long will I have to watch my every thought, my every word, in case Trayne is lurking in them, waiting to pounce on me, waiting to make me his goddamn slave again." She blinked, as if surprised by her language.

"Donna, don't. Don't distress yourself. Just know what the traps are, and be on guard against them. You can do it."

"But for how long?"

Tom wanted to lie at that moment, but he feared what a lie might begin, feared the weakness in himself that even such a small, white lie might generate.

"Perhaps forever," he said. "You may have to fight him for the rest of you life. Be on guard always." He saw the fear in her eyes and raised his hand to cup the gentle curve of her cheek. "But you'll do it, Donna. You'll fight, and you'll win."

"I wish I had your faith in me, Padre." She leaned back in the chair. "It seems like my inability to avoid obvious traps is what got me into this mess in the first place." She sighed, holding up before her a hand that trembled in the glow of the dying fire. "I really could use a drink. A few hundred drinks, actually, but one good long one to start. I feel like hell." It was not an exaggeration. The backs of her eyeballs were coated with coarse sand. All her teeth were too big for her jaw. Everything was disproportionate, painful, wrong.

Just one drink. One or two at most . . .

Tom shook his head. "No."

"No." Donna nodded. "When did I take the pledge without noticing?"

"When I realized you're an alcoholic." He put a hand to her arm. "I think you should go back to bed, Donna. Get some rest."

She heard the deeper meaning in his words. "It's going to get bad again, isn't it? Not my needing a drink, I mean. That's bad already. The business with Trayne."

"Yes. Yes, I think it's going to get very bad."

"You . . . can't think of a way to stop him, can you?"

"No. I read up the rites of exorcism again. There's nothing there that covers this. Not that I can find, anyway."

"Because Paul isn't possessed, you mean?"

"Yes. We can't drive the evil spirit out of Paul Trayne, because Paul Trayne is, himself, the center of the evil."

Donna was still not entirely convinced of that. But she said, "There must be something we can do. A weapon. A . . . an antidote to the power of Paul Trayne." As she said those words, that precise phrase, something passed quickly across Donna's mind. Something she realized she'd thought before but, like a song lyric known so well and yet failing to come to mind, the thought would not gel.

Tom shrugged. He urged her from her seat and walked her back toward the bedroom. The somber faces of the old photographs looked down as they passed, and Tom thought he might sense their disapproval, were he inclined to open himself to it. He helped Donna into bed and pulled the blankets up. Without thinking, he smoothed the tousled hair back from her brow. Even with the darkness under her eyes she looked child-like, he thought, snuggled down under the thick covering of blankets and comforter.

"There must be something we can do," she repeated. "A weapon."

Tom nodded, crossing to the door. He smiled. "Yes. There must be."

"And you'll find it. You'll destroy Robert Trayne?" *And free Paul,* she thought, but kept silent. She did not entirely like the way that sounded, even in her mind. If Tom was right . . .

"Yes." She heard the grim set in Tom's voice, the total commitment. "Whatever it takes, I will destroy Trayne. You have my word on that." He paused. He looked into Donna's face, and she saw in his eyes something of the looks she'd been given by Walker Stone. She'd resented them then, but she found she did not now.

"Something else?" She was almost afraid of what he might say.

"I promise you I will destroy Trayne," Tom said again, "but I want a promise from you in return."

"A trade?"

"No. I'll destroy Trayne, if I can, no matter what you say now. But I do want this promise from you. A bond of faith, if you like."

Donna sighed. "All right. Do I get to know what it is, or do I have to promise blind?"

"St. Timothy's has an alcohol abuse clinic. We run it every Tuesday and Thursday, alternating days with our drug abuse clinic. It's set up very much like AA. If I succeed, if I destroy Trayne, I'd like you to come by for a session." He shrugged. "More than one, really. I'd like you to commit yourself to a complete program."

Donna pushed the back of her head deeper into the pillow and stared up at the ceiling, wondering what Walker Stone would think if he could hear what she was about to say. "All right, Padre," she said. "You beat Trayne, and I'll let you do the best you can to dry me out."

"I want that as a promise, Donna."

She nodded. "I promise."

18

Clayton Garber had never been so eager to leave anywhere as he was Faulkner. He paced back and forth in Maurice Zeldenrust's office, reminding even himself of the big cats he'd seen at the Chicago Zoo stalking relentlessly up and down the claustrophobic confines of their cages.

Pete Hay and the old doctor had exchanged a night's worth of questions and answers with Clay, subject: Paul Trayne. In those hours the police commissioner learned for the first time the present condition of Walker Stone.

"And this is all true?" Clay said at last, dropping his bulk onto a corner of Zeldenrust's desk. He found he trusted Zeldenrust far more than the nervous, angry policeman.

"Every word," Zeldenrust said. "I've got a morgue full of corpses, some of them in very nasty condition, if you need more proof."

Clay shook his head. "I'd better get back to Chicago as fast as I possibly can." He pushed himself up, rising to his full height, filling the small office. He should be tired, he knew. It was nearly twenty-four hours since he last slept, nearly that many since he sat in the kitchen of his quiet house and learned of the grim death of Charles Addison Kilgore. But he was running on pure adrenaline, the street cop rearing up, ready to battle until the job was done. "There's a string of dominoes I had not a small part in pushing over," Clay said. "I've got to do what I can to stop them. And I want to talk to Stone, right now."

"I cannot guarantee that is a practical possibility," Zeldenrust said. "He's in a bad way. Heavily sedated. Plus, the tracheotomy . . ."

"We can try, at least," Clay said.

Zeldenrust shrugged and rose. "I'll take you to him, then. Pete?"

"Two minutes," Hay said. "I want to look in on Alice Nickerson."

Zeldenrust nodded and fished in his pocket for the big key chain he always carried. He sorted out the key to the security ward and handed it to Pete with the rest of the keys dangling. They set off in two directions, Clay following Zeldenrust down the darkened halls until they came to Walker Stone's private room.

"How well did you know Stone?" Zeldenrust asked.

"Pretty well," Clay said, finding it difficult to quantify his relationship with the *Advocate* editor. They were not so much friends—Clay was very sparing with that term—as friendly adversaries. Although he had never had a bad moment with the press, Clay had a politician's natural distrust of the Fourth Estate. Newspapermen were, he thought, dedicated solely to the acquisition of *bad* news. The Woodward-and-Bernstein syndrome, Clay called it. They all wanted that big story, deep and dark and dirty, full of the kinds of secrets that made for big fat books and bigger, fatter movie contracts. They all wanted to be played by Robert Redford.

"You will find him changed," Zeldenrust said, drawing Clay's wandering thoughts back to the hospital, to Faulkner, to the occupant of the room outside which Zeldenrust had stopped.

He opened the door. Clay stepped into the room and looked at Walker Stone. He'd tried to imagine the worst, and found now he'd fallen far short. Stone was frail and haggard, a translucent gray-blue. His breathing was a rasping, mechanical sound, a faint gurgling at the place where the tracheotomy tube pierced his throat. He looked several weeks dead, Clay thought.

"Mr. Stone?" Maurice Zeldenrust leaned close to Stone's head, his voice a calculated whisper, not enough to wake Stone if he were deeply asleep, but enough to draw his attention if Stone were on the edge of wakefulness. "Mr. Stone, there is someone here to see you. Commissioner Garber."

Stone stirred. Clay saw his eyelids flutter. Stone's left hand tried to rise from his side. It was lashed, gently, to the chrome-plated rail along the side of the bed. Clay watched as the muscles tensed along the length of Stone's arm, then relaxed, surrendering. Stone opened his eyes. His gaze was not firm; his pupils wandered. Clay realized they would not have much time to find out what he needed to know before Stone drifted off again.

"Clay Garber . . . ?" No sound came from Stone's mouth, though the tracheotomy gurgled disturbingly in a faint imitation of words. But Clay recognized the shape of his name on the bearded lips.

"Hello, Walker," he said, trying a small smile. He did not like the feel of it on his face and abandoned it. "How do you feel?"

Walker cocked an eyebrow. He needed only that disdainful expression to tell Clay his question was more than a trifle redundant.

"Yes"—Clay nodded—"I can see you probably don't feel very well at all." He moved closer to Stone's head, Zeldenrust opposite him. "Can you manage to tell us anything, Walker?" Clay asked. "Anything at all about what happened to you?"

"Nickerson," Stone mouthed. Zeldenrust recognized the chief's name, said it aloud, for Clay's benefit. Stone nodded.

"The one who attacked you?" Clay asked. He'd been told something of what was believed to have happened in Gunner's Field and the cellar of the old Tempest place. It had been unnerving, hearing that part of the story. Clay had entered Faulkner from the north, along Black Rock Highway. He realized, there in Stone's room, that without knowing it he had passed through the nexus of the horror that had descended on this unsuspecting town.

Stone nodded his reply to Clay. Then he mouthed something Clay was not certain of. For a moment he thought it might be "mommy." Then something Stone had mentioned many years before percolated into the front of Clay's brain. "Tommy?" Clay asked. Stone nodded, mouthed something else.

"He's getting tired," Zeldenrust said. "I don't think . . ."

"That's all right, Doctor," Clay said. He laid a big hand on Stone's shoulder, careful of the tracheotomy tubes. "I understand, Walker. I'll do what I can."

Stone smiled, already drifting away from them.

They left the room in the silence in which they'd found it, walked in silence back to Zeldenrust's office. Pete Hay was waiting outside the door.

"Who is Tommy?" Zeldenrust asked Clay as they went back into his chambers.

"I'm not sure. I have to call Chicago."

Zeldenrust nodded toward the telephone on the desk. "Help yourself."

Clay lifted the phone from its cradle, dialed his home. It was a rotary dial, and for a moment it confused him. He'd grown so accustomed to Touch Tone dialing he thought of phone numbers as patterns rather than digits. He had to force the actual numerical sequence out of his mind and into his index finger. The phone rang six times and a voice he did not recognize answered.

"Mandrake."

"This is Commissioner Garber," Garber said. "I need a make on Walker Stone. Anyone connected with him whose name might be Thomas or Tommy, or any variant."

"Stone the newspaper guy?"

"That's him. How long do you think it will take?"

"Two seconds," Mandrake said. Garber heard the sound of the telephone receiver being put down. In his mind he could see the man—a generic cop-shaped form—crossing the bustling office to the wall of computer terminals. Would he be facile enough to work the keyboard himself, or would he call for help? Garber heard no voice raised above the general background noise. In a few moments—more than two seconds, but not a lot—Mandrake was back. "Stone's first cousin is a priest named Thomas Sylvestri. He sound like your man?"

Clay nodded, smiling. "Yes. Thanks." He paused.

"Something else, Commissioner?"

"Paul Trayne. Do you have anything recent on him or his father?"

"Who?"

Then it had not reached that far. Should he put out an APB, have the Traynes found and arrested?

No. It would be an abuse of power. There was no way to connect them to the horrors Clay had seen in Faulkner. It was, in fact, a kind of madness even to suggest they were connected. Teenage boys with fantastic powers did not belong in the real world. And even if they did, there was nothing implicitly illegal about what Paul did. Nothing Clay knew about, at least.

"Never mind," he said at last. "Thanks for your help."

He hung up. He looked at the phone, drummed his fingers on the black plastic.

"Someone else you wanted to call?" Zeldenrust asked.

"My wife. With all this . . ." He rotated his head to encompass what he had seen and heard of Faulkner. He'd left Marjorie seeming right as rain last night, but with what he'd learned, could he ever think her all right again? She'd been touched by Paul Trayne, and Clay now understood that to be every bit as dangerous, as poisonous, as his first instincts had told him.

He dialed his home number. After two rings the recorded voice of Marjorie Garber answered, the greeting she'd taped over a year ago. Two rings meant there were messages waiting, but Garber could not retrieve them from a rotary phone. He left a message of his own, promising to be home soon. He hung up, feeling no better. Garber wondered where everyone could be. Anne was still missing apparently, and it was possible Rose was out shopping.

But where was Marjorie?

With Paul?

The thought was a dagger in Clay's soul. He looked at his watch. It was nearly eight in the morning. Gray light spread through the venetian blinds over Zeldenrust's windows. When Clay looked out through the horizontal slats he saw low, heavy clouds and dark smoke drifting across the sky. Something was burning to the west. Something close. Something big.

"I have to get back to Chicago," Clay had said. "I have to tell Stuartson about this." He remembered Mannie Stuartson's enthusiasm for Paul, and wondered if his tale could have any effect.

He dialed again, Stuartson's private home number. The phone rang twenty times without answer. He pressed the cutoff button and dialed the public line. The sharp buzz of a busy signal sounded oddly angry in his ear. Clay hung up again. He rose and paced.

How far has it gone, in the time I've been away? Only a few hours, but if what these two told me is true the madness consumed Faulkner in very little more than that. If only the goddamn phone wasn't busy . . .

"I have to go back. Now."

"I'll escort you to the edge of town."

Clay turned to look at Pete Hay. "That's not necessary, Deputy. I can take care of myself. You're needed here."

Pete shook his head. "I don't think you'll get far without me, Commissioner. We told you about the barricade. I don't think that's gonna prove an isolated incident." Pete heard the iron in his voice, the edge of hard resolve. He wondered what Clarence would have thought to hear it.

I promised you I'd kill the bastards who fucked with you, Chief, Hay thought, *but now I've got something else to do. Something you'd never have thought you'd ever see me volunteering for, I'll bet.*

"What do you anticipate, Deputy?" Clay asked.

"Just . . . trouble. So I'll take you to the edge of town. Then . . . well, then I have to see what I can do about saving this place. Saving these people from themselves."

Clay nodded. "That's a big job, Deputy."

Hay snorted. "You've got a bigger one, Commissioner, if Paul Trayne is already doin' his nastiness in Chicago. He turned this town inside out in a month. What's he going to do in Chicago?"

Clay thought about the image that had greeted him when he arrived in Faulkner: filthy streets, garbage, burned-out buildings. He'd seen rats running across the snow, big and fat, made bold by the stench of offal and decay. And Chicago . . .

Clay Garber loved Chicago with all the passion of a man dedicated to the life of a city, but he knew as only a cop knows that there was a terrible black rot there, below the surface, behind the gleaming glass and steel of the bright new towers. People were not meant to live in big cities, he'd thought more than once. They were not meant to be pressed together like that, piled on top of each other. Even in a small town like Faulkner there was so much for Paul Trayne to prey on. He'd twisted almost everyone—seventeen thousand!—in barely a month. Chicago was bigger, but also darker, meaner, more prepared for what Paul gave.

"All right. I'll take that escort." He looked at Zeldenrust. "Will you be all right here, if Hay comes with me to the city limits?"

Zeldenrust shrugged. "If I'm not, I'm not. I'm a fatalist. If something's going to happen to me, I think it will happen with Pete here or not."

Clay wondered aloud about bringing Stone back to Chicago, but Zeldenrust warned against it.

"He'll be all right here, as long as he isn't moved," he'd said. "A car trip, along these winter roads, without anyone with proper medical training to look after him if something should go wrong . . . No. Leave him. He'll be all right. As all right as any of us."

A few minutes later Clay climbed behind the wheel of the BMW and waited for Hay to pull up alongside in the patrol car. Hay leaned over to roll down the passenger side window.

"Follow me," he said. "And keep it slow and easy."

Garber nodded and pulled out behind Hay. Slow as a funeral procession they began to make their way through the middle of town. The smoke was thick across the sky. How much of Faulkner was ablaze? he wondered. And, with the fire department completely uninterested in dealing with the blaze, how long before the whole town was razed?

The streets were still, empty. No one was in sight. Nothing, not even a stray cat or dog, moved anywhere in Clay's line of sight. Bare trees lined the avenues, drab and skeletal, looking in the morning light as if they had never held leaves and never would. Garbage was piled around their trunks. A stench like none he'd ever known began to assail Clay's nostrils. He rolled up the window he'd lowered to talk to Pete Hay and turned on the heater.

Clay's heart was full of foreboding. Whatever lay ahead, he thought, it had very little to do with spring and summer, with green leaves and life returning. He saw only death. Hopelessness.

And then, as they passed under the highway overpass and rose up onto the ridge of Black Rock, just short of the turn onto Pine Tree Road, he saw something else.

The patrol car stopped. Clay slowed the BMW, halting a few inches short of Hay's rear bumper. Hay was already out of the car, a riot gun at his side.

He trotted back to Garber, said, "Stay put."

He turned and jogged back toward the barricade that blocked their way. In intent it was similar to the one Hay and Zeldenrust had encountered on Albert Street, but very different in structure. Where that had been old sofas and two-by-fours stacked in a haphazard jumble, this was made up of tractors, combines, and huge plows with great circular blades that made Clay Garber think of the shields of a Roman army. The barricade stretched from one side of the highway to the other. Even the drainage ditches to either side were blocked with big machines, incongruous in their bright colors, looking to Clay more like circus floats than the weapons of war they had clearly become.

Clay watched as Hay reached the leading edge of the barricade. He wondered what Pete Hay was feeling, thinking. He glanced to the left. A small sign nailed to a fencepost said "Pine Tree Road."

So this is where it all began, Clay thought. *Amazing. And I passed this road on the way in. Why didn't I feel the evil in that field?*

Hay walked back to the right, looking for some space between the machines. Clay watched until the deputy found the gap he was seeking and disappeared behind a big old International Harvester combine. Clay realized he was gripping the wheel of the BMW with all his strength. His knuckles were a dull ocher across the darkness of his hands. Painfully he forced his stiffened fingers to relax. He flexed and stretched his hands wide on the wheel.

He looked at the dashboard clock. The digital face told him Hay had been gone one full minute now. When five had passed without event, Garber climbed out of the car and began walking slowly toward the wall of machinery. He'd heard no sound of violence, no cry from Pete Hay. No shots. The tangled mass of steel and rubber, one machine blending indecipherably into the next to his city eyes, was silent and cold in the morning light. He slipped his hand under his coat, around his back. He closed his fingers tight around the butt of the .38. It seemed suddenly very small. He wondered if it packed enough power to penetrate all this steel.

Clay was within ten paces of the barrier when one of the tractors fired up its engines. An explosion of sound punched a red hot fist through Clay Garber's chest. He stiffened, heart pounding, breath choking against the back of his throat. His cop's instincts kicked in. He pulled the .38, assumed firing stance, gun hand braced by the other.

The tractor lurched—he could see a man at the wheel now, inside the glassed-in cabin—and began to roll toward him.

Ben Carpenter awoke, a single dull ache. His head ached. His fingers ached. His back felt as though it had been twisted like taffy between monstrously powerful hands. He rolled his legs off the sofa in his office and pushed up on his right arm. Painful tingles shot up and down the arm. He'd slept on it, and now the blood returning to the deprived arteries was pushing ground glass before it.

Ben leaned forward, arms dangling on either side of his knees. His heart pounded, his head felt light. He hated this feeling. It came more and more often, more and more frighteningly, whenever an arm or leg—or worse, two—went to sleep. He felt as if he was going to have a heart attack, although never having had one he was not at all sure what the actual warning signs would be. It seemed as if all the blood in his body was pumping into the arm, and the rest of him would die for lack of sustenance. He waited for the spell to pass. After what he guessed to be a little more than a minute he felt well enough to sit up. He leaned back on the couch and raised his right arm, flexing the hand until life felt fully restored. He rubbed the arm with his left hand, rubbed his face with both hands. His cheeks were thick with stubble; he'd been asleep for quite some time by the angle of the light through the window. He forced himself to his feet and crossed the two paces to his desk.

Ben looked at the typewriter. He had vague memories of spending a long and frenzied time banging away at those old manual keys. Now, as if the action had emptied him of whatever caused it, he had no memory whatsoever of what he had typed, or why it had seemed so important. As the fog of sleep drifted away and portions of his brain normally associated with cohesive thought manifested themselves, he realized he remembered little of the last twenty-four hours. He sat behind the desk and looked for some sign of what he had been typing. He found nothing—no paper, no crumpled discards. He wondered if he had dreamed the typing or—worse—if the compulsion he associated with the action had not included feeding paper into the typewriter. His shoulders ached. He'd worked a long, long time on whatever it had been. He did not care for his work to be pounded into the black rubber face of the roller.

Ben squinted at the pitted surface, leaning close over the keys. It looked no worse than it always did, but it always looked pretty bad, Ben thought. He could have typed the *Encyclopedia Britannica A* to *Z* onto that old roll without adding appreciably to the overlapping pattern of letters absorbed in its long lifetime. Old newspapers were strewn around the office. He realized from their quantity that he must have raided the morgue, the narrow, dark room next to the storage closet. He could not have had this many papers stored in his office no matter how neatly they might have been stacked. He wondered what he'd been looking for and felt his brows draw into a tight, painful frown as the information refused to reveal itself.

He left the office, crossing the newsroom to the bathroom. Inside, it was cold and dark in the little windowless room, but he waited a moment before turning on the light. He was not at all sure he wanted to see what the mirror would show him. He reached for the light switch and confirmed his worst fears. He looked as if he was coming out of a three-day drunk. His hair rose in curious spikes, oily and dark. His face was dusted with a gray-white stubble that caught the light like powdered sugar. His shirt was grimy with droppings of Chinese food. His chin was covered with the stuff, dry and caked.

Christ! I look like I was on some kind of feeding frenzy.

He ran hot water into the small sink and splashed his face. The bar of soap on the dish was a tiny, ineffectual thing, and in any case it would have taken more than hand soap to rectify everything Ben Carpenter found wrong with himself that morning. He was going to have get back to his apartment, get a shower and shave and a change of clothes. He dried his hands and face, wiping off most of the Chinese debris. Then he went back across the newsroom to the enclosure in front of his office. He lifted his hat and coat from the rack and pulled them on. The newsroom was a ruin, despite his best efforts not to notice. He sighed, crossed to the door, and carefully locked it behind him. Halfway down the front stairs he stopped, considering. He did not want to be seen on the street looking like this. He frowned for a moment. It seemed odd—and oddly welcome—that such considerations should occur to him. He waited for the sound of the little voice, but the familiar *Never mind* did not come.

Ben went on down the stairs and turned hard left at the bottom. He walked back along the narrow corridor to the back door. He unlatched it and stepped out into the alley. Shielded from the small warmth of the sun, the alley was a valley of cold. Ben's breath filled the air before him. He pulled the collar up on his coat and turned to lock the door behind him.

He saw Mae Ellen and froze.

Her body hung from the fractured leg, muscle and sinew pulled out into a long, tapering ribbon, punctuated at either end by jagged, bloodied bone. Her dress had fallen back under the weight of gravity and soaked-in blood. Her torso was almost completely covered with dark, dry blood. Her head was turned on the pavement. Her face was covered with rivulets of blood that had dripped from her dress. Her eyes were open, fixed. Ben remembered the sound that brought him to the window above, hours before. He remembered seeing the twisted

figure in the alley, remembered—a painful, bitter memory now
—not caring.

He crossed the two steps to Mae's side, stooped beside her,
tears running down his face. One dropped from the edge of his
jaw and splashed against her cheek. It loosened some of the
dried blood and created another rivulet, tiny red-black crumbs,
no more than specks, floating in the clear stream of his tear.
Ben lost his balance and sat down hard on the pavement by
Mae Ellen Faber. He put out a hand to touch hers. Her skin
was cold as stone, her muscles hard.

Ben huddled into his knees and began sobbing.

Donna's sleep was punctuated with uneasy, fragmented
dreams. It seemed to her she had lain awake for hours, days,
before sleep had finally come. She really needed a drink, now.
Really. Really. Her fitful doze was breaking in a jumble of
half-conscious hallucinatory flashes. As she drifted toward
wakefulness they seemed to coalesce, to be drawn together
into a single form.

"Hello, Chow," said Walker Stone.

Donna could not find her voice to answer. She knew Walker
was dead, but the face and form before her were exactly the
man she'd loved and hated and ultimately loved again. He was
standing three feet from her bedside. He wore his usual slacks,
plaid shirt, suspenders. Even the red socks, Donna noted. His
glasses had slipped down to the end of his nose. His beard was
dark in the dark room. It was still the bedroom Father Tom
had put her in, still in the residence behind St. Timothy's.

"Walker . . . ?"

The image of Stone took two paces forward and lowered
itself into a sitting position on the edge of the bed. Donna
shifted automatically, but the mattress did not sink under
Stone.

He has no weight. Ghosts have no weight.

"It's me," Stone said. The voice was right, the smile. He
seemed solid in her eyes.

"You . . . you are dead, Walker? I mean . . ."

"Yes, I'm dead." He smiled again and raised his hands to

either side of his head, wiggling the fingers furiously. "Booga-booga."

Donna swallowed in a dry throat. "Not funny."

But very, very Walker.

"Sorry." He lowered his hands and put the left out to cover her right, where it rested on the top blanket. Donna saw the stubby fingers cover her own but felt nothing.

"I shouldn't be kidding around, I guess," Stone's voice said. "I need to say a few things to you, and I don't know how long I've got."

"Walker . . ."

He raised his other hand. "Don't try to understand it, Chow. It's not something that's going to make much sense, however much you look at it."

"Walker, I think I'm dreaming this."

He smiled. "I'd make book on it. For one thing, you've never believed in ghosts. But you remember what I always said dreams were all about? They're for sorting things out, Chow. For putting things in order." His face darkened slightly. Donna wanted to put out a hand to his shoulder, his cheek, but something made her hold back. "They're for clearing out the psychic deadwood, Chow. For throwing away the things you don't need cluttering up the old attic anymore."

"Like you? Don't you think I still need you, Walker?"

"Maybe. I'd like to think you do, Chow." The use of the nickname no longer bothered Donna. In fact, she realized, she welcomed it. It was something more of Walker Stone. Another detail to make this phantom real. "But I don't want you getting all bent out of shape over what you think was your part in my death."

He paused, frowning. Then he smiled, and the expression was so real, so familiar, it brought tears to Donna's eyes. "No, no. Don't do this, Chow-Chow. Don't mess yourself up over me like this. You used to be able to switch me off pretty good when I was alive . . ." The smile again. "I am never gonna get used to this kind of talk."

"Are you . . . going to have a chance to get used to it, Walker? I mean . . . are you here to stay?"

"I don't know. I don't think it is *Randall and Hopkirk, Deceased*."

"Is that another TV reference?"

"Yes. Late sixties. British show about a private eye who gets bumped off and comes back to help his partner catch the man who killed him. Hangs around too long and gets stuck on earth for a hundred years. In American syndication it was called *My Partner, the Ghost*."

"I like the British title better."

"Yes, that's what you said when I told you about it four or five years ago."

Donna leaned back, sighing. "You told me about it?"

"Is there a TV show in the world I didn't tell you about at some time or other?"

"I guess not." The tears were coming again, driven by bitter nostalgia.

"What? Chow?" He put his hand to her face. Donna felt nothing where his fingers touched. She pulled back.

"When you started talking about some goddamn television show I thought I'd never heard of . . ."

"Ah! You were ready to convince yourself I was really the ghost of Walker Stone? Now I'm back to dream status?" He shrugged. "I'll accept either, if it will let me say what I have to say."

"And that is?"

"Be careful of Tommy. He's . . ." Stone shook his head. It was a familiar movement, telling Donna he was sorting through words in his head, looking for just the phrasing. "He's just the teeniest bit driven," he said at last.

"You're making light of this to cover your real concern," Donna said. "Typical Walker."

He smiled. "But, then, I am a typical Walker, if you're dreaming this."

"What do you mean about Tom being 'driven'?"

"Oh yes? 'Tom' is it? What a pity he's a priest. I could see you two together. He'd be good for you, if he wasn't off on a mission from God."

"He's gay, Walker. Didn't you know?"

The phantom's eyebrows shot up toward its hairline. "No!

Are you sure? Son of a gun! His mother must be spinning in her grave!"

"Get back to the point." Donna was feeling quite exasperated with the roundabout way her dream was presenting its information.

"The point," Stone said, "is that Tommy is looking to handle the Traynes all on his own, without any help. He sees this as some kind of holy crusade. You know he thinks they're both demons or some such rubbish."

"I know," Donna said. "I think he feels this is some kind of test. He blames himself for the suicide of his lover. He sees this as something he can do to maybe make amends."

"Sounds like my cousin. And I think that's dangerous. I think you should find someone to help you."

"Who?"

Stone shrugged. "You were looking for a weapon. A weapon to use against Paul Trayne. There is one, you know. Right here in Chicago. A very potent weapon."

"Riddles, Walker?"

"I don't seem to be able to say it outright." He shook his head again. "What a remarkably ineffectual visitation I am. I hope I *am* just your dream. I'd make a crummy spook."

Donna smiled. "But you make a good dream. I'm . . . sorry you're dead, Walker."

The ghost shrugged. "Think real hard, Donna. Think about me and about what you've done for me. Stories you've written. That's the answer. Think about stories. Recent stories."

"And you can't be more specific?"

"No time. I think you're waking up."

"Walker . . ."

"So long, Chow. Maybe we'll get to chat again. I hope so."

"Walker . . ."

He was starting to fade, becoming more like the ghost Donna no longer believed him to be.

He was gone.

Donna sat up and threw aside the covers. The floor was stone cold beneath her bare feet. She pulled on Tom Sylvestri's robe and crossed on tiptoe to the door. As she opened it she looked back at the bed, half expecting to see herself still there, to find this to be as much a dream as the visit of Walker's ghost. The bed was empty.

She turned back to the door and the first spasms hit her.

Donna grabbed the doorknob and leaned on it as her legs started to topple out from under her. She pressed her forehead against the cool wood of the doorjamb. Her stomach made a very good try at climbing up her throat. She hiccuped and tasted bile. Her arms were no more inclined to support her than her legs. Her elbows bent suddenly, and Donna dropped to her knees. The doorknob came up under her chin, a small, brass fist. Her teeth clacked together and she tasted blood. The right side of her tongue had been in the way of those slamming molars. Donna slumped back. Her head seemed to roll down the length of her body, as another spasm came up, bringing the horrible taste of vomit to mingle with the salty blood in her mouth. She shuddered, head low, one ear against the floorboard.

Her stomach was still doing flip-flops, but the worst of the nausea was abating. She pulled one leg up and tested her weight on it. The other. She grabbed the doorknob with sausage fingers and pulled herself up. She leaned against the door again, waiting to see if she would collapse again.

When she didn't, she stepped out into the hall. Somewhere between the visitation of Walker Stone's "ghost" and the churning of her gut she'd found a single crystalline thought dropping into place.

She had to talk to Tom. Now.

Because she knew what their weapon was. What she didn't know was how they'd ever get their hands on him.

Clay Garber put little stock in psychic phenomenon, in mind reading, clairvoyance, the whole bag of conjuring tricks. But when he entered the big house by the Lake, he knew Marjorie was gone. And not out with friends. Not off on one of her lunches. Gone.

It seemed a particularly cruel jest to tag onto the end of his trip back from Faulkner. He'd been so sure he was going to die in that moment when the big farm machine began to roll toward him. But Pete Hay had been walking along behind the machine, laughing and joking loudly with the men who were manning the other side of the huge barricade. Clay had lowered his weapon and slipped the hand holding it into a big pocket of his coat. He did not release the butt, did not take his finger from the trigger.

Hay confirmed Clay's deduction when he strolled over, his face split with a toothy grin that had nothing at all to do with the tone of his voice. As he came within earshot he hissed at Clay. "Get in your car and drive through, Commissioner. And whatever you do, don't look back." Hay laughed, clapped Garber on the back, and stepped away.

Puzzled, but not enough to question, Garber climbed back into the BMW, backed away from the rear of Hay's car, and drove carefully through the opening provided in the wall of steel. The men on the other side laughed and bowed, waving him through with huge flourishes that looked to Garber like schoolboys trying to play French courtiers. He wondered what in the world Hay could have told them. Ultimately, as he drove back toward Chicago, he decided it did not matter. He'd glanced in the rearview mirror only once, to see the big tractor roll back, resealing the wall. As it shuddered into place Clay Garber had his last glimpse of Pete Hay.

He knew in that moment he would never see Hay again, and he felt a sudden, unexpected sadness in the realization. He did not like Deputy Hay, but he felt a growing respect for him. Hay was one of the few sane people left in Faulkner. An oasis —a very small oasis—in the midst of seventeen thousand madmen, each and every one of whom might at any moment decide it would be interesting to see how Pete Hay looked with his head on backward. And with the decision would come the act, for there was nothing, no single shred of human decency or morality left to stop them.

Clay pushed the pedal down and drove the BMW into darkness, leaving Faulkner behind, bound, at one hundred miles per hour, for something his every thought told him was likely to be worse.

He did not know how much worse until he walked into the big house by the Lake.

He knew she was gone, but he called his wife's name anyway, a deliberate rebellion against the psychic certainty of her absence.

Rose appeared in the door of the kitchen. "She's not 'ere, Commissioner," she said.

"Where is she?" Clay could not recall ever having used a tone so brusque with the cook. Nor could Rose, if her expression was anything to judge by.

"I'm sure I don't know, sir." Rose's accent thickened with each word.

"Didn't she leave a message? Something?"

"I didn't see anything, sir."

Clay stormed past her down the hall, and climbed the back stairs to the landing just outside the master bedroom.

Only Wednesday I came down these stairs to let Donna in.

He went into the bedroom. Everything was neat, tidy. The bed made. The closet doors closed. He crossed to Marjorie's closet and took a deep breath before seizing the handle and pulling open the wide door. Her clothes were still there. It seemed strange now that he might have thought they would not be. Yet . . .

He looked around the room. Everything was as it always was. Everything. Everything.

Except Marjorie's dressing table. It stood where it always stood. From this angle the oval mirror above it showed Clay the view of the room it always showed him. But the dressing table was clear. All of Marjorie's makeup bottles, jars, brushes —the bewildering array of things she used every day, sometimes more, sometimes less, but in some combination each day. They were gone. The top of the little table was clear. Only the old Princess model phone remained, pushed back against the wall.

Clay crossed to the table and sat heavily in the frail little chair before the mirror. He stared at his reflection, big and dark in the oval glass. Stared beyond his reflection, trying, somehow striving to will a message to appear.

Mirror, mirror on the wall . . .

Shouldn't she have left him some kind of message? Any kind of message.

She's with Paul Trayne. She's gone to Paul Trayne. And the thing he did to her, the thing he did to all those poor, stupid fools in Faulkner, that takes away the little niceties like leaving a message for your husband when you leave him.

Thirty years. Could it really be thirty? It was, and yet it was all like yesterday.

Clay shook his head. No. Nothing was like yesterday.

He reached out for the telephone and rested his hand on the pale pink plastic for a long time before he pulled the instrument toward him, picked it up, dialed. After three rings an answering machine picked up and he heard the voice of his oldest daughter's roommate.

"Hi, this is Kate. DiAnne and Kelly and I are all out partying hearty, dude"—girlish laughter—"so leave a message and we'll, like, dig you later. Here's the beep." More laughter, then the single elongated tone.

"This is Clay Garber calling for DiAnne. Honey . . ." His train of thought died. What could he say? How could he phrase it? If Marjorie had already contacted DiAnne, already brought her under the influence of Paul Trayne . . . "Call me if you have a chance," he said finally, lamely. He hung up.

He looked at the phone in his hand for a while. He turned it back and forth, watching a small spot of reflected light trace a slow curve over the smooth plastic. Back and forth. Back and forth.

Next? He tried the mayor's phone again. The private line rang without answer. The house line was still busy.

For the first time in his career, even in his life, Garber was beginning to feel helpless. He was, by anyone's reckoning, one of the most powerful men in one of the most powerful cities in America. He should have been able to reach out and swat Paul Trayne and his father like a pair of annoying gnats. In another time, and not so long ago, a man with Clay Garber's power might well have done just that. But that man would not have been Clay Garber. Garber played by the rules. Even when the rules kept changing. Even when he did not know what the rules were.

He dialed directory assistance. "Looking for a Thomas Sylvestri," he said. "Father Thomas Sylvestri."

* * *

"One hundred and twelve." Marjorie Garber beamed, a child with a straight A report card presented to proud parents.

Robert Trayne looked at the list, the long tabulation of names in Marjorie's neat, precise hand. He smiled. "Paul will be very happy," he said.

They were in the living room of Emmanuel Stuartson's big town house. Stuartson was in the parlor, making the last few calls that might add a dozen more names to the list. Paul was asleep on the big double bed upstairs, preparing himself. The house was bright and sunny, as Marjorie remembered it. Stuartson, the perennial bachelor—enough that there were sometimes stories about him, whispered rumors about his personal predilections that Marjorie could silence so easily now— kept a perfect house. Or at least his staff did.

Perfect house, perfect day, Marjorie thought.

"Will he be strong enough?" she asked. *Never mind,* said the voice. Of course, it did not matter, unless he should be too weak to complete the task at hand . . .

"He will do what he has to do," Trayne said. He looked again at the list. One hundred and twelve of the most powerful, most influential people in Chicago. In Faulkner they'd had to begin with the dregs, the foolish, useless people who wandered into his tent by chance. Of all who came in the first few days only the police chief had been of any real use. Now he was gone, left behind to do his last useful deed.

One hundred and twelve names. Called by Marjorie and the mayor, told of the wonderful thing that would be happening soon. Of the special dinner that would be held as soon as the mayor could make the proper arrangements. A thousand-dollar-a-plate dinner, but worth ten times that. A hundred times that. That was what Marjorie told the people she spoke to. Trayne had stood by, silent, attentive, smiling.

A thousand dollars a plate to give their souls to Paul. To begin in Chicago the fine and terrible purging he had brought to Three Forks, brought to Winsonia, Kansas, to Happenstance, Oklahoma. Tiny towns, now busily burning themselves off the face of the earth.

And Faulkner, of course. Faulkner, the big town, the big test, before Paul was ready for Chicago. And he was ready.

Because he was growing stronger. Trayne could see that. He could see that each session weakened Paul less and less. He could see the change that was building in his son's eyes, his face, his very posture. As if he were growing up as he grew stronger. As if he were becoming a man, as he took into himself all those adult thoughts and fantasies and terrible, terrible dreams.

Growing up. Growing stronger.

"Paul will do what he has to do." Trayne smiled. "He is my son."

"Father Sylvestri? We've never met, but my name is Garber. Clayton Garber."

"Commissioner Garber?"

"Yes. Father, I need to talk to you. About Walker Stone."

"I know all about Walker Stone, Commissioner. Donna told me."

"Wojciechowski?"

"Yes." Tom recognized the tone in Clay's voice. "Don't worry, Commissioner. She's no longer a pawn of Paul Trayne's."

A long pause. "You know about him, too? Jesus, how far has this gone?"

"Not very, yet. I take it you want to be sure it goes no further?"

"Yes. Can we meet, Father? On . . . neutral ground?"

"I'm speaking from the rectory of St. Timothy's, Commissioner. I don't think you get more neutral than that."

Another pause. "All right. I'm at my house. I can be there in . . . half an hour?"

"We'll be waiting."

"And . . ."

"Yes?"

"You're sure about Donna?"

"I'm sure about Donna, yes."

"All right. Good-bye, Father."

"Good-bye, Commissioner."

Tom hung up the phone and turned to face Donna. She wore a pair of his old jeans that were two sizes too big, and one of his big cable-knit sweaters. With the jeans rolled up about her ankles, she sat with her legs tucked up on the edge of the chair, looking, Tom thought, like a pinup out of the 1940s. Not so risqué, perhaps, but a model a Varga or a Petty might well have appreciated.

"Clay?" she said, clearly rhetorically.

"Yes. He said he had to tell me about Walker."

Donna frowned. "What could he have to tell you, unless . . ." Her eyes widened. "You don't suppose he's been to Faulkner?"

Tom stroked his chin and felt the stubble from not having shaved that morning. "I wonder. I think that would be a good sign, if it were true. It might indicate he was checking things out for himself. And that would suggest he was outside Paul's influence still."

"I hope so. The police commissioner could be very handy to my mad scheme."

Tom frowned and crossed to sit in the chair across from Donna. They were in the study again. A fire crackled merrily on the hearth, ignorant of the misery in the world around it. Tom looked into the flames and thought of the curious innocence of fire. The most destructive of all the elements, yet it had no malice of its own. The fire that cooked a Boy Scout's hot dog and the fire that burned a martyr were pieces of the same eternal force, unchanging, timeless.

"Your scheme . . ." Tom said. Of course Donna had told him of the dream visit of Walker Stone, and how, somehow, it had triggered the last steps of her struggling thought processes and given her the name of the weapon they could use against Paul Trayne. "It would have to be under the most stringently controlled circumstances," Tom said, coming back to the point they'd been at when the telephone rang and interrupted them.

"Of course," Donna said. "Just to have him there, out of police custody . . ."

"No. I mean the situation under which he was exposed to Paul. Or vice versa. We'd have to control the moment very carefully. If I am right in my judgment of who and what Paul Trayne and his father may be, a human soul would be placed at hazard. A soul not ours to use."

"A soul about to be rather forcibly evicted from its present domicile anyway," Donna said. "But the perfect soul. All that anger. All that grief and guilt. Enough for a hundred souls. Like a laser beam. A laser beam aimed right into the heart of Paul Trayne's power."

Tom leaned back in his chair, rested elbows on the broad arms, and steepled his fingers. "Errol Keane Warner." He shook his head. "It's just dreaming, of course. There's no way we could get him released in our custody. It's madness even to think it."

"No," Donna said, "we couldn't get him. But Clay Garber could. He's the commissioner of police. The top cop. He could get us Errol Warner. And if we could get Warner within range of Paul . . ."

"It would have to be at one of the sessions." The idea was absurd, but Tom could not resist playing it out, running the scenario through his mind. "In a crowd of people, all giving Paul their 'needings.' It would be like a cyanide pill slipped into a bag of candy. Candy you'd wolf down in handfuls so you'd never notice . . ."

Donna nodded, vigorously. She found herself doing everything vigorously now. Whatever the visitation of Walker Stone was, ghost, dream, or flat-out hallucination, it had cleared her brain just enough to give her this idea. And with the idea had come a renewed vigor, a sense that maybe, just maybe they were not going to end as sacrificial lambs, slaughtered in the name of Paul Trayne and his unholy gift.

"If it can be done," she said, "Garber can do it." It even seemed appropriate. A piece of this had begun with Garber, with meeting him in the lobby as she left for Faulkner, three thousand years ago. Donna was not much for believing in fate, but it certainly seemed to her now that Clayton Garber was spun into the weave of this right from the start. Before the start. Meant to be part of it. An important part.

That was why you took Paul to him. Because you knew he had the capacity to resist Paul's power, and you knew he had the clout in this city to get things done, amass the forces necessary to undo Paul. You knew that. You just didn't know you knew.

"It's all quite amazing," Tom said. "I've been praying for

some kind of sign, some kind of arrow to point us in the right direction. Now you have your revelation, and within twenty-four hours a means to accomplish it delivers himself to our doorstep. Amazing."

Donna smiled. "Maybe the good guys are supposed to win this one after all, Father."

PART THREE

The Day of Evil

19

The glass wall was supposed to make the hospital lobby bright and cheery, keep it flooded with sunlight. There was no sunlight today. The sky was a solid sheet of roiling black smoke, red-bellied to the west where a third of Faulkner burned. The glass wall seemed now nothing more than a huge and completely indefensible hole in Pete Hay's armor. Armor that was flimsy at best.

With Zeldenrust's keys in hand he'd found and locked every single outside door, the big Sturm Ruger heavy on his belt, ready to be snapped out, ready to blow its terrible cavernous hole through anyone who might be trying to get in through one of those doors.

Now Pete was back in the lobby with the inescapable feeling that he was a specimen on a slide, the big glass panes of the outer wall the lens, the brooding black sky the eye that peered down the long barrel of the microscope at small, squirming Pete Hay.

He was not squirming yet, but he felt he might at any second. His skin felt ready to crawl off his body. Every move, even his breathing, shifted some part of his clothing, the fold of a sleeve, the pocket heavy with spare ammo, to make Pete twitch as if someone had reached out a hand to touch him.

His range of defense was severely limited. He'd swung by the station house on his return from escorting Clayton Garber to the edge of town—swung by the end of the block, that is. He'd needed to get no closer to see the police station had been taken over by the citizens of Faulkner. The desks had been carried to the front door and pitched down the steps. Drawers had either fallen or been pulled out, papers blowing everywhere. There was no chance to get the weapons Pete had hoped for. He was limited to those in the trunk of the police car, and while Clarence Nickerson had always insisted his vehicles be well equipped, that left Pete Hay with a noticeably small arsenal.

As he'd driven away from the station, Pete thought for the first time in many hours of Marcy Kavelhoff, still—so far as he knew—locked in one of the cells behind the front office. Was she all right? Would the vandals who'd sacked the station have freed her? Killed her? Pete felt a cold spot where the fires of his passion once raged. He knew that Marcy was as much a victim of the monster called Paul Trayne as anyone else in Faulkner, knew that her casual murder of her children should not necessarily be read as a true representation of her personality, but he could not get past the fact that she had so obviously disobeyed him. Lied to him, in fact, about visiting the Traynes' tent show. If she had obeyed, stayed away, her children would still be alive, and Marcy would not have been locked in the cell, at the mercy of whoever came to the station house.

This Pete Hay told himself—albeit not in so many words, or in fact quite consciously—as a way of excusing the fact that he had more or less abandoned Marcy to her fate. He'd not given her more than the most fleeting thought since locking her in cell 3. There were too many other things, he told himself, of much more pressing concern.

He had the weapons arranged in careful rows along the back of one of the couches he'd dragged across the lobby to form a bulwark against the glass wall. All were fully loaded, none more than a quick stretch away. He had one conventional rifle, one shotgun, two flare guns—which might be handy in a last-ditch effort, after all—the automatic he usually carried, and the big Sturm Ruger. He was as ready, he thought, as it was possible to be.

Considering that he was one man. One man versus a whole town gone mad.

Seventeen thousand, he thought. *I might know every one of them, by sight at least. And they're all out there. Doing whatever it is they're doing. Whatever horrible, nasty things they'd kept all bottled up inside until now.*

The drive back from the barricade had been a nightmare. He'd been able to joke his way through with Garber—the men marshaled at the steel wall were obsessed with keeping people *out* of Faulkner—but as he drove back to the station house to collect the additional ordnance he'd need to protect the hospital, Pete had expected every turn, every street to spew out a horde of shrieking, ax-wielding demons, each and every one of whom was, a month ago, a friend—familiar faces, people he'd been to school with, played baseball with on Sunday afternoons in the park, gone to football games with. Lived with.

And now I'm gonna die with you, you stupid fucks. Pete was very much aware that the space of his life had become something most likely measured in hours, maybe days if he was very lucky. And he was determined he would take as many of the people of Faulkner as he could with him. It no longer mattered that they were the innocent victims of Paul Trayne's terrible gift. There were no innocents anymore, Pete thought.

And when it came down to it, who wasn't a victim?

Who?

The knock on the door was so soft Marjorie was not certain she'd heard it. She stepped closer and listened for a moment before she said, "Yes?"

"Mrs. Garber?" It was Paul.

Marjorie opened the door. "Paul, dear! What on earth are you doing, sneaking around like a mouse? I barely heard your knock."

"I wanted to talk to you. In private." Paul glanced over his shoulder. Beyond the door to Marjorie's room, the mayor's room on the third floor of the brownstone, the landing was empty. The stairs curved away behind Paul, and the sound of Emmanuel Stuartson's and Robert Trayne's voices in the study below drifted up the open stairwell.

"Well, come in then." Marjorie smiled. "Would you like me to ring for some cookies?"

"No." There was a biting edge in the single syllable that surprised Marjorie. She would not have thought Paul capable of such a tone.

"Whatever is the matter, dear," she asked, putting an arm around his bony shoulders.

Paul stepped away from her touch. "Close the door," he said. There was little doubting it was a command, and one not to be hesitated on.

Marjorie closed the door. Paul crossed to the center of the room. He turned slowly, rotating, looking at the tall windows, the big bed, the dresser, the closet door. He seemed, Marjorie thought, to be studying them, memorizing them.

"Do you know what we did to my mother, Father and I?" Each sound was a drip of ice water on Marjorie's skin. She could not believe this was truly Paul's voice.

"Did to . . . ?"

"We killed her," Paul said. "At the time it was terrible. I was only five, you see. But I had my power. Full-blown. And Father made me use it to kill her. But slowly. We tortured her first. For a long time."

"Paul . . ."

"Shut up." The words bit into Marjorie. "Father says women are all evil. It was through the weakness of a woman that humanity fell from grace. You are all the daughters of Eve, he says. And *you*, black people, he says you are the sons of Cain."

Marjorie frowned. She had, of course, heard that there were some who believed the dark pigment of the Negro race was the mark God had placed on the first murderer. She could not believe she now heard this stupid, barbarous thinking spewing from Paul Trayne. "That's . . ."

"I said shut up."

Something with long, cold steel claws reached into Marjorie's soul and squeezed. She gasped and staggered back a step. She came up against the closed door, lost her footing, and slid down heavily to an awkward sitting position.

"Father made me kill my mother with my power," Paul said

again. "Very slowly. Over days. I cried the whole time. I screamed. I begged him to stop, to let me stop. But he wouldn't let me. He made me keep twisting her, twisting her." As he spoke he stepped closer to Marjorie, until he stood over her. "When we found her she was with a man. A young man. Not much older than I am now, I suppose. Father had me kill him quickly. He wasn't any more than a stupid dupe, after all. But Mother . . ."

Paul squatted down and brought his eyes level with Marjorie's. "She was naked. I'd never seen a naked woman. I didn't even understand what it meant. Being naked. But the image stayed with me. The picture, in my mind." He reached out a hand, stroked the side of Marjorie's face. A gentle touch, the barest flutter of a butterfly's wing. Such a contrast to the snap she'd heard in his voice.

"The picture stayed with me," Paul repeated. "All down the years, it stuck in my mind. My mother. Naked. Tied to the bed we'd found her in. Writhing. Screaming. Sometimes that picture would come to me just as I was going to bed, just as I was starting to fall asleep. Then it would stay with me all night. Her screams would stay with me. The way she stretched and twisted on the bed. The way she pulled and tore at the ropes until her wrists and ankles were rubbed raw."

Paul's brain filled with the terrible imagery as he spoke. So clear. So vivid. And yet—fearfully he tested the boundaries of his feeling, the ragged edges left by the trauma, and found them less ragged. There was something like a healing going on, as if his own wondrous gift had been somehow turned on this pain, to smooth it, soothe it. Paul could easily envision a time when the thought of his mother's torment would bring him no distress at all. When—and here his gut tightened to a cold, hard knot—when he might *enjoy* it, as his father had so clearly enjoyed it at the time. Confusion filled Paul's mind. Fear filled his heart. But the fear was less than it had been. Less, he knew, than it should have been.

"Paul, that's so . . ."

"Shut up." This time the hand slapped across Marjorie's face, a gunshot sound in the closed room. Paul was surprised by his own violence. Surprised and frightened by the speed, the ease with which it came. Voices not his own whispered in his mind, urging him, encouraging. He shuddered and pushed the alien feelings away. But the anger remained, not alien now. Once, but no longer. "I'm not telling you this so you'll feel sorry for me. I don't want your pity. I don't want anyone's pity."

His voice was so changed, Marjorie thought. Not a child's voice at all. A grown man's voice, now and then catching on some word, some syllable, the way a boy's voice might, comically in any other context. But not a child's tone, not a boy's words.

"All my life I remembered my mother," Paul said. "Then Father made me do the same thing to Donna. Not to kill her. Only to punish. And I was afraid at first. I was afraid she'd scream and writhe and it would be just like my mother all over. But then, when it started and she did scream, and she did writhe and twist and beg me not to do it, beg me to disobey my father . . ."

The pause stretched out. Frightened, Marjorie did not speak. She stared into Paul's eyes, eyes bright and hot, burning, flaming. Eyes that had no place in the freckled face framed by tousled red hair.

"I looked at Donna's nakedness, and it was different," Paul said. "Not just because she wasn't my mother. Not just because she was shaped differently. Donna is tall and lean, my mother was short and fleshy. Donna has long legs and small breasts. My mother's breasts were huge. At least, when I was five they were. But it wasn't just the physical difference. It was the way I felt. The way I felt inside, in my body, in my mind . . ."

He seemed confused. Marjorie, thinking she understood, risked speaking. "You're body is changing, Paul. It happens to all boys. When they become men."

"No." Paul did not strike her this time. He put his hand on her shoulder and drew her face closer to his. "No, I'm not talking about that. I know about that. I'm talking about in here." He tapped Marjorie's forehead with the stiffened middle finger of his free hand. "Inside my mind, something was different. When I hurt my mother, when I killed her, it made me feel terrible. But with Donna, the more we tortured her, the more we punished her, the more I liked it. The more I hoped she would be disobedient again, so I could punish her again. And each time she needed punishment it was better, stronger, the feeling. Watching her twist. Watching the way her body sheeted over with sweat, the way the light caught on the wetness, the way her arms and legs twitched, the way her breasts moved. I liked it. More and more."

He was gripping Marjorie's shoulder hard now, digging in the tips of his fingers. Marjorie's heart pounded. None of what she was hearing made any kind of real sense to her—none of it would fit with the image of Paul Trayne carved so clearly in the surface of her mind—and it frightened her. Frightened her to see him so changed, to see the hot, scalding intensity in his young eyes. She tried desperately to keep the pain she felt in her shoulder from showing in her face, fearful of what that might do, what reaction that might elicit, based on what Paul was saying. She was not successful. As his fingers tightened she winced, and Paul smiled.

"Now you understand," he said. The words were coming all in a rush now. The alien thoughts and feelings swelling up to overwhelm the fears that still dwelt in the mind of the boy named Paul Trayne. The boy who was beginning to feel himself consumed by another, a different Paul Trayne. "This is a wonderful thing, this gift of mine. The way I can twist people. The way I can hurt people. I can hurt you, Marjorie." It was the first time he'd used her given name. Part of Marjorie told her she would have been thrilled, at another time, in another place. But now she was only frightened. Terribly, terribly frightened.

"I can hurt you as much as I want," Paul said. "As often as I want. Because that's the best thing. I know now. Hurting. I don't know why I didn't understand that before, but it is. Hurting. It's so wonderful. It feels so good."

He grabbed her wrists, rising suddenly, pulling her to her feet. Marjorie was astonished by his strength. He twisted her arms, rotating the wrists outward until sharp pain shot through the joints of her elbows and she gasped despite herself.

"What shall we do, Marjorie?" It was almost the child's voice again, a child's voice asking a playmate what game they should play. "What would you like me to do to you? Just to start? I don't want to do too much the first time. That would spoil the fun. Tell me what I should do to you, Marjorie. What are you most afraid of? What kind of pain?"

"Paul . . ." The pain in her arms was really intense now. Marjorie could barely speak. Her knees were weak. In a moment, she knew, she would fall. "Paul, please . . . don't do this. I love you. I'd do anything for you. But not this. Please. Not this."

Paul shook his head, slowly, his face now that of a disapproving parent. "Come over to the bed." It was all so clear in his mind. What he had to do. What he *wanted* to do. As if it was something he'd done before, thought of, dreamed of before. He sensed a specific mind, a specific set of needings guiding, driving him. He saw the dark face of Mayor Stuartson, saw the big teeth bared in a most unpleasant grin. He grinned himself, and was only a little disturbed by how strange, how utterly alien it felt on his young face.

"Paul, please . . ."

"You said you'd do anything for me," he said. He pulled her to the edge of the bed and pushed her down onto the high mattress. He grabbed her skirt and pulled it up to bare her thighs. He ran his hand over the curve of her flesh, too adult a move, too sexual. Marjorie tried to twist away. Paul's hand flashed up and out, into her hair, grabbing, twisting.

"No, no," he said. "You only want to make me happy, remember?" He looked into her eyes. "And this will make me happy."

The abyss opened for Marjorie Garber.

"No, Walker isn't dead. He's in a bad way. A very bad way. But he's not dead."

Donna stared at Clay Garber as if she fully expected him to sprout a second head. This was extraordinary news, wonderful news. But how could she believe it? How could she trust this was not something Robert Trayne had cooked up? Some new trap, laid in Garber's mind that first night, perhaps. If Garber's resistance had been feigned all along . . .

"That's good news," Tom said, articulating at least a part of what Donna felt. She heard the small reservation in his voice, knew he was thinking as she was.

"If we can believe it," she said, when Tom did not.

Garber frowned. "I hardly think you're in any sort of position to be distrusting me, Donna," he said. "More the other way round, I should say."

"Trust is a difficult commodity to come by in these times, Commissioner," Tom said. "It's all part of what Paul Trayne does."

Garber nodded. "I saw Faulkner. I couldn't believe it. It was . . . it was like a piece of hell had been puked up onto the earth."

Donna compared this with her own memory of the town. "It was pretty scuzzy when I was there. It's worse?"

"There aren't more than a dozen people in the whole town who were untouched by Paul Trayne's power. And them only because they were in the hospital at the time he arrived. Appendicitis, broken limbs. One accidental gunshot wound. That sort of thing. But all the staff except Dr. Zeldenrust were affected. And all the police except Pete Hay."

Donna twisted her mouth, remembering Hay. "Now I would have thought him a prime candidate for Paul Trayne's power."

"Me too, based on what I saw of him," Garber said. "But I was left with the impression he was untouched. I wouldn't have trusted him to guard Walker and the others, otherwise."

Tom nodded. "And Walker somehow told you to get in touch with me. Why, I wonder?"

"Because you're a priest, I suppose," the commissioner said. "Walker was never much for religion as I remember . . ."

"Not much," Donna and Tom said almost in unison.

". . . but after seeing what the Trayne boy can do . . ." Clay shook his head. "I guess I've always had a sort of layman's feeling about religion. I believe in God, maybe in some kind of afterlife. But hell, the devil . . . that I'm not so sure about. But after seeing what Paul Trayne did to Faulkner—"

"I'm more or less convinced Paul Trayne and his father are not of this earth," Tom said, regretting the hoary phrase at once. "Donna thinks Paul is a mutant of some kind, but the scope of his power seems too great to me."

"But then," Donna said, "since we've never seen or heard of anything like Paul before, there's no way to be sure what would be too great. And remember, it's Robert Trayne who drives Paul. Drives him beyond his natural endurance levels, I should think."

"You think so?" Garber was clearly not impressed by this line of thinking. "I wonder if it can really work that way. If the old man can really exercise that much control over the boy, over his power."

Donna shrugged. "Either way, we think we may have a weapon to use against Paul, against Paul's power anyway. If we can work it right."

"Weapon?"

Tom told him, then saw Garber's eyes go wide.

"You're joking."

Tom shook his head. "Deadly serious, Commissioner. If we could persuade the Trayne boy to use his 'gift' on Errol Warner, it would be very much as Donna described it, a laser beam striking right into the heart of the evil."

Clay frowned. "I know you wrote all those powerhouse articles about Warner, Donna, but . . ."

"It would work," Donna said. "Paul is like this big, empty barrel. The 'mouth' that the needings go in through is huge. I don't think he can stop the flow, once it starts. He said when he did me that he couldn't just skim off the top of our troubles, the pond scum. He had to take everything. I believe that."

"Even though other things he told you were lies?"

"Like not being able to take against people's will, you mean? Yes, I know there's a lot of falsehood to be separated out of this, but bits and pieces seem true to me somehow because . . . well, because there doesn't seem any logical reason for them to be lies. I mean, I can see why Trayne wouldn't want me to know Paul could force the issue if he needed to. That was something of an ace in the hole. But this, this business of not being able to stop taking until it's all gone? That I think is true."

"It has to be true, in fact, or we have no plan." Tom's face was set into an unreadable mask.

"I'd say you have no plan anyway, Father," Clay said. "Not

if it hinges on getting custody of Errol Warner. You can't expect to walk into the holding cells and say, 'We'd like to borrow Errol for the weekend,' can you?"

"No," Tom said. He looked at Donna.

"We kind of thought that might be where you came in, Commissioner," she said.

"It wears off," Ben Carpenter wrote. He wrote in longhand, the stub of a pencil small in his thick fingers, the bitten-down end of the eraser pushed into his palm. He wrote on a legal-size pad of yellow lined paper. His hand trembled. It was not easy to keep within the slender blue lines.

It wears off. Sooner or later. I think maybe for everyone. For me, definitely. The gift of Paul Trayne is temporary. It unleashes you, lets loose all the rotten, stupid things you keep inside. Then, when you've run rampant, when you've gone off on an orgy of self-indulgence or cruelty, the gift wears off and you can look at everything you've done. And this time it's worse. You can see all those terrible, horrible things you'd kept buried inside for God knows how long. Buried down deep, where maybe even you weren't sure they were there, until Paul Trayne let them out and you went mad and then the gift went away and it all came back. Like it's all come back to me. Mae is dead.

He stopped. He was seated at his secretary's desk, and he looked across the room to where Mae Faber's body lay on the old horsehair sofa. He'd put a jacket over her face and arranged her broken leg so that it looked, at this distance, almost normal, her skirt draped across it. She might have been asleep. But she wasn't. Only a sentimental poet would call this sleep, and there was nothing sentimental left in Ben Carpenter.

"Faulkner has gone mad," he wrote. He was almost at the bottom of the page now. He had no real idea how much he was going to say. He just wanted to get it all out, on paper, in his own hand, before . . .

Faulkner has gone mad. The sky is black with smoke. I think half the town may be burning. The whole west end. I don't know how much. If it spreads, the whole town could go. Maybe it should. When Paul Trayne's gift starts to wear off on everyone else—if it hasn't already—they'll never be able to go back to their normal lives. Their old lives. They've done too much. They've killed and looted and raped. They've tortured. They've acted like animals, worse than animals. Animals don't have the kinds of moral codes humans do. They don't need them. Because they don't have the imaginations we do. They don't have the kind of minds that can start to wondering how a neighbor's kid might look as a lampshade."

Now, where had that come from? Ben paused, stared up at the ceiling for a long while before he remembered the conversation he'd had with Clarence Nickerson when the Errol Warner case started to break in the newspapers and on TV.

"What makes somebody do that, Clarence?" he'd asked, as they shared a few beers and contemplated the nature of the universe. "You're a cop. You're supposed to understand."

Clarence had snorted, slugging back what was left of one beer and signaling for another. "It doesn't come with the job, Benny," he'd said. "I mean, understanding like that. I became a cop because I wanted to do something for this town, something good. Not because I thought I had any special plug into people's brains or special notion of what makes 'em do the rotten things they do."

Ben had lifted the newspaper from the table between them and scanned again the lines of Donna Wojciechowski's first article on the Warner case. "All those women. Just barely women. More like children. What could make someone do that? Torture. What makes somebody want to hurt somebody else? Not out of spite or anything. I can almost understand that. Just out of sheer bloody-mindedness."

"Too much time on their hands," Clarence Nickerson said. He ran a thick finger across the top of the newly arrived beer, leveling the foam. He stuck the finger in his mouth and sucked for a moment. "That's what's wrong with people altogether, I think. I bet they didn't have things like this a hundred, two hundred years ago."

"Jack the Ripper," Ben offered.

"Yeah. But look how famous he got. And he only killed six, seven women, right? All of them whores. He got famous because he stood out, because what he did was so outrageous, so terrible, back there in quaint old England where people had lots of other things to keep them occupied. But nowadays, no. There's just too much time, people have too much time on their hands. They sit around. They watch TV. Maybe they read a book, although there's some people in this town who can't keep their concentration focused long enough to get through a whole article in *TV Guide*. So they have a lot of time on their hands, and maybe pretty soon they start letting their imaginations run away with them. And maybe not long after that they start wondering how the neighbor's kid would look as a lampshade."

Yes, that was where it came from. Too much time on their hands. And after Paul Trayne, nothing to stop them from doing the things, all the things, that might have passed through their minds with too much time on their hands.

Ben thought about Trina and Ed Keene, running their little hardware shop right under his feet. Thought about the looks he'd seen go between them, over the years since Ed's wife died, since Trina had blossomed into her vaguely slovenly womanhood. He'd never wanted to believe what he saw in those looks, but sometimes he remembered a line he'd heard attributed to Charles Laughton, when he was told the movie censors were insisting the studio downplay to the point of elimination the incest theme of the book his latest movie was based on. "They can't censor the gleam in my eye," Laughton had supposedly said.

Ben shook his head. That was right there, right in front of the whole town, Ed and Trina, what was churning under the surface. But nobody paid it any heed because, well, they were all decent, proper folk in Faulkner, Illinois, population 17,964. Things like that didn't happen in decent, proper towns filled with decent, proper people.

Like murder didn't happen. Rape. Like kind, gentle women

running off with their bosses and leaving their invalid mothers to starve to death, all alone in their apartments, growing weaker and weaker until they couldn't even call for help.

Ben's chin fell to his chest. It was not going to be easy to write any more, but he had to. He had to get his thoughts on paper. And then he had to get that paper locked in the big fireproof safe set into the rear wall of his office. Because Faulkner was burning itself to the ground, and Ben Carpenter wanted everyone to know, when it was all over, what had happened and why all those decent, proper folk had gone completely insane for a few short, terrible weeks.

He wanted it all in writing, in his own hand. Because something deep inside told him he wasn't going to be able to tell the tale in person.

Emmanuel Stuartson climbed the stairs to his bedroom. He'd spent nearly three hours talking with the Reverend Robert Johnston Trayne, working out the details of their master plan, how the gift of Paul Trayne could be brought to the hundred and twelve people they'd selected to begin, and how each of them would be able to bring in a dozen, two dozen more, and each of them two dozen, and on and on.

It would take next to no time to have the highest strata of Chicago exposed to Paul's gift, given the wonderful sense of freedom and joy it brought. As their conversation wore on, though, Stuartson began to lose interest in Trayne, in his slow, methodical approach to detailing the many subtle layers of the plan. He'd begun to think of Marjorie again. She'd gone upstairs to take a nap, she said, just as the conversation with Trayne began.

Stuartson's mind began to fill with thoughts of Marjorie. She was so beautiful. So perfect. So surprising in bed! It was as if she'd kept all her desires pent up inside her for a lot of long, long years—unlikely as that seemed, married to Clay Garber—and now they were all gushing out and there was nothing she would not do, nothing she would not try, the two of them thrashing about on the big bed like teenagers, screaming and shouting and carrying on.

Stuartson smiled as he climbed the stairs. Tonight there were a few more things he wanted to try. Things he'd read about, heard about, that had seemed too terrible, too hurtful, too shocking. They didn't seem so now. They seemed only like things he wanted to try. Things he wanted to do with Marjorie. Do to Marjorie.

He stepped up onto the top-floor landing and crossed to the bedroom door, hand reaching for the knob.

He stopped.

A sound came from behind the door. A squeaking sound, quite loud even through the thick oak, the heavy walls of the old brownstone. He tipped his head, listening, recognizing the sound. Bedsprings. His bedsprings.

He turned the knob and stepped into the room. The picture spread before him would not quite take hold on his retinas. Marjorie was there, as he expected. She was on the bed. She lay on her back, fully dressed, her legs pushed up and back, her skirt pulled up to show her thighs and buttocks.

Paul Trayne leaned over her, frozen as a statue. His arms were hooked under Marjorie's knees, pulling her legs up. His trousers were down around his skinny ankles. His face was twisted in a wide, wild grin, frozen like the rest of him as he stared at Garber.

"Mr. Mayor," he said, and his voice was a croak, his throat obviously dry.

"Paul? What's going on here?" It was nothing more than a question. Already a voice in Stuartson's head was saying *Never mind.*

Marjorie lifted her head from the comforter. Her face was smeared with the ruined mascara she'd worn about her eyes. Tears ran down her cheeks. "Mannie . . ." She could barely speak. "Mannie, help me. Please."

Stuartson stroked his chin. As near as he could tell, Paul had been raping Marjorie.

"Help me," Marjorie said again.

Paul's face relaxed from the broad grin. "Mr. Mayor?" he said again.

Stuartson stepped into the room and closed the door behind

him. He took off his jacket and hung it on the back of the chair by the door.

"That looks like fun, Paul," he said. "Mind if I take a turn?"

The glass wall was broken. The wind whipped through the gaping holes, the long shards like the teeth of some crystal dragon. It should have been a cold wind, this deep into February, but it was almost balmy.

Pete Hay peered over the back of the long couch in the hospital lobby and watched the flames marching across the skyline of Faulkner. Better than three quarters of the town was burning or had burned, he guessed. The flames covered two thirds of his field of vision, left to right, and what remained, to the right, the west, was thick with smoke even if there were not flames.

Pete thought about all that would have perished in that conflagration. Not just people—and the days and nights were full of enough screams that he knew people were dying—but memories, pieces of seventeen thousand lifetimes.

Pete hated fire. As a boy he'd watched his uncle's house burn to the ground, right next door to the house he shared with his mother. The flames had climbed high into the night sky— *why do houses always burn at night?*—and the firemen had come to the door and bustled Pete and his mother out into the street. The little houses were set so close together there was a real danger that the least gust of wind would turn Pete's house into the same kind of tinderbox that blazed where Uncle Ira's home had stood.

Pete stood shivering in the cold—*why do houses always burn in the winter?*—watching the last vestige of the house crisp and blacken in the midst of the flames. And all the time there was a dog barking. Ira's dog, Scottie, locked in the basement as he always was. Locked in the basement of the burning house.

Pete was only ten, but when he heard the barking he'd tried to rush into the flames, push through the firemen to get to the back of the house, to the big doors that opened into the basement. Scottie would be right there, he knew. They only needed to open those doors and he'd bound up out of the basement and escape the flames.

It took two firemen to hold Pete back. "You gotta save him," he'd yelled as the barking rose to a frantic, terrified and terrifying pitch. "You gotta save him!"

"We can't get near the house," one of the firefighters said. "It's too dangerous. It could collapse anytime."

And it did. As if waiting for a cue, for the signal of the fireman's words. Pete remembered a terrible cannon boom, a sudden whoosh of flame and scalding air as the center of the house gave way and the whole inferno collapsed into the basement. The barking turned to an all too human scream that Pete Hay could still hear in his darkest nightmares.

Pete crouched behind the couch in the lobby and remembered the screams and watched the fire, and his heart filled with the old fear. The fear that he would die as Scottie had died, burning, his flesh blistering, bursting, peeling back from his bones as he screamed and screamed and would not, could not die until he was completely consumed.

"Pete?"

Hay snapped out of his bitter reverie. "Doc. Keep back."

"Are they still out there?"

"No sign for a while. I think those"—he nodded at the five bodies strewn across the hospital steps—"have given 'em food for thought." Pete Hay had never killed anyone before. Never even had to draw his gun in anger. Now he'd killed five men, three of whom he knew by name. Men armed only with crude clubs, baseball bats, and the bricks they'd brought to throw through the windows.

And it had been easy. The necessity of survival made it easy.

"You think they won't come back?"

"Don't know." Pete shook his head. "Don't want to think about it a whole lot, Doc."

"Pete . . ."

Hay turned to look directly at Zeldenrust. "What's on your mind?"

"This is a hospital," Zeldenrust said. "They might need it.

With the fire. With everything. I never thought they'd attack a hospital."

"That wasn't a real attack," Pete said. "They didn't have guns. They haven't gone round the back or sides. I think they're just . . ."

He stopped. He looked out across the blackened face of his hometown. Something had caught his ear. He squinted left, right. There was nothing to see. Nothing to hear. Maybe it was his imagination?

Then he heard it again, and it was no hallucination. An engine. An automobile engine. A big one. The sound was coming from somewhere off to the left, the east, out of the line of Pete's vision. He scuttled to the end of the couch, crab walking, low against any sudden renewal of the assault. The attackers might just be playing games, as he'd started to say to Zeldenrust, but they were games that could leave Pete Hay very dead.

He lay down to look around the end of the couch. A truck was moving up the long avenue in front of the hospital. A big service station vehicle with a crane mounted on the front. There were fifteen or twenty men and women walking around, following the truck. They still had no firearms that Pete could see.

What he did see was bad enough.

There was a naked man hanging upside down from the hook of the crane.

The truck stopped suddenly, and the naked man swung back, his head hitting the truck's big bumper with a *bong* loud enough for Pete to hear from half a block away. The man started screaming profanities. One of the other men, the walkers, hefted a baseball bat and swung it with all his force against the hanging man's dangling, exposed genitals. The man screamed, thrashing. Pete saw a stream of bright yellow vomit spew from his mouth.

"Shit," Pete said. "What the fuck are they doing?"

"Pete Hay!" One of the walkers had a megaphone. "Pete Hay, do you see who we've got here?"

Pete frowned, cocked his head to the side to see the face of the hanging man. It was Billie Pollock. The same Billie Pollock Pete had known since grade school. They'd played G.I. Joe together when they were kids. Leered together at the big-breasted beauties in the magazines Billie's dad kept hidden in his sock drawer. They'd smoked their first cigarette together. Got drunk the first time together. And, as a degree of sensibility came with age, gone bowling together every Wednesday night for the last ten years.

"What do you want?" Pete shouted.

"You," said the man with the bullhorn. "You killed five of us. We want you to come out and pay for that."

"Go fuck yourself," Pete shouted.

"Wrong answer," the man said. He turned and nodded to the driver. A screech and whine sounded up and down the street. The crane began to pull back, up and back, so that Billie Pollock rose, his head banging against the front edge of the hood.

"Help me, Pete," Billie shouted. "For Chrissake, don't let them kill me!"

The crane swung around to the side. Pete saw now that a litter basket, one of the city litter baskets that lined the main streets, had been placed alongside the truck. The crane stopped turning when Billie Pollock was hanging directly over the basket.

Pete knew with sickening, instinctive certainty what was coming next.

Someone dropped a match into the trash in the basket.

They must have doused it with gasoline, Pete thought. It went up fast and bright, a huge tongue of flame that rose high enough to lick Billie Pollock's face before it settled back to a steady, sun-bright glow. Billie screamed.

That scream.

The crane whined and screeched again. One link at a time the heave chain began to drop over the big pulley. One link at a time Billie inched down toward the flame.

"Pete! For Chrissake! Please! Pete!" They were barely words at all, he was screaming so. He thrashed about, arms pinned behind him.

"Come on out, Pete Hay," said the man with the bullhorn.

Billie's head was in the flame. Pete saw his hair ignite. Heard him screaming. Screaming.

Pete raised his rifle and shot his best friend, his bowling buddy, once through the heart.

Then he shot the man with the megaphone.

20

They spent an interminable fifty-six hours, waiting, watching, trying to guess, to intuit where and how Paul and Robert Trayne were going to strike next.

Now they knew, and it was only by accident that they knew.

Garber went to his office as usual, turning at once to Sally Pini as the fount of all knowledge. She'd had little to tell, as Garber reported that evening back at the rectory of St. Timothy's, and Garber—fearful always now of even the most innocent people, people who might turn out to be acolytes of Paul Trayne—found it necessary to be so careful in asking her, in phrasing his questions, that he could not be sure he'd really learned everything Sally might know. He'd paged through every report filed in the last two days, even the most routine, looking for anything that might say "Trayne." But there was nothing. The boy and his father had vanished, gone to ground, and in a city the size of Chicago there were a million places they could hide. Especially—as Garber knew was almost certainly the case—if they were under the protection of Mannie Stuartson.

How much easier it would have been to have simply gone up to his old friend's office, to have laid out for him the terrible details of all he'd seen and heard in Faulkner. But that was out of the question. The risk, should Stuartson in fact be within Paul's power, was too great. Garber found himself hovering at the very brink of utter despair. There was no doubt he had lost Marjorie to Paul Trayne. There was also no doubt that Stuartson, if lost, was lost only because he, Clay, had brought the boy into his life and opened him to the trap of Paul Trayne's power. Wife and best friend, then, almost certainly in the enemy camp now. Possibly salvageable—if Donna could pull herself out from under Trayne's thumb, why not Marjorie? Why not Stuartson?—but until the miracle happened, until they *were* free, these two who had been more close, more dear to Clay Garber than any others outside of his two daughters and his long dead son, could only be considered as hazards, menaces to the plan, the puny, paltry plan the three conspirators were patching together in the rectory of St. Timothy's.

So Garber waited and watched, reading the new reports that crossed his desk, keeping his ears open, asking carefully shaded questions. Avoiding the mayor. Avoiding those directly in contact with the mayor.

Nothing revealed itself.

Donna called in to the *Advocate,* played her best reporter's games, pretending no knowledge of Walker Stone's trip to Faulkner, no knowledge of his failure to return. It was possible —seemed likely in fact, from Stone's secretary's response to Donna's questions—that she did not know where Stone had gone, or that it was any real reason for concern that he was not back yet. But Donna learned nothing.

Then the sought-for answer dropped into Clay Garber's lap when he wasn't even looking for it. The telephone rang in the outer office. Clay heard Sally answer, heard the tone of her exchange. He could not hear the words, but he recognized her shifting into her Most Official mode. Someone was giving her a hard time. Someone who wanted to give him a hard time, he suspected, and Sally was doing her usual incomparable job of protecting him.

Up to a point. The door opened. "Man named Clifford," Sally said. "Says he's Alexander Reddington's private secretary." Her small voice managed to conjure a roll of thunder as she pronounced the second name.

Clay's eyebrows rose. *"The . . . ?"*

"Is there another one?"

Clay picked up his extension. "Commissioner Garber. How may I help you, Mr. Clifford?"

"I just want to be sure everything is shipshape for this do tonight, Commissioner." Clifford's voice was odd, hollow, as if he was pulling his cheeks away from his teeth with his fingers, Clay thought. "I mean, that all the security is laid on and all. Mr. Reddington doesn't like to go out, as you well know. But for something this special . . ."

"Yes, of course," Clay said, not having the least notion of what the man was talking about. "I don't have the exact arrangements in front of me just now, though. Could I have someone call you back in twenty minutes or so?"

"Mr. Reddington would prefer you to call yourself, of course." Reddington was one of the richest men in the city, by any numbers Clay had seen. Once the friend of statesmen, artists, brilliant, bright lights from all over the country, the world. Now a notorious recluse who, to quote Walker Stone, "makes Howard Hughes seem like Hugh Hefner."

"Of course," Garber said. He was about to hang up when something jelled in his mind. Something of astonishing clarity. What could cause Alexander Reddington to come out into the cold, cruel world? What, except . . . "Just to check now, to be sure. This is for the mayor's . . . ?"

"For the mayor's dinner. Tonight." Clifford's exasperation was abundantly clear. He was dealing with a complete imbecile, and he wanted Clay Garber to know it.

"Of course. I'll be back to you in twenty minutes."

Clay hung up.

It had to be. It had to be.

Donna said Trayne wanted to start at the top this time. Alexander Reddington was the top. Along with perhaps a hundred others he formed the crème de la crème of Chicago politics and power. With them under his thrall, there would be no part of the city into which Paul Trayne could not extend his tentacles.

"Sal!" Garber bellowed at the closed door.

"Commissioner?" Sally appeared instantly.

"Something's on tonight. The mayor's having a dinner. Know anything?"

She frowned. "Nothing's come across my desk. I'll ask." She closed the door.

Clay sat back in his chair. He looked at the plaque, the Kipling quote. *Yes, Paul Trayne. You've struck a real city. And it's going to strike back. If I have anything to say about it. Anything at all.*

He reached for the phone and dialed the number of the Cook County Prisoner Transfer Authority. The timing could not have been better. Errol Warner was due to be shipped to Joliet tomorrow at nine. But tonight, Clay thought, smiling, tonight he had something else to do.

Marjorie Garber tried to segregate the pain into recognizable moments of time. There was a gnawing hunger in her belly—a pain within the pain—that made it seem days since she'd eaten.

She tried, too, to segregate the monster who was the main instrument of her pain from the sweet-faced boy who had come to her house barely a week ago. How could this be Paul? She tried to focus on what he'd said about growing to like the inflicting of pain. She thought, dimly, that she understood something of what Paul meant. Mirroring without knowing it the very idea Donna Wojciechowski had suggested to Tom Sylvestri, Marjorie thought about all the evil, the terrible evil Paul had drawn from others into himself. He understood, he'd said, the source of each and every pain, each and every bit of grief and anger he'd drawn away. And if he truly understood, as only an adult can understand . . .

Marjorie lifted herself on her elbows. She was still lying on the big bed in Stuartson's private room. The bed that had been the center of so much pleasure when she first arrived.

She slid to the edge of the bed and stood up, leaning on the edge of the mattress, arms and legs barely up to the task of taking her weight. She was naked now. Her clothes were strewn in tatters across the room. There were angry weals across her back, from when her bra strap dug into the flesh before it snapped as Emmanuel Stuartson tore at it, at her.

She moved slowly to the end of the bed, gauged the distance to the bathroom. She needed a drink of water. Her tongue was dry, swollen. She needed food too, but most of all she needed water.

She essayed a careful step toward the bathroom door. Her legs held through three steps. Four. She made it to the door and leaned heavily on the knob. She opened the door and stepped through into the bathroom. It was a big room, marble walled and masculine. The tub was wide and sunk low into the floor. The counter was black marble, the sink a hollow in its surface. Marjorie turned on the cold tap, bending to put her mouth to the flow. She drank, and choked. She slowed herself, drinking carefully, lapping at the water like a cat.

After a while the terrible thirst drew back enough for her to turn off the tap and straighten. She looked at herself in the mirror. Her makeup was ruined, her hair askew, but, surprisingly, she did not look all that bad. Stuartson and Paul had traded off, first one, then the other, assaulting her, using her. Their attack had risen to a frenzy that actually brought Reverend Trayne crashing into the room at one point. He'd stood looking, frowning, his face almost Lincoln's face, almost kind. As she had when Stuartson entered—Stuartson atop her now, bearing down, his big teeth white against lips drawn back in a horrible rictus—Marjorie called for help. Trayne threw back his head and laughed. Mercifully he did not add his own efforts to her agony. He looked to the side and saw the chair on which Stuartson had draped his coat. He sat, crossed his long legs, and settled back to enjoy the show.

She looked around the bathroom. She did not know where the three men—impossible to think of Paul as a boy now—might have gone, but she was certain they would be back. They had not begun to test the degree to which they could torment her. Stuartson had said so in as many words.

She wondered how he could behave so with her, after his professions of love, after their passion. But, she reminded herself, love and hate were not so distantly separated as some might wish to think. They were parts of a great circle, and the gap between them was a slender thing indeed.

She knew now, understood completely all the feelings Stuartson had kept bottled up for all those years. Of course she'd known, when they met, that Stuartson desired her. But he was such a strange, stick insect of a man in those days, too intense, too eager. And when he'd introduced her to Clay Garber . . .

Clay.

Was there some way she could get in touch with Clay? Not the phone, she knew. That would not be safe. The phone on the bedside table was Stuartson's private line, and she did not know how many extensions might be scattered through the house. Certainly he would have one in his study. The bedroom phone was an old rotary model, too, and Marjorie knew from experience in her own house that a rotary phone being dialed could make other units on the same line jingle. Such a sound would surely alert Stuartson or the Traynes that she was trying to call out.

So there was no chance of contacting Clay unless she escaped. Odd to think of it in those terms; escape from Paul Trayne would once have been the last thing Marjorie Garber desired.

Now it was all.

She continued her survey of the bathroom. She'd been in here a couple of times since she came to Stuartson's house, but now she saw it as if for the first time. Because, on those other occasions, she had not been looking for a weapon. She had not been looking for something she could use to kill Emmanuel Stuartson and Paul and Robert Trayne.

Errol Keane Warner did not look like a man who could have murdered nearly forty young women. He looked like someone who should be working in an athletic supply shop. Tall, but not overly so, well muscled, but not overly so. His face was round, his dark hair long but tidy, pulled back into a short queue at the base of his skull. He wore wire-rim glasses over large brown eyes, and when Donna, Tom and Clay entered his cell, he rose and thrust a hand to Donna.

"Miss Wojciechowski. Come for my last thoughts before I leave Chicago forever?"

Donna shook the offered hand. "Not exactly. Do you know Commissioner Garber?"

"I've never had the pleasure. How do you do, sir?"

"I'm . . . fine." Clay, in turn, shook Warner's hand. The flesh was firm, slightly moist. The courtesy seemed too much, Clay thought. He was reminded of the psychologists' reports, the ones that compared Errol Warner to a tightly wound elastic band. A too tightly wound elastic band. That was the impression, to be sure. That he was screwed up as tight as he could be, and at any moment . . .

"And this is Father Sylvestri," Donna said.

"Father." Again the eager handshake. "I'm afraid I don't have any use for your services. I'm sure Donna has told you I'm an agnostic."

Tom nodded, though Donna had mentioned no such thing.

"Perhaps we should get down to business," Donna said. She motioned for the three men to sit. They were in the interview room, the same one in which Donna had gathered the information for her stories on Warner. There was a wooden table in the center of the green-walled room, and three chairs.

"Donna . . ." Clay said, indicating one of the chairs.

"I'd prefer to stand," she said. She felt too nervous to sit. She was afraid if she did she might start bouncing, as had been her habit as a very young child. The habit Viveca Wojciechowski cured by the simple expedient of tying Donna to her chair.

The three men sat.

"Well," said Errol Warner, "if you haven't come to interview me, why have you come, I wonder?"

"To enlist your help," Tom said, and noted there was no change whatsoever in Warner's face. He sat opposite Tom, hands clasped on the table before him, head forward, shoulders slightly rounded.

"My help?"

"Yes," Donna said. "Although I suppose we should begin by admitting there is absolutely nothing we can offer in exchange." She looked at Clay. "Right, Commissioner?"

"No," Clay said. "Nothing. This is not an official visit. I have the power to take you from this place, and if you agree to what we ask I will use that power, but I have neither the power nor the authority to offer you any sort of release or pardon or commutation of sentence."

"My goodness," Warner said. "What a speech! Well, maybe you'd better tell me what it is you have in mind."

There were fifteen bodies now, sprawled across the steps of the hospital. Fifteen dead men—no women, yet—who had been Pete Hay's friends and neighbors. The newcomers had been added in the wave of attack that followed Pete's shooting the man with the megaphone, long, long hours ago now.

A shriek had ripped through the crowd. A horrible animal sound. They'd come at the steps in a single surge, a monster that scrambled and clambered toward the hospital on many legs, many heads screaming, shouting faces twisted so that Pete scarcely recognized some of them.

He'd not hesitated to fire. He knew there was no point. Ten shots had rung out, loud in the lobby. Ten shots fired by a man who was as proud of his marksmanship as anything else in his life. Ten shots, ten new corpses.

The mob had broken, scattering up and down the snow-swept street. The pall of smoke made it look like twilight. With the mob dispersed—however temporarily—the town looked peaceful again. The warmth made Pete think of late spring evenings, of walks with Marcy Kavelhoff. Of the warmer times after the walks. He wondered what had happened to Marcy. Was she alive? Was she dead? Horribly dead? Was there anything at all he could have done, might have done to deflect any of this?

He'd slumped against the back of the couch, breathing hard fighting off hot, stinging tears.

"That was . . . easy enough," Zeldenrust said. He was crouched to Pete's right, reloading the spent weapons. Although his words suggested he thought they had won a decisive victory, Pete noticed the old doctor did not stop the reloading until all the weapons were ready again.

"Killing unarmed people has to be easy," Pete had said. "But they'll be coming back with guns. Count on it. They've sacked the station. They can get all the weapons they want there. And most of 'em have rifles of their own, hunting weapons. And then this couch won't be worth shit for cover."

Zeldenrust frowned. "Maybe if we piled up some of the chairs, the tables . . ."

Pete shook his head. "This isn't a TV show, Doc. Real bullets don't stop conveniently at the first thing they hit."

He remembered now a trip to Chicago with Clarence. They'd gone up for a demonstration of assault rifles, at that time only starting to make their devastating presence felt. They were taken, along with some two dozen other local enforcement officers from all over Illinois, to the huge Cook County police firing range, a vast mixture of field and woodland that looked to Pete Hay to be about half the size of Faulkner.

The officer in charge had led them to a wide open space, in the center of which, parked against a low, sandy hill, was an old Pontiac. One of the big ones, built before cars started shrinking. Behind the wheel, looking just as it did in the Volvo ads on TV, sat a crash dummy. The driver's door was closed.

A police marksman assumed a firing stance some twenty feet away from the driver's side and pulled back the bolt on his weapon.

"Now," the cop in charge said, "you've all seen Clint Eastwood and Charlie Bronson duck down behind the door of their cars to return fire. This is why movies are movies and real is real." He pulled the sound baffles, like a stereo headset, down over his ears and nodded to the officer with the assault rifle.

The man started firing.

Pete could not remember ever having heard such noise. The car lurched under the impact, sparks and shards of shattered metal screaming off the points of impact, a wail like ten thousand banshees filling the air.

And inside the car the crash dummy danced and twitched as the fusillade of fire power punched through the door and on through his cloth-and-plastic body.

The officer in charge raised his hand, stopped the fire. He crossed to the car and opened the driver's side door. The crash dummy was very nearly cut in half, its fibrous innards spilled into its lap, white and frothy, like snow. "As you can see," the cop said, "a car door isn't much use against this kind of ordnance. Now, come and look at this."

He led them around to the other side of the car. The passenger door was riddled with exit wounds, still smoking in the cool morning air.

The shots from the rifle had gone through the door, the dummy, and the other door. Several layers of metal, plastic, cloth, foam—all the things that made up the car and its ersatz occupant.

So what possible good was a couch going to be? Two couches?

Now it was nearly sixty hours since the last attack. Sixty hours in which Pete Hay had slept not more than two. Sixty hours of eating nothing but stale sandwiches and candy bars from the hospital cafeteria's vending machines. Of drinking black coffee and crouching in the lobby that had become the whole world to Pete Hay. He'd been in that lobby, in that hospital, maybe twenty times before, delivering people who'd hurt themselves or suffered sudden appendicitis attacks, kidney stones, heart attacks. Once even bringing a pregnant woman racing through town, siren wailing, praying he would not find himself caught in the colorful—but, he fancied, thoroughly disgusting—cliché of delivering the baby himself in the backseat. In those twenty-odd visits he'd paid very little attention to the lobby. Now he knew it by heart. Knew every square inch. Every crack in the plaster. Every detail of the bland, boring paintings on the walls. He knew every line of the Red Cross posters, every word of their warnings, their stern admonitions. The rest of Faulkner—his one-room apartment, the station house, the coffee shop, the bowling alley, Marcy Kavelhoff's farm, her bedroom—all these were fading into a kind of hazy dream, no longer real. No longer important. But Pete knew every square inch of the lobby, of his new world. Knew it because he understood only too well that he *had* to know it. His survival might well depend on some detail, some minor, seemingly insignificant thing that he might have missed about this lobby, this world.

Then he heard the sound. Car engines. More than a dozen from the noise. Coming toward the hospital.

He looked over the couch. His guess was right. There were fifteen cars barreling straight toward the hospital steps. Their front windshields were gone, all of them. Rifles poked out from the shadowed interiors.

"Here they come," Pete said.

Marjorie found her weapon.

She'd searched the bathroom, the bedroom, the closets. There was nothing of a conventional sort—no gun hidden conveniently in the sock drawer, such as she knew Clay kept—but the search did yield one of Stuartson's robes, so she was able to cover herself. There were no large blunt instruments. The furniture, when she studied it, was too strongly constructed for her to break. No handy wooden stakes would be produced by the breaking of chairs.

In fact, she realized, there was nothing she could break, nothing that would shatter to produce sharp points and edges without creating enough noise to alert the whole household to what she was doing. And since Stuartson, Trayne and Paul—it was so hard to think of Paul this way!—were all strong enough to overpower her easily, it could not be a subtle weapon. A garrote, for instance.

She'd returned to the bathroom in mounting despair and sat on the lowered lid of the commode, looking around, her fingers running nervously back and forth, back and forth along the hard edge of the toilet seat.

The hard edge of the toilet seat.

Marjorie rose. She turned and looked down at the dark, imitation marble seat and cover. She blinked, as the idea slipped into place in her mind. Could it really work?

She dropped to her knees—carefully, for every joint still flamed with pain. She lowered her head into the narrow space between the commode and the washstand. There were two large butterfly nuts holding the toilet seat in place. Marjorie tested one and found it turned easily. She unscrewed it, then tried the other. A little stiffer, but after a moment—a long moment, as heat rose in her face, as something like panic tried to claw its way out of her—it relented and turned.

Marjorie lifted the toilet seat from its place and hefted it. It was not real marble, but it weighed a good twenty pounds, she estimated. Quite possibly more. She tipped the cumbersome ovoid back and forth, testing the weight, finding places she could grip it. It was not an easy thing to hold. The two pieces were not designed for this kind of movement. The lid kept slipping sideways on the seat. That, Marjorie realized, was the sort of thing that might unbalance her swing and make her miss.

It seemed an odd thing to be thinking about, to be realizing so quickly. She'd never before brained anyone with a toilet seat, or given thought to doing such a thing. Now it was the total focus of her existence, and Marjorie Garber found her brain was able to work along remarkably clear lines, considering the act. The gift of Paul Trayne, no doubt, she thought. Allowing her to contemplate murder, her mind turning not to the immorality of the act, but only to the details that would make it happen most efficiently.

She set the toilet seat on the broad marble counter and opened the cabinet below. In a box marked with a large red cross Marjorie found the thing her racing brain told her she needed: a large roll of surgical tape, the paper wrapper unbroken.

She ripped open the package with her teeth, squinting to find the beginning of the tape. She pulled out a strip and tested its stick on the surface of the toilet seat. It seemed fine.

With tape and toilet seat in hand she crossed to the edge of the bathtub, sat, and began wrapping the tape around the seat, loop after loop, until the tape ran out and the whole unit was swathed—a strange mummification effect, as though this were no longer a fake marble toilet seat, but some ancient treasure plucked from the tombs of some great king of millennia past.

Marjorie stood and tested the feel of the improved weapon. Much better. She tried a few practice swings. Good. Good.

She was ready for them.

Emmanuel Stuartson stood by the tallest of the three tall windows looking out from the second-floor living room of his big brownstone. Outside the Chicago night was darkening fast, and a light snow formed fleeting, shimmering nimbuses around the streetlamps.

Stuartson grinned into the darkness, seeing his reflection in the window glass. Seeing the dark skin, the huge teeth. Seeing much more than that. Seeing himself as the centerpiece of a wonderful new Chicago, and—he would not deny it; why should he?—the centerpiece of a new and better America.

"President Stuartson."

He'd played the words over and over in his mind. He'd imagined the news anchors of all the networks, broadcast and cable, saying the words.

"Speaking from the White House, President Stuartson said today . . ."

"After his meeting with the Soviet premier, President Stuartson announced . . ."

It was real, it was true. This was the place in history reserved for Emmanuel Stuartson. He'd fought his way up from the slums of the South Side, to the courts of Chicago, to City Hall, to the highest office in the city. Now, leaping over the gubernatorial seat he knew Clay Garber eyed occasionally, Mannie Stuartson was on the verge of landing himself in the highest office in the nation and—as he saw it—therefore the highest office in the world.

"You remember what you have to say, Mr. Mayor?" Robert Trayne's voice spoke from just outside the range of Stuartson's daydreaming. "Mr. Mayor?"

At the more insistent tone Stuartson turned. "Hm? What?"

"You remember what you have to say?"

"Yes. Of course." Stuartson ran through the litany in his mind, just to be sure. "Yes, of course," he repeated.

"Good." Trayne placed his hands on Paul's slender shoulders. They stood on the other side of the room, in front of the big fireplace with the massive mirror above it. Turning to look at them, Stuartson was again confronted with his own reflection, above and behind the Traynes. Stuartson looked into Paul's face and smiled at the calm strength, the serenity he saw there.

"This is exciting," Paul said. His voice was soft, but it carried well, Stuartson noted. It would have been a good voice for a politician. It inspired trust. More. It inspired hope. "I've never worked with the kind of people you've assembled for me. People with such power." He smiled, a very grown-up smile,

Stuartson thought. "It must be a fine thing to have that kind of power. To have people in your control. Afraid of you. Afraid to say even the tiniest thing wrong, because they know you can reach out and crush them, crush their whole lives, because that's the kind of power you have."

Stuartson frowned. These were odd words indeed from the boy who was going to save the world from that kind of thing. But he could not get his brain to pursue that thought. *Never mind,* said the voice, and Stuartson was quite content to follow its suggestion. He had other things to think about.

I am the gift bringer, he thought, *and they all know it. They know I have delivered Paul Trayne to them.* He smiled.

"Following his audience with the Pope, President Stuartson said . . ."

"How soon should we leave?" Robert Trayne asked.

Stuartson forced his brain to disconnect itself from the pleasantly addictive hypothesizing. He looked at his watch. "The car will be here in—forty-five minutes."

"Good," Trayne said.

"Good." Stuartson nodded. A thought passed quickly across his mind. Forty-five minutes. Time for . . . ?

"If you'll excuse me," he said, striding past the Trayne's toward the central staircase, "there's one last thing I want to attend to before we get on our way."

21

Errol Warner agreed, smiling. His face was boyish, open. A lock of hair fell across his smooth brow. He sat back in his chair, unselfconscious, relaxed.

Was he plotting an escape, Garber wondered? Garber had made it quite clear there would be no moment when Warner was not under observation, surrounded by a police escort.

What struck Garber as especially strange, though, was the ease with which Warner had accepted everything they said. Of course they'd had to tell him the whole story. Or Donna had. Clay was impressed by the remarkable precision with which she outlined the whole sordid mess. She spared no one's feelings—least of all her own—laying out the procession of events from Ben Carpenter's first encounter with Paul Trayne to the realization that Warner himself was the perfect weapon to use against the boy.

"Because of all the guilt the doctors say I must have bottled up inside of me?" Warner's face was smooth, expressionless. Each of them—Donna, Tom, and Clay—tried to read what was there, and found there was nothing. For that moment it had seemed he would surely reject their mad scheme.

"Yes," Tom said. "Your soul carries a great burden, Mr. Warner. We believe it too much of a burden for Paul to take, concentrated, focused as it is."

Warner nodded slowly. "You understand that I don't really

hold with what the doctors say." He smiled. "I really don't feel bad about any of what I did." He shrugged, the gesture seeming to dismiss his actions as inconsequential.

Donna nodded. "We—or at least, *I*—think that will work to our advantage, Errol." Both Tom and Clay had been aware of Donna's repeated use of Warner's first name. They'd resisted following her example. They could not get so familiar with a monster like this.

No, Tom thought, *not a monster. Only one monster in this.*

"You think because I don't feel bad," Warner said slowly, "but the doctors say I *should* feel bad, that maybe there's some kind of cover over my emotions, over this guilt I'm supposed to be feeling. And that will . . . ?"

". . . hide it from Paul Trayne until it's too late." Donna could scarcely contain her emotions now. With each word, each item detailed in their plan, it seemed to her more sure, more absolutely certain of success.

Warner nodded. "Right. You said he can't turn off this power of his once it's started." He leaned back and looked from Donna to Clay to Tom and back to Donna. "Okay," he said. Again the boyish grin. Walker, Donna thought, would have been reminded of a young Andy Griffith—or Howdy Doody.

" 'But . . . ?' " Donna said.

"No 'but.' This is interesting." He smiled again. "And I like you, Miss Wojciechowski. I'd like to help you."

Donna let out her breath in a long, slow sigh. "Thank you, Errol."

"And," Clay said, "you understand there is no payoff in this for you?"

"Sure." Warner leaned forward. "I'm not a bad man, you see, Commissioner. I know that seems like a kind of foolish thing to say, but it's true. I've never done a single bad thing. I like to help people. Do good for people. So if I can help you, I'll help you." The eagerness in his voice and posture seemed genuine.

Tom rose. "Then we'd better get a move on. It's all going to start happening very quickly now, and we haven't even got through the most awkward part."

Clay nodded. "We still have to get Mr. Warner here released into my custody. And that, if you'll pardon my French, is going to be the queen bitch of the whole business."

Marjorie heard footsteps on the stair. She took the position she'd prepared, standing on the chair on which Stuartson usually draped his jacket.

She needed the height, though she realized the normal peripheral vision of whoever came through the door would reveal her presence and allow only one shot, one swing. If there was more than one—if it was all three of them, for instance—Marjorie was depending on the confusion of the first attack to allow her the chance to regain her balance and be ready for the others.

She pressed herself back against the wall, thankful for the light color of Stuartson's robe, which blended better with the pale wallpaper than her naked flesh would. She raised the bound toilet seat high over her head, waiting.

The door opened.

She saw a dark brown hand on the knob.

So it would be Stuartson who would die first.

Mannie Stuartson. Clay's best friend. DiAnne's godfather. Her own bed partner. Marjorie shuddered at that thought. It was Robert Trayne who had driven her to it, of course. When he came to her house, he'd told her what needed to be done. Not specifically. He was too clever, too careful for that. But his words—his words and the effect of Paul's power—made it quite clear to Marjorie that she had to do everything she could to make sure Mannie Stuartson was completely and irrevocably their slave.

Stuartson stepped into the room. "Going to be getting on our way in about forty minutes, Marjorie." His hand was on the buckle of his belt, loosening it. "Just time for a quick . . ."

Marjorie swung the toilet seat. The bandaged surface came down on Stuartson's head with a muffled *swoosh*. A crack like a coconut hitting concrete accompanied the jolt of impact in Marjorie's arms. A second sound, smaller but distinctive, came so close on the noise of the blow it blended with it: the sound of Stuartson's big tombstone teeth clacking together.

He toppled and landed with a dull thud on the dark carpet.

Marjorie jumped from the chair. Stuartson was still breathing, though the sound was ragged. Marjorie knelt down at his side, raised the toilet seat again, and brought it down in a long, hard arc, one, two, three. The seat was heavy. By the third swing it took all of Marjorie's strength to raise it.

By the third swing, Stuartson was not breathing anymore, ragged or otherwise.

Marjorie leaned back and slid the toilet seat to one side. There was a glistening darkness in the salt-and-pepper curls of Stuartson's hair. She was aware of small hot spots on her cheeks. Across the front of the light terry robe dark red blobs were spreading into the fabric.

"Witch!"

The word snapped across her. She'd been so sure Stuartson was alone.

And he was, she saw now, for Robert Trayne was still on the stairs, bounding up, doubtless having heard the sound of Marjorie's attack. He was on the landing, across it in two strides of his long legs. Marjorie pushed herself to her feet and raised the toilet seat again. She swung hard, but Trayne was not an unsuspecting victim as the mayor had been.

He danced back and reached over the curve of her swing with his long arms. The big hands clamped Marjorie's shoulders. The talon fingers dug deep. She yelped in pain and pulled the toilet seat weapon back up. Pinned by Trayne's grip, she had no room to swing, but the seat smashed into his left elbow, and he barked at his own pain. His left hand lost its grip. With his right he pushed, and Marjorie spun back, still unbalanced from the weight of the toilet seat.

She fell full length, and Trayne was upon her, his big hands making even bigger fists, pummeling her shoulders, the back of her head. Stars sprang out of the air around Marjorie. The room tipped and swam. She tried to get her hands into the stream of blows to deflect them. She was too weak, and Trayne was kneeling on her right arm.

"Father!"

The rain of blows stopped. The pressure on her back eased,

vanished. Trayne stood up. Marjorie turned her head and looked toward the door. Paul.

"The witch has killed the mayor," Trayne said. He kicked out at Marjorie, and his booted foot dug deep into the soft flesh of her abdomen. She gasped, retched, tasted vomit.

"We don't need him anyway," Paul said. So adult his tone! So sure his posture! "He's set everything up. We only need to take advantage of it."

Trayne was trembling with rage, his face scarlet, his neck corded with muscles pulled taut. Marjorie tried to pull herself away from him. Trayne shifted and brought his foot down on her arm, pinning it. She screamed as the bone snapped under his weight.

"The witch must be punished," Trayne said.

Paul smiled. "Yes. I think she should." He crossed to Marjorie and hunkered down barely a foot from her side. He reached out to touch her hair. He ran his hand over her shoulder, the smooth skin of her arm, sliding the soft fabric of the robe down across the dark satin of her flesh. He touched a finger to the curve of her exposed breast and circled the dark nipple. Marjorie shuddered at the touch and shrank back.

"Punishing is a very good idea," Paul said.

The abyss opened beneath Marjorie Garber. As she fell, she knew she would never again see the world beyond that terrible pit. Her last conscious thought was of her husband and her daughters. Then there was only pain.

The first car hit the bottom step and kept coming, powering up the long, slow slope, bouncing across each riser, its rear bumper crashing up and down, up and down, like the war drum of some impossible robotic race.

Pete Hay said a small prayer of thanks for the bouncing. The man in the passenger seat was blasting away all the way up the steps, but the vibration of the car made his shots go wild. Plaster exploded from the wall above Pete's head. To his right a thickly upholstered chair jumped back, coughing white stuffing.

The car crashed through into the lobby, snapping off the crystalline teeth of the window, sending bright, sharp shards spinning ahead of it. Pete ducked as the shower of fragments hit the front of the couch. It was lucky he did. A second car was coming up the steps already, and the boom of a twin gauge was followed almost immediately by a piece of the couch as big as Pete's chest ripping itself to shreds. Right where Pete's head would have been. A spring, freed from the restraints of the Naugahyde-and-wood back, popped loose with a sound that belonged more in a Bugs Bunny cartoon than on a battlefield.

Pete poked his gun hand around the edge of the couch, keeping his body low to put as much substance between himself and the attackers as possible. He fired Nickerson's Blackhawk in a blind arc, guessing where the first car would be, where the passenger side window would be. The first three shots *whanged* loudly into the metal of the car. The fourth broke glass and brought a scream of pain.

Pete pulled his hand back and grabbed one of the pump-action riot guns from the floor at his side. Zeldenrust was no longer there to hand him the weapons. As soon as he'd seen the cars coming Pete had ordered the doctor to cover, back deep in the shadows of the hospital. Zeldenrust took two rifles with him, though Pete suspected they would serve the doctor little, if it came to that.

Pete snapped up over the top of the couch, took in the scene in a glance, and pumped off two quick shots from the riot gun. A third car was coming up the steps, bouncing, its bumper screeching. Pete's shot took out the driver of the second car, not quite all the way up yet. He slumped sideways. The car turned into the path of the third. The third car hit broadside, pushing the second car on up the steps, its front end folding like a steel accordion as it plowed into the obstruction. The second car bucked up, looking to Pete for one moment as if it was going to slide right across the top of the impacting car. Then it rolled, turning once over completely to crash into the lobby doors sideways. Bright yellow flame spat from the underside of the rear. Pete ducked his head and ran for the back of the lobby.

The explosion caught him full force, lifted him, threw him. He hit against a corner wall and felt something snap in his right shoulder before the concussion pushed him on past the corner to the corridor beyond. Pete came down hard, skidding along the linoleum. New pain joined the one spreading in agonizing waves from his dislocated shoulder.

He pushed himself up on knees with his left arm and tried to crawl to the closer wall. Another blast—the third car?—knocked him from his precarious tripod perch. He fell full length, coming down hard on his injured side. The broken shoulder found a new way to hurt, something Pete would not have considered possible, given the pain already there.

He tried to get up again, tried to crawl away from the clear view of the lobby. Something white-hot smacked into the back of his right thigh. Pete had never been shot before. He would have expected a sharp, stabbing pain. Instead it felt more as if a scalding-hot club had smashed across the back of his leg. He yelped like a kicked dog and grabbed instinctively with the only hand working, his left. That unbalanced him, and he went down again.

He did not get up a third time. There was another crash from the lobby—another car bursting through what was left of the windows—and Pete heard voices shouting. He twisted to look, saw five or six heat-distorted shapes moving toward him, backlit by the flames of the burning cars.

The shapes became men. Men Pete recognized. Men carrying baseball bats and huge steel monkey wrenches.

The first blow caught Pete across the side of the head. If there was a second, he did not feel it.

"You're good at this, Commissioner. I'd hate to sit across from you in a poker game."

Clay Garber turned to look at the speaker. Errol Warner smiled his increasingly familiar, increasingly discomforting smile. He was clearly enjoying the machinations, watching Clay work the men under his command. Not quite lying to them, but not telling them anything like the truth, either.

"I'm glad you find it all so entertaining," Garber said. He did not try to disguise the sarcasm in his voice. He saw Donna frown and shake her head almost imperceptibly.

Careful, Clay, her face said. *Don't antagonize him. If he changes his mind now . . .*

They were in the main hall of the Prisoner Transfer Authority building, a massive marble-floored vault that looked to Tom Sylvestri like something more properly belonging in an opera house. The building dated from a period of grandeur in Chicago architecture when everything was writ large, simply because it could be. When municipal buildings were monuments, built to commemorate the power of the infamous political machine.

"Where's our escort?" Tom asked, his voice low, his face close to Clay's.

"They'll be here," Clay said. "Don't worry. We have to play this by the book."

Except nobody's written the book for this one. Clay sighed. He'd managed to convince everyone he was taking Errol Warner on the direct authority of the mayor, for the function the mayor was holding tonight. A check of computer records confirmed the mayor had something going, something that required the diversion of a large number of uniformed officers for security detail. And since Clay was the police commissioner, he could get away with the demands he was making without any written authorization. His right hand ached from the number of times he'd had to sign his name in the last half hour, but now they were on their way, and Errol Warner, their secret weapon, was theirs.

The tall glass doors opened at the front of the broad, high vestibule. A small army of uniforms—at least fifteen by Donna's quick head count—marched in, huge and dark in their bulky winter coats.

"Commissioner?" said the one who reached Clay first.

"Yes. Have you brought the cars around?"

"Three cars," the man nodded. "And a wagon."

Garber frowned. "I didn't order a wagon."

"Can't do it any other way, Commissioner," the officer said. He was young, Clay thought, to be heading this detail. But, then, all police officers looked young to him these days. Some time about his fiftieth birthday his whole force had turned into babies. "With a prisoner of this nature, we're not authorized to use a car for transport. You know that."

Clay ignored the petulance he heard in the man's voice. "All right. I'll ride in the wagon with the prisoner, then. Father Sylvestri and Miss Wojciechowski . . ."

". . . will ride with you." Donna set her jaw in a way she hoped Clay would know meant she was not to be argued with.

Clay ignored her message, if he got it. "No," he said flatly. He lowered his voice and aimed a harsh whisper at Donna. "You've done your part, Donna. You've convinced Warner of our . . . well, our cause. Now you have to get out of the line of fire."

Donna blanched. This was the first time anything like this had been mentioned. "What . . . ?"

"Clay's right," Tom said. "We discussed it out of your presence, and I apologize for that, but you surely must have realized there's no way you can walk into the lion's den. It's absurd."

Donna could not believe what she was hearing. "It's hardly a lion's den. There'll be a hundred other people there."

Tom shook his head. "We have no assurance of safety in numbers. You have been in Paul Trayne's thrall. We are *assuming* you are now free of it. But that remains nothing more than an assumption. And it's not an assumption any of us—you especially, I should have thought—are prepared to risk our lives on."

"But . . ."

Clay reached out a huge, brown hand. "Listen to me, Donna. There's more to this than worrying that you're going to fall back into Paul Trayne's grip the moment you're in the same room with him again. It's not like we think you're some kind of spy or something." He paused and glanced at the policemen gathered around them. Their focus was on Errol Warner. Clay turned back to Donna. "But the simple fact of the matter is, you're the only one who knows the truth. If anything happens to Father Sylvestri and me, you'll have to be the one who starts this again. Maybe from scratch."

Tom nodded again. "Don't you see, Donna? I know part of the story. Clay knows part. But you know all of it. You've lived through it."

Donna's mouth moved without sound. She felt so tense she fairly vibrated. This could not be happening. To have been in on it all, to have been part of the planning, the scheming. To have been instrumental in the recruitment of Errol Warner, and then to be told she had to sit out the last dance? No. It was utterly unacceptable. She would not tolerate it. Absolutely would not.

"All right," she said. "You win. What do you want me to do?"

Tom narrowed his eyes, studied her. "You're sure? You genuinely understand?"

"Sure," Donna said. "I'm sort of outvoted and outnumbered, anyway." She looked at Clay. "I suppose you could always have me tossed in the clink, if necessary. Protective custody."

"I could," Clay nodded. "Though I don't think it would be wise. We need you free, if we fail."

Donna nodded. "All right. What then?"

"While Clay takes Warner on to the dinner, you and I will take a short side trip back to St. Timothy's," Tom said. "I think that will be the safest place."

"Hallowed ground," Donna said.

"Yes," Tom said, and there was no suggestion in his tone that he meant it as a joke.

"Then let's go," Clay said.

The uniforms closed into a tunnel wall around the four of them, Clay, Tom, Donna, and Warner. Warner's face still wore its bright, broad jack-o-lantern grin. He looked, Tom thought, like a mischievous schoolboy, cutting classes, heading off with a party of his friends to do something his young mind considered wicked.

And what is really going on in that mind? Tom wondered.

He had been trying for weeks, off and on, to fathom the thought processes of someone like Errol Warner. Watching the news on TV, reading Donna's stories.

He looked at Donna. It was difficult, sometimes, to connect this frail, vulnerable woman, trying so very hard to be strong and brave, with the keen wit, the insightful mind that had crafted the articles in the *Advocate*. It showed, he thought, how very different people could be in different situations. On the job, he'd decided, Donna must be all business, hard as nails.

Only when she let her guard down—involuntarily, in this case —did something of her other side appear.

Tom slid into the seat beside Donna. The squad car was full of stale odors. Tom wrinkled his nose and saw Donna smile. "First time?" she asked.

"In a police car? Yes, as a matter of fact. Do they all smell like this?"

Donna sniffed as if, Tom thought, making an actual assessment of the odors in the confined space. Like a wine expert tasting a vintage, looking for this element, that.

Donna nodded. "Pretty much standard issue. Old plastic, steel and Lysol. And, of course, the ghosts of all the things the Lysol is supposed to have eradicated. Sweat. Urine. Vomit. It's not too many upright, clean-cut citizens who get to ride where we're riding, Father."

Tom wondered about that. "I'm surprised they don't have a special fleet for—well, 'civilians' is the only word that comes to mind."

"They do," Donna said. "A small one. And you can bet every one of them is tied up with the mayor's shindig." Their escorting officers had climbed into the front seat while she spoke. A small kick at the base of Donna's spine signaled the gunning of the engine, the beginning of acceleration. She twisted in her seat to look out the rear window and saw the big wagon pull away from the curb and pull in behind them.

The movement of her body brought Donna's leg up against Tom Sylvestri's. She jerked back, memories of their meeting flooding her brain, twisting her stomach. Tom put a hand out to hers.

"Don't think about it." He smiled. "It was your cry for help. If I'd been a little more alert, it wouldn't even have gone as far as it did." He'd read every nuance of Donna's thought processes in her face. The contact had reminded him of the same moment. That was not something to be considered now. It would only cloud their purpose.

"Was it St. Timothy's, Father?"

Tom turned in his seat. The speaker was the policeman on the passenger side, immediately in front of him. He was looking back through the wire grill that divided the car in half.

"Sorry?" Tom said, not having caught all that the man said.

"The church the Commissioner said you wanted to be taken to first," the officer repeated. "Was it St. Timothy's?"

"Yes. On West Addison."

The driver nodded silently and eased the car out into traffic. "Guess we won't need the siren," his partner noted.

"No," Tom said. He studied the young officer's face. Round and boyish, much as Donna had described Paul Trayne. But with something missing in the eyes, Tom thought. Some element of humanity. *He has barriers around his soul. He's put them up, one by one, little by little, every day he's been on the force. In a city the size of Chicago, it must not take long to find your senses being dulled, your normal reactions being wound down, pulled back. Not if you're a cop.*

"This must be some do the mayor has cooking," the young cop said. "It must be something pretty big. I've been hearing about it for a couple of days now. A real choice assignment, they were saying. Everybody wanted to get in on it."

"Why so many cops?" Donna asked, knowing the answer, but wanting confirmation of a more official kind.

"Lots of VIPs," the cop said. "I said to Murph here"—a quick nod at the driver—"the other day I said, boy, I said, if somebody was to toss a bomb into that party, it would hurt Chicago pretty bad. There'd be an awful lot of big companies without their top people, all of a sudden. Not to mention the city government."

"You've seen a guest list?" Tom asked. A foreknowledge of the people who were going to be at the dinner might give them some sense of what to expect, what kind of action to take.

"Not a real list, no," the cop said. "But you hear things. And I mean, the commissioner isn't exactly small potatoes, huh?"

"Not exactly," Donna nodded. *But, then, he's not on the guest list.* She wondered what might be going on in the armored van, far behind them, right now. What sort of exchange —if any—would be passing between Clay Garber and Errol Warner.

"I'd've thought you'd be covering it for your paper, Ms. Wochowski," the cop said.

Donna nodded, ignoring as she always did the mispronunciation. "No. Not really my style." It wasn't even a lie.

"Here we are," the driver said. He swung the car in a broad U-turn and pulled up at the foot of the church steps.

Obediently, Donna reached for the handle of the door and started to open it.

"I'm sorry, Donna," Tom said. "But you understand . . ."

". . . it's all for the best. Yes." She leaned over and kissed him quickly on the cheek. "For luck," she said. She climbed out of the patrol car and slammed the door behind her. She turned away, walked quickly up the low steps, and paused at the church door to wave. Tom returned the gesture. The car did not start to pull away until Donna stepped safely into the church.

She leaned back against the door, counting slowly to one hundred.

She opened the door and looked out into the street. The patrol car was gone.

Donna ran back down the steps and started jogging down West Addison, looking for a taxi.

It was cold in Faulkner. The fires that had burned for so many days seemed to have run out of kindling. The black smoke that hung above the town was breaking apart, tearing into long dark streamers, black on black against a sky filled with stars. The full moon painted the edges of the cloud with mother-of-pearl and spilled inky shadows across the streets.

Maurice Zeldenrust ran from shadow to shadow, darkness to darkness. He carried a loaded shotgun under one arm, though he had not yet fully convinced himself that he would be able to use it, if the time came. He'd spent his life saving lives. Could he now so easily end them? Loading the guns for Pete Hay was one thing. Pointing a gun, selecting a target, pulling the trigger —no, he was not sure he would be able to do that.

Yet if Pete Hay was to see the light of tomorrow's morning, that was exactly what Zeldenrust knew he had to do.

From his hiding place in the darkness of the unlit hall, far back in the hospital, he'd seen them shoot Pete, seen them fall upon him with clubs and fists. Zeldenrust estimated a good twenty to thirty swings connected with some part of Pete's fallen form before a man he did not recognize called off the attack.

"Don't kill him," the man said. "Not yet."

A laugh came from the group standing around Pete. A sound Maurice Zeldenrust could not quite convince himself was human.

They'd picked Pete up and swung him shoulder-high to carry him back out to the lobby and down the steps. Someone had found a fire extinguisher and sprayed the burning cars, dousing their flames. Zeldenrust wondered why—why would they care if the hospital burned to the ground?—until he realized the flames would otherwise have impeded their own escape from the building. As the tops of their heads dropped below his eye level he stepped from his place of concealment. Nothing moved anywhere in the hospital. The pistol Pete Hay had forced him to take grew heavier, tucked into the doctor's waist band.

He'd listened for the sounds of the car engines drawing away outside, then moved slowly, silently through the darkness to the edge of the lobby. There was no one there. The two cars lay like some bizarre modern sculpture, welded together by force and fire. Zeldenrust chanced a step into the lobby, into the marginally better light, beyond the darkness of the hall. If anyone was watching, he would be shot and killed instantly, he was sure.

He took a second step and, when he did not die, a third. He crossed to the couch behind which Pete had prepared for his last stand. The last stand he'd had no chance to make. The attackers had taken all the weapons.

Or had they?

Zeldenrust dropped to his knees and felt under the couch for the shotgun Pete had placed there. "Just in case we need an ace in the hole," he'd said. The gun was still there. Zeldenrust pulled it out and checked the load as Pete had showed him. He patted the pocket of his coat, confirming the three boxes of extra shells were still there.

He hefted the shotgun and considered his options. Rescue Pete, of course, if such a thing was possible. He didn't feel foolishly heroic enough to add "or die trying." But there was something else he should do too. There were people still here, in the hospital. All confined to their beds by illness or injury. They would have been hearing the terrible sounds from the lobby, but no one had yet gone back to tell them what had been happening. And, Zeldenrust thought, if he went now to do just that, they might not let him leave. And they would be perfectly justified in taking such a position, helpless and unarmed as they were.

But he had only the shotgun and the pistol in his belt. If the attackers returned, he would be unable to defend them properly anyway.

He'd halfway convinced himself to temporarily forget his proper charges and get after Pete Hay—all this debate passing through his mind in a matter of seconds—when he remembered Walker Stone. Stone, of all the people still here, would certainly be the most vulnerable. Paul Trayne or his father had somehow compelled Clarence Nickerson to attempt to kill Stone. Clarence, who, despite his gruff exterior, was one of the sweetest, kindest men Maurice Zeldenrust had ever known. If such a man could be turned into a killing machine aimed specifically at Stone, who else might be out there programmed with the same deadly mission? It was possible the Traynes did not know Clarence had failed to kill Stone. It was equally possible they did. Either way, the best defense was a good offense.

He'd slung the shotgun under his arm and trotted back toward Walker Stone's room.

Now he moved from shadow to shadow through a town grown more alien to him than it had been the first day he'd set eyes upon it. A Faulkner that had nothing to do with the long summer evenings, the crisp winter nights that had filled his life for many years now. Nothing to do with boys and girls playing in the green parks. Nothing to do with summer skies filled with birdsong. If it had been transplanted whole from Mars, it could not have seemed any less familiar, Zeldenrust was sure.

The fires had gone out, but the wind still carried their smell. No breath could escape the charcoal odor and the stench of burnt flesh that drifted just under that, not strong, but strong enough to notice, to recognize.

The streets were strewn with garbage. More than the trash that had begun to pile up since the Faulkner Department of Sanitation lost all interest in its job. There were wrecked cars, overturned trucks. Windows were broken. As far as his eyes could see in the light of the intermittent moon, Zeldenrust could make out not a single window that was not smashed, no matter how tall the building that housed it. He walked carefully stepping around broken glass lest a foot put wrong make a sound that would betray him.

Not that such a small sound would be too likely to be heard over the noise he moved toward. It was a roar like dinosaurs in heat, but it was very much a thing of the twentieth century and, he thought sadly, even more a thing of the dreadful here and now of Faulkner, Illinois.

Automobile engines. The same noise that had told Pete Hay the final attack was heading toward the hospital. The same noise, but magnified, increased tenfold. It came from the direction of the town square, the broad patch of winter-brown grass and trees centered on the marble pedestal from whose base the ancient bronze of Elihu Faulkner looked down. Zeldenrust wondered if there might be any modification in that dour expression, etched there unchanging since he'd come to Faulkner as a young man. He wondered if the spirit of old Elihu might be looking out through those smooth metal eyes and despairing at the sight that lay before him, despairing at all that had happened to the few hundred acres of real estate that bore his name.

Zeldenrust came to the corner of Varney Street and pressed himself back against the wall of the courthouse.

It was not dark beyond the corner. The park was flooded with yellow light, the light of a hundred cars parked in a huge circle, facing in to mingle their beams in a great sea of luminescence. This was what confronted Zeldenrust as he poked one fearful eye around the corner of the courthouse. A few hundred people stood within the ring of cars, whooping and cheering, their combined voices just loud enough to be heard over the gunning of the engines of all those cars.

No one was looking his way. Zeldenrust stepped away from the side of the courthouse and moved as quickly as he could to the shadow cast by the big oak that stood across from the narrow mouth of Varney. The shrieking and whooping grew louder as he approached, and his shift of position was not solely responsible for the increased volume. The people were cheering and chanting, repeating over and over, louder and louder, the single word "Pull!"

Zeldenrust stepped away from the tree and moved around the outer edge of the parked cars. Still no one paid him the least attention. All eyes were focused toward the center of the ring, and as he looked through the gaps in the wall of pressed flesh, Zeldenrust saw there were four cars inside the hoop of people, four cars forming the points of a cross, their lights pointing out toward the ring of people.

"Pull PULL pull PULL pull," went the chant, louder and louder.

Zeldenrust pulled his collar up around his head, his hat down. He pushed the rifle inside the folds of his big coat and tried very hard to saunter, to stroll to the circle of people.

"Pull PULL pull PULL pull PULL!"

They were shouting, chanting so loud, the engines of the four cars roaring so loud, that Zeldenrust at first did not hear the other sound. The anguished wailing.

He came abreast of a break in the crowd and saw what was in the center.

"Gonna be a bitch to find anywhere close to park, you know," said the driver of the patrol car. He did not seem at all concerned by the fact that he was addressing a priest. "With all them bigwigs it's gonna be Rolls-Royces and Cadillacs as far as the eye can see."

"Just get as close as you can," Tom said to the back of the man's head.

"Do you know why the mayor wants Warner?" the other cop asked.

"Showing off?" Tom suggested. He was suddenly slightly paranoid, not knowing exactly what part of which story Clay had told might have reached these ears. Was the question meant as a test? Were these two men, perhaps, already in the control of Robert Trayne? He dropped his hand to the door handle and curled his gloved fingers around the cold metal. If he jumped and ran . . .

"Yeah," the cop said, defusing the moment, "I guess the mayor is pretty pleased to have Warner get nailed under his administration. A real feather in his cap."

A feather that cost thirty-eight lives, Tom thought, saying nothing.

It came to him now how small and inconsequential a number was thirty-eight. Here were these young women, all in the prime of their lives, all from good families, snatched out of lives that had in no way prepared them for the horror of the last days and hours of their time on earth, the unspeakable horror unleashed upon them by Errol Warner. Here they were, thirty-eight of them, such a big number when a TV newsman said it, or when a newspaper blasted it across a headline, and yet, compared to the kind of devastation Paul Trayne and his father were capable of unleashing, compared to what Clay Garber reported having seen in Faulkner, what were those thirty-eight lives? Almost nothing. Paul Trayne's power, let loose in Chicago and the world beyond, could claim thirty-eight thousand lives, thirty-eight million. Human beings stripped of all their inhibitions, all the blocks and restrictions created by a lifetime of "proper" living, could create havoc and destruction on a scale that would make Errol Warner seem nothing more than the naughty schoolboy he seemed so much to resemble, at least in Tom's mind.

"Here we are," said the driver. The car stopped rather abruptly. "Fucking parking lot," he said, "like I told you."

"Do the best you can," Tom said. They were a good two blocks from their destination, and there would be no way, he saw, that their transport would ever get them all the way to the door. He looked over the cars ahead to the pool of light they wanted to reach. The South Shore Armory, rising like a Hollywood set designer's idea of a medieval fortress: huge granite walls smoothed by more than a hundred years of Chicago weather, tall, slender windows like archer's ports, filled with colored glass, ablaze now with light. Tom could see the well-dressed dignitaries strolling—hobbling in some cases; there was a lot of very old money here—toward the Armory, strolling toward a wall of dark blue greatcoats that fronted the sidewalk before the old structure.

"There's the paddy wagon," the driver said. "And the commissioner."

Clay had evidently had better luck than Tom in getting fairly close to the Armory.

"Good," Tom Sylvestri said. "I'll walk from here, then."

He pushed open the door of the car and slipped out into the ink-black cold of the Chicago night, looking for Clay Garber.

Pete Hay.

Zeldenrust stepped to the front of the watchers and saw what they had done with Pete Hay.

He was spread-eagled on the ground, lying on his back, his wrists and ankles joined by long ropes to the bumpers of the four cars. He was naked. His body was covered with bruises and abrasions. A woman was squatting on top of him. A blond woman, full-fleshed. Marcy Kavelhoff. In a flood of annoyance, Zeldenrust realized that both he and Hay had, in the insanity, forgotten her, locked away in the back of the police station.

These people must have discovered her there and released her. Now she sat astride Pete Hay, her broad thighs clamped tight around his middle, their position uncomfortably sexual. Especially given the way she bounced up and down.

But there was nothing sexual in her mood, her intent. Her face was twisted with fury. It was normally a pretty face, but not tonight. Not in the harsh light of the ring of cars. Not with that expression.

With each "PULL" from the crowd the drivers nudged their accelerators, and Pete was lifted from the ground, a wail torn out of him. Marcy rode up on him, rose like a child on some fairground ride, lifted from the ground as he was. Pete's head hung back, jerking from side to side as the scream came from him. Marcy's hands drummed on the taut skin of his chest, making the scream vibrate, undulate, as if Pete Hay were some kind of musical instrument and his pain a sound for her to manipulate.

Zeldenrust could tell by the attenuation of the darkening flesh that Pete's right shoulder was already dislocated. His hands and feet were almost black from the tightness of the ropes that held them. The ground beneath him glistened with blood from his bullet wounds.

The tension on the ropes eased. Pete dropped back to the ground. Marcy bounced, drumming.

"Pull PULL pull PULL pull PULL!"

The engines revved again. Pete Hay screamed again. Marcy whooped with joy, pounding.

Zeldenrust fingered the shotgun stock under his coat. Two shots only. And fifty, sixty people in the ring around Pete Hay.

"Pull PULL pull PULL pull PULL!"

The engines revved hard. Pete Hay's other shoulder wrenched out of its socket with a sound like nothing Maurice Zeldenrust had ever heard or imagined. Marcy squealed, writhing atop him. The crowd cheered. Zeldenrust quailed inside the terrible noise.

"Pull PULL pull PULL pull PULL!"

The cars lurched. Marcy braced her feet. The ropes sprang to their terminal tension. The strength of Pete Hay's muscle and flesh was enough that one of them even spun its wheels as it surged away. Then there was nothing restraining them. The crowd jumped, parting in four places as the cars zoomed away from the center of the park. Brakes squealed. As Zeldenrust watched in horror, one car was unable to stop. It plowed into the outer ring of vehicles. A plume of bright orange flame launched straight up from the point of impact. The crowd scattered, fleeing the flames. The driver jumped from the car, but his trouser leg was already on fire. He screamed and fell, swatting at the flame. His pants must have been polyester, Zeldenrust thought. The flames spread up the leg like a thing alive, consuming trousers, flesh, ultimately consuming the man. He rolled, screaming. No one moved to help him. Some even cheered and clapped.

Zeldenrust made use of the distraction to approach what was left of Pete Hay. Marcy had run off to see the fire, like the others. Zeldenrust could see her footprints on the ground leading away from Pete. The brown grass was a sea of blood. The remains of Pete Hay were gray-white where not spattered with red. Pete's face was slack. Half his right arm and his left leg above the knee were still attached to his torso. The tearing free of his right leg had taken half his pelvis and pulled out his intestines in a slimy, snaking string that looked to Zeldenrust like nothing quite so much as the worms squirming in the tin can he and Clarence Nickerson used to hold bait when they went fishing in Pine Tree River in the sweet summers that would not, could not ever come again.

Zeldenrust knelt by Pete, his knees sinking in the sodden earth. He put a finger to Pete's neck, felt the flicker of a pulse. Pete was still alive. Unconscious, but alive. At any other time, in any other place, Zeldenrust was almost certain he might have been able to save the young man's life. By Herculean effort, yes, but with the wonders of modern medicine at his command, even injuries so gross as this could be dealt with.

Anywhere else.

Any other time.

Zeldenrust knelt, sobbing, his fingers on Pete Hay's throat, feeling the last shuddering spasms of the deputy's heart. Feeling him die.

22

Just walk in. Just walk in and look like you belong. Like you belong.

It was fast becoming a mantra in Donna's mind. A chant she hoped would steel her soul against whatever lay ahead. Like the prayers she was sure Tom Sylvestri was repeating to himself, wherever he might be right now.

She walked slowly down the cold street, a light snow swirling, lamplit yellow pools at equal intervals. She blended into the trailing edge of the people moving toward the Armory. She was glad she'd thought to borrow one of Tom's best coats for the trip to meet Errol Warner. It did not look quite so elegant as the furs and finery around her, but it was dark and long, and the broad shoulders—filled out with the sleeves of the big sweater she wore, pulled up as high as they would go—were passing fashionable. At least she did not stand out, she felt, as she would have if she were wearing only the old sweater and rolled-up jeans she had on under the coat.

Tom in his clerical garb and Garber in his traditional dark suit looked good enough to blend with the crowd. She was reasonably sure they'd had no trouble getting inside. The only thing Donna worried about now—at least, the *latest* thing she felt the need to worry about—was her swollen face. She'd raided Mrs. Buck's limited supply of makeup earlier that day, but she'd not allowed herself the opportunity to patch the job since. It seemed unlikely to Donna, who wore little makeup as a rule, that such patching would be necessary. She had now as much Max Factor layered on her face as she might normally use in a year. In this light, though, she was reasonably sure the bruising she'd received at the hands of Robert Trayne would go unnoticed.

She flowed with the crowd and tried to figure out just what she would do if someone at the door asked for an invitation. She was guessing—hoping—that with this crowd, this most elite of the elite, there would be no formal check for written invitations, only a scan for faces that did not seem to belong in such an assemblage. And if she was recognized, Donna hoped her small slice of fame—well, notoriety—in Chicago might get her through. With the speed with which this seemed to have happened, it was unlikely any written invitations would have been prepared. Plus, the people who moved now all around Donna were not inclined to be stopped at doorways, any doorways, by officious little men looking for tickets.

Donna took a deep breath, tried to will her face and hair into their very best, most stylish configurations, and pressed on toward the door.

"You're still sure about this?" Tom asked Clay, close by his right side. He'd told Tom what he wanted to do, the plan that had formulated itself as he rode in the wagon with Errol Warner.

Clay looked at the crowd around them, looked at their escort of police. "I don't think I have a whole lot of choice, Father," he said. "With these policemen all around us—not to mention those already stationed around the Armory—we can't hope to sneak in. I've got to play my bluff. I've got to find Mannie and convince him I've gone over to his side."

"And you're sure that will work?"

"I can only hope. But, on the basis of what Donna said . . ."

Tom nodded, remembering. "There's nothing she'd seen to indicate Paul or the old man can tell either way, whether you're with them or against them. Neither can read minds, though Robert Trayne sounds like something of an adept in reading body language. Still, if you say you've gone over and don't do anything too overt to show them that you haven't, they may buy into it." He studied the crowd around them. A hundred people, he guessed. A hundred of the finest Chicago had to offer. Wealth and power. Everything Paul and Robert Trayne were after. He looked back at Clay. "Your wife . . ."

Clay shook his big head. "I'll be honest with you, Tom. I haven't even thought through that part. If Marjorie is here—and I have every reason to believe she will be—I just don't know how I'll react."

Tom saw the way the Commissioner's hands were flexing, fists balling and unballing as he spoke. "You will need every bit of restraint you can muster," Tom said. He laid a hand on Clay's shoulder. " 'Surely the wrath of man shall praise thee: the remainder of wrath shalt thou restrain.' "

"Yeah," Clay said. If there was more he wanted to say, he did not.

"We'll have to move fast, now," Tom said, letting the moment pass, the tension. "We'll have to have everything in place, everything ready, before Paul has the chance to work on these people."

Clay looked at him. Donna had been right, he saw. Tom was still convinced of the Old Testament nature of Paul's power, of his evil. Tom was shielding his soul against a threat of Biblical proportions. Donna, on the other hand, was worrying about a fifteen-year-old boy whose misaligned genes had given him the power to destroy the world. Clay was not sure which story he was prepared to buy into; he knew only that the power of Paul Trayne had corrupted and quite likely destroyed the life he'd built for himself.

Paul Trayne, Robert Trayne, or both, would somehow, some way be made to pay. If he was convinced of nothing else, Clay Garber was absolutely convinced of that.

The last time Walker Stone held a gun in his hand it was a Fanner-50, by Mattel. He was twelve years old.

Thirty-some years later, he sat in his bed, in the dark room at the back of the dark hospital in the southernmost part of the dark town, and realized just how absurd his position really was.

Zeldenrust had given him a pistol to protect himself; a .45 snub-nosed thing, dark blue steel, heavy in his usable hand. For the twentieth time since Zeldenrust departed, Stone raised the revolver, sighted on the door of his room. If they came for him, as Zeldenrust said they'd come for Pete Hay, what could Stone honestly hope to do? Zeldenrust said there were dozens of them. This pistol held six bullets.

Stone sighed and let the gun fall back into his lap, his strength too low to hold it up for long. He listened to the silence of the hospital, a frightening sound. A lifeless sound. Stone had remarked once or twice that the most silent thing in the world was a dead telephone. That plastic implement, held against the ear, no familiar buzz to indicate the lines working properly, always seemed to him the deadest kind of silence, so wrong, so absolute.

He was learning differently now. The silence in his room was more complete, more oppressive than any he'd ever experienced. He could hear his own heartbeat. He could hear the rasp of his breathing. Beyond that, there was nothing.

A silence emphasized, made all the more terrible, by the things Zeldenrust had told him in the few moments before the doctor departed. Told him of the horrors being unleashed in Faulkner. That made the silence here worse. Knowing that the town outside these walls was burning, screams filling the air. Knowing that all the madness could come bursting through that door, his door, and consume him at any moment.

Stone had never been afraid of death. There was, he said, nothing in the time after the body ceased to function. No more than there was anything in the time before conception. "Dust to dust," he'd said. "We come from nothing, and we go to nothing."

This was something else Walker Stone was learning to reevaluate. Alone in the darkness, trapped in that bed, so weak even raising the handgun taxed him, he was looking at death from a whole new angle. There might be nothing after, he found himself thinking, but getting there could be a very nasty trip indeed.

He thought about Errol Warner. He thought about the thirty-eight women who had died at the hands of that unrepentant madman, their deaths slow, full of pain. Warner saw himself as an artist, Donna had determined. He saw human suffering as his art, the human body his canvas. He claimed—and medical examination seemed to suggest—that he could prolong an agonizing death for hours, even days. He could *coax* the soul from the body, inch by inch. Stone shook his head. It seemed impossible a human mind could work that way, but Warner had managed to find a new and different pathway to death for each of his victims. A new and different agony.

Stone shuddered and wondered if he might not be better served by reversing the direction his small weapon pointed. By saving the first and only shot for himself.

Then he heard the sound in the hall outside his room.

There was nothing small about Velma Fantuccio. She weighed close to two hundred and fifty pounds and had a pair of trunk-like legs that looked to all who saw them as if they would have no difficulty supporting ten times that weight.

Likewise her voice was large, a big, booming noise that Velma had long since given up any hope of modulating. If there was anything like a whisper in Velma's catalog of sounds, no one had heard it in years.

Paul Trayne started when the big voice thundered across the great dining hall of the Armory. It seemed to roll around the darkly paneled walls, rumbling up from the floor, down from the vaulted ceiling, pummeling him. As Velma's corpulent mass bore down on him, surging through the people already milling about the hall, Paul took a step back, horrified. Immediately he found himself missing Marjorie Garber. Her small-ness, her softness. Missing, though in no way regretting.

"Paul," Velma bellowed. She seized him, hugged him to her. Paul would not have been in the least surprised if that mountain of flesh had proved enough to engulf him, consume him. He felt with great relief the grip of his father's big hand on his arm, pulling him back from the morass.

Something flashed across Paul's mind. Something dark and formless, but leaving in its trail an image of Velma Fantuccio sprawled on the dark stone floor, the thick layers of her fat flesh pared from her bones in long, slimy slabs that shuddered like slick, white snakes as the last spasms of her death agony went through her. Like everything else that filled his brain now, Paul did not know the origin of this image. He knew only that it did not frighten him as much as it would have, not so very long ago.

"And you would be?" Robert Trayne asked, his voice soft but stern.

Velma identified herself. "It's so wonderful that you could be here. Marjorie told me so much about you." The big head bobbed, the amazing fright wig of colored hair dancing to the movement. "But, where is Marjorie? And the mayor?"

"Briefly detained," Trayne said, smiling now he knew the identity of this grotesque woman. It would be interesting, he thought, to learn what evils she kept bundled up inside that obese form. "They will join us before the evening is half over. But Mayor Stuartson felt we should come and make a start."

"There is so much to do," Paul added. He felt unclean, dirtied by his unwelcome contact with the gross woman before him. He wanted to run away from her, but there were too many others here, too many of interest. Looking past Velma, he studied the people entering the hall, men and woman, old and young, a broad spectrum of ages and races. There was a beautiful Asian woman some sixty feet to his right. Small, slim, with dark almond eyes and skin that shone like polished ivory. Paul let his gaze run up and down her slender form, revealed so perfectly by the lines of the sleek, dark velvet gown she wore. And there was a blond woman beyond her, taller, bigger, with bright red lips and a dress whose décolletage plunged low enough to reveal the under curve of her full breasts.

This was all new to Paul, this ability to see women in this way, to see them as sexual things, objects to be used. New, yet increasingly familiar. Increasingly comfortable. He was constantly discovering new avenues in his mind, routes and pathways unguessed. He knew, when he gave it any thought at all, that it must all be coming from the things he'd taken from those who had received his gift. This was the manifestation of their needings, and so much of it was physical, sexual. Lust was something new to Paul Trayne, but he learned very quickly to enjoy it.

His mind filled now with a clear image of the small Asian woman and the big blond together, naked, their limbs intertwined, writhing, flesh glistening with sweat. He had no idea which of his many "patients" put that particular imagery in his young mind, but it came complete, fully detailed. He heard their moans of pleasure, wondered immediately how close in sound would be moans of pain. The image in his mind changed accordingly, darkening.

Still, Paul felt something was holding him back, some element of his past self, his dwindling, dying self that clung on, as Donna Wojciechowski had imaged herself clinging, dangling from the precipice, terrified of what lay beyond and below. But Paul was no longer terrified. He sensed—a false sensation? More a wish?—that something was waiting for him here, tonight. Something that would banish the last of the old Paul, and set him free.

Even as he thought this, as he saw for the first time the changes in him as a release, a freeing of his spirit from the burdens of his father's preached morality, Paul sensed too that his other self—why did he want to think his *true* self?—was screaming as it shrank, screaming as it died.

Paul smiled. "We should get started," he said. "We should get started as soon as possible."

Clay abandoned all hope of guessing how the next few minutes would go. His rank got him past the police guards outside the Armory without resistance. He'd given instructions that Tom and Errol Warner be taken to a small waiting room he knew lay just off the side of the rear of the dining hall. He'd surrendered his overcoat to one of the attendants waiting inside and joined the people flowing through the tall oaken doors into the dining hall.

Clay could no longer count the number of times he'd been here, been in this great chamber, attending the endless dinners, the formal civic functions. Sometimes with Marjorie on his arm, sometimes alone. Sometimes in white tie and tails, sometimes in his uniform. He always felt foolish in the uniform. As if he were playing policeman instead of actually being the highest ranking police official in the city.

He smiled and nodded as he moved through the Armory, putting on the good show, shaking hands where hands were extended, exchanging pleasantries where such pleasantries needed to be exchanged.

A variety of emotions ebbed and flowed in his breast. It was good, on the one hand, to be here in the old Armory. The huge stone building always seemed a safe haven to Clay. The medieval castle motif was carried throughout, massive blocks of carefully hewn masonry standing alongside elaborately wrought wood and iron. A strong and, to Clay's way of thinking, very masculine place. There was a weight of age in the old walls, as if the whole history of Chicago had seeped into the thick rock, filling it with magical power. Clay remembered the first time he'd come here, in 1959, as a neophyte police officer, escorting Mayor Daley—the first Mayor Daley of the unbreakable political machine—to make one of his famous speeches before a throng of eager supporters. Clay had begun to understand then the power inherent in public office, the great power to shape the minds and will of men to one's own needs.

A puny power, compared to what Paul Trayne could do.

Then there came the other emotion Clay felt, the one that stood in direct juxtaposition to the normal strength and confidence he drew from this old building. For this fortress structure could *contain* as easily as it could repel. While Clay might once have felt completely safe within these impregnable walls, he understood only too well now that the evil he was here to destroy was inside, within the walls. And he was in there with it.

He entered the dining hall. A huge room, a hundred feet long, fifty feet wide, a broad stage at one end, dark curtains closed across its open space tonight. The floor was slate, dark enough to reflect the lights that blazed in wrought iron sconces along the walls. Those walls alternated stone and wood, dark brown and pale gray, and portraits of long dead city fathers glowered down at the tables set out before the stage. There was one long table, long enough to seat fifteen or twenty people, Clay judged, and twelve round tables arranged randomly before it, eight chairs set around each. Crystal and silver glistened on the bright white tablecloths. Beautiful arrangements of flowers decorated the center of each table. Waiters in white coats circulated, pouring champagne for those who were already seated, offering glasses from trays to those who continued to circulate.

Clay took a glass from a passing waiter and tried to make himself look as if he belonged as he made his way across the center of the hall toward the main table. He saw no sign of Mannie Stuartson yet. No sign of Paul or Robert Trayne. No sign—his heart sinking here—of Marjorie.

"Clay! Clay Garber!"

Clay cringed. He knew the voice, knew what to expect as he turned. Or thought he did. Velma Fantuccio looked every bit as overwhelming as she ever had. What Clay had not anticipated, though, was that she would be bracketed by Paul and Robert Trayne, a fat arm linked with each of them, seeming almost to be dragging them across the floor toward him.

"Hello, Velma," Clay said, summoning a smile he hoped was every bit as convincing as it needed to be. "Good evening Paul, Reverend Trayne."

This was the moment. It would all fall apart, right here, right now, if it was going to. Clay thrust a hand toward the older Trayne and felt the long moments tick by into what seemed hours as it hung there, unreceived.

Trayne reached out his own big hand and grasped Clay's. "It is good to see you again, Commissioner Garber," Trayne said. The Lincoln face was calm, serene. A friendly smile played in the hooded eyes. "And where, might I ask, is your lovely wife?"

Clay felt his insides turn to ice. Was this a gibe, a dangling of bait? How should he respond? With the kind of oblique answer he might use had he and Marjorie separated under different circumstances? He was sure she was with Paul—enslaved by him, if not actually here with him now—but was he supposed to know that? He'd not told Marjorie he was going to Faulkner, so there was no way she could have informed the Traynes of his trip. Could someone there have contacted them, told them Garber knew their secret? Knew all of it now?

"My wife and I have . . . separated," Clay said, noting the reaction in Velma's fat face, the widening of eyes, the flash that told Clay Garber this news would be all over the hall within minutes, all over Chicago within days. "I'm not sure where she is." Almost as an afterthought he added, "It doesn't matter, really."

Paul had been paying little attention to the conversation, studying as he was the many women around him. At Garber's last words he turned and looked up at the tall commissioner. "Really? It doesn't matter?"

Garber tried to keep calm, tried to keep his hand from trembling, remembering Tom's warning, the quote from Psalms. He drained the champagne glass—untouched till this moment—in one draught. "No," he said. He shrugged his broad shoulders. "I really can't find it in my heart to give a damn."

Paul smiled. "You have joined us, Commissioner. I'd hoped you would."

Clay feigned momentary surprise. "Have I? Well . . . yes. I guess that's right. Over the last couple of days, it seems . . ."

"The old worries have seemed less and less important?" Reverend Robert Johnston Trayne placed a hand on Garber's shoulder. "You have come to see how utterly unimportant are the trivialities which vex us daily?"

Garber nodded, offering a small prayer of silent thanks to whichever benevolent deity had planted in his mind the impulse to say he did not care where Marjorie was. "The slings and arrows of outrageous fortune, yes," he said. "Whatever you do, Paul," he said, looking back at the boy, smiling his broadest smile, "it seems a pretty good suit of armor against such things."

Velma seemed puzzled. "Marjorie said you didn't want whatever it is young Paul here has to offer," she said. "She said you . . . what? Resisted the gift?"

"I guess I didn't resist hard enough," Garber said, realized the choice of words was poor. He smiled, dived at his last chance to shift the course of the conversation back into his control. "I thought I might be able to offer you a special service, Paul," he said.

"Service?"

Garber nodded. "I've brought someone with me. Someone who should prove quite a handy tool in convincing all these people how wonderful your power is."

The police, the attendants at the doors all saw her, all seemed to recognize her. None moved to bar her way.

Donna walked up the worn sandstone steps of the Armory toward the three big black doors and felt the age and warmth of the old place enfold her as she entered. She kept as far to the right of the right-hand door as possible. Inside, she kept close to the wall, letting the last of the elegant people flow past her toward the great dining hall. Their talk and laughter rose to the dark vault of the ceiling and was swallowed by the shadows above the chandeliers. Donna smiled and nodded, keeping her face pleasant, happy, acknowledging the looks, the silent greetings of those who saw and recognized her.

She declined the offer of one young female attendant to take her coat. "I won't be here long," Donna said. She kept close to the north wall and moved in a slow half circuit of the lobby.

She knew the Armory very well. Like Clay Garber, her job had brought her to this place many times. She did not date back—professionally—as far as the Daley administration, but she'd covered one or two of Jane Byrne's speeches and had been in the crowd of reporters the first time Harold Washington spoke here. Chicago's first black mayor, he'd paved the way for Emmanuel Stuartson. Donna felt a twinge, a pain under her heart as she thought of the tall, gangling, oh-so-easily caricatured mayor. He was firmly at the center of Robert Trayne's web, according to Clay, and that was her fault.

If there was a way, any way, to save Stuartson, Donna would seize it. It was, she saw now, quite possibly the only way she might ever find to redeem herself, to make up for the horrors she had so deliberately, so calculatedly unleashed when she had brought Paul and Robert Trayne to the Garber house.

The pain she felt was a welcome thing indeed. If she was still under the complete influence of Paul, she knew, she would not have felt the least bit of compassion for Mannie Stuartson or anyone else.

Strengthened by this conviction, Donna made her way at last

to the tall, dark door set into very nearly the center of the west wall of the wide lobby. Beyond that door, past experience told her, was a short, narrow hall leading to a steep, curved flight of stone steps. Those steps opened at their top into a glass-faced booth, a commentator's booth, looking down onto the dining hall. From there, Donna would be able to see all that transpired in the hall. If anything went wrong, she would see and be able to act. If Tom and Clay missed some chance, she would, she was convinced, see that too. And be there ready to act on it.

Once it had been a cloakroom, and the wooden pegs poking from the walls just above eye level remained as mute testimony to this former function. Sometime in the last half century it had been converted to a projection booth, a narrow, glass-fronted slot carved into the thick stone of the wall between the small room and the big dining chamber, a platform suitable for supporting a movie projector bolted into the wall below.

Tom, two policemen, and Errol Keane Warner occupied all the floor space left by the projector table. A half dozen more uniformed officers lingered in the lobby beyond the door, adding their number to those already ordered here by and for the mayor.

Tom leaned close to the glass window and peered into the dining hall. He could not begin to name everyone there, he thought, but he knew them, nonetheless. All the rich, powerful men and women, all their wives and husbands. There were some older children, college kids, brought along by proud parents always eager for a chance to display their brood. Tom studied the faces, old, young, everything in between. He looked at the waiters gliding among them.

He looked for, and did not see, anything that suggested the mark of Paul Trayne's power. People talked, joked, laughed. A small but intense argument was going on a dozen feet in front of him—two men Tom Sylvestri knew would never voluntarily breathe the same air snarling at each other as their wives did the best they could to prevent a full-fledged explosion.

No sign of Paul Trayne there, he thought. *If Paul had touched them, they wouldn't care anymore. Wouldn't be both-*

ered, one way or the other, whether their old rival was here or not.

As he watched, Paul Trayne and his father separated themselves from a small knot of people, a hugely fat woman walking with them, apparently playing escort. It was the first time Tom had seen either Trayne, but he could have picked them out of a crowd a thousand times this size. Robert Johnston Trayne was unmistakable, of course. Donna's repeated references to his resemblance to the sixteenth president had not been exaggerated. Trayne was tall, gaunt, handsome in the same craggy way Lincoln had been.

The boy, too, was unmistakable. His face and form were completely that of a fifteen-year-old youth, but, Tom thought, there was something in his eyes, his posture; something that spoke of a wisdom beyond his years. Not surprisingly, to Tom, since he was still convinced of Paul Trayne's otherworldly origins.

That made a difficult place in the center of Tom's thoughts, their grand plan. A place with rough edges that marred the smooth perfection of all he and Donna and Clay Garber had worked out. Tom believed the evil in Errol Warner would be enough to temporarily throw the Trayne boy off his footing, to perhaps disorient him, but he was equally sure such a disorientation would last no more than a few moments. It was in that time, Tom was sure, that a more direct action would have to be taken. An action he, as a priest, was quite prepared to take. A physical action.

Without telling Clay or Donna, Tom had prepared himself for battle with this evil one. He'd read up again on the various rites used in dealing with demons. He'd brought, under his coat, the heavy old crucifix Father Percival willed to Tom as his last act in the world. The same exquisitely wrought cross that had come to Percival from his predecessor, and to that man from his, and so back some five hundred years. If the power in which Tom Sylvestri placed his faith and conviction could be quantified, summarized, Tom felt it was within that cross, that treasured symbol handed down through so many generations by so many devout men.

Tom only hoped—and here was the rough place, the flaw—

that the corruption he knew lay upon his own soul would not weaken the power he hoped to see transmitted through that holy artifact. He had failed his vows, and though he was determined such a thing would never happen again, Tom could not escape the nagging thought that all of this—Paul Trayne, the madness wrought by his "gift"—might be part of the punishment meted out to him for his transgression. He recognized it as a kind of hubris that he should even give credence to such a thought, but try as he might he could not fully divest himself of the conceit.

I am setting myself up in opposition to a force I believe to be as old as the universe itself, he thought, *and the only shield I carry against it is my own faith. My conviction that, despite my lapse, that faith has not been damaged.*

He was haunted by the sixteenth Proverb, by the lines that seemed, in Tom Sylvestri's mind at least, to apply to himself, to Errol Warner and, perhaps, to Paul Trayne.

All the ways of man are *clean in his own eyes,* Tom quoted silently to himself, *but the Lord weigheth the spirits. Commit thy works unto the Lord, and thy thoughts shall be established. The Lord hath made all* things *for himself: yea, even the wicked for the day of evil. Everyone* that is *proud in heart is an abomination to the Lord: though* hand *join* in hand, *he shall not be unpunished. By mercy and truth iniquity is purged: and by the fear of the Lord* men *depart from evil.*

I fear the Lord, Tom thought, understanding as he had been taught that such fear was not meant to be the terrible, consuming dread that could seize a man's soul in any of the situations he might confront in his daily life, but a fear that came from willing acquiescence to a power one understood as greater than anything a mortal mind could ever truly comprehend. *I fear the Lord, and I pray that the stain He may perceive upon my own spirit will not be so great as to weigh against me. I pray that we may come through this place of darkness and find the light. That this day of evil, if such it is, will not be the last day for the world.*

He frowned at the inherent melodrama of the words, but what choice was there but to couch his thoughts thus? Whether Paul Trayne was a blight set upon the world or a test sent down against Tom Sylvestri, he and his power could have come only from God, as everything came from God, and whatever part Tom played in all of this, it was the part he was meant to play. He only hoped, when the time came, he would be strong enough—strong in spirit, not in body—to carry through whatever he was meant to do.

He brought his thoughts back to the Armory, the narrow projection window. The main doors were away to his left. Clay would have to come twenty paces or more into the room for Tom to be able to see him.

The presence of the two policemen was something of a problem, Tom thought. If he had to act in some way, to go to Clay's aid or to defend himself, it might be awkward having them there. He turned. "I don't suppose you gentlemen would like to go get a cup of coffee? I don't think you'll be needed until Commissioner Garber wants Warner escorted into the hall."

The closer cop shook his head. "Commissioner Garber said to stay with you," he said. "I don't much feel like facing him down if we don't."

Tom cursed softly to himself. Of course Clay had said that. He'd *had* to say it. Anything else would have seemed wrong. Now they were stuck with a bodyguard, and Tom could see no way to get away from them. Even if he did, there was the problem of the guards in the lobby.

So he could only wait and watch and hope the moment, when it came, would be clear to him.

Tom turned from the window. Errol Warner sat by the door, perched like an attentive schoolboy on the only chair in the room. He'd offered it to Tom, of course—always so polite, this murderer, this butcher of young women—and seated himself there only when Tom declined. The second cop leaned against the wall, his hand on the gun in his holster, his eyes riveted to Warner's every movement.

"When do you suppose Commissioner Garber will need me?" Warner asked. Tom could still not quite believe this part of it was happening so easily. Why was Warner so agreeable? So keen to help?

Because he doesn't care, Tom thought, finally. *He's a man who knows exactly how many days he has left in his life. He knows there's nothing he can do to alter the progress of those days. If this provides him with a little diversion, all well and good. He doesn't believe in Paul Trayne's power. He thinks this is all some sort of game.*

So much was staked on what they thought they knew of the innermost workings of this man's mind and soul. Tom remembered Donna's words, spoken with such enthusiasm. The good guys might win this one yet, she'd said.

Tom was no longer so sure. He closed his eyes and began to pray.

The door opened slowly. A flashlight beam stabbed through the darkness. Walker Stone raised the small pistol and tightened his finger on the trigger.

"Stone! Is that you?"

Stone let his hand drop. "Carpenter?" His voice was a croak, a gurgle, not a human sound at all. Pain shot through Stone's throat, making his gasp aloud, adding new pain.

Ben turned the flashlight back on himself, confirming visually what Walker's ears had told him. "It's me, Ben Carpenter. I didn't know you were still here."

Stone gestured with his gun hand, indicating his condition.

"Guess you didn't have much choice." Ben crossed to the end of the bed and leaned heavily against it. "Better do something about getting you out of here. Whole town's gone to hell. Mae's dead." He shuddered. Stone felt it through the bed frame. "Think you're fit to travel?"

Stone gestured again, pointing to the intravenous feed in his arm, the tubes snaking into his nose and throat.

"Guess not. Damn. Wish Zeldenrust was here. Looked all over the hospital for him." Ben paused. "Brought Mae's body. Didn't know what else to do with her. Didn't want to leave her alone at the *Observer*." He shook his head, his face strangely lit in the flashlight glow. "Everything's gone to hell."

"Paul?" Another gurgled croak, as much as Stone could manage.

"Long gone." He looked at Stone. "Oh, you mean he caused all this? Yes. Of course I can see that now. Wish I could find him. Might be my one chance to make amends. I started all this, really, with my stupid article. Up to me to finish it." Ben shook his head. "Wouldn't ever have thought it would come out like this, would you? So much horror. Things I've seen, just driving here. Bodies everywhere. Mutilated. Not a lamppost on Jefferson that doesn't have somebody hanging from it. Or pieces of somebody. Wouldn't think there was that much pure evil inside a normal human being. Just wouldn't believe it."

I'd believe it, Walker Stone thought. He did not think himself a terrible pessimist, but he'd long been convinced that ninety percent of the evils of the world happened not because of extraordinary actions on the part of his fellow humans, but because of very ordinary, very human things that our cultures and faiths, worldwide, taught us to deny. Why were we always surprised by war, by cruelty, by people like Hitler, Saddam Hussein, John Wayne Gacy, or Errol Warner? Because we were taught to think of human beings as basically good, basically decent. Yet there was nothing, Stone felt, in the long lesson of history to support such a belief.

Humankind was basically rotten, he thought. Well, not rotten, maybe. But self-centered. Sigmund Freud thought sex was the driving factor in human nature, but Walker Stone had another idea. It was not the need to procreate that powered human activity. If it was, we should see it in history, see old men and women slowing down, growing kinder and gentler as their ability to reproduce faded. But that was not the case. Instead, there was something else, something far stronger than sex at work. The territorial imperative, he'd heard it called. The need to seize and hold territory. Dogs did it, peeing on trees to mark their terrain. Birds did it with their songs that inspired poets to such eloquence in the name of beauty, but were really nothing more than declarations of war. *Cross this line,* the birdsong said, *and die.*

That was in every man and woman, Stone knew. The drive to make a mark, to seize a piece of the world—the bigger the better—and mark it as one's own, for all eternity. That was why men built castles, bridges, all the myriad monuments to themselves. That was the reason for the bitterness in Shelley's "Ozymandias." If it were the tale of a man who had lost his wife, his harem even, it would not have been so sad, so profound, as the story of a king whose kingdom had been swept away by the ruthless and uncaring hand of Time.

But we denied all that, Stone thought. We denied the need to grab and hold, to build and defend. We read the Bible, and Jesus told us we were all basically good. We read a hundred books in a hundred different faiths, and the message was the same: we are basically good.

And even when we were confronted with the truth, when a Hitler or a Napoleon came along, when a man showed just how far he was willing to go to seize and hold, to crush, we put it down to aberration. Man is basically good. So the "gift" of Paul Trayne, taking away all the guilt and grief, leaves only goodness.

Stone sneered in the darkness. A pretty theory. The evidence of Faulkner stood against it, though. But even there, even confronted with all this madness, he was sure there would be people—lots of people, everyone perhaps—who would insist this was somehow a massive aberration. That something in the power the boy unleashed twisted the souls of men and made them do the things Ben Carpenter had seen. That the evil lay not in the people of Faulkner, lurking below the surface like a serpent in a still pond, but in Paul Trayne.

But Stone, with his encyclopedic memory for old TV shows, had picked up a piece of philosophy that worked very well for him in defining humanity. It came from *Star Trek,* from a speech Captain Kirk delivered, pompous and overbearing as always, but hitting very near the mark in Stone's mind. Mankind was a race of killers, the captain of the *Enterprise* said. But we had the power to make the decision *not* to kill. "We're killers," he said, "but we're not going to kill today." That was what separated humanity from the beasts. We could make that decision. We could *choose* not to kill.

Paul Trayne eliminated that ability, robbed us of the power to make that decision. If killing seemed a good idea, an efficacious solution to a given problem, then kill we would, and think no more of it than swatting a fly.

There was a metaphor to which Walker Stone had given considerable thought, lying alone in the dark silence. *We swatted flies with no thought at all of the life such action extin-*

guished. How many flies does a man kill in his lifetime? How many ants, spiders, mosquitoes? Were any of them any less alive than a man, a woman? Is life something to be quantified by size, dimensions? If it's so easy to kill a fly, is it then not just as easy to kill a bird? A gopher? A cat? A cow? How many of these deaths, deaths we never gave the tiniest consideration to, deaths we took as part and parcel of our place as rulers of the universe —how many of these tiny deaths add up to the numbing of a man's soul that allowed a creature like Errol Warner to come into the world?

Stone had gone through many periods of long concern over the inherent sanctity of life. Was it right to swat a fly? Was it right to slaughter a cow? He was strongly opposed to the use of animals in research, especially what he considered utterly useless cosmetic research. He was not comfortable either with much of the research done in the name of medicine. Animals, he had been told by people who should know, were too different in too many ways. If a process was successful on a dog, a cat, or a chimpanzee, it did not guarantee any success when used on humans. "The only study of man is man," Stone thought, and he believed it.

So, in this town gone mad, this bastion of civilization now surrendered to the lowest instincts of the human race, how much blame could truly be laid at the feet of the boy called Paul Trayne? How much of the groundwork, the preparation for Paul's coming, had been done by a thousand generations of human indifference? He thought of his library of videotapes, all the treasured sitcoms collected so painstakingly over the years. Half hours designed to bring laughter to those who watched, yet how many had derived their humor from the suffering and death of animals, pets? How many movies generated laughter from the killing of animals? How many yappy little dogs had been "killed" to get a laugh? And, extrapolating, how many people? He remembered himself laughing at *Kelly's Heroes,* one of his favorite movies, and only later coming to realize that not a little of that laughter had come from watching people—evil Nazis—being blown up en masse. Now audiences cheered at murder and dismemberment. Seemingly upstanding, decent men and women were drawn to the darker side. He needed only the increased circulation numbers Donna's articles in the *Advocate* had generated with her in-depth reporting on Errol Warner and his crimes to prove his sad thesis.

Stone sighed. He thought of Donna. He'd sent her here because the words in Ben Carpenter's article had suggested, even to one with his cynical viewpoint, that there might be something in the power of Paul Trayne that would save her from the evils that were slowly destroying her soul. Maybe even bring her around to the way she'd been when they had been together. Stone saw now the selfish motivation that tinged his action. Donna had been his, once. The territorial imperative had made him claim her. When he lost her, it made him look for a way—even a ridiculous, farfetched way—to get her back.

So he'd sent her to Faulkner. Against her will. Against any kind of common sense. Then he'd come himself. Because he loved her? Maybe. Or maybe to see if it had worked. To see if what she said was *true*. If there was something in the world that might undo the strand of cruelty and carelessness that seemed to thread its way through all of human history.

But he'd found it was true in a way he'd not considered. Now he did not know where Donna was. Did not know if she was even alive. He hoped—almost prayed—the story Clarence Nickerson had used to lure him out to Gunner's Field was entirely a lie. But it might not be.

"Chicago," he croaked.

Ben Carpenter did not hear at first, lost in his own bitter thoughts. Stone tried again.

"Chicago?" Ben said. "What?"

"Call." It took three tries for Ben to get the small word.

"Who?"

Stone had sent Clay Garber after Tom Sylvestri. At least, he was almost certain he had. He'd been losing it pretty fast at that point. He had to try that course again. "Garber," he croaked.

Ben didn't get it, being unfamiliar with the name. Stone sighed, then had an idea and pantomimed writing. Ben nodded, flashing his light around the room. There was no paper, no sign of a pen or pencil.

"I'll check the front desk," he said, and left.

Walker Stone would never see him again. Somehow he sensed it, knew that whatever demons now bedeviled Ben Carpenter would soon consume him. Alone again. Would he ever see Tom Sylvestri again? Or Clay Garber?

Or Donna?

Most of all, he would have sold his soul—if he believed he had one—right then and there, to see Donna just one more time. To know she was alive. To know his foolishness had not destroyed her.

"I do not think the mayor would want us to wait any longer." Robert Trayne's voice boomed from the microphone mounted on the speaker's dais at the center of the long table. The microphone squealed. Trayne leaned back from it. "When he realized he was going to be delayed," Trayne said, smiling, looking from eye to eye, taking in all the people assembled before him in the great hall, "he asked that we wait no longer than this. There are many needings here," he said, "and it was Mayor Stuartson's desire that Paul be allowed to attend to them as quickly as possible."

Watching alone from the converted cloakroom, Tom Sylvestri swallowed hard against the pounding of his heart. The moments of the plan were ticking by, one by one; he had no way of seeing how it was all going to come out.

Clay had come back to the cloakroom nearly an hour earlier, leaving the Reverend Trayne and Paul with Velma Fantuccio. He'd opened the door, poked his head in and said, "Now."

Tom's first instinct was to step toward the door, but Clay put out a hand to stop him. "I'll call you out later, Father," he said. Tom understood. Clay wanted him as a line of reserve. He could not say as much in front of the policemen guarding Warner, but now, with the plan in full gear, with their brains linked almost telepathically on the same course, he did not need to.

Garber had convinced Robert Trayne that Errol Warner was a perfect demonstration tool for Paul's power. If they wanted to convince this room of hard-boiled, no-nonsense power brokers that the tale the mayor had been telling them was true, how better than by freeing Errol Warner of his own terrible burden. They'd all read the stories, heard the news reports. They knew what Warner was supposed—*supposed*—to be carrying around inside him.

Now Tom looked out the narrow glass portal again. He was a long way from the center of activity, but he could see the head table clearly enough. Errol Warner sat next to Clay, the two of them occupying chairs that had been hastily summoned from somewhere behind the stage. The two cops, Warner's closest guards, stood at either end of the long table, watching, Tom was sure, for the tiniest sign of mischief from Warner. One kept fingering the small metal button that secured the leather flap of his holster across the top of his revolver.

What a surprise Warner's entrance had been! Tom could still see the faces on the gathered hundred as the most famous, most infamous man in all Chicago's well-laden history walked coolly and calmly into their midst. Al Capone himself could not have created such a stir, Tom thought, for about him there was the stuff of legend, the veneer of envious respect. Errol Warner had no such camouflage. Those who turned, those who looked—and that was everyone in the hall—saw only evil.

Now he sat listening to Reverend Trayne, smiling as he looked around the room, seeming completely calm, at rest, uncaring.

Paul sat at the other end of the table, next to Velma Fantuccio. The boy kept looking down the table length at Errol Warner.

What are you thinking? Tom wondered. *You've never come up against the likes of him before. But you must know the stories. Know what he's done.*

Tom's thoughts slowed, hesitated. He felt a weakness form at the center of his carefully maintained resolve.

What if Paul refused? What if Donna's assumption was right, that Paul was no more than a mutated human, and at the last moment, what if this poor, innocent, naïve young boy realized the enormity of what he would be taking from Errol Warner and flat-out refused to do it?

* * *

Donna was still clinging to the conviction that Paul was a pawn of Robert Trayne and that he could be saved from the web of evil at whose center he'd found himself. She felt this even now, as she leaned as close as she dared to the glass face of the booth, high in the heavy stone wall of the dining room's north end, looking across the heads of the chosen, looking at Paul Trayne.

It was not her intent to harm Paul. She felt certain there was every chance the massive bolt of concentrated evil he'd pull out of Errol Warner would overload his power, burn it out perhaps, but she was certain too that Paul himself would not be harmed. He might be left disoriented—after all, he'd had the power almost all his life. Losing it would have *some* effect, like losing the sense of touch—but Donna was sure he would recover, would be able to go on from this terrible place to live a normal, healthy life. The kind of life he would have had if he'd been born to normal parents, to a normal life.

She frowned as she thought this.

There was still that nagging notion that Robert Trayne was himself a victim of Paul's power. Perhaps the first to feel it. If that was true, it was a pity, for Donna could think of no way to free Robert Trayne from the effect of Paul's power. It had worn off on her. She was at least partly convinced it would wear off on anyone after a long enough time, but could this really be expected to happen to Robert Trayne? The evil she had seen in him was so total, so complete, she could think only that his exposure to Paul's power had been much greater than hers, than anyone's. Perhaps, she now thought, Trayne was exposed anew at each of the sessions Paul held, so that the effect of the son's power was reinforced in the father each time Paul used it, wiping away whatever small shred of decency might have grown back along the familiar pathways of Robert Trayne's corrupted brain.

That was how Donna had come to think of it. The brain was like some incredibly complex pattern of tubing, looping, and curving, interconnecting, filled with a vital fluid that flowed from one point to another through this amazing circuit, carrying feeling, emotion—life. Sometimes that fluid became polluted, poisoned. What Paul did was drain off the poison, so that some of the passages, some of the narrow tunnels, became empty and dry. Still there, still a vague awareness in the mind of the one touched by Paul's power, but no longer of serious consideration.

But slowly the vital fluid would find its way back into the passages. Slowly, as had happened with her, the power would shrink until the full function of the brain was back. If the person was lucky, nothing more would occur than the return of those griefs and guilts, those angers and annoyances that Paul Trayne had briefly sponged away. But if, in the time the barriers were down, the person had gone on to add more things to feel guilty about, more griefs to bear, the return of function might be more than a human brain could handle.

This, more than anything, was why Donna felt Robert Trayne could not, in the end, be saved. This, she had decided, was why all the attention should be focused on Paul. He was the one who was truly the greatest victim in all this. But he was the one who could yet be brought back to the sanity of the real world.

Now, as she thought of this, she thought too, for the first time, of all the channels that might have been opened in Paul's young mind. The effect of all the debris he'd siphoned from the souls of others. Not a pleasant thing to contemplate. Paul's effect on others was proving temporary, an elastic time frame that stretched or shrank according to the psyche within which it operated. Or so she was guessing, based on her own experience.

But how would Paul be with his power gone? Surely—*surely* —the things he had absorbed would go with the power. The power was, she was sure, the bottom of the bucket, the base of the unimaginable psychic container that held all the evils of Paul Trayne's fellow men. With the power, the bottom of the bucket, gone, everything would pour out.

But if those channels, those newly opened passages, remained, what would be their effect on Paul Trayne? If the passages that Paul emptied in others remained, what if the new thoughts, the new sensations introduced to Paul's brain remained in him?

If all that did not go when the power went, Donna suddenly

realized, the Paul Trayne who was left could very well be a creature of more concentrated evil than Errol Warner had ever been.

Paul listened to his father speaking. The old man droned on, the familiar recital, crafted and shaped carefully as Paul's power was tested here and there, on this one and that one. Making everyone in the audience understand what a terrible burden it was the poor, sweet boy would be taking. At each point, at each preplanned cue, Paul turned his face, lifted an eyebrow, summoned a brave smile.

Wanted to scream.

He had never felt so frustrated. The fat woman at his side kept squirming in her chair and putting out a flabby hand to touch his where it rested on the tablecloth. The people in the audience muttered and mumbled, nodding, taking in what Robert Trayne told them.

Paul was bored with it all. Bored with the game, the subterfuge. This was no burden he took upon himself. At first he thought it might have been, though he could no longer remember, no longer summon the exact feelings he'd had when his power manifested itself. It might have been the terrible burden Robert Trayne spoke of, once, but no longer. Paul savored the things his power had brought to his mind. The anger. The cruelty. It was intoxicating that he could open a piece of his brain and out of it would spill such wondrous thoughts, such images and imaginings as he had never dreamed could be.

There was rage here, building and building with each session. Great and potent fury that curled and roiled around his brain, making him bounce his knees together, under the table, so eager was he to get to the center of this matter, to let this rage boil out.

And the sex! Here was something he had barely begun to comprehend; now he understood all of it, all the twisted, dark, and dangerous pathways down which the drive for sexual gratification might lead him.

The Fantuccio woman revolted him, but in the audience there were so many women, so many beauties. How strange that in a world so full of women, so full of beauty, the major source of the frustrations, the angers, and the griefs that came to him should be sexual. He could not understand it at all, that a man should feel frustrated, feel himself pent up inside like some caged beast, when all the women he might want were there, fresh fruit upon the vine, to be plucked and used as he needed.

Paul thought about Donna Wojciechowski. What a pity he had never had the chance to have his way with her as he had with Marjorie Garber. Marjorie was in wonderful condition— he knew this from the memories, the comparisons that had come with his acceptance of the thoughts and feelings of others —but Donna was so much better. He wished she had not escaped him. But then there was every chance, every likelihood, in fact, that he would be able to recapture her. Then he would be able to use her as his newfound desires told him he should.

His father droned on.

Paul licked his lips and looked again at Errol Warner. Paul had heard of the man, of course. He remembered, as one remembers a fragment of a fading dream, how terrible it had seemed, the things Warner had done. All those young women! But now, now it seemed not nearly so bad. Why not torture? There was much sexual gratification in this, Paul had discovered. The inflicting of pain was a great aphrodisiac. Errol Warner must have explored avenues of delight that Paul—even Paul, with his burgeoning awareness—could only begin to guess at. And soon, soon, Paul would be able to open himself to that mind, to those delicious thoughts and memories.

He would learn so much! He would feel so much!

If his father would only get on with it! If his father would only stop talking!

"Ladies and gentlemen," Robert Johnston Trayne said at last, at long, long last, "Paul."

23

Here it comes.

Donna felt faint. Her heart pounded so hard she could barely breathe. Down a pink-tinged tunnel she watched Paul Trayne rise and walk the length of the table to where his father stood waiting, the biggest, warmest, kindliest smile splitting his great Lincoln face. He reached out a hand and placed it on Paul's shoulder as the boy came alongside him.

The crowd was applauding, the sound echoing in the big hall, doubling and redoubling until it seemed to Donna, even behind the shelter of the thick glass, that it must be a thousand people slapping their hands together down there, five thousand people.

She pressed her hands over her ears and leaned back against the side wall of the booth. She forced herself to breathe slowly, carefully. She knew what this was. Panic. Raw panic, welling up inside her. All the madness, all the stress of the past days catching up at last, magnifying her senses, making everything too loud, too bright, too sharp. The rounded edge of the commentator's desk, pressing against the outside of her right thigh, felt like a knife through Tom's thick coat. The lights of the hall were suns exploding.

Donna crouched down and put her head between her knees, breathing, breathing. She was not going to lose it now. The image of a silent serial heroine clinging to the cliff by her fingernails came to her mind. Walker would have been proud of her, she thought.

She found the strength she needed in the thought of Walker Stone. He was alive! He was in Faulkner. When this was all over, she could get a car, drive down there, find him, be with him. That much, at least, she had been given by the power of Paul Trayne.

When this was all over.

She rose, sliding her back up the wall. She'd missed some small portion of the action. Robert Trayne had evidently introduced—unnecessary in this crowd—Clay Garber. Clay was walking toward the place where Trayne and Paul stood. He seemed to Donna to be moving in slow motion, his huge form an icebreaker crashing through an arctic sea.

He reached the podium. He shook hands with Robert Trayne. Donna marveled at the strength contained in that simple, everyday gesture. He turned to face the audience.

"I've never been much for believing in fate," Clay said. "Capital *F* Fate. The Fate that manipulates people's lives. When people fall in love and say they were 'fated' to meet, the image just never works for me. I always find myself thinking that for them to be 'fated,' then their parents would have to have been 'fated.' And their parents, and their parents, and all the whole history of the world, back to the very beginning. Maybe that's too literal an interpretation, but then, I'm a pretty literal guy."

A smattering of laughter and applause. Clay drew strength from it, from the support—however unconscious—of his fellow human beings.

"But in the past few days," he went on, "I've started to take something of a different look at the idea of Fate. This boy"—a nod to Paul Trayne—"and the amazing sequence of events that brought him here, now, have made me think there just might be something to Fate after all." *And if my dear old mother's looking down from heaven right now, she'll be wanting me to wash my mouth out with soap by the time I'm done with this lie.*

"It must have been Fate that first brought Paul to the attention of Walker Stone," Clay said. "And Fate that made him send Donna Wojciechowski down to Faulkner to investigate the story. Fate that made Donna bring Paul to my house, when she brought him back here to Chicago. Because, you see, we were both in a perfect position to do Paul a great service, right here, right now. Donna had just completed her brilliant articles on Errol Warner. I was the top police official in the city. And Mr. Warner"—Clay used the polite title with deliberate effect —"is, you might say, just what the doctor ordered, as far as Paul Trayne and his gift are concerned."

He turned to Warner and gestured for him to approach. Warner rose slowly so as not to aggravate or alarm his guarding policemen, whose hands were still close to their holstered pistols. He walked the same distance Clay had crossed a few moments earlier and took his place at one side of the Commissioner.

"You all know this man," Clay said. "Perhaps you'll be surprised, knowing what you know of him, to hear that he has come here tonight, at my request, freely and without any sort of deals being made. Perhaps," Clay said, summoning the biggest part of this big, big lie, "he understands the power Paul possesses. Perhaps he realizes the wonderful gift of this boy will give him the only chance he will ever have in this life to be free of the terrible burden of guilt we all know he must bear. The anguish we all know must be writhing around in his soul." He looked at Warner as he said this. Warner smiled his schoolboy smile. In that moment Clay felt a coldness at the center of his chest. *If we're wrong on this, if we're wrong . . .*

"My pleasure, Commissioner," Warner said. He turned slightly, thrust a hand toward Reverend Trayne. "Hi. We weren't properly introduced. Errol Warner."

Trayne shook the offered hand and brought Paul closer with his free hand. "My son," Trayne said.

"Hi," Warner said.

"Hello," Paul said. Clay had the distinct impression of the two sizing each other up, gauging each other's strengths. What would Paul see in Warner, Clay wondered? And what would Warner possibly see in Paul? What *could* he possibly see?

"How do you want to do this?" Warner asked. His voice was calm. He sounded very normal, Clay thought. His tone was so mundane, so very much of the ordinary, everyday world. He might have been a furniture mover saying, "Where do you want this chair?" Helpful, but not really concerned, not really plugged into the moment, the event.

"Perhaps," Paul said, "if you could stand in front of the table?"

"Over there?" Warner tipped his head toward a spot about ten feet directly in front of where Clay stood, between the two closest tables, the two most distinguished parties of dignitaries.

"That would be fine," Paul said.

Clay hung on Paul's every word, every syllable. If anything went wrong now, it would have to be detected almost before Paul himself was aware of it. The least nuance, the tiniest hint would be all that stood between Clay Garber and—what? Clay was not altogether certain what the outcome of this evening might be, should their desperate gambit fail. Despite what Tom might think, Clay could not bring himself to vest Paul Trayne with truly supernatural power. He did not believe Paul would be able to do very much if the trick failed. No calling down of lightnings. No summoning of earthquakes. Mostly, Clay knew, it would depend on just how much influence Paul had already worked in this crowd. They had no way to be sure to what extent Paul's power operated on an unconscious level. Just how much had already seeped into the people sitting around this hall, drinking their drinks, eating their dinners, wondering how much of what they'd been told could be true?

Clay was certain there was a key in that, in the degree to which people came to Paul Trayne *prepared* to believe in him, in what he offered. Donna had gone to Faulkner, she'd told them, wishing something like Paul Trayne could come into the world and sweep away all the bitterness, the human foibles that so despoiled what could be, what might be.

But Walker had sent her to debunk the boy, Clay believed. Walker had never for a moment believed in the power of Paul Trayne. Neither did Clay, himself. How many of these familiar faces might be here eager, willing to believe? Many of them, in fighting their way to the top of the heap, had done things to be ashamed of, things that would carry tremendous burdens of guilt. Those who had not done the deeds themselves might be troubled by what their fathers and grandfathers had done while carving out the empires over which they now held sway. There was a price, Clay knew, that came with wealth and power; that price was a peeling away of one's humanity, layer by layer, until only the hard, unfeeling inner core remained.

"This okay?" Warner had sat down on the long table, swung his legs up and around, and dropped to the floor on the other side. In three paces he'd taken the position Paul indicated.

Paul nodded. "If we could just have a moment of silence, now."

Clay took a deep breath, measuring distances. Paul. Robert Trayne. The door. He looked at the narrow slot on the far wall, the projection window behind which Tom Sylvestri waited.

Now, he thought. *Whatever happens, it happens now.*

Paul frowned. He was having trouble concentrating. This was something new. His head was so full of distracting thoughts he was having great difficulty focusing on the man in front of him, on Errol Keane Warner.

There was a woman just to Warner's right. She had curly, blond hair and a long neck above broad shoulders accentuated by the cut of her gown. Her lips were full, pink against pale skin. Her eyes were large, and they did not stray from Paul Trayne. Much as Paul tried to bend his concentration to the task at hand, his eyes kept slipping away from Errol Warner, slipping to the curve of the woman's bosom above the top of her dress, to the swooping line that accentuated the soft, shadowed Y of her cleavage. His brain filled with streams of consciousness over which he had no control. One image piled up against the next, all dark, sexual. A piece of his brain was still sufficiently unsullied that he could remember a time when these images, these thoughts would have frightened him. They made him think of his mother, of what his father had made him do to his mother. They made him remember a time when the things he thought of now—the things he'd done to Marjorie Garber—made him weep for the memory of his mother, the child-bride, so afraid of Robert Trayne. As Paul himself was afraid, until he learned his power could control his father, at least to the point of deflecting Trayne's rages. Many had suf-

fered since Paul Trayne came to his power, but Paul himself
was no longer one of them.

"What's wrong, boy?" Robert Trayne, close at Paul's shoulder, leaned forward to bring his mouth close to his son's ear.
"What's wrong? Why don't you do what you have to do?"

Paul did not turn to look at Trayne. He tried to keep his eyes
on Errol Warner.

But that woman. The blond woman. Her soft skin. The way
the light caught her shoulders, the long curve of her collar-
bones.

The man sitting next to her was older than she, Paul thought.
Not enough to be scandalous, but enough that his face showed
more years than hers. Paul did not like the way he angled
himself to be as close to her as the curvature of their table
allowed. The way he put his hand on hers, where it rested on
the tablecloth. Paul's brain burned with images of these two
locked in coital passions. Of her body bending, arching under
his. Sometimes the man's face changed in Paul's mind, and it
was his own face he saw, his own passions that vented themselves on the woman's eager flesh. But then the face of the
stranger would return, the face of this rich man, powerful man,
who could command the company of such a woman.

Power? Paul thought, as the stream of pictures raced
through his brain. *You think you have power? With your
money. Your fancy clothes. Your big houses. You have nothing!
I have power. I can show you power.*

He turned his eyes back to Errol Warner.

"I don't feel anything yet," the murderer of young women
said. He smiled.

"You will," Paul said. He reached into the part of his brain
that controlled the power. He turned the center of it toward
Errol Warner.

"You will," Paul said again. He reached out with invisible
tendrils, one mind reaching for another. He always saw it like
this, as if slender filaments were growing out of his forehead,
invisible, intangible, probing into the mind of the one who had
come before him. It was always the same. The sensations were
the same. The weakness he felt. The look in the faces of those
he touched. Always the same.

Expecting nothing to be any different here, Paul reached into the mind of Errol Warner.

Tom snapped back from the window. He felt the touch of Paul Trayne's power in his mind as a physical thing, a wind blowing across the innermost recesses of his psyche.

He stepped back from the window, but the feeling remained, strengthened. Paul was unleashing everything he had, Tom realized. He was not focusing his power on Errol Warner, as their plan required. He was opening himself to the whole room, everyone, simultaneously.

Why? What could have driven him to such an act? What could be its possible purpose?

He reached inside his coat and seized the shaft of the ancient crucifix. He felt the contours of the filigree against his hand, the shape of the figure of the Savior, so very different in its studied realism from the abstract form that hung above the nave of St. Timothy's. He drew strength from the familiar shape, the honored meaning of the object. He looked back out the narrow window. He squinted to see Paul's distant face more clearly. There was something there. Something that hinted of an answer to his question. Surprise, Tom thought. Even shock. Paul was experiencing something he had not expected. His power was out of his control. Tom was sure of it.

But there was nothing he could do. Not then. Not as he felt his soul twisting inside him, as all the griefs, pains, guilt, anger, envy, bitterness, pettiness—everything came boiling up, surging up, pounding against the front of his skull as if that curve of bone were a stone wall, a dike built up to hold back the relentless pounding of a poisonous sea.

There was Joseph. Poor, sweet, foolish Joseph. Every word they'd ever spoken, every touch they'd ever exchanged. It was all there, spread across the forefront of Tom's mind, across the breadth of this moment of his reality, as if it were all here and now. The soft words, the harsh words. The anger. The love. At one and the same moment Tom lay in the arms of his gentle lover and looked down at his sad, dead face. At one and the same moment he heard the sound of Joseph's laugh—so free, so uninhibited—and heard the cold, echoing thud of the morgue drawer sliding back into place, bearing Joseph's body into darkness.

If Paul stopped now, Tom knew, stopped with everything pulled to the front, pulled to the outer edge of the mind, it would be as if he'd been thrown into hell. It would be that way for everyone there. All the things they'd ever tried to repress, every bad moment, every emotional scar suddenly ripped open, smeared with salt.

It would be an unspeakable horror if everyone should be left like that, stripped bare, torn ragged by Paul's unleashed power. Tom knew he must do something. He must act. He must find a way to undo this, to break the spell. He staggered under the weight of his own released emotions, but in the cross he held he must find the strength to act.

Now. While there was still time.

Donna lurched back, stifling a scream with both hands thrown hard across her mouth.

Paul Trayne was everywhere in her mind. There was not the least corner of her brain that did not hold his presence.

She came up against the rear wall of the booth, and the back of her head slammed hard against it. Lights swam before her eyes. She took her right hand away from her mouth and put it against the wall at her side, steadying herself. Through the wall of glass before her she saw Paul Trayne facing Errol Warner. In Donna's eyes Paul seemed to burn with cold, white fire. He was a center of pain, a focus of agony, and it seemed, every bit of it, directed solely at her.

So much so that it took her nearly a minute to come to the same realization Tom Sylvestri had arrived at almost immediately. Paul was unleashing the full vigor of his power on the whole crowd, perhaps the whole building. Donna prayed it was not the whole city, the country, the world. She did not believe Paul was that powerful, but she did not *know*.

In the minute it took her to understand what was happening, the string of dominoes set tumbling by Ben Carpenter's article came to a sudden end on the slate floor below the commentator's booth. Donna was too lost, for that minute, too lost in her own anguish, to understand fully what had happened.

* * *

Paul blinked.

Clay had taken two steps back when the first wave of Paul's unleashed power hit him. He had not known what to expect—Donna's most vivid description could not have prepared him—but it was not this. He'd seen Paul's power in action. He understood it to be a focused, directed thing. But this was the power gone wild. This was the power reaching out to everyone, all at once without warning. At tables all around, jaws went slack. People jerked back in their chairs, eyes wide. Mouths opened to speak, to shout, perhaps to scream. But no sound came. Everyone was trapped in the sudden impact of Paul Trayne's power.

But why had the boy unleashed it like this?

Clay stood now firmly rooted, pulling back against the physical sensation, the feeling of razor-sharp fingers tearing through his brain, through the shields he'd built there in fifty years. He gritted his teeth and forced himself to think straight, to ignore the relentless pounding of his own emotions.

Paul was wavering!

He could see it. Clay was sure it was not wishful thinking. The boy was trembling. A shudder ran up and down his slender frame, growing stronger. His eyes were wide. The tendons of his neck stood out like ropes, as if straining to keep the boy's head from flying off his shoulders.

Clay looked at Errol Warner. He was a mirror image of Paul, stiff, shaking, his face contorted almost like a child's, an exasperated child holding his breath to win what he demanded.

Clay found the strength to take a step forward, then another. He regained the ground he'd lost to the first impact of Paul's power. He was within striking distance of the boy now. The imagery of the corded neck was so strong Clay almost believed a good, solid swing of his right hand would indeed dislodge the head, send it sailing back to crash against the faux medieval tapestries above the head table.

But he did not swing. He waited. Waited one second, two. And in that moment came a sound. A scream. But a scream like nothing Clay Garber had ever heard. Not in all the years of his life. Not in war. Not in one horrible, never-to-be-forgotten visit to the great Chicago stockyards.

Clay turned his head away from Paul Trayne. He looked back at the man standing before the head table. The murderer. The man with the incongruous, innocuous schoolboy face.

Errol Warner was holding his breath no longer. His head was thrown back, his mouth opened wider than Clay would have believed a human jaw could spread. The flesh of his cheeks and jawline creased into accordion folds, bleached white from lack of blood.

From that awful, gaping, distended maw issued forth a cry that Clay Garber did not believe could have been equaled by the voices of a hundred souls pitched headlong into boiling tar.

Nothing in Paul's experience prepared him for this. Nothing.

If he believed himself to have drunk deep the heady draught of unexpurgated evil, now he learned he had merely sipped from a crystal goblet of the most purified water.

What came from Errol Warner's psyche was beyond measure, beyond description. No guilt at all. No grief. No shame. No pain. Only pleasure. Joy. The screams of his victims echoed forever through the dark corridors of his brain, and with each resounding, Errol Warner rejoiced.

The memory of each moment, each long, agonized hour with each victim, was as clear and fresh in Warner's brain as if it were unfolding now, this moment. Flesh that peeled away in long, slender strips did so by the manipulation of Paul's own fingers, gleaming, chrome-plated instruments held in his own hands. Warm blood flowed across his own flesh. Pleas for mercy—ever softer, ever weaker—fell upon his own uncaring ears.

Paul reeled before it all. He felt himself lifted, rising on his toes, the force of all that came from Errol Warner pushing into him, blasting away his own small defenses, knocking down all thought or hope that Paul might have of drawing things only to the surface and leaving them there.

That had been his plan. That had been the way he'd thought to punish all these smug, rich, powerful people. The men with their expensive women. The women, too, for their own lack of character.

But that was no longer Paul's choice. The floodgates of his power were indeed opened wide, but the flow through those floodgates had turned into a raging torrent, a surge driven by hurricane force, filling Paul Trayne, expanding him, stretching him beyond his small capacity to contain.

Paul gasped for breath. He staggered. He reached out, blindly, his fingers digging into the only support he could find, the shirt fronts of the two men standing closest to him, his father and Clay Garber.

He hung onto them, leaning back as the weight of Errol Warner's terrible joy pushed down on him, as the fire of it burned through him, as the electricity of it blasted open every synapse of his brain and all the universe opened itself to Paul Trayne.

Opened like a black and bottomless mouth. An abyss.

He trembled at the edge of it. The edge crumbled.

Paul began to fall.

Errol Warner had given no consideration at all to what this evening might bring. He was, in his own way, a man firmly grounded in the reality of the everyday world. He could not have done the things he'd done, he was sure, had this not been absolutely the case.

His mother and father had raised him in a strict fundamentalist Christian household. They had taught him the truth of the Bible was in every word, in every line, as stated. There was no room for interpretation. If the Bible said God created the heavens and the earth in six days, it meant six days, six periods of twenty-four hours each. If woman was made from man's rib, she was made from man's rib, and man, every man, to this day, would have one less rib to show this.

They would not let the weight of any mundane evidence sway them. They taught Errol Warner that there was no room for interpretation. If the Bible said there was a Devil, there was a Devil, and he was a fallen angel, and he tempted Jesus, and he ruled over a kingdom to which all lesser, tainted souls would be inevitably condemned.

Errol Warner believed all this, deeply, fully, until his sixteenth birthday. Then two friends—friends only in the broadest possible terms, he supposed, since he was too introverted then to really have friends—decided that everything that could ever be wrong with young Errol could be solved completely by the most simple and direct expedient: they decided to get him laid.

That was how they put it. Such phrasing was strange to Errol then. The whole concept of sex for pleasure, for its own sake, was unknown to him, even at what his friends considered such an advanced age. Sex, as much as he knew or understood, was wholly and solely for the procreation of the race. It was something humans endured, but the most exacting reading of the Bible—the kind of reading his parents insisted upon—told Errol Warner it was not something to be enjoyed.

His friends, though, that day seventeen years ago, were confronted with something of a problem: how to accomplish their goal? They could not afford to hire a prostitute for Errol's initiation. If they could, in any case, they would have seen the money best spent on themselves.

Nor were the girls they knew, the girls in their various classes at Maine Township High School, in pleasant, suburban Park Ridge, particularly inclined to the kind of activity they had in mind. They were free enough with their favors, with those boys from whom they felt they had the proper degree of promised commitment, but for the kind of one-night event his friends planned for Errol, this was not good enough by half.

Except that there was Carolyn Shawn, and Carolyn Shawn was known—reputed—to have two elements about her that made her an ideal subject for the assignment. She had a known weakness for sob stories, birds with broken wings, and she had no tolerance for alcohol whatsoever.

If they could convince her Errol was to be alone and miserable on this most significant of birthdays, she might be enticed into joining him for a highly illegal drink in his parents' garage.

The trick, the friends knew, was to keep the uptight, anally retentive Errol from discovering what they were about until it was too late.

Errol had surprisingly little actual memory of the event that was to so change his life, so shape his young psyche. He remembered joining his friends in the loft of the garage, the dimly lighted mold-scented sanctum he'd created for himself out of carefully arranged cardboard boxes and an old rug and mattress his mother had set out for the trashmen to take away. There, in the slats of horizontal light that filtered through the vent above the doors of the garage, Errol Warner would sit among the cobwebs and think, wondering about the mysteries of life that lay beyond the strict boundaries proscribed by his parents, fearing the bolt of lightning that would surely strike down from the heavens, obliterating him forever if he let his thoughts stray too far.

Never had he allowed his thoughts to reach the point of what confronted him as he climbed into the loft space on the afternoon of his sixteenth birthday. His friends had cornered him after school, scurried him home before either of his parents would get back from work. It was a warm, late September day, and they knew very well Errol would have loitered on his way home had they not impelled him.

They waited below as he climbed the ladder to his loft. They watched as he reached the top, stopped, and looked back at them in a mixture of wonder and disbelief.

"Hello, Errol," Carolyn Shawn had said. She was sitting on the box they'd brought up for her, a vision in pale pink and white in the afternoon light, dust motes dancing all around her in the divided darkness. "Sure is stinky up here, isn't it?"

That much Errol remembered. Beyond that, there was a darkness, a red-tinged blur that came back into something like the real world only when a scream and a sharp pain pierced the shroud across his memory. Then he saw himself lying atop Carolyn Shawn. He saw the way her pink sweater was pushed up. He saw the way her breasts looked, nearly as pink against the stark white of her bra.

He felt again the pain of the slap, the second slap, as Carolyn struck out at him. He felt himself roll away from her. Felt new pain as his head thumped against the unadorned wall of the garage.

He saw Carolyn scramble to her feet. Saw the fury in her eyes. Heard her screaming at him, threatening him with all the fires of damnation. He saw her start to climb down the ladder and pause to shout at the boys still waiting below, telling them to get away, to stop trying to look up her dress.

Errol crawled to the edge of the loft floor and looked down. He saw and heard the heated exchange below. The boys realized the seriousness of their situation. They would go down along with Errol unless they did something, here, now, fast.

What they did was to kill Carolyn Shawn.

Errol was amazed by the speed at which it happened. One boy grabbed Carolyn and pushed her back against the rear wall of the empty garage. The other grabbed a shovel from the rack by the door. He swung. The edge of the blade caught Carolyn Shawn under her chin, the corner biting deep into the flesh of her neck.

The boy pulled back.

Errol saw a spray of blood spit across the dimly lighted garage. It drew a line of remarkable length and straightness across the dirty, dusty floor.

Carolyn's hands flew up to her throat. They clutched at the wound, her eyes wide, her fingers scrabbling as if to somehow hold together the ruin of her throat. Her mouth opened to scream, but her windpipe was severed below her vocal chords. All that came out was a gurgle.

She fell forward. Blood sprayed again as her hands came away from her throat, arms snapping out to block her fall. She went down on hands and knees, each fraction of a second like an hour now to Errol Warner.

She tried to crawl, two, three feet. Her hands left bloody prints on the cement.

The boy with the shovel raised it again and brought it down hard on the back of Carolyn's head. She pitched forward full length, rolling, hands up to block the next blow. The next blow went between her hands. Errol heard the wet crunch of bone as her face collapsed under the force of the swing. There was blood all over the front of her pink sweater. A trail of blood on the floor.

The boy swung again.

Again.

Carolyn lay still.

The boy looked up.

"Well, don't just lie there," he snarled. "Come down and help us get rid of this." He kicked Carolyn's side. Errol was not then sure if the boy was making a great show of not caring to bolster himself against the horror of what he had done, or if the boy really did not care.

Errol climbed down the ladder. It was hot and still in the garage. He wondered what time it was. The hairs on the back of his neck prickled as he waited for the automatic garage door opener to make its characteristic *thunk* as the chains locked, as the door opened.

"Where can we put her?" It was the boy who did not hold the shovel. Errol could not give him a name for a long moment. He seemed, then and there, utterly unconnected with the boy whose name seemed to belong to that face.

"Where . . . ?" Errol could remember quite clearly the way his brain refused to function, the way even the most simple of concepts seemed now strange and untenable.

"We gotta hide the body," the shovel boy said. He, too, had become a nameless thing, not connected in any way with school, with baseball, with life.

"Hide the body," Errol said.

"If anybody finds the body," the shovel boy said, "they'll know you killed her."

Errol blinked. "I didn't . . ."

"This is your dad's garage," the shovel boy said. "Your dad's shovel. Who else coulda killed her?"

"They'll know it was you," the other boy said. "They'll arrest you. An' you'll get hung. And then"—a brilliant touch here, Errol was sure the boy thought—"you'll burn in hell forever."

Errol Warner was quite sure he understood what that was meant to do to him. Everyone knew about his parents, his upbringing. Most of the neighborhood kids had Christian families who taught relaxed versions of the dogma drilled into Errol Warner. They feared that vague, uncomprehensible thing called Hell, though not so much, they would have said, as they were sure Errol Warner did.

But if it was their scheme to draw him into an inescapable

web and place him at the center so they might themselves escape, it was not fated to work to their plan. Errol Warner was already at the center of a web, a web spun by his parents, so vast and strong these boys could never begin to understand it. So vast and strong, in fact, that there would never be a hope of escape for Errol unless—a mighty and insurmountable "unless"—the web itself somehow vanished.

It vanished then.

Errol Warner could not trace the precise course of his thoughts, the avenues along which his brain raced in those few moments in that hot garage in September of his sixteenth year, but the place at which his thoughts ended, the destination they had perhaps always been aimed for, was a place without the stark restrictions of his upbringing. A place where he was not threatened with eternal hellfire and damnation.

Faced with the near certainty of such everlasting agony, Errol Warner's young mind took the only route it could to save itself: it banished any possibility of such things being real. It drove them out, suddenly, completely, in less time than it would have taken him to express the thought. Confronted with damnation, Errol Warner, then and there, decided there was no such thing as damnation. Confronted with an act of unspeakable evil, Errol Warner understood there was no such thing as evil.

He reached out a hand to take the shovel from the boy who held it. They were right on one score, of course. The rest of the world, having not had the experience of Errol's sudden revelation, would seek to punish him for this deed.

He took the shovel. He swung the shovel. The first boy fell, half his skull sheared away by the force of Errol's blow.

The second boy almost made it to the door.

Errol dragged them both to the foot of the ladder to his loft. He went back and started to drag Carolyn Shawn's body over too. He knelt beside her. Her face was smashed in, broken, and bloodied. Her throat was ripped from side to side.

He reached out and touched the jagged wetness. He lifted his fingers into the light, turning his hand so sunlight drew gleaming lines up and down the dark, wet blood.

He wiped his fingers on Carolyn's sweater. He stroked the

sweater, the breasts confined by the bra beneath. He ran his fingertips over the hem of the sweater, the top of her skirt.

He scowled. There was no time for anything but hiding the bodies. His mother and father would be home soon.

He rose and pulled Carolyn's surprisingly heavy corpse up onto his back, pulling the arms around his head. He felt her face and neck fail wet against his head. He carried her across the garage and struggled up the ladder to his loft.

He laid her out on the old, musty mattress. He climbed down, got the boy who'd swung the shovel, and heaved him up the ladder. Errol was strong even then. His strength served him well that afternoon as the shadows lengthened and he struggled and sweated in the furnace of the garage.

He got the second boy up to the loft. He was not sure what to do beyond that, certain only that the bodies could lie there for a while, a few days, at least. His parents never looked up here. There was the problem that they would start to stink— Errol remembered coming home from three weeks' vacation to find ruined hamburger in a refrigerator that had failed while he and his parents were gone. He had no reason to assume human flesh would be any different from beef.

Still, it was stinky enough in that loft, as Carolyn had said. And there was a way, Errol knew, to cover both the coming stench and the blood on the floor of the garage.

He climbed back down the ladder. Carolyn's blood was mingled with the boys', drying on his back, flaking. He ignored it and moved quickly, purposefully. His father always kept a can of gasoline in one of the many racks he'd built around the garage. Errol found it and lifted it out. He unscrewed the top and tipped the can. Three gallons of gasoline gurgled through the opening, splashing across the floor. It washed the blood from the cement. Most had soaked into the dust and dirt that was a constant layer on the hard floor. What little had soaked all the way through left a stain quickly disguised by the flood of petrol.

The gas washed the floor, carrying the evidence to the edge of the concrete apron, where a half-inch gap opened between cement and wall. The gasoline and the gore ran over the edge and soaked down into the earth below.

Errol set the can on one side, on the floor. He positioned it carefully, trying to make it look as if it had been dropped carelessly.

Satisfied, he left the garage, went into the house, and stripped off his clothes. He washed his shirt and slacks in the big tin tub in the basement and poured the stained water into the drain in the center of the floor. He tossed the clothes into the dryer.

In his underwear he went back upstairs, to the second floor, the bathroom. He took a quick shower and was just drying his hair as he heard the distant *thunk* of the automatic garage door opener. He dressed quickly and ran down to the garage to apologize for the spilled gasoline. He'd been trying to clean up the garage, he told his father.

Lying, as with a great many other things, was coming to Errol Warner with increasing ease.

Everything in his life from that moment on became easier. He decided the best way to dispose of the three corpses in his loft was to cut them in pieces. He stole a large butcher's cleaver from K mart—theft presenting no barrier to him now —and chopped them up, bit by bit, over the next several weeks.

In that time the investigation raged through the neighborhood. Three kids missing. Where were they?

Errol, seeing no reason not to, volunteered that Ray and Steve—yes, those were their names—had tried to get him to go with them and Carolyn. They were going to go into Chicago, downtown Chicago, he said. It was his birthday, and they wanted him to go.

The center of the search shifted to downtown Chicago.

Errol continued chopping up the bodies, scattering them bit by bit. The neighborhood dogs did well by Errol Warner that September.

Errol Warner began to learn there were pleasures he had never guessed. After those first two, the rest were easy—easier each time, in fact. So easy, eventually, that *not* killing, *not* torturing, maiming, destroying, became more difficult than doing it. To restrain himself from the act was a greater task than simply letting it happen.

And in all the years since, with all the killings since, he'd never once felt anything but pleasure. The screams and pleadings of his victims were a gourmet's feast. The sounds of torture—the strange, unique *skritching* of skin pulling away from flesh—were symphonies orchestrated for his delight. He took pleasure in the pain of his victims. He took delight in the cold, smooth feel of the instruments.

Until now.

Until he faced Paul Trayne.

Tom reached the main doors of the hall. He stood staring, shaking, his knees barely strong enough to support him as the contents of his soul were torn from him, pushed back, torn out again.

Fifty feet away Paul Trayne faced Errol Warner, and for all Tom could see there was no visual evidence that anything unusual was happening. The boy faced the man, the man faced the boy. A few paces to Paul's right, Clay Garber stood, broad and dark, a mountain. A few paces to the left, Robert Trayne, also dark, but slender, a serpent.

All around the hall people remained in their places, frozen in their places. Here, if anywhere, Tom thought, was the only suggestion all was not as it should be. Everyone was stiff and still. No one seemed even to breathe.

And Tom knew why. If they were experiencing even a fraction of what he was feeling, they would have no strength to move.

Every emotion Tom Sylvestri had ever known, every thought, every memory, was being dragged up from the most distant reaches of his inner being, dredged up and spread across his conscious brain, a vast, numbing ocean of joy, pain, grief, delight, all surging and slamming against him simultaneously. And like an ocean there were tides in this flood. The sea of sensation drew near, high, crashing down on him before it suddenly pulled back, back, almost to the limits of his awareness.

Tom tried to understand, tried to force some semblance of sanity from the torrent. He concentrated on the face and form of the boy, Paul. He focused his strength, his will, into a single

eam, like the beam of a lighthouse beacon, he thought,
unching through the miasma of emotion, giving him a center
bout which he could turn his thoughts.

Paul was trying to take the weight of whatever evils lurked
1 the heart and soul of Errol Warner. But something was
rong. This much Tom was sure of. Something had gone com-
letely wrong with the plan—their plan, perhaps even Paul's
lan.

Paul and Warner faced each other, and Tom guessed
Varner's face must be as blank and uncomprehending as the
xpression he saw on the boy's face. They were at the nexus of
he riptide of emotions. Whatever Tom felt was flowing back
nd forth between them magnified a thousandfold. He was
nly at the very edge of the cyclone, and his heart and mind
vere almost torn in two by what he felt. For Paul and Warner,
vhat must it be like?

He's no demon, then, Tom thought.

Warner's simple human evil wouldn't be enough to cause
his effect, were Paul Trayne really the monster Tom had suspected. Nothing in the soul of Errol Warner could begin to
equal the unexpurgated evil a true demon would have within
tself. So Donna was right, after all. Paul was nothing more
han a boy, a mutant boy. And now, because of their scheme,
heir plan—the plan Tom had at least partially endorsed—that
poy was being thrown into a maelstrom of grief and guilt, pain
and anguish such as Tom could only begin to guess at.

He pushed himself away from the door frame. He forced his
ellied knees to take his weight. One step. Another.

Paul Trayne was a boy. An innocent boy.

He must be saved from the horror Tom Sylvestri had allowed to be unleashed upon him. Tom pulled the cross from
the folds of his coat and advanced toward Errol Warner's back.

Clay felt what Paul felt.

Not as strongly, for he was not the center of power from
which this nightmare spun, but he saw what Paul saw, felt what
Paul felt, as he knew the older Trayne and perhaps a dozen of
the closer observers must also be seeing and feeling.

He knew what had happened to Marjorie.

In all the whirling madness of emotion that surged and roiled about Paul Trayne, that image, perhaps because it was so dear and important to Clay, sprang out as if lit by hellfire.

He knew what Marjorie had done with Paul. Knew what Marjorie had done to Stuartson. Worst, worst, worst, he knew what Paul Trayne had done to Marjorie. Hot tears stung his eyes.

"Baby," he said, his brain filled with a lifetime of happy memories turned suddenly to bitter bile.

His big hands reached out for the back of Paul Trayne's neck.

Robert Trayne, too, was weeping.

For nearly ten years, since he'd first known the touch of his son's power, there had been nothing in Robert Johnston Trayne's life that elicited from him the least degree of sorrow.

Especially not memory. Memory, for Robert Trayne, had become a thing insubstantial, a fleeting, unimportant thing that had no bearing on his daily life. In memory, after all, lay only sadness, remembrance of those things he had done, those terrible things he had done, since Paul's power freed him to do them.

All in a good cause, of course. He had never doubted that everything he did, from the least to the greatest evil, was in a good and righteous cause. This was what he told Paul. This was what he believed.

Until now.

Now his son's power had gone wrong, gone out of control. He'd seen the stillness come into Paul's face, seen the way his fingers curled—the way they always curled—as he prepared to take on the guilts and griefs of the infamous Errol Warner, and then . . .

Then the floodgates opened, and everything Robert Trayne had done in the last ten years—beginning with the slow and agonizing murder of his dear, dear wife—had come back, come back full flame to sear his soul and make him want to scream as his wife had screamed, beg as his wife had begged.

Then it was all gone, again, and there was peace, and nothing he looked at in the long scroll of his memory caused him the slightest pain.

Then it did, all at once, all again, pounding down on him, crushing him.

Then relief again.

Pain.

Relief.

In one of those fragments of relief, in one of those moments when Paul's power was doing what it was supposed to do, Robert Trayne saw Clay Garber move, saw him reach out for Paul's throat.

Robert Trayne moved too.

Donna stumbled as she walked. She reached the stairs and clung to the banister as she tried to make it down the steep flight, but the world rolled like a small ship on a stormy sea. Her feet would not stay squarely beneath her.

Finally she lost her footing altogether and would have pitched headlong down the unforgiving stone steps had she not grabbed with both hands at the smooth wooden rail at her side. She caught the rail, almost twisting her arms from their sockets in the process. She did not stop her fall, but at least turned so she went feet first, bouncing from worn stone step to worn stone step like a child, bouncing on her buttocks, each impact a blast of pain up her spine.

She reached the bottom, her fall not more than ten steps. It might have been a hundred, from the way she felt.

Donna pushed herself back onto her feet, pushed out into the foyer. She did not know what it was that drove her, what she felt she needed to do, but she knew she had to get into the hall, had to get to Paul. When she got there, she hoped, she would understand what it was she had to do.

Paul screamed.

A high, wailing, banshee shriek that started deep, deep in his narrow chest and came boiling up and out before he had any chance to control it.

He screamed, his head thrown back, his shoulders crowding up against the sides of his head, his arms stiff, his hands like claws before him. And as Paul began to scream, so too did Errol Warner, his deeper voice taking a fraction of a second longer than Paul's to rise to the same keening note, the same piercing wail.

The screams rose from both of them, bouncing back from the stone walls, echoing around the hall, rising and rising in pitch until they went far beyond any sound a human throat should ever have been capable of making. Higher and higher, shriller and shriller until there was no sound, until the two stood facing each other, faces twisted and stretched by the gape of their distended jaws, a silence in itself more piercing, more horrible than the screams crashing down around them.

In the heart of the silence, Clay Garber's hands closed around Paul's throat.

In the heart of the silence, Robert Trayne seized a steak knife from the table beside him, seized it with both his gnarled hands, and drove it as hard as he could into Clay Garber's chest.

In the silence Tom Sylvestri hurled himself against Errol Warner, raising the heavy crucifix and swinging it down hard across Warner's back. Warner cried out and fell forward. The impetus of Tom's swing carried him on and over. Both went sprawling on the cold slate floor.

In the silence Donna Wojciechowski slumped to her knees at the main door of the hall, understanding what had happened, and knowing, knowing fully, there was nothing in the world she could do to change it.

Errol Warner was crying.

Tom looked down at the face of the murderer, the face that had been so calm, so empty of emotion, and scarcely believed what he saw.

Warner's face was contorted into a mask of such consuming grief Tom felt all anger, all grief of his own dissolve and shrink away before the wave of compassion that rose inside him. It had been his intent to strike down Errol Warner, to kill him with his bare hands if necessary, to break the cycle of emotion ricocheting back and forth between Warner and Paul Trayne.

But that was gone now, that intent, the rage that fired it, powered it.

Tom pulled back from Warner and shifted his weight to free his hands. As a priest, he placed one of those hands on Warner's head, on his sweat-sodden hair, stroking.

Warner looked up, looked into Tom's eyes; all that Tom Sylvestri ever needed to know or understand was written in the young man's face.

"Help me, Father," Warner said, his voice a whisper, a rustle of dry leaves. "Oh, Jesus, help me!" He dropped his face on his outstretched arm, and the sobs overwhelmed him once again.

"It's all right, my son," Tom said, the words small against the size of what he knew now filled Errol Warner's soul. He picked up the fallen cross with his free hand and hugged it to his bosom. He felt the power he believed to be there flow from the cross, filling him, strengthening him. "Be still. Be still."

Clay bellowed as the knife buried itself in the heavy flesh of his chest. It was not a knife made for the work to which Robert Trayne directed it. Almost as soon as the swing was completed, as soon as the point dug through Clay's jacket, Trayne's fingers slipped on the handle and lurched forward down the blade. He mixed his own cry of pain with Clay's as the edge of the blade sliced deep into his leathery skin. The blood of the two men mingled on Clay's dark jacket.

Clay released Paul at once, swinging his thick arms against this new assault. He caught Robert Trayne full across the chest, sending him sprawling. The force of the blow pulled the knife down and across Clay's chest, opening a wide gash and slicing most of the flesh from the inner curve of two of Robert Trayne's fingers.

Clay tottered back and came up hard against the stone wall behind the table. He lost his footing and slipped sideways, sliding down the wall. He reached instinctively for anything that might stop his fall, caught the tasseled hem of one of the faux medieval tapestries. The rings that supported the cloth were made to hold its weight, but not the additional poundage Clay brought to bear. With a sound like firecrackers popping the rings broke free and the long strip of fabric fell from the wall, landing across Clay Garber, hiding him in its folds.

Trayne scrabbled to his feet, breathing hard. The blow taken from Garber, though poorly aimed, had blasted the air from the old man's lungs as if some godly fist had squeezed his chest flat. Trayne leaned heavily on the table before him, panting, waiting for the room to settle into a more familiar stability. He looked about, eyes darting here and there. He took in the lump of tapestry covering Clay, the commissioner's feet thrust out from the tassled edge like those of some huge, carelessly discarded toy.

Trayne assessed the small distance between himself and his son. Paul did not seem aware of him. His narrow back was ramrod straight, his head tipped slightly, as if he were gazing into some unseen cosmos beyond the dark ceiling of the hall. Trayne took a step toward the boy, big hand out to grab his arm.

"No."

The voice was calm, ice cold, from Trayne's left. He took his eyes away from Paul, turned slowly. Donna. Standing on the long table, her feet too close together for good balance, her fists clenched at her sides. One of the overhead lighting fixtures was centered directly behind her head, its light filtering through the hair, which had come loose about her face. The coppery strands shone like a golden halo in Trayne's eyes. Trayne could not read her expression, but Donna's posture told him all he needed to know. This woman was no longer under his son's thrall, and therefore no longer his to command. Still, she was only a woman, and the touch of Paul's gift had left Robert Trayne absolutely convinced there was no woman —or man, for that matter—who was his match.

"Do not interfere, woman," Robert Trayne said. "I mean to take my son away from this place. I do not mean to let you, or anyone else, stand in my way."

Donna's response was simple and direct. Trayne understood instantly why she had not placed her feet wider, for greater stability. She needed them directly under her center of gravity, so she would be balanced for the kick.

The kick came lightning fast, completely without warning.

The toe of Donna's right foot came up under Trayne's big chin so hard his teeth snapped together with a sound like gunshot. Pain shot through his head and he tasted blood. He'd bitten into his tongue—through his tongue, in fact. The force of Donna's blow lifted him bodily, sent him staggering back, and as he went a plume of dark blood arced across the air, spewing from his mouth.

Donna leaped from the table, her face set, her mouth drawn in a bloodless line. She kicked again, this time aiming for the spot his awkward backward-leaning angle thrust at her. The right toe buried itself this time deep in the folds of black cloth over the place where Trayne's legs joined his body. He howled, spraying blood, doubling forward as Donna, ready for the switchblade motion, brought her knee up to meet his face. She felt his nose shatter under the blow and snapped her foot out and up, under the curve of his ribs as the old man's body jerked now back again.

Trayne stumbled three steps back and came up hard against the stone wall. Donna laced her fingers, building one large fist out of her two small ones, and swung hard at the right side of Trayne's bloody face. His head snapped hard to the left, but Donna's hands were faster, coming up already from that side and smashing into his face again. As his head snapped back and forth with the force of each blow, Donna doubled and redoubled her efforts. Her hands burned with an agony such as she had never known, but only a small part of her brain was concerned with such things. As only a small part of her brain was aware of the shift in the old tapestry piled to her left, of Clay Garber extricating himself from the heavy folds.

It was not until Garber's big arms folded around her, drew her back, and lifted her away, that the red haze passed from Donna's eyes and she was able to see what she had done to Robert Johnston Trayne.

The old man lay on one side. His face was a mask of blood, his eyes open, staring without seeing. There was a long arc of blood down the dark stone wall, marking the place his face had hit, driven by Donna's last blow, sliding like a bloody brush over the rough canvas of the wall, a long slow curve that seemed, in Donna's mind, suddenly a wonderfully symbolic thing. A line on a graph—the parallel layers of mortar between the big stones did almost suggest graph paper—that marked the decline of Robert Johnston Trayne and his unholy crusade.

Donna drew a deep, slow, steady breath. She unlaced her fingers and learned from the bolt of pain that at least one on each hand was broken. She leaned back into Clay Garber, letting her heart regain its normal pace.

"Son of a bitch," she said, looking, finally, away from the place where Trayne lay. "Paul . . ."

But Paul was gone.

Paul was only barely aware of the events around him.

Something new had come into his life. Something odd. Frightening for only the moment it took him to notice it was frightening, then that emotion vanished and Paul Trayne looked upon the world with new and different eyes.

He looked around the hall. People were stirring in their places. The gathered powerful, the ones who had come to see him flex his magic and disport himself for them. Some rose, staggering, as if drunk. Others gripped the edges of their tables, eyes wide, faces pale.

The effect of Paul's power had been more dramatic than usual. More extreme. Normally, he knew, they would hardly realize anything had happened until they moved back into their normal lives and began to notice how things that had bothered them once bothered them no longer. How a course of action once anathema to them now seemed perfectly acceptable.

As things now seemed to Paul Trayne.

Was there anything in the world that seemed wrong to him? Any deed, any thought from which he might shrink? His brain was full of many deeds and thoughts, culled from the minds of those on whom he'd worked his power, but search them as he might, he found nothing that repelled him, nothing that disgusted him. And there were so many new things here, so many rich and different images, taken from the life experience of Errol Warner.

The same Errol Warner who now lay sobbing in the arms of a man in the dark clothing and bright white collar of a priest.

The priest stroked Warner's hair and seemed, Paul thought, to be trying to comfort him.

As if there could be any need for such comfort. Why would Errol Warner need comforting? What had he ever done—and Paul paused in his train of thought to contemplate the precise details of everything Warner had done—what had he ever done that he should feel so bad about?

Nothing. Paul found nothing in all of Warner's deeds, in all the deeds of everyone there assembled, that caused him the smallest discomfort. They were all quite normal, petty, commonplace things. Murder. Embezzlement. Adultery.

Puny things.

Paul smiled.

Nothing at all, in fact, compared to the sort of things he now felt himself quite capable of doing. He stepped away from the table, away from the people. He jumped over the still mound that marked the place Clay Garber lay. He slipped past the uniformed policemen, no one moving to stop him.

He came to the door that opened on the long, white hall leading to the service rooms, the kitchen, the pantries. He walked down the hall, opening doors, until he found one that led to the outside.

Paul stepped into the cold Chicago night, feeling the wind bite into his poorly protected flesh. He jogged down the four steps to the pavement, the side alley opening onto the street at either end. He turned left, away from the street the Armory faced, away from the police cars and reporters that might be there.

He went off into the cold, dark night, alone, unafraid. The first order of business would be to find a coat to protect him from the cold. The second—the smile on Paul's face grew broader—might be to kill the person from whom he took the coat.

Paul laughed and ran off into the darkness of his astonishing new world.

After

The tent was gone. The area churned up by the wheels of countless cars had been ploughed into dark, straight lines. The smell of earth and new-mown grass filled the air. A tiny piece of yellowed, frayed cardboard was still stuck to the gatepost by a rusting nail. No trace of its message remained.

Donna Wojciechowski stood at the gate to Gunner's Field, remembering.

Summer had come and nearly gone. That night, that terrible, mad night, was done and gone, all the ramifications of it fading into a morass of civic red tape. Amazingly, some of the anguish of it, the madness of it, had even begun to fade too, dulled and diluted by the distance of time.

It could never pass entirely, of course. Though Paul Trayne was gone, there remained too much of his works, too much of his evil—ever to pass completely from the world, from memory.

Marjorie Garber was institutionalized, insane. At least, to those who examined her, those who professed knowledge of such things, she seemed insane. But Donna knew better. Donna had gone with Tom Sylvestri to the mayor's house to find Marjorie. Clay had begged them to go, as he was carried from the hall on a stretcher, his loss of blood too great to allow him to undertake that grim mission himself.

So Tom and Donna—after Tom turned Errol Warner over to

the police once more—took a patrol car to the mayor's house and found it dark and unlocked. They made their way through to the mayor's bedroom and found Marjorie and the remains of Emmanuel Stuartson.

Donna looked into Marjorie's eyes and knew she was not insane. Not as mere mortals understood insanity, at least. Donna knew the look in Marjorie's eyes. Knew it as one who had looked out through eyes like that. Marjorie was lost in the abyss, and there would be no saving her, no gallant rescue.

Certainly Paul would not save her. Paul did not care.

Paul, as Donna had so clearly understood in that moment as she slumped by the door of the dining hall in the old Armory, had become a recipient of his own gift.

Tom worked out what he thought to be the actual mechanics of it. Errol Warner, contrary to their expectations, carried no guilt, no grief at all for Paul to draw out. Instead, reaching into that black oblivion, Paul Trayne's power had been sucked from him, as air will rush into a vacuum, unstoppable until the container is completely emptied. The power of Paul Trayne had drained out of the boy and into Errol Warner, but Warner had not possessed in his genetic code the intricate pattern of molecules that had created Paul Trayne's power. The power poured out and, finding nothing and nowhere to nest, had begun to feed upon itself, had begun the nightmare of seesawing emotion that had possessed everyone in the hall that night.

No, Warner had not received the power, but it was clear to Tom he'd received something else. He had become what Paul could no longer be, the receptacle of all those many griefs and guilts, those angers, pains, and furies that Paul had drawn from all the people of Faulkner and all the uncounted souls before and since.

The man who had known no guilt in all his life bore now the burden of guilt normally divided among twenty thousand souls. If there was a fitting punishment for what he'd done, Tom had said to Donna, this must surely be it.

And Paul?

Paul was gone. Slipped away in the time of disorientation that followed the event. Donna searched her memory but found no trace of his departure. He must have slipped out one of the side doors, abandoning his father, abandoning his Cause.

But the Paul Trayne who had slipped away from the Armory was a far cry from the boy who'd been introduced to Donna Wojciechowski here, in this field, nearly seven months ago. If what Tom deduced was true, the Paul Trayne who'd escaped them might no longer have the power his mutant genes had given him, but he had—or more exactly, *lacked*—something else.

"Hardly looks like the end of the world might almost have started here, does it?" The voice was a whisper at Donna's side, like sand falling against the bottom of an old tin bucket.

She turned and looked down into the eyes of Walker Stone. He was almost fully recovered from his ordeal. He'd survived the long night in Faulkner until the morning light brought Maurice Zeldenrust back to the hospital. Their rage vented against Pete Hay and the town, the once good people of Faulkner had lost interest in the hospital. Stone and the few patients untouched by Paul Trayne had survived until Zeldenrust summoned help to transport them to other towns, other hospitals. All that remained to remind Stone of what had happened was the tracheotomy scar and the permanent change in his voice.

"No," Donna said, "it doesn't look like much of anything but a farmer's field." She reached out a hand and took Stone's. "Where is he, I wonder?"

"Paul Trayne?"

Donna nodded. "If what Tom guessed was right . . ."

"And I'm sure it was."

". . . then Paul has been touched by his own power. The effect of it being sucked out of him like that . . ."

". . . would have left him as emptied of simple human decency as anyone he touched." Stone shuddered. "What kind of a mind does that create, I wonder? What kind of creature, that can move through the world and be completely untouched by it?"

"Not completely untouched," Donna said. "Those things we're supposed to worry about, care about, they won't bother him at all anymore. Those things that we're supposed to find horrible, repulsive . . ."

". . . become compelling. Even pleasureful. As they did with Warner."

She nodded. "So Paul's out there, somewhere, a sweet-faced boy who can lie and cheat and steal and kill, and never think once about it. Never even think that he *should* be thinking about it."

"Nothing's happened yet," Stone reminded. "It's quite possible he did not survive that night. If he wandered out into Chicago with no more sense in his head than you think, than Tommy thinks—well, he might have walked right into a mess of trouble right then and there."

"There was nothing in the police bulletins."

"There might not be. You know how that works as well as I do. There's a dozen murders in a city the size of Chicago every year that go undetected, unknown. People who just . . . vanish."

"I wonder . . ."

"Hmm?"

"I just wonder if Paul might ever come back, looking for his father. That 'assault with a deadly weapon' charge will put Trayne behind bars for a long time, but if Paul came looking for him . . ."

"I doubt that he will," Stone said. "Why would he care?"

Donna nodded and turned away from the broad brown rectangle of Gunner's Field. "So he's out there. And, if we're right, he's more soulless, more empty of simple human decency than Errol Warner ever was." She shook her head. "Hard to believe it started here. Hard to believe it happened at all. The power of Paul Trayne has worn off the people of Faulkner. They've buried their dead, they're rebuilding their town, and I'll bet it's all starting to seem like some kind of nightmare, like something that didn't really happen."

"It happened. You and Clay and Tom—and I—will always be around to remind them of that. To remind everyone. There might not be any realistic way to bring charges, to prosecute these people for what happened—after all, no one really believes what happened, what Paul Trayne did, like you said—but there's no reason to let anyone forget."

They strolled back to Stone's Mercedes and got in.

"But he's out there," Donna said. "Like some kind of time bomb. And when he goes off . . ."

"We'll know," Stone said. "If he's really still alive, if he acts as we expect, we'll spot the signs, if no one else does. Senseless things. Pain, killing. That's what Paul Trayne will sow across the country. And if we watch for them, track them, we'll know where he is, where he's going. And we'll find him."

"We'll find him," Donna said. She turned and draped her arms around Stone's shoulders. "I'm glad Tom made me give him that promise," she said. "I feel better. Not a whole lot better—I always feel like I need that drink, that one drink— but I feel more in control of my life than I have in a long time."

"You look better," Stone said. He stroked her hair, shorter now around a face that was still spectacular in its beauty, at least in his eyes.

"I never could have done it without the gift of Paul Trayne," Donna said. "That's the worst thing about it. That I went through it all, and in the end I'm a better person for having been touched by Paul Trayne."

"You're a better person because you always were a better person," Stone said. "No witchcraft needed."

Donna smiled. "I knew you'd say the right thing." She kissed him lingeringly. "I love you, Walker." That she could say it, and did not need to fight against it, she knew, was a last vestige of the power of the boy named Paul Trayne.

"I love you, too," Stone said. He started the car and pulled into Gunner's Field to make his turn. Donna looked at the field one last time. No trace at all. No trace of the tent. No trace of Clarence Nickerson's prehistoric Buick. Across the plowed earth the old Tempest house stood tall and forlorn, windows looking down on them, black eyes that saw everything, but cared not one whit.

Walker guided the Mercedes back onto Pine Tree Road, bouncing in the sun-dried ruts until they came up to the highway. Donna looked right, toward Faulkner. She thought about Clarence Nickerson, and Pete Hay, and Ben Carpenter. She thought about Mae Ellen Faber, her mother, the faceless, nameless lives destroyed by Paul Trayne.

"What do you suppose happened to Carpenter?" she asked, expecting no real reply.

"I don't know," Stone said. "Back in my room, in the hospital, he said something about making amends. Putting things right. I've halfway convinced myself . . ."

"What?"

Stone shrugged and turned toward Chicago, accelerating onto the highway. "I've halfway convinced myself he's gone looking for Paul. Looking for . . . vengeance, I guess." He turned to glance at Donna. "How do you feel about that? What you said about Paul and the way his power worked . . ."

"Paul was an innocent victim in this as much as anyone," Donna said. "He didn't ask for the power. He didn't ask for the slime and corruption using the power poured into him. But . . . well, that Paul is dead, isn't he? We used one evil to destroy another, and in the process we killed the innocent victim who was Paul Trayne. What's left . . ."

"What's left is something, someone else, altogether," Stone said. "So if Ben Carpenter is really looking for him, if he finds him . . ."

Donna watched the summer green fields slip by. She leaned against Walker Stone, feeling his warmth, his strength. "I hope he does," she said. "I hope he finds Paul. I hope he kills him." She felt the tears coming but did not try to hold them back. "It's the only way we can ever be finally free of it all. The only way Paul can ever be free."

"Free?" Stone did not look away from the road ahead.

"Free, as we can never be," Donna said. "Because, if there's nothing else that is to be learned from the 'gift' of Paul Trayne, it's that we can't ever be free of the guilt and grief and rage and lust and general shittiness we carry around inside us. Paul took all that away, and that was exactly the wrong thing. Exactly the thing we—humanity—does not need. It's having all that, but always being aware of it, always fighting against it, that makes us human in the first place."

Stone nodded. "It seems like I've been trying to tell you something very much like that for a long time."

Donna smiled, a small but very real thing. "Yes, you have." She leaned her head on Stone's shoulder. "And now, after all this time, I think it's finally sunk in."